# AVAILABLE DARKNESS: BOOK THREE

## DAVID WRIGHT

*For Todd.*
*April 1970 – April 1996*

# Prologue

*2011*

CALEB CAME TO. The world was upside down, his feet knotted in an ancient tree's twisting, gnarled branches, the ground five feet or so beneath him.

He struggled to look up at the tangled mass holding him prisoner, trying to figure out how he'd wound up in this trap, and whether it was manmade or natural. The darkness was absolute, save the two fat moons hanging bright in the sky.

Caleb wasn't sure how long he'd been out, but he was cold and soaking from landing in a river alongside his brother, Jacob after they'd fallen through the portal from Earth into this world. The rapids had shoved them toward a waterfall. Caleb could barely gulp a mouthful of air before going under to an assault of rocks and debris along the riverbed. The last thing he'd seen before slamming into a giant fallen tree was Jacob tumbling over the waterfall's edge.

Caleb had stabbed his brother with a blade designed to kill vampires, but Jacob had somehow managed to stagger away, escaping through the portal. Caleb, in what seemed like a good idea at the time, chased him down to finish the job. Now, stuck in a tree on another world, full of God only knew what breed sort of monstrosities, the idea seemed anything but good.

He wondered if Jacob had survived the waterfall. Caleb would need to do a cursory search for a body before setting back upriver to search for the portal home — assuming it hadn't winked from existence.

Caleb didn't want to consider the alternative: the portal was temporary, and he was now stuck.

*No sense in worrying about things beyond my control. One thing at a time, starting with getting down from this damned tree.*

Caleb struggled to look around and gather his whereabouts — maybe he'd gone over the waterfall, too, before somehow landing in this tree. But if that were true, he should've seen the waterfall's imposing precipice bearing down on him. Yet he saw no such thing, nor heard the rushing river.

*How far did the river carry me?*

*How long was I out?*

He closed his eyes and listened, scanning the world around him for clues to his location — not that anything was recognizable across the unfamiliar landscape.

He heard what sounded like normal forest noises: insects, small animals, and a cold breeze tickling the branches. Nothing out of the ordinary. The scents on this world — the trees, the soil, flowering plants, and things he couldn't quite place — were far more pungent than Earth's.

Caleb wondered if he should call out for help.

Wondered if his other brother, John, or any of John's men had followed. He'd seen John reach out, trying to stop him from getting sucked into the portal, but then the world was gone, replaced by this one.

He wondered if John would follow him over.

Caleb didn't know his brother well, or *even remember having a brother* twenty-four hours ago, but something about John said he was loyal, and that he would follow Caleb to bring him back.

*Unless he got himself killed.*

Caleb thought about calling out, but the last thing he wanted to do was draw attention to himself in this helpless position — especially when Jacob might be lurking nearby.

He struggled to pull himself up, to reach for the branches holding him. Then he heard movement, the creaking of tree limbs above him. At first, he thought it was only the wind, but the movements were sustained and deliberate.

*Something is pushing the branches aside.*

He looked up, heart racing, to see a large dark shape shifting behind the thick branches, slowly spreading them apart. Then the branches fell back into place, and whatever it was seemed to recede back into the darkness — for now.

*What the hell is that?*

He had to get down.

*Now.*

Ignoring the pain in his back and ribs from the tumble in the river, Caleb bent forward at the waist, reaching toward the branches that had him tangled so he could free himself. As his hand grasped a branch and he steadied his position, he thanked Agency training requirements and the countless crunches he'd spent a lifetime loathing.

As he pulled his head up to get a closer look at what he was tangled in, he felt a sudden sickness. What had *appeared* to be boughs in the darkness above was instead some sort of sticky substance binding his feet, and then trapping his fingers the moment he touched it.

He struggled, trying to withdraw his hand.

Movement above made him freeze.

*Oh, God, it's back!*

The branches slowly peeled back again, this time revealing his trapper.

At first, his eyes couldn't decipher the large, black round shape. His mind was insisting that this was a giant rock moving above him, as unlikely as that seemed. It was at least ten feet wide, with glimmers of shifting light piercing the darkness.

Only when the branches parted, and the shape moved closer, did Caleb see that the rock was covered with dingy knots of blood-clotted hair, and eight nightmarish eyes.

*Not a rock — a giant spider!*

The spider scurried closer, and about six feet away began to make an ungodly clicking. Whether the sound came from its mouth and twitching palps or somewhere else, Caleb didn't know. Nor did he intend to find out. Caleb had never heard a spider make noise, but then again he'd never seen one with a ten-foot-wide head. He dreaded knowing the creature's total size.

The branches spread as more of its slowly descended toward Caleb, as if purposely going as slow as possible to allow Caleb to marinate in fear.

His heart pounded, adrenaline claiming his body, every nerve burning with a plea: *escape*.

He tugged at his stuck hand, but it refused to budge.

Images collided inside him, from his youth and movies, nature documentaries of insects and animals trapped in a spider's web and struggling without hope — Caleb had never seen anything escape once trapped.

His first instinct was to reach up and try to yank his arm out, but Caleb didn't want to get *both hands* stuck. Instead he twisted and turned, awkwardly and painfully, his left arm blindly reaching out to his sides and below, searching for something, *anything*, he could use to either ward off the spider or pry his hand free.

He found a branch with his free hand. He gripped it tight, pulling.

The creature descended, perhaps sensing Caleb's plans, or excited that its prey was moving.

This time, it wasn't slow. It surged, branches and leaves shaking in a flurry as its head and large furry fangs came closer to Caleb.

The branch Caleb was trying to break off wasn't cooperating. Though not particularly thick, it was barely bending and seemed unwilling to break.

*What the hell is this tree made of?*

The spider was moving fast. It would be on him in seconds, likely injecting Caleb with a poison a heartbeat after its jaws found flesh.

The branch finally gave, snapping with a loud *POP!* as the spider opened its jaws.

Its giant head was on him, palps moving like furry tentacles pressing into his flesh, preparing Caleb for fangs.

He brought the broken branch upward in a stabbing motion and screamed, both to buy himself a few seconds by scaring the arachnid, and because he was scared shitless.

No time to aim as the spider was moving fast and erratic. The branch pierced something, but Caleb couldn't see what.

He only heard the scream and felt a rush of cold blood, or *something,* gushing down onto his body.

He closed his mouth before any of the bug's juice found its way inside.

The spider jerked its head so fast that Caleb lost his grip on the stick, still stuck in the creature, robbing Caleb of his only weapon.

He hoped the spider would scurry away to lick its wounds in the canopy of branches, but those hopes were dashed as its legs began to batter him, with either attack or reflex. Caleb screamed again, pounding his fists against the creature's thick, fur-covered head.

And then he felt it.

A bite in his abdomen.

"No!"

Caleb cried out in defeat, knowing he'd soon be dead. Images of spiders devouring their prey careened through his mind. Maybe it would wrap him tightly in web, like a burrito, then feast on him later.

He continued to fight back, though, this time clawing at the creature's flesh, fingers raking across a row of eyes.

He dug in, tearing at the beast's eyes, puncturing them.

He might die, but he'd be damned if he was going without a fight.

The spider screamed and finally retreated back into the darkness above.

Caleb smiled at Pyrrhic victory; he could already feel the toxins working their way through his blood.

His head was dizzy.

His body beginning to stiffen.

And above him, Caleb could see the spider peering back through the bushes with whatever was left of its eyes, waiting for its victim to finish struggling.

Then the feast would begin.

As darkness swam at the edges of his vision, inviting Caleb into its embrace, he flashed back to happier times.

Before he accidentally killed his wife with nothing but a touch.

Before he realized he was one of the very monsters he was tracking, brought to this world as a child, his memory wiped, vampire abilities somehow squelched by The Guardians.

Caleb's recall was a mess of his forgotten past, what he'd been told, and memories from both John and Jacob he saw in flashes — probably from some sort of psychic bond — when he joined hands with his brothers to create the portal.

He wondered if he still shared that bond. If his brother — the good one — could sense his danger, then maybe he could find him and spare his death.

But those thoughts screeched to a halt.

Caleb realized with a sickening, helpless horror that he could no longer feel anything. Not the cold from his soaking clothes, not the air's frozen kiss, not the pain in his back or sides, and not even the bite.

Caleb was frozen.

The spider, perhaps sensing his prey's paralysis, descended.

Caleb lost consciousness.

~

CALEB WOKE, surprised by four things at once: he was still alive; he was no longer paralyzed; his arms were bound behind him; and … he wasn't alone.

He was lying on the floor of a horse-drawn caravan. A young light-skinned black woman with long straight hair, golden eyes, and blue symbols painted (or tattooed) onto her forehead and cheeks sat across from him, staring intensely at him. She was wearing all-white: pants, shirt, cape, and cowl, reminding Caleb of a ninja.

She sat knees to chest, white-taped hands resting on a sheathed sword, still staring at Caleb as he struggled to sit up and looked around. There was one other person in the covered wagon, a man in similar white garb and markings, crimson symbols on his face.

"So the Valkoer is awake," she said.

*Valkoer?*

Then Caleb remembered, though he wasn't sure if it was something he was told or from memories belonging to his brothers — the vampires in this world were called Valkoer. How did this woman know he was one? Did the Valkoer appear visibly different?

Caleb said nothing, not knowing who these people were, or if they were friend or foe to the vampire race.

"Why were you with the prince?"

The woman's accent had an odd lilt that sounded slightly Irish, mixed with something guttural.

They must've seen him chasing Jacob when they crossed through the portal. He considered telling the truth, that he chased the evil fucker from Earth in an attempt to kill him. But he didn't know where the woman's loyalties lay. She called him Valkoer, which seemed to indicate that *she* wasn't. Yet she called Jacob the prince, which could mean he was *her* prince.

Instead of answering, Caleb said, "And *you* are?"

"I'm Sister Raina, of The Hand of the Seven Gods. And you will regret stepping outside of your Kingdom, *Valkoer!*"

She spit the final word with disgust.

*Okay, definitely not one of Jacob's people.*

Caleb was about to tell her who he was when she

rushed forward, shoved a dirty rag into his mouth, and slipped a hood over his head.

He tried to speak, to explain that he wasn't an enemy, but merely earned a hard knock on the head for his effort.

Then Caleb saw nothing but darkness again.

# ONE

## Jacob
------------

*Now (2013)*
  *Castle Valkoer*

JACOB SAT on the hard black metal-and-bone bench outside Father's Royal Chambers. It was similar to the King's throne, made from the armor and bones of enemies who'd attacked The South during The Great Purge ages ago.

The North had sliced through The South and killed or exiled every potential threat — most of the Valkoer, The Magick Guild, and the Were-Beasts of No Man's Land. Exiles were herded onto the island town, The Forgotten City — a ten-square mile territory of ramshackle buildings stacked atop more of the same. Organized chaos that only Jacob's father, King Zol Graymare, could control.

Zol gathered the freaks, thieves, monsters, and other undesirables forced to live in the ghettos, and though the island had no such recognized designation by The Realm's other kingdoms, he demanded it be called The Forgotten *Kingdom.*

The castle was a walled-off fortress within the walled city, giving its most important residents and shop owners an additional layer of protection from the riffraff that comprised most of the Kingdom's denizens. The Keep — the Kingdom's largest residence — rested in the castle's heart, sitting atop a large motte, giving the King a bird's eye view of his empire of shit.

King Zol had gone from King of the Valkoer, a race of vampires numbering in the tens of thousands, to ruler of less than a hundred remaining of his own kind, and a few thousand other freaks and criminals who lived on the island. Neither The North, nor The Forgotten Kingdom Council, would ever allow Zol to turn anyone else into Valkoer, save for those unlucky enough to become thralls to the elite.

The Valkoer's days were ending.

But they didn't have to.

Jacob carried the answer in a small black leather pouch within a pocket of his long dark coat. He couldn't wait to see Father's face when he revealed that his last trip to Earth hadn't just been a success, but it had been the kind of success that would solve *all* their problems. The Last Great Wizard's power stored in the crystals would be a turning point for the Valkoer, *and* the world.

Perhaps *now* Jacob would finally have his father's respect.

The King would see that his son *wasn't* a source of shame and disgust as he'd always been treated. He would see Jacob as the worthy successor he was. Not just to The Forgotten Kingdom's throne, but as heir to the true dominion over both worlds.

The large double wooden doors to Father's chambers opened, and Viceroy Calbot Mason entered the hallway. Mason was barrel-chested with a bushy red beard that

Jacob found disgusting. He often imagined bugs crawling through the greasy tufts in search of food.

"The King will see you now."

Mason had been Zol's right hand since The Last Great Wizard, VVessolff, had betrayed him decades ago. Mason wasn't Valkoer but was one of the Old Ones, around for thousands of years without visibly aging past his fifties. He had once been a good-looking man, before gluttony claimed him, a trait that Jacob found repulsive. Mason had traded weapons and a battlefield for whispers with the elite, establishing himself as a legendary politician whose charm and gift of gab had helped Zol secure a peace treaty with The Hand of the Seven Gods, and The North.

The chamber was long and narrow, with several rooms off to both sides and the King's throne at the end — black and gold, made from his enemies' bones, and brought from their old mountain castle by Zol himself. The King sat on his throne reading, not so much as glancing up from his book to greet his son's triumphant return.

At a table in front of the throne sat Sir Tomas Barron, head of the Valkoer Knights. He was studying a map, surely planning a mission.

If Mason was Zol's second, Barron was his third. He was also a vampire who'd sworn allegiance to *his* Master, Zol, ages ago.

The man was deceptively small, particularly for a leader of the knights, but what Barron lacked in size he delivered on the battlefield. No person in all of the lands owned more kills.

Despite his greatness, and being vampire kin, something about Barron wore at Jacob's trust. Perhaps it was his clinging to youth, choosing to keep his appearance at no older than twenty. The man was vain, reportedly using many spells to achieve his renowned good looks — he had no shortage of women offering to be his thralls. Rumor had it that Barron had no less than thirty beautiful Valkoer who lived to serve his every need.

Though Jacob found the knight's vanity offensive, he was still easier to deal with than Mason.

But the presence of both Barron *and* Mason made Jacob want to wait until later, perhaps in the evening, when he could possibly talk to Father alone.

Jacob didn't want them around during the presentation of his Earthly gift. Nor did he want their input when he revealed his plans for the crystals.

Barron looked up from the map, flashed his handsome smile, then stood and circled the table to greet Jacob with a big, warm hug.

"Prince Jacob! How were your travels?"

"Great," Jacob said, annoyed at the man's kindness.

Damn it if Barron's smile didn't seem genuine. It was hard for Jacob to hate the man while standing beside him.

Mason walked past them, having offered no warm welcome, taking a seat at Barron's table. Mason had a silver tongue, but never feigned kindness toward the prince. He was almost openly hostile, which Jacob attributed to the man raising him for some time as a child after Jacob's mother had fled to Earth with John and Caleb.

Mason hated children, so being saddled with raising the King's son had bred years of contempt.

Jacob approached the throne. Father finally — *barely* — looked down.

"Hello, Father."

"Hello," he said, then returned his gaze to the tome.

Jacob stifled his sigh. "Father, I need to speak with you, alone."

Father, who had once been large and muscular, was starting to look frail, and old. Long black hair had given way to pure white. His flesh sagged, particularly in his jowls and the puffy bags beneath his dark and sunken eyes.

While the Valkoer, as well as the rest of The Realm, could live for thousands of years before looking elderly, when age finally caught up, it hit hard and fast. The effect was even more noticeable with Valkoer who failed to sufficiently feed. Jacob wondered if his father had lost the appetite. If so, his decline would be rapid.

Jacob could almost feel Mason licking his chops.

Jacob was King of the Valkoer by birthright, but all of that changed when most of the Valkoer were killed off, and their home Kingdom rendered null.

This was a new Kingdom, made up of all the Forgotten City misfits, and ne'er do wells relegated to the ghetto. The Council no longer honored tradition. Hell, until Zol fought to form this city into a recognized power in The Realm by forcing a treaty, most citizens hated the Valkoer, seeing them as a threat to their existence.

If Zol were to die, Mason's popularity with the Kingdom's various factions would certainly enable him to mount a coup and claim the throne.

Father looked down at Jacob as if he hadn't heard his request.

Louder, Jacob repeated, "I need to speak to you alone, my King." He hated calling his father "my King" but knew that the old man preferred it in the company of others. Or perhaps he just hated being reminded that Jacob was his son.

"What is this about?"

"My trip to Earth."

Father looked up, voice slightly slurred. "My Inner Council stays."

Jacob wanted to argue, but Father's agitated expression warned him not to. He didn't want to start this important conversation on shaky ground, and needed Father on his side to push through his agenda.

"Very well, my King." Jacob stepped in front of both the throne and the table with Mason and Barron.

"So," Father began, "how did this trip go?"

Jacob looked at Mason, wishing the bastard wasn't there, then reached into his pocket and drew the black pouch.

"I found them."

"Found what?" Father asked.

"The answer to all of our problems."

Jacob retrieved one of the six crystals from the bag and held it up. It was small, the size of a few cherries, glowing a brilliant red in his hand.

Father's eyes widened, then, almost immediately, they looked tired again. "This has better not be another of your *games.*"

"Did you come all the way back with *magick tricks?*" Mason said, clearly annoyed.

Jacob was about to hand them the golden key, and still they treated him like a feckless child.

He fought the urge to argue or to tell these men how damn grateful they ought to be — the crystals could end centuries of Northern oppression. Then they could *easily* conquer Earth and have an endless supply of food.

"It's the wizard."

"What?" Mason said, confused.

Father also seemed baffled. "What wizard?"

"VVessolff."

The King's eyes were suddenly alert.

"VVessolff. After he helped Mother run away with John and Caleb, we forced him to create another portal. You'll remember he did so after he vanished. Since you could no longer connect to him, we thought maybe he killed himself to protect whatever remaining knowledge he had about their location. We were partially correct, but didn't know he had his apprentice kill him, then store his soul inside the crystals. His apprentice then took them to Earth and found human vessels to hide the crystals inside."

"His apprentice?" Father looked appalled. "That stable girl? What was her name?"

"I don't know. She vanished at the same time. We should have known he was up to something then."

"So," Father said, "you're saying that his soul is in these crystals?"

"Yes, my King. And, more importantly, *his power*. He was The Last Great Wizard, able to create portals to Earth. Raise the dead. Do nearly anything. No one after The Great Purge has had a hundredth of his power."

Father stared at Jacob, a glint in his eye.

Jacob smiled. "Do you *see* what we have here?"

"Here." Father held out his hand, waiting for Jacob to fill it.

Jacob approached the throne, resisting an urge to give Mason a *fuck-you* smirk.

*I've finally done something that will make Father proud of me, and there's nothing you can do to fuck this up.*

Jacob withdrew a crystal and placed it into his father's hand.

The crystal brightened, then withered to black.

Father jumped and dropped the crystal.

Barron leaped from his seat and grabbed the crystal, clutching it tightly as if it might harm the King. "How dare you bring this in here?"

"The wizard can't harm us!" Jacob yelled.

Father held out his other hand, waiting for the pouch and the rest of the crystals.

Mason blurted, "I don't think that's a good idea!"

"Relax," Jacob said, doing his best not to smile at Mason's ruffled feathers. "The wizard is a prisoner in that crystal and can't do anything to us. But *we* can make him do things."

Jacob handed the pouch to his father, wanting to wave his victory like a flag — it was all he could do to keep from racing through his carefully plotted plan, knowing he had to be careful. With Father, and his advisers.

"*Make him do things?*" Father stared down at the pouch, seemingly afraid to look inside.

"Yes, I've already used him to do a few things."

"What sorts of … *things?*" Mason asked suspiciously.

Jacob smiled. "Whatever I wanted."

With Father's eyes still transfixed on the pouch, Jacob winked at Mason.

*May as well get the portly pisser to back the fuck off.*

Mason stared, surely not wanting to give Jacob any satisfaction. Barron stood, still holding and staring at the first crystal, which was now turning blue enough to match his eyes.

Mason turned to Zol. "We ought to lock these things up immediately. Elder Ponson can bar them in a spell."

Father looked up. "Ponson will do no such thing."

"But, my King, we don't know what sort of threat these crystals pose. We must contain them before they are a peril to the Kingdom. Elder Ponson is the only one equipped to contain such magick."

Father was getting angry, finally at Mason rather than Jacob.

"Why would I ever trust Ponson with these? I will *never* give that much power to a *wizard* again."

"Elder Ponson is the oldest, most trustworthy member of what's left of the Magick Guild. He is loyal, and has helped us *every time* we've asked."

"You know whom else I trusted?" Father raised then shook the pouch. "This fucker!"

Mason looked to his feet, then turned his accusatory eyes on Jacob. The prince resisted every urge to smile, or wink, again, now unwilling to risk being seen as an aggressor by his father.

"And what would *you* have us do with this … *this abomination?*" Mason asked Jacob.

The Warriors Guild, which Mason had once led despite his not being a warrior, hated all things magick, except of course when they asked magick users to bless their weapons with some ability or another. But Mason's disgust was practically choking him.

Jacob was loving every moment, but he had to be careful. If he came right out and said, "Hey, I think we ought to invade Earth and enslave its people as livestock to feast on!" he might overplay his hand and give Father a reason to lend Mason his ears.

He played it subtle instead — he could always work on Father later, when the Big Red Fucker wasn't hanging around.

"I would have you do whatever *you* wanted, my King," Jacob said, making a point to remind Mason who held the power. "At the very least, you could push back The North, perhaps reclaim the lands taken by The Hand of the Seven Gods, return it to *our people*. Why live behind these walls, on this forsaken island, when we can have *our mountain homes* back?"

Mason responded, "We have a tenuous agreement in place with The North, with The Hand, and with The Free People of The Southern Realm. Why instigate another war? Our people are tired of fighting. Tired of dying. We go to war, and The North will destroy us. The North's technology and army is too much for us to fight. Hell, The Hand of the Seven now outnumber us!"

Jacob wanted to respond, to put Mason in a position where he seemed cowardly or perhaps in disagreement with Father. But it wasn't necessary. The King was already there.

"So, you'd have us remain here, Viceroy Mason? Forever subject to The Hand?"

"*Subject?* They let us be in peace. How are we *subject* to them?"

"Because we are still beholden to them for our existence. Because, if you remember, they wished us all dead. Because we cannot freely leave this island! Because they have taken our homeland. We may be left in peace, but make no mistake, Viceroy Mason, *we are their property.*"

Mason, perhaps sensing that he couldn't win the argument, or trying to conjure a reasoning that wouldn't set off the King, nodded then looked to the ground.

Jacob, sensing a victory, tested his limits. "We all know it's only a matter of time before The North, or The Hand, deems our presence inconvenient. Before they find some reason to take our land, to finish the job of exterminating us and the others."

Even if Mason wouldn't argue with the king, he wasn't about to be bested by the prince.

"If they could so easily *exterminate* us, then they already would have! We work hard to maintain this kingdom, and they're not about to pick an unnecessary quarrel. Well, *some of us* work hard, while *others* go galavanting on Earth."

Jacob snapped.

"*Galavanting?* I'm sorry, I didn't see anyone else, least of all the *Fearless Former Head of the Warriors Guild*, standing in line to risk their life to do what had to be done. When was the last time you actually did anything more than lap at my father's feet?"

Mason lurched forward, fists clenched, ready to draw blood.

*Good. Let's play!*

Jacob reached up, hand ready to catch the man's fist. The moment his flesh touched Mason's, he would gladly drain the bastard of his life, and forever remove this thorn from his side.

Barron, smartly, got between the two men, raising his hands to each of their chests.

"Calm yourselves. The *both* of you."

"Enough!" Father screamed, thrusting his arms forward, fingertips touching before he thrust them apart, using his magick.

Mason and Jacob flew backward, each man landing on his ass — shocked and embarrassed.

Father stood from his throne, then floated above the table, casting his eyes down upon the fallen men. Though Zol's frail frame swam in his all-black garb, he was alight with a new fire. Whether it was anger at his right hand and son arguing, or a desire to use the crystals, Jacob wasn't sure.

But he was pleasantly surprised to see that Father still had some life inside him. Perhaps that would delay whatever designs Mason and The Council might have on the throne.

"I want you out!" Father yelled, pointing at Jacob.

"What? *Me?* He started it!"

"Yes, you! There is no place in this room for your impetuousness. I will not have you assault my Viceroy!"

"He came at me!"

"Enough!" Father shouted again.

Jacob seethed at being treated like a child, particularly

in front of Mason. But only compliance would shrink the gulf between himself and his father.

Better to get up, lick his wounds, and return later.

He rose to his feet in concert with Mason, who was still eyeballing him as though expecting Jacob to attack.

Either reading the situation, or Mason's mind, Father warned Jacob, "Leave, now, while I'm still asking."

"Yes, my King," Jacob said, skulking out of the room.

He didn't look back as he heard Mason close the doors, surely smirking. If Jacob had seen such a thing in his current state, the man would be dead.

Jacob needed release.

He headed to the back stairwell, used a key to pass through a red door, then quickly descended the steps until he found himself beneath The Keep.

There were three levels under The Keep. The first was an armory where the King's Guard were stationed. The second was a dungeon where enemies were kept. The third was the Castle's most secret of levels. Only the King's inner circle and select Valkoer knew of its existence. If any of the common folk in the Kingdom knew what lay beneath, they would've overthrown Zol long ago.

At the bottom of the stairs, Jacob reached another door.

He opened it and found himself in an antechamber with a beautiful brunette Valkoer wearing a red silk robe and nothing underneath. She had a tattoo of a rose on her right cheek. She was sitting in a chair behind a desk. A crow sat atop an ancient globe behind her, eyeballing Jacob.

"Hello, Esmerelda."

"Jacob? You're back?" Esmerelda smiled, then stood to greet him with a warm embrace.

The crow looked at Jacob, head tilted ever so slightly.

Jacob wasn't sure if this was the same crow from the last time he'd been here, or another of the dirty beasts she'd tamed with a psychic connection.

He closed his eyes, inhaling her intoxicatingly sweet scent.

"Did you come to spend time with me?" she asked as they parted, biting her lip at the corner. She let her robe slip a bit, revealing the swell of her right breast.

If he'd been in the mood for sex, he would've gladly accepted her offer. She was accommodating to most desires.

"I've come for something different."

"Ah," she said, returning to her spot behind the desk, playing wounded at his rejection. "So then, what *are* you looking for?"

He told her, then asked what she had in stock.

She told him what was available, and Jacob made his choice.

"Enjoy," she said, reaching into a desk drawer and pulling out a heavy iron key cast with the number *11*.

He stepped past the desk and through another doorway, finding himself in a long hallway bathed in red magickal light seeping into the stone walls. The hallway buzzed with the depravity taking place beyond the many doors. He could feel sin on his skin like soothing warm water. Though he normally rejected such vulgar displays, there was something about being in their proximity before he engaged in his own sins that excited him.

He came to a black door with a number *11*.

He slipped his key through the knob, unlocked it, and entered the room.

It was slightly larger than a jail cell but offered more amenities — a comfortable bed, a lantern, running water for a primitive toilet and sink, and a small cupboard where the prisoner was allowed to stow a few personal items.

He looked at the room's lone occupant sitting on the bed reading a book. She looked around ten, well fed, and not like the poor trash one usually found in The Forgotten Kingdom.

"And who might you be, young lady?"

"My name is Jessa," she said, smiling.

"And where are you from?"

"Calladian Mountains. My family has a farm there."

"Ah, Calladia, quite a beautiful place: lovely, pristine lakes," Jacob said, reliving memories of his home before the usurpers stole it for people like this girl's family.

He closed the door behind him, though he didn't need to. Thanks to Esmerelda's powerful magick, The Keep's prisoners didn't realize what had happened to them, and thus would never try to escape — at least not before the magick gave way to the pain.

Some of the Kingdom's Elite came for sex. Others to torture, and then some to *be* tortured. But Jacob liked to think his preferences were above the uncultured waste that sucked at his father's teat.

Jacob was here to steal the girl's memories, to live vicariously through her experiences. Some of the others who used Esmerelda's services would turn their victims into Valkoer before extracting what they wanted — whether it be sex or memories. It was a way to keep the prisoners alive, a way to rent the same prisoner to multiple clients.

Jacob thought it cruel, especially with children. Better to end their misery. It wasn't as if they were worth anything after he extracted their memories. Stealing their memories wholly as he did, it usually left a human in an almost catatonic state. And if he turned them into Valkoer, they'd only become sex slaves to the deviant fuckers who came down here.

His time on Earth had more or less soured him on sex. Humans were filthy. So unclean. The thought of these innocent children who offered such joy in their memories becoming nothing more than sperm receptacles for the filthy degenerates who frequented this place seemed too cruel a punishment for their gifts.

So he gave them a gift of his own: *freedom in death.*

He looked at the girl, an adorable blonde with big blue eyes and the happiest of smiles. Esmerelda was excellent at finding gleeful children to take.

Jacob hated draining the life from children of sorrow, like those wastrels raised in The Forgotten Kingdom. He'd had enough sadness in his life, and didn't want to experience *more.*

"Do you want to play a game?" Jacob asked, smiling.

Jessa sat forward on the bed and closed her book, folding her hands on top of it. "I'd love to, mister."

"Good. I want you to close your eyes and remember the happiest moment of your life."

"Hmm," she said, squeezing them tight.

A smile lit her face, visible even in the chamber's gloom. Jacob looked down at her, so pure, so innocent, and wondered how the monsters in the other rooms could be raping such a thing.

Especially when the real prize wasn't their body, but rather their memories. There was such pleasure to be had in their memories, a happiness Jacob hadn't felt authentically for as long as he could remember.

"Do you have a good memory?" he asked.

His body tingled with anticipation, wondering what beautiful moment he was about to experience. Would it be a swim in a pure lake beneath a warm sun he could no longer enjoy? Time spent with a loving mother or father instead of the two wretched fucks he'd been saddled with? Perhaps it would be something he couldn't imagine, some enjoyment or feeling of love he'd yet to experience in his own life, or vicariously through another.

The girl was ripe with possibilities. His heart raced as he stepped toward her.

She beamed, "Yes, I've got a *great* memory!"

"That *is* great," Jacob said, reaching out to touch her face.

TWO

## John

JOHN CROUCHED in the bushes along the gas station's perimeter on the corner of Fisher and Twelfth across from Omega's temporary headquarters, waiting. He pulled his black hoodie away from his eyes for a better view.

It was six a.m., and he knew his target would be arriving soon, as Special Agent in Charge Serena Sanders was a woman of habit. For the past week, Sanders had stopped at the gas station to get coffee each morning, a few minutes past six.

John didn't want to come, but didn't have a choice. It had been nearly a week since he'd seen the video of Abigail entering the portal — the next day the portal was barricaded by the military and surrounded by ultraviolet lights to keep vampires out. He might be able to cross it with enough force, but he wasn't sure if he could come back through if the military buffed up its protection even more. Plus, he didn't want to kill soldiers merely doing their job.

Yet, he still needed to cross through the portal.

He had to find Abigail. Had to find his brother, Caleb.

Then had to find his brother, Jacob, and retrieve the crystals — all before Jacob returned to Earth with more monsters.

In short, John had to save the only people he cared about, and the planet. But he couldn't do it alone. Or with just Hope and Larry.

John needed help.

*But is the FBI in a helping mood?*

Following events at the old Omega headquarters, and the murders of Commander Mike Mathews and their boss, Director Bob Cromwell, John knew he was WANTED by the FBI. All caps.

The *shoot first, ask questions later* kind of WANTED.

Ironically, it was because John had helped the FBI's Omega division for the past couple of years, arresting their "enemies of the state," that John couldn't turn to his old contacts — Otherworlders, Halfworlders, or even Tiny's crew. They all saw him as a traitor, turning on his own kind. Of course they didn't know that he'd been forced to help the Agency that had threatened Hope and Abigail if he didn't.

But still, a traitor was a traitor, and John had few remaining friends. His last chance was the very Agency he'd been running from before becoming their colleague.

His fate, as well as that of those he loved, and possibly the planet, rested with the results of these next fifteen minutes.

He watched the black SUV pulled up to the station, then the fiftysomething-year-old black woman got out — not a speck of lint on her suit.

Sanders entered the station.

John sprinted from the bushes to the SUV, broke the lock with a minor feat of magick, then hopped inside.

JOHN SAT in the SUV's rear, using a cloaking spell to shroud himself while Sanders chatted with the cashier until the gas station door finally opened and she emerged with two coffees in hand.

Sanders walked around the front of the SUV, unlocked the door, and got inside. As she placed her coffees in the center console, John dropped the spell.

"Coffee? You shouldn't have." John's gun was at the back of Sanders's head before she could react. "Close the door; we're taking a drive."

THEY WERE PARKED in the rear of a Walmart parking lot, a place granting them ample privacy and unlikely to invite attention from cops that parking along the roadside might.

John had explained the situation to Sanders — though not his request — as they drove. But he had yet to get a read on the woman's emotions. Sanders held her cards close. Sure, John knew the agent would love to turn around, rip the gun from his hands, and arrest him, but he couldn't tell from her zen exterior.

Sanders turned off the truck. "So, what do you want from me?"

"Help. I want you to assemble a team, with me on it, to go after Jacob and recover the crystals."

"And what are *you* going to do with the crystals?"

"*I* don't want them. You all do whatever it is you do with your Otherworldly artifacts. But we both know that Jacob can't be allowed to keep them. He killed many people to get them, and from what I can tell, they're extremely powerful. Do we really want to wait and see what he's planning to do once he unleashes their power?"

"How do you know he hasn't already? That he's not waiting for *us* to come through the portal? That this isn't some sort of trap? How do I know *you're* not working with him to lead us *into* that trap?"

John met Sanders's eyes in the rearview.

"Come on, Serena. You know better than that."

"What I *know* is that you and your friends are responsible for the deaths of several agents, as well as the former director."

Her tone revealed her anger. John had to tread lightly, appeal to the good agent he knew the woman to be.

"What happened with the director wasn't intentional. But I think *we both know* those agents weren't the good guys. I watched Mathews kill an innocent woman in cold blood just to keep her quiet, a woman who had just lost her daughter. Is *that* the kind of Agency you want to be part of?"

"So you kill a bunch of people, and I'm supposed to take *your* word for it that *they* were bad?"

"No, Serena. You don't need to take my word for anything. I think you know damn well that things weren't right. It's why you've turned down so many promotions, isn't it? Figured you'd lie low as an agent until you got a corporate gig or retired. Right?"

Sanders stared back in the mirror, hard. She wasn't used to someone reading her so easily.

"I don't know who's calling the shots, but I'm guessing they don't want the world to end any more than I do. If we don't go in there and get those crystals, Jacob will return. And *nobody* is prepared for what he'll bring back."

Sanders didn't need any intel on Otherworld's

monstrosities. She'd been with Omega long enough to have tracked down a few of the minor beasties and freaks, ones created on this world using Otherworldly magick, to understand exactly how much trouble they'd be in if the real things started spilling in through the portal. With Jacob as the Pied-Piper, it would be nothing less than a mass slaughter of humanity.

Serena's silence said she was contemplating the offer.

"I'm here because I trust you. You're not at this job for power. You want to help others. I can tell from the few times we've worked together. Women like you are rarely in charge for very long. Eventually some power-hungry dipshit will come gunning for you, or the Agency will find someone more willing to kiss ass and kowtow to the Guardians. That leaves you with a narrow window of opportunity to act and to do something good."

"How do I know I can trust *you?*"

"Because if all I wanted was to go through the portal, I wouldn't be asking for permission, or help. I'd just find a way through."

Sanders nodded. "Let me run it up the chain and see what we get from the bosses. How do I get in touch with you?"

John handed her a cell phone. "Call me on that. Number's already in there. Just one thing before I go. Your bosses will try and convince you to not go through with this. Maybe they'll even tell you to act like you're going to help, then capture me at the last minute and bring me to their godforsaken "research" facility. But you'll be betraying humanity if you do. I need you make this happen, even if that means standing up to your bosses. Can you do that, Serena?"

"I'll see what I can do," she said, not meeting his eyes.

John sighed. "Well, I guess that'll have to be good enough for now."

He opened the door and escaped into the night.

# THREE

# Abigail

Abigail could hardly believe her eyes as they crossed from one world into the next.

Skies were purple here instead of blue. The grass was so bright green it felt like a cartoon. And the world smelled so different — the air rich with sweet scents she'd never smelled on Earth. Abigail wasn't sure if they were smelling food in some nearby town or fruits and flowers from unseen fields that she couldn't even imagine.

It was nighttime back home, but daytime here.

Abigail's skin wasn't burning from the sun.

She looked over at her friend Talani, then at Judith and Solomon, Judith's husband. The women wore matching long, plain brown dresses with dark hoods and cloaks, while Solomon was in brown pants and a plain gray shirt, no cloak or hood, and a leather pack strapped to his back. Their clothing reminded Abigail of early American settlers, and it felt odd being in a dress and uncomfortable leather shoes that were nothing like her usual sneakers.

They stood in awe of the world around them,

absorbing the myriad sights that Abigail was still trying to process.

"Why aren't we burning?" she asked the other vampires.

Talani looked over to Abigail, her dark skin practically glowing.

Abigail looked down at her own pale skin. It was also glowing, as was Judith's and Solomon's sheer white skin, which only seemed to brighten their white hair.

Talani smiled. "Solomon used a spell to keep us safe from the sun."

Though the sun wasn't harming her, Abigail could still sense its warmth, and it felt fabulous. Between the years she'd spent imprisoned in Randy Webster's closet and those following John turning her into a vampire, she'd almost forgotten the feel of sun on her skin.

She fell to the ground, running her hands through the thick green grass, digging her fingers into the rich soil, tears of joy streaming down her cheeks.

"This is soooo beautiful," she said to Talani.

Talani fell to the ground beside Abigail, embracing the girl and holding her tight. "Aren't you glad you came?"

Abigail flinched from the hug, used to avoiding contact with everyone but John — whom she rarely ever saw — lest they die by her touch. But then she remembered that Talani was just like her, a vampire. She hugged her new friend back, and felt even warmer.

She'd been on this world less than five minutes and already felt at home.

She'd been reluctant to leave everything she knew behind, especially leaving with these people she didn't know. But John was busy with his government work, and she couldn't stay with Larry, not after she accidentally killed her tutor, Katya, the first girl Abigail had allowed into her heart since her mother's death, a woman she could tell that Larry was falling for. He might have eventually forgiven Abigail, but he'd never fully trust her. How could he, when *she* didn't even trust the monster inside her — the one that needed feeding to keep her alive?

*Better to be with others like me, even if they're strangers.*

While she wasn't sure what to make of Judith — the woman felt a bit icy — or Solomon, who seemed so quiet, Abigail thought she could really come to like Talani.

The girl was only a few years older than Abigail. And she, more than anyone, seemed to understand what Abigail was going through — her pain at having killed innocents, and someone close to her.

"Yes," Abigail said. "I'm so glad I came."

Talani stood, offered her hands to Abigail, then helped her to stand, then began to spin her around. Abigail felt carefree, like a little kid on a playground.

They collapsed to the ground, laughing.

And laughter had never felt better.

As Judith and Solomon surveyed the clearing, Abigail and Talani lay staring up at the sky and its woolly white clouds.

"The sky looks so cool," Abigail said. "I wonder why it's purple."

"I don't know, but you're right: it *is* cool."

Abigail looked at Judith and Solomon — standing near the tree line, hands held, eyes closed, faces turned to the sky.

"What are they doing?"

"Probably trying to find a bird to hijack its sight so they can find the town."

"They can *do* that? Tap into animals to see through their eyes? Can *we* do that?"

"Judith and Solomon can, yes. Solomon tried to teach

me, but I haven't been able to get the hang of it. But they've been vampires a lot longer than I have."

"How long?"

"I dunno. Thousands of years?"

"What about you?"

Talani didn't answer.

Abigail rolled over to see her friend's face. Talani stared up at the sky as if wrestling with whether she wanted to talk about herself.

"Long enough," she finally said. Given her lack of eye contact and tone of voice, Abigail decided to drop it. The last thing she wanted was to make her new friend uncomfortable.

Abigail rolled back over, stared at the sky, and tried to think of a way to transition from the awkward silence.

"Sorry, I didn't mean to —"

"It's okay. Just not something I like to think about. But hey, I'm sure none of us has a good story on how we turned, right?"

Abigail thought about her own turning — shot in a motel parking lot, dying until John gifted her with his curse.

She told Talani her story.

"And are you glad he turned you?"

Abigail kept staring at the clouds, even though she could tell that Talani was now lying on her side, looking at her.

"I dunno. I mean, I guess I'm glad I'm not dead, but at the same time, I don't like feeding on other people to survive."

"Yeah, it can be tough."

"How do *you* do it, Talani? You seem nice. How do you decide whose life to take so you can live?"

"At first it was tough. I didn't want to feed. But I was young."

"How old were you when you turned?"

"Five."

Abigail sat up, met her friend's haunted eyes.

"Five?"

"Yeah."

"But you look sixteen." Abigail remembered Judith saying she could use a spell to age them. "Did Judith age you?"

"Yeah," Talani said, plucking fat green blades of grass from the ground and running them through her fingers.

"Oh, wow."

Abigail stared at the blades, her mind turning the possibility of Judith aging her. Talani, either sensing Abigail's thoughts or invading them again, said, "You want her to age you, don't you?"

Abigail felt guilty, though she didn't know why.

"Maybe. Why?"

"Just asking."

"Do you think I should?"

"I dunno. Why do you want to be older?"

"I don't know."

"Sure you do," Talani said, meeting her eyes, challenging Abigail.

"I don't like being a helpless child. First my parents died, leaving me all alone in the world. Then my only family, my jerk of an uncle, sold me to a man who kept me in a closet as a sex slave. And then I got kidnapped by this evil vampire, Jacob. Then I wound up staying in a house with John's friend, Larry, who was super nice. But, as you know, I then accidentally killed a family of innocent people, and then my only friend. Nothing good has come from my childhood. The sooner it's over, the sooner I can start a new life."

Talani looked at Abigail, her smile kind. "Everything will be better now. I promise."

Abigail wanted to ask her how she could be sure. They hardly knew one another, and were on a world that neither of them was familiar with. How could she be confident enough to promise what she couldn't possibly know?

But Abigail said nothing.

There was something comforting about Talani's blind optimism that made Abigail almost believe her. She certainly *wanted* to believe her, anyway.

"Thank you," Abigail said, wanting to hug Talani, but not comfortable enough to initiate.

Talani reached over and hugged Abigail again.

Abigail wasn't sure if the girl was in her head and knew she wanted a hug, but oddly, she didn't even care. The thought of someone else being there gave her comfort, especially after John being gone from her head for so long.

The sound of footsteps broke the moment.

Judith and Solomon were heading toward them.

Talani stood and helped Abigail to her feet. "What's up?" Talani asked. "Did you find the town?"

"Yes," Judith said. "We're about a day's walk from Jonah."

"Jonah?" Abigail asked. "Is that a town or person?"

"Both," said Solomon. "My sister, Cassandra, lives there, with other Outcasts under the town. We'll be safe."

As they walked, Judith explained that the town beneath the town was a refuge for other vampires and freaks shunned from The Forgotten City, and hunted in The Freelands by The Hand of the Seven Gods. They were given safe passage under The South's oldest town, Jonah.

Abigail wasn't sure how much she liked the idea of

living in an underground town, but didn't want to seem whiny. She could take things one day at a time. So long as Talani stayed by her side, things wouldn't be too bad.

ABIGAIL COULDN'T STOP GAWKING as they made their way out of the woods then traveled along a brick-paved road toward Jonah. Everywhere she looked, there was something she'd never seen — from giant, ancient trees to birds and other animals that looked both odd and somewhat familiar at the same time, like evolutionary cousins to animals on Earth. There were large white birds that looked like cockatoos, but far larger. Long rodent-like beasts scurrying along the brush on either side of the road. Creatures that she couldn't quite make out scampering in the shadows of the brush.

Abigail also heard exotic noises she'd never heard: chirps and birdsong, insect-like buzzing and clicking, the occasional unidentifiable animal yelp that made her jump. The sounds made her think of an old black-and-white movie she'd seen on TV one night when she couldn't find anything else to watch, about a man named Tarzan who grew up in the jungle.

She remembered his yell and had to stifle a giggle as she imagined herself swinging on a vine and doing the same thing.

Talani looked over and smiled. "What?"

"Nothing, just thinking how weird everything is here."

Of course, given her age and how much of her childhood she'd spent indoors, Abigail couldn't be certain that at least some of these animals didn't also exist on Earth. Most of her worldly knowledge had come from books, after all.

So far, thankfully, she hadn't seen anything too scary. She hoped their luck would hold out until they reached Jonah. Despite her unease, she wasn't genuinely afraid because she was with Judith, Solomon, and Talani, who had easily dispatched the soldiers outside the portal despite their many guns and security measures. Surely, they could put down a few scary animals if they had to.

After what felt like hours of walking, they stopped along the roadside, and Solomon slung his backpack onto the ground.

"Anybody thirsty?"

Talani said yes, and Abigail echoed.

Solomon handed them each a bottle of water then shared his with Judith.

Abigail drank, not wanting to mention her hunger, wondering if the other vampires even ate food or if they filled up on the soldiers guarding the portal. Abigail's human and vampire appetites were very different things. But she didn't know if that was true for others. She'd seen John eat but wasn't sure if it was something he *needed* to do. She remembered seeing a movie with Larry one night called *Let the Right One In*, where the vampire girl got sick after eating. But it wasn't exactly a documentary, and even if it had been, Abigail, John, and the others were different kinds of vampires — with these weird parasites that totally grossed her out whenever she thought too much about it.

Her vampire side wasn't yet hungry, but her stomach was growling.

Abigail couldn't remember the last time she'd eaten solid food. Her growl only grew louder as she drank, enough to widen Talani's eyes. "Is that *you?*"

Abigail nodded. "Yeah. Sorry."

Talani turned to Solomon. "The poor kid is starving. Do you have anything in there to eat?"

The fact that Talani asked Solomon if he had food made her wonder if maybe they didn't eat. She couldn't imagine not eating, then she started thinking about all the yummy foods she'd had since John saved her from Randy's closet of horror — french fries, milkshakes, pizza, and those cheese sticks that Katya had loved.

Of course, thinking of these things only made her hungrier.

Solomon reached into his backpack, pulled out a banana, and threw it to Abigail.

While she hadn't expected him to throw it, her instincts were surprisingly quick, and her hand flicked forward to seize the banana.

She was surprised by her reflexes. Abigail was definitely faster, and her instincts sharper than ever, but she hadn't realized how much had changed since becoming a vampire. She wondered if being around this group was enhancing her abilities. Nobody else seemed to notice, maybe because it wasn't impressive to them.

Abigail said, "Thank you" and peeled her banana.

After Solomon slipped back into his pack, they continued on their way, drinking and eating as they walked.

"When you're done, give your bottles and banana peel to Solomon," Judith said. "We don't want to leave any evidence."

"What *would* people do if they found our stuff, or found *us*?" Abigail asked.

"I don't know," Judith said. "And I'd prefer we not find out. That's why we're all wearing these clothes, to blend in with the natives. It's been a long time since I've been here, so I don't know how much has changed. But I do know that we can't let people know we're from Earth. They may take us as enemies, or want to know the portal's location. It won't end well. Fortunately, Solomon has been talking to his sister, and she's going to create covers for us to live under the radar."

"How did he talk to his sister?" Abigail asked. "Telepathy?"

Solomon looked at Judith, as if seeking approval to respond.

She nodded.

"Magick. Specifically a book he's had since he came over to Earth ages ago."

"Cool." Abigail wondered if she could use it to reach John. She didn't want to ask, *yet*. "How does it work? And how were you able to find your sister?"

Solomon answered, "It's a family book. We've been writing back and forth for millennia."

"Wow. And you haven't seen her since you left Earth? She never crossed over?"

"No. All the portals were closed."

"Until John and his brothers opened one," Abigail said. "And then Jacob opened the other."

"Yes."

"Do you think there will be more?" Abigail asked.

"I don't know. But I figured if we were going to return home, we ought to do it before either someone closes it, or —"

Solomon stopped.

Abigail caught Judith giving him a glance — like he'd said too much.

"Or what?" Abigail said, undeterred by Judith's glare.

Judith responded, "We don't know what's going to happen with the portals. But it could get ugly."

"How?" Abigail remembered John and Larry discussing the terrible things that could happen if Jacob unleashed his monsters on Earth, but that seemed like worst-case speculation. It wasn't as if Jacob had *told them* of his diabolical plans. Maybe Judith or Solomon had inside information.

"I've seen the things King Zol does to his enemies when I lived here before," Judith said. "If he goes through the portals, no one on Earth will be safe."

Abigail wondered if John and Larry would be in danger, but didn't want to voice her fear. She felt hesitant to mention them, though she wasn't sure why.

Talani was looking at her but not saying anything.

*Are you in my head, Talani? Should I avoid mentioning John and Larry?*

She waited for a response that never came.

But Talani *did* have a conspiratorial gleam in her eye, a *let's just keep this between us* sort of look. She wondered if Talani could read her thoughts but couldn't broadcast so close to Judith without Judith *overhearing*.

Talani gave the subtlest of nods.

Abigail smiled, comforted by their shared link rather than feeling violated as she initially had at the thought of a stranger rooting through her memories and thoughts.

Abigail looked at Judith walking with Solomon. "If the King is such a scary guy, why are we even coming to this planet?"

"Because sometimes it's better to hide in plain sight. The Outcasts, most of them expelled from the walled-off King's Forgotten Kingdom, have been living under the city of Jonah for a long time."

"Why do the Outcasts live under the city? Hiding from the King?"

"No, the King doesn't care about them. They're not his concern if they've left his flock."

"Then who are they hiding from?"

"The Hand of the Seven Gods."

"Who are *they*?" Abigail asked, confused.

Solomon suddenly stopped.

Judith paused in response, and for a moment time seemed to freeze, until Abigail saw the black arrow sticking out of the back of Solomon's skull.

Abigail screamed.

Time pitched forward in a gut-churning lurch as Solomon fell face forward to the grass. Screams erupted in the woods.

And then, as Solomon's spell died with him, the sun unleashed hell upon them.

FOUR

# John

It wasn't an army, but John guessed it would have to do.

It was daybreak, and he was standing just outside the portal, in the mobile control center with Special Agent in Charge Serena Sanders. They were looking out the truck's window at the assembled team of twelve agents who would join John, Larry, and Hope on their trip to Otherworld to retrieve the crystals.

John thought it would be hell trying to convince Omega and The Guardians to allow civilians Larry and Hope to join them. But John made it clear that he wasn't going alone, and if he couldn't bring his most trusted people, then he wasn't going at all. The Agency could take their chances with humans. To his surprise, he didn't get much of an argument from Sanders, though they *did* have a lengthy discussion establishing the mission's ground rules.

While they saw eye to eye on the primary objective, they disagreed on the others. There was only one for the Agency: to retrieve the crystals and find a way to close the portals.

But John wasn't coming back without Abigail or his

brother, Caleb — assuming Caleb hadn't, as Jacob had boasted, been turned bad by their father.

"So, these are your best?" John surveyed the field of agents. There were eight men and four women, all of them, save for a couple, looking too green for a battle against Jacob and whatever other hellish beasts waited on the other side.

"This is who the bosses would let me take," Sanders said with resignation, hand on her hip as she looked at them through the window. "After all, we've got to keep our best people defending both portals in case Jacob, or anyone else, invades while we're over there."

John supposed it made sense, though he wished their number was greater. He remembered seeing the video showing how easily the vampires with Abigail had dispatched the soldiers guarding the portal; the battle lasted only seconds.

"This crew is more experienced than the ones that *were* guarding the portal before, right?"

"Yes. They have field experience dealing with Other-worlders."

"How many of those Otherworlders were vampires, as opposed to some halfassed magick user or thief?"

"Enough to give us hope, but not enough that we should be counting chickens."

"Well, thank you for your honesty. And hey, at least they're letting *you* go."

She shrugged as if it wasn't any great honor. Hell, maybe they wanted her to go because they saw her as expendable. Gotta keep her position open for someone a bit more willing to play ball, after all.

"There's one other thing you should know, John. You see that one?" Sanders nodded toward a petite young woman sitting cross-legged on the asphalt smoking a cigarette and anxiously eying the portal. Everything about her looked like she either needed attention or rejected authority, maybe both, from her purple pixie cut, multiple facial piercings and black lipstick, to the tattoos covering her hands and creeping up her arms under the Guardian uniform.

"Her name is Emma Crowe, a Halfworlder thief whose twin brother, Logan, was with a group we sent through for recon."

"He was lost?"

"Yeah, along with six other agents, four days ago."

"So, why are we bringing her? She's just a kid."

"Don't let her looks fool you. She's one of the best at getting in and out of places. A master of shadows, as your people say."

John laughed. "I hadn't heard that one, but okay."

"She's also got a telepathic bond with her brother, so she might be our key to getting around over there."

"Assuming he's alive?"

Sanders nodded. "Emma said she felt his presence. That he's still alive, and once we're over there she hopes to contact him."

"Does she even *want* to go? She looks pissed."

"Emma's pissed at the world. Her father was a magick-using troublemaker who died when she was fourteen. She and her brother lived on the streets for a while until we caught them breaking into a black site where we were holding a friend of theirs."

"And, what, you decided to *hire* them?"

"Long story short, we persuaded her brother to work *with* rather than *against* us. We offered them a chance to have normal lives, something they never could've had otherwise. Gave them new names and a house, set them on the straight and narrow."

*No, the agency saw a couple of kids with powers they could exploit. Let's not pretend you all are rehabilitating people out of the goodness of your hearts.*

John didn't say that, of course. Serena wasn't like the others in her position before. She probably hated exploiting Otherworlders as much as anyone.

John looked at the girl and wondered how much pain she'd seen in her young life living among Otherworlders and Halfworlders. John hated that so many of the criminal Otherworlders couldn't keep to their own, finding humans to breed with. Why bring kids into a world that wasn't meant for their kind? Under a government that actively sought out their marginalization and extinction?

He found himself thinking of Abigail, and how she'd had that same lost look when he found her.

John asked, "Think she'll be up for this?"

"Think *your people* will be?"

John nodded as he looked at Hope and Larry just outside the truck and getting outfitted with Agency gear and uniforms. He wouldn't tell Sanders, but John *was* worried about their odds of survival.

Larry was habitually out of shape, had bushy hair and a beard that looked like he didn't give two fucks about grooming, and a body built by Mountain Dew and Doritos, though he'd proved himself a scrappy survivor many times over the years. But Hope was another story.

She was in decent enough shape for a civilian, but Hope hadn't been through the battles that he and Larry had. And, so far as John knew, she had little training with weapons. Sure, Hope had saved his life when putting a bullet in Greg, but that was a close shot, against one man. How would she fare against *multiple inhuman enemies that ran so fast they were a blur to the human eye?*

Still, she insisted on coming. And what else could he

do? Have someone wipe her memory and hide her away, *again?* Even if she'd allow it, which she wouldn't, they didn't have the time, and John could no longer trust the Agency to protect her. They'd probably hide her away again, wipe her memory, then use her as leverage to get him to continue doing their bidding, *again.*

But maybe there was more to Hope than he knew.

Ever since his discovery that she was, in fact, an Otherworlder sent over shortly after he and Caleb, John wondered how much she'd been through. He also wondered who originally wiped her mind, to keep her ignorant of her heritage. It had to be someone with The Guardians, maybe even the late Duncan Alderman, the man who had protected Caleb, and kept John locked in government research labs trying to turn him into an Agency asset.

Whatever the case, he had to trust that Hope could take care of herself — that she would find a way to survive in Otherworld, particularly if something happened to him. Perhaps her instincts were razor-sharp and would awaken in a moment of crisis.

"Ready?" Sanders asked.

John sighed. "Yeah, let me talk with Larry and Hope one last time, make sure they're good."

"Okay, I'll call the boss and get this thing going."

John stepped outside of the truck and approached Hope and Larry.

Larry was struggling to strap a bulletproof vest over his black Guardian uniform. "They really ought to make these fuckers a bit bigger for us plus-sized guys."

"Or maybe you could slow down on the Mountain Dew?" John suggested.

"Screw you, buddy. You just hate me because I'm sexy.

It's okay. I've lived with the pain of being beautiful all my life. You know how it is, right, Hope?"

She laughed and joked, "Yep, it's rough to be so pretty."

"See?" Larry said. "Maybe someday you'll understand, John."

Larry leaned over and unzipped a black tactical backpack on the ground. In addition to supplies needed on their trip, he revealed two bottles of Dew.

"*Really?*" John asked.

"Hey, I'm guessing we're gonna need all the caffeine we can get."

John shook his head then turned to Hope, also decked out in Guardian black, staring out at the horizon and seemingly lost in thought.

He wondered if she was having second thoughts about the journey, or hell, maybe second thoughts on being with him.

It had only been a few days since she'd remembered her life with him in the nineties, and how he'd betrayed her by wiping her memories and hiding her away. She'd been plenty pissed, and he couldn't really blame her. He also couldn't blame her if she'd lost whatever love she'd once felt for him. It had been a long time since they'd been together as a couple, and who knew how much she remembered, how much of her more recent life clouded out her old life, or if their love could survive such a break.

*He* still loved her, but it was easy for him. John had devoted his life to protecting her, even if they couldn't be together and his touch spelled her death. Something about that kind of sacrifice placed her on a constant pedestal in his heart.

But back together, pedestals were out of place. Now he

had the hard work of earning her trust, trying to reignite whatever embers might still be burning.

"You okay?" John put a gloved hand on her uniformed shoulder.

Hope met his eyes, blinked as if trying to snap back to the moment. "Yeah, just thinking this could be the last time I see our sun rise."

"We're going to make it back."

"Don't do that."

"Do what?"

"Make promises you can't keep. You don't know what's going to happen over there any better than I do. So, please, let's not pretend."

Larry looked at them, realized they needed space to talk, then walked over to Emma with the purple hair, and started to chat.

John turned back to Hope. He *really* didn't want to start their trek to another world with an argument. Besides, wasn't it just a few nights ago that Hope had begged to come, said if he died, she wanted to die with him? Maybe she was finally coming to her senses.

"You don't have to come. I can have Larry stay with you. I know he looks like a slob and his sense of humor is crass, but he's a great guy, and you couldn't ask for a better bodyguard. Maybe we could even get some other Guardians to protect you."

It wasn't his favorite option, particularly since he didn't trust them not to take her again. Still, dancing with the devil he knew *might* not be the worst idea.

"No, John. You're not pushing me away again. I lost more than a decade of my life because of you! Do you know what it's like to have your life stolen? To be given a false history, a past, a family, and memories that aren't even yours?"

"I wouldn't need to wipe your memories this time."

"I don't care. I'm going with you."

"Even though we could die?"

"I'd rather die fighting than live hiding."

Noble talk. John wondered if she had any sense of just how dangerous this was, and that neither he, nor their small army, might be able to protect her.

He flashed back to their life in Saint Augustine in what now seemed like forever ago. There had been a time when she was sure that a cook in the kitchen at the restaurant where she worked was abusing his girlfriend, one of the servers. She was determined to end it, even if that meant incurring the guy's wrath. She came to John, not asking what to do so much as making sure she would be doing the right thing in confronting him. She had such a fire in her eyes, standing up for a coworker.

It was dangerous, but John knew there was no talking her out of it. He offered to handle the matter, but Hope had refused. Said she would take care of it, and if she couldn't, *then* John could be a tough guy.

But he never had to.

Hope scared the guy straight. He started going to anger management classes, and last anyone knew, had actually changed for the better.

She had that same fiery look in her eyes now, on the cusp of war with Jacob and whatever forces he surrounded himself with.

Hope was pissed, partly at John, yes, but even more so at his brother Jacob, who had brought this hell into their lives.

"Okay. I won't try talking you out of it. But before we go in, you've got to promise me something."

"What's that?"

"If anything happens to me, anything at all, you can't

try to save me. Go with whoever is left, and get somewhere safe."

She met his eyes then shook her head. "No. We're in this together, for better or for worse."

John was thinking of something else to say, but the command unit door opened and Sanders stepped out, gear bag slung over her back.

"You all ready to kick some ass?" she barked.

John wasn't sure what to expect, maybe a Marines "Hoo-rah!" battle cry. Instead, he saw only solemn nods.

John looked at Larry and sent a telepathic message to his friend: *This is a suicide mission.*

Shaking his head, Larry sent one back: *"Then let's make sure we take as many of these fuckers as possible."*

# FIVE

# Abigail

THE AGONY WAS intense and immediate, like being doused in flames.

"Down!" Talani shouted, throwing herself atop Abigail and covering them both with her cloak.

Arrows hissed overhead as Abigail surrendered to Talani's darkness, hoping her friend wasn't getting hit with arrows.

Judith screamed. Abigail didn't know if it was pain from the sun, because she'd been hit with an arrow, was reacting to Solomon's murder, or was launching an attack of her own.

A man shrieked then choked: Judith was striking back.

"Get up!" Abigail shouted. "We've gotta help her!"

Talani was frozen. Abigail wasn't sure if it was her fear of being hit by the still-flying arrows, exposure to the sun, or an urge to keep shielding her.

After a long moment, Talani launched herself up as she pulled her cowl around her face and seized on an enemy.

Abigail leaped to her feet, secured her hood, and looked around.

The sun was blazing, but the cloak and hood provided enough shelter to keep Abigail from burning. She didn't dare expose any flesh for fear of both seeing what damage had already been done *and* getting burned again.

The arrows had ceased. Dozens of men and women, dirty and dressed in tattered leathers and cloth, rushed toward them clinging to all matter of weapons — blades, spears, long staves, and axes. Some of the blades were a deep, dark black, which some part of Abigail sensed was dangerous to her kind. She wasn't sure what these people were — bandits, pirates, savages, or what. Their look reminded her of wild animals.

*Bandits.*

Abigail's eyes caught sudden movement to her right.

She turned in time to intercept a skinny, filthy man swinging a knife with a chipped blade, then fell backward, hand reaching out to balance herself and catching hold of the man's forearm.

Her fingers locked on. Energy coursed through Abigail.

No matter how many times she fed on another, there was no getting used to the euphoria that flooded her mind and body.

A part of her wanted to freeze time and live in the bliss.

But she knew the dangers of staying too long.

Victims' memories followed the energy, and given the man's appearance — a poor beggar who'd been forced to do God only knew what to survive — his memories would surely infect her spirit, spinning Abigail into a depression that would make her useless in battle. There was also the danger of being frozen in the feeding for so long that she'd be blind to the world, and any threat hurtling toward her.

She flung the man away as his memories crossed into hers, then spun toward the footsteps behind her.

An axe swung at her gut.

She fell backward again, but not soon enough.

The blade licked her stomach, a trail of blood following the tip as it finished its arc.

Abigail wasn't sure of the wound's depth, but her body was on fire as her back slapped the grass.

Her hood askew, the sun assaulted her face.

A shadow fell over Abigail and graced her with protection.

Time seemed to stop again as she looked up and locked eyes with her attacker — a girl, not much older than her: grimy-faced; eyes wide and dark with fear; dark, rotting teeth in a savage snarl.

The girl grunted as she dove blade first toward Abigail.

She rolled out of the way. The girl hit the ground with a grunt, then turned on Abigail, too late.

Abigail's hands found her throat, and again she drank.

*More energy!*

Abigail could feel the burns she'd suffered already repairing.

Abigail disengaged, but instead of shoving the corpse away, she let the girl's burned but not yet ashen body fall on her, shielding Abigail from the sun and hiding her from enemies as more scurried from the tree line into the clearing.

She stayed perfectly still, her face buried in the girl's grimy blouse, playing dead, eyes closed, hoping none of the bandits saw through her ruse and rushed to finish her off with a well-placed blade through her chest or head.

Staying still was almost impossible. She'd surely

hyperventilate under the dead girl's weight and the raw panic clawing at her insides as footsteps multiplied around her.

How many of them had stopped to look down, to consider the dead girl? How long before one of the bandits realized she was faking? Or maybe pulled the body off of Abigail and exposed her to the sun? She could never play dead through that.

Abigail had to stay calm. Had to be still, like death, long enough to heal her quickly knitting stomach wound and take the enemy by surprise.

*If they don't kill Talani and Judith first!*

*No, don't think of that.*

*Think of something happy.*

Her mind flashed back to that night that she, John, Larry, and Tiny had taken the van out for their "last meal" before going to war with Jacob back on Earth.

She was enjoying her chocolate shake, and the giant man named Tiny told her to dip her fries into the shake.

At the time, it sounded like the grossest thing ever. Until she actually tried it.

She had tried to shove fries into John's mouth, but he closed it, grossed out.

"Don't be so lame," Larry had said.

John shot Larry a look then turned to Abigail with a reluctant sigh. "Fine."

And he liked it.

It was the last first time Abigail had felt part of something since her family had died. And while dipping fries in a milkshake might be a silly memory not amounting to much for most kids with awesome lives, it was one of her most cherished.

Soon the memory's warmth turned to ice as Abigail remembered accidentally killing her instructor and friend,

Katya, before running away from Larry and John, the only family she had.

Talani's scream tore Abigail from her self-pity.

She turned toward the battle sounds, her heart sinking as she saw a small crowd of at least twenty bandits surrounding Judith and Talani, wildly swinging their blades.

The crowd was a wall — she couldn't see how much damage they'd done, or how close they were to killing her friends.

Abigail looked around and saw that nobody was paying her any mind. All of the bandits — at least those who had come from the woods — were circling her companions.

She ignored the pain in her gut and ran toward the chaos.

No time for planning. Abigail simply acted, laying hands on the necks of two men closest to the edge.

Her touch was fire.

She let go as they screamed, knowing she wouldn't have long before weapons were on her, too.

That meant injuring, not killing, or draining the men dry — *yet*.

She flung the screaming men far away from the circle, hoping they were too injured to get up and fight back.

Three others, two men and a woman — all scrawny, filthy, and wild-eyed — turned on Abigail, gripping their weapons and sizing her up.

She had seconds before one, or all, would strike her, or call out to the others still focused on Judith and Talani, whom Abigail could no longer see.

Surveying the situation, Abigail lost her advantage.

Two of the bandits started forward, one with a spear and the other with a blade.

Adrenaline, and the fiery life force of those she'd

already attacked, fueled Abigail as she rolled forward, beneath their weapons and between the bandits.

She popped up behind them, grabbing their bare arms and squeezing tight.

Energy flooded her system, and she held on longer.

*Just a little more to heal my wounds, to give me …*

Lightning split through Abigail's back.

She screamed, releasing her prey and falling to the ground.

Something was lodged in her back — the most intense pain she'd ever felt. She reached around awkwardly to find it with blind fingers. With her sleeves falling away from her hand, the sun punished Abigail's efforts, burning her fingers.

She pushed through the torment as her fingers felt the hilt of what was surely a blade lodged in the small of her back.

*Have to get it out!*

Something then struck her hard in the back of the head.

She fell, face-first into to the grass with a whimper.

The pain in her back radiated fire, a different kind than the life force she fed upon — more like the sun, threatening to devour her entire body.

If she didn't get the knife out, she was going to burn alive, just like her victims.

She struggled through the pain to pull at the blade, doing God knew what kind of damage to her insides, but her hand refused to cooperate.

It was locking up.

Paralyzed. Maybe the skin burned to a crisp, inflexible.

She cried out.

*Have to get away!*

Footsteps behind and above her.

A hand ripped her cowl back, grabbed Abigail by the hair, yanked her to standing.

She screamed, the sun's rays searing her face, sure she would burn to a husk and crumble in the coming breeze.

Her attacker yanked the knife from her back with a grunt.

He threw her back to the ground then rolled Abigail over and dropped atop her, straddling her, one large beefy gloved hand on her neck, choking the life from her body.

He was a mountain of a man, his weight impossible to flee.

At least she was momentarily cast in shadow, staring up at his horrible bucket of a face, a big black messy beard covering where a neck might have been. An awful scar gashed his lips and twisted them in a permanent snarl.

His eyes were most terrifying — milky white and surely cursed.

Yet he was staring straight into Abigail's eyes, spittle flying from his mouth as he snarled, "Time to die, monster!"

"Please, mister," Abigail cried, tears streaming down her hot cheeks, hoping she could appeal to whatever part of this man might think twice about killing a child, monster or not.

Attempts to reach his humanity failed.

With his other hand, he brought the knife back into view — it was short, the same magick-looking black that she'd noticed before — then raised it, ready to plunge it into Abigail's chest.

She gasped, trying to move, but the pain in her body, coupled with the man's weight and vice-like grip on her neck, was too much.

She reached for his face, but her hand was burned and bloody, barely able to move.

She was trapped.

This was how she would die.

Abigail closed her eyes.

Thought of John and Larry.

Wished she'd never left them behind.

She waited to die.

Then a gurgle.

She opened her eyes to see the man's body violently shaking, red fissures breaking through his skin as his body burned from within.

Talani — clothes, cloak, and hood coated in blood — was seizing the man's face, snarling, "Get off of her!"

The man's grip on the knife opened, as did the one on her neck.

Abigail grabbed the weapon, rolled out from beneath him, and struggled to stand, ready to fight.

But the rest of the bandits were dead.

Judith stood behind Talani, pulling her bloody, tattered cloak around herself.

Abigail couldn't tell how much blood belonged to them versus the bandits, but both women looked like they had barely escaped death.

Talani let out an animalistic scream as she drained the last of the big man and let his burned husk fall to the ground.

Then she collapsed, body heaving as she gasped for air.

Abigail stood, staggered toward her — the pain from the blade, or perhaps the sun's assault, now spreading from her back to her arms and legs.

Every step felt like it might end her, but she had to reach her friend, to hug and thank her.

Talani looked up, and there was a light in her eyes that said how glad she was to see Abigail alive. But then it vanished, and Talani's mouth went agape.

"What is it?" Abigail asked, afraid to turn and see another two dozen bandits behind them.

But Talani wasn't looking past Abigail. She was looking right at her. She stood, approaching Abigail, not to embrace her but to look closer.

"What is it?" Abigail asked, suddenly terrified. "What's wrong?"

Talani looked back at Judith, now approaching. "Is she going to —"

"To what?" Abigail cried out, afraid to know what the women were seeing.

*What did the knife do to me?*

Abigail had to ask, even though she was afraid of the answer.

"Am I going to —"

She never finished the question.

# SIX

# Abigail

ABIGAIL WOKE to the sound of footsteps in sand.

She opened her heavy eyelids to blurred darkness.

Movement to her right.

She tried to scramble upright but was held in place by someone bringing her back to the cold ground as they sat beside her.

"Get off of me!"

"Shh, shh." A familiar voice in her ear as hands touched Abigail's shoulders — the only place she didn't hurt.

*Talani.*

"What's going on? Where are we?"

"We're in a cave," Talani said. "And you're sick. The bandits had poisoned blades, deadly to our kind."

"Am I going to die?" Abigail asked, voice cracking.

"Not if we can help it."

"Where's Judith?"

"Out getting help for you."

As Abigail's eyes adjusted to the scant light, she could see that Talani's face was no longer burned and was relieved to see that the burns weren't permanent. Though that didn't mean *Abigail's* weren't.

"I want to see what I look like."

"That's not a good idea. And besides, I didn't pack a mirror."

"Tell me what I look like."

Talani's eyes could barely meet Abigail's.

"I wanna know."

"Well, you're burned, but we can fix that."

"Okay. What else?"

"There are dark veins showing through your skin."

"Dark veins?"

"Black veins."

She held up an arm, but everything was blurry, so she could only make out vague dark lines on her skin.

Abigail did her best to stifle tears, her mind racing for explanations of what was happening to her body, or how she might end up dead.

Talani continued, "The blades are poison to the things inside us."

"The parasites?"

"Yes. The blades kill them with a magickal poison, then — well, you know we can't live without them now, right?"

Abigail nodded.

"So, Judith is out looking for someone to heal you."

"Does she know someone here?"

"Solomon's sister. She's trying to reach her."

"Is Solomon still …?"

"Dead? Yes."

"Will his sister still help us?"

"I hope so, because I don't know if we have any other contacts."

Not knowing what to say, Abigail said nothing.

"How do you feel?"

"Not good."

"Are you hungry?"

"For food or … *the other?*"

"Yes, *the other.*"

Abigail nodded.

"Hold on, then."

Talani stood, then disappeared around a corner. Abigail listened to her footsteps echo off the cave walls before growing closer again.

Only Talani didn't return.

It was someone else. Though blurry, Abigail was pretty sure it was a bandit.

*What? How?*

Abigail's eyes widened as she leaped to her feet then nearly fell over in a dizzy heap, her body rebelling against the movement. Trying to figure out how she could fight back, Abigail realized she wouldn't need to — the bandit's hands were tied behind his back. And he was even younger than her, no older than ten.

Talani entered, smiling. "I got you some lunch."

Abigail stared at the child, her eyes finding a bit more focus. He was filthy, like the others, wearing rags with God only knew how much dirt caked onto them. His hair was dark, long, and matted, reminding her of a neglected animal more than a child. He looked around with nervous glances, perhaps evaluating his odds of escape.

Abigail could feel an intense heat radiating off of his body, practically begging her to feed. Despite his condition, he was still full of energy that would make her feel better.

But when his eyes met hers, she flashed back to her time as a prisoner in Randy's closet. A few months in. His girlfriend, Stacy, had been out of the house, and he had been feeling particularly monstrous. He came into the closet, grabbed Abigail — who had already learned that resistance was futile — picked her up, and carried her to his bed.

It was one of countless such abuses, but something about this particular time stayed with her. Abigail had been trying to decide if that would be the time she'd fight back, try and escape. She'd spent countless nights imagining how she might be able to get away, most of her ideas involving a pair of scissors on the dresser, a knife left on a plate, or something she could use as a weapon.

But Randy was a giant, way bigger and stronger than her. And even if she managed to gain a weapon, Abigail wasn't sure if she could hurt him.

Yes, she had hate in her heart for the things he'd done to her, but she wasn't sure if she could actually kill him.

Worse yet, what if she had failed to hurt him enough? What if the scissors didn't puncture his skin? What if all she did was make him mad?

Surely, he'd grab her awkward weapon then show her how it was *really* used.

But as Randy was taking her to the bed on this particular night, she caught her reflection in the dresser mirror — the one with the scissors — and saw a look in her eyes that chilled her.

She was no longer human.

She was, like the kid before her now, a hopeless animal.

"What are you waiting for?" Talani asked.

"I … can't."

"What do you mean *you can't?* I saved him for you. You need to feed, Abigail."

She looked at the boy, who was staring at her, maybe even feeling a bit of hope on the rise. His eyes were wet with tears, lips trembling, but he was too terrified to speak, or attempt escape.

"Let him go. He's just a kid."

Talani pushed past the boy, stepping up to Abigail, eyebrows furrowed. "We're *all kids!*"

Abigail shook her head.

"He is the enemy. He and his group tried to kill us! They *did* kill Solomon! They almost killed me and Judith! And you!"

"He doesn't know any better. Let him go."

Talani got in Abigail's face, lowering her voice to a whisper. "What's going on, Abigail?"

Tears stung her eyes, but Abigail did her best to hold them in. "Nothing. I just … can't. He's not like them. He's innocent."

"None of us are innocent. You need to get that through your skull. It's us against them. You let him go, and you're handing them one more in their war against us. How long before he comes back, maybe kills me or you for your kindness?"

Maybe Talani was making a good point. But as Abigail eyed the scared, dirty boy, she couldn't get past the truth that he was a child, hurled into a life he didn't ask for, or choose.

"Let him go."

"I'm not letting him go," Talani said, a determined look in her eyes. "If you don't eat him, I will."

An idea came to Abigail. Possibly awful, but the only way she might save the child.

She threw her arms around Talani, hugging her tight.

At first, Abigail made it seem like the kind of hug you give someone when needing comfort, resting her head on Talani's shoulder and closing her eyes.

Then she tightened her arms.

Without looking at the kid, she yelled, "Run!"

Talani pulled back, eyes wide in shock as she squirmed to break free.

Abigail held on as the boy's footsteps bounced off the walls in retreat.

"Let go!" Talani shouted.

Abigail met her eyes and shook her head.

Talani's face turned stone cold, serious and on the verge of an anger that Abigail never wanted to trigger.

"Let me go, Abigail!"

Abigail held tight.

On one hand, she didn't want to alienate her only friend, but on the other, she couldn't let Talani kill the boy.

"No."

Talani stared into her eyes. "You'll die to save your enemy?"

"He's not my enemy."

"Then you're either dumb or blind." Talani broke free, shoving Abigail to the ground.

She hit it so hard, the air was knocked from her lungs.

She could only watch helplessly as Talani raced after the boy, faster than any person should be able to run. Seconds later, while Abigail was still catching her breath, she heard the boy's death cry.

The tears Abigail had been holding back finally broke free.

She sat in silence staring at the cave floor, shaking.

Talani returned, walking slowly.

Abigail couldn't look at her.

"You know I had to do it."

Abigail said nothing, staring at the ground, head down, not wanting Talani to see her tears.

Talani's footsteps drew nearer.

Abigail refused to acknowledge her.

"Come on, Abigail. We only kept him alive to feed you."

Still, Abigail said nothing.

Talani drew closer.

Suddenly Abigail felt Talani's hand on her head, a gentle scalp massage. It felt good, but Abigail refused to acknowledge it. She kept her face down, tears flowing faster.

She hated how easily she cried.

Hated how emotionally unhinged she felt.

Hated this world.

Hated that she left John and Larry.

Hated everything.

"I did it because I love you, Abigail. You're like a sister to me. And I don't want to lose another sister."

Suddenly, Talani's hand gripped tighter on Abigail's skull, followed by a white-hot flash.

At first, Abigail screamed, thinking that Talani was trying to feed off of her. Then she realized Talani was doing the opposite. She was feeding her the boy's energy, along with his terrible memories.

Abigail had no choice but to suck it all in.

JUDITH RETURNED JUST before dawn with news. A witch in the village of Kovar — on the way to Jonah — might be able to help Abigail.

They would sleep through the day and leave at nightfall.

Lying between Judith and Talani on the cave's cold floor, Abigail couldn't help but feel as if each day here was pulling her farther from her true family — John and Larry.

# SEVEN

# John

IT HAD BEEN morning on Earth when they crossed, but it was night in this other world, with two bright moons and a cold howling wind filled with sounds born from nightmares.

There were sixteen of them in total, all on horseback — the only means of reliable travel and carrying gear.

John was wearing a black Guardian uniform like the others, except he wore a helmet and dark visor, and his uniform was made to block the sun. His visor was up, the night allowing him to inhale the fresh air — sweet and unlike anything he'd ever smelled on Earth.

He looked back from his position beside Sanders and the Halfworlder, Emma Crowe, to see how Hope was doing.

If she was anxious, or scared by the sounds of alien wildlife, he couldn't tell — she was laughing at whatever stories Larry was telling. John was glad Larry came along. Not just because Larry was his best friend, but because he was good at things like this — easing Hope's mind as they ventured into a dark and unfamiliar world.

"Got anything yet?" Sanders asked Emma, who had been trying to telepathically connect with her brother Logan.

"I've found him!"

The three of them stopped in their tracks, then the others followed, all eyes on Emma.

John watched the girl's pupils racing beneath her eyelids as she communicated with her lost brother.

Tears streamed down her cheeks, and suddenly her smile broke.

Eyes still closed she said, "He's alive. Some of Jacob's men attacked them, but they managed to escape."

"Does he know where he is?" Sanders asked. "How many of them are still alive?"

She was quiet for a moment, likely relaying the questions to her brother.

John kept watching, heart racing, hoping for any information they could use to find Jacob.

Watching Emma, he couldn't help but think of Abigail, also lost somewhere on this world. Part of him wanted to break off this search for Jacob and the crystals, go find Abigail, and secure her safety first. But that was a dumb idea. Sanders would never abandon their prime objective, not when the crystals posed a threat to Earth. And Abigail *chose* to leave. From the video of her crossing through the portal, she didn't appear to be held against her will or in immediate danger. Abigail was probably sad, lonely, and confused. The other vampires found her, took advantage of her mental state, and convinced her to join them. But he had to assume she was safe, for now.

But of all the unknowns racing through his mind, there was one he couldn't reconcile: Who were these other vampires, and how did they find her? Were they random

Otherworlders she'd run into, or were they working for Jacob?

Emma finally spoke. "Two others are alive. They're hiding in an burned down houses just outside of a place called The Citadel. They're afraid to leave. We have to find them."

"Can they tell us where Jacob is?" Sanders asked.

"They can help us once we find them." Emma opened her eyes, tears falling. "The connection is gone."

John asked, "Did he tell you how we can find them?"

She shook her head. "No, but I can feel him."

John sat up straighter on his horse. "Where?"

"That way." Emma pointed southeast.

"How far?" Sanders asked.

She shook her head. "I'm not sure."

Sanders spoke loud enough for everyone in the party to hear. "We've got a location. Southeast. Not sure how far. We need to hurry."

They set off in their new direction, eager to catch up.

As their horses trotted, John found himself beside Emma. He noticed her watching him from the corner of her eye. She caught him looking and turned back to the path, face flushing.

John wished she hadn't been a Halfworlder, as their auras were never easy to read. They changed too quickly and were rarely accurate. Her colors were a roiling blend of grays and bright pink, two colors that were opposite in humans — sickness and health.

Finally Emma turned back to him, and clearly nervous, she spoke. "You're John, right? A Valkoer?"

"Yes."

She nodded then looked down, avoiding his eyes.

He figured one of two things was happening. Either she knew he'd been working for Omega and was responsible for capturing people she knew, or Emma, like many Halfworlders, didn't care for the vampires among them. John couldn't blame her either way.

He decided to pass the awkwardness with small talk. "How long have you been working with Omega?"

"This is the first time. My brother went to work for them so I wouldn't have to. So I could have a normal life."

"Sounds familiar," John said, thinking of how they leveraged Hope's and Abigail's lives to force his cooperation.

"How's that?"

"They did the same to me, to someone I care about."

Her face warmed, ever so slightly. Maybe she *was* holding his former job against him.

"Oh, I'm sorry."

"We'll get your brother back," John promised. He was nowhere near certain but figured a bit of false confidence might help Emma feel better — maybe strengthen her telepathic bond with her brother. Telepathy was a mental game — the more desperately you tried to connect with someone, the more likely the ability would fail you. Any reassurance could help.

He'd already made his own attempts to connect with Abigail but had so far failed. He couldn't even get a feeling that she was out there. The silence was disturbing, but John couldn't let his doubt take root. Not now. There had to be another reason that he couldn't feel her, something other than her being dead in the woods. If Abigail *was* dead, he felt certain he'd feel it, no matter how far away she was. He'd felt Tiny's death, and his bond with Abigail was much deeper.

"Was it her?" Emma asked, nodding back at Hope, still side by side with Larry, laughing at another one of his stories — about the time he was on a stakeout and had to follow a woman into a female locker room.

John nodded. "Yes."

"Well, you're together now, at least," Emma said, her tone bittersweet.

"We *will* find him," John reiterated. "You're twins, right?"

"Yes, though by virtue of being born twelve seconds later, I'm forever the little sister."

"It's good having someone who always has your back, right?"

"Yeah, it is," Emma said, now melancholic.

Clearly, she wasn't convinced that they'd find her brother. John wondered again what hell she'd been through, and how much had been at the hands of Omega. And again, he thought of Abigail, focusing on her, sending telepathic signals to no response.

*Hey, Larry, you tuned in?*

"You got it, Bro. What's up?"

*Just checking. Trying to reach Abigail.*

"Sorry, man. Why don't you come back here and hang out with us a bit?"

*On it.*

John excused himself from his awkward conversation with Emma and slowed his horse until Larry and Hope were beside him, Hope taking his left and Larry his right.

Larry whispered, "What's Wednesday Adams's deal?"

"Wednesday Adams?" Hope looked at Larry. "You can't think of a reference more recent than that?"

"Sorry," Larry laughed. "I loved The Adams Family."

"She doesn't look anything like her."

"All right, so sue me for a bad joke. At least John never calls out my terrible references."

"That's because he doesn't watch TV."

John added, "And *my* pop culture references are centuries old."

Larry pointed at John. "Yeah, you *are* an old fucker."

They rode for a while just like that, shooting the shit and joking like old friends, even though Larry and Hope hadn't known one another all that well in Florida. Larry was the sort of guy who became an instant buddy, assuming you passed his asshole test.

Suddenly, everything went wrong.

John sensed something in the dark woods, beasts of some sort, drawing closer.

The horses smelled danger.

Hell erupted around them.

The horses freaked, all of them neighing and most of them bucking, throwing their riders to the ground.

John somehow managed to hang on, as did Hope.

And then the beasts came.

Flashes of shadow, hair, claws, and bright crimson eyes moving in the darkness at the speed of murder.

Chaotic screams and movement everywhere at once as horses and people attempted to find safety, and the beasts closed in for the kill.

To John's left, one of the horses came barreling toward him, causing his mount to rise up in an attempt to escape.

Then, before the horses collided, the oncoming steed was split into two, hot slaughter splashing John and his horse.

*Shit!*

As the horse fell into halves, its murderer stopped, eyes finding John and his mount — another two meals.

Then John saw the nature of the beast — a giant wolf, as large as the horse but thicker, stronger, deadlier.

John's horse bucked again, sending him to the ground before it galloped away. He was momentarily frozen as the wolf looked down at him, then at the escaping horse, as if trying to determine whom to kill — easy target or fleeing prey.

The wolf leaped over John, so fast that he barely had time to react, then charged into the woods behind the horse.

Automatic gunfire erupted. Adrenaline and fear coursing through him, John scanned the chaos searching for Hope.

In the chaos, he saw wolves tearing humans and horses to shreds; saw Omega agents blasting away, having killed at least one of the giant wolves; and then, from the corner of his eye, he saw Hope being carried away by her horse, with a pair of wolves in pursuit.

John had no time to look for Larry or ensure anyone else's safety. They were on their own.

He had to save Hope.

John ran into the woods, his heart pounding. He had to outrun the beasts before they caught up with his love.

EIGHT

## Caleb

*2011*

Caleb woke, flinching to the sound of a cell door creaking open.

*Time for pain.*

His heart raced.

His naked, battered body tensed in the chair, muscles bulging against the straps. He itched to break free, but after three weeks of struggling, he knew it was pointless. The binds were tightened after every interrogation.

*What will today's torment bring?*

Caleb couldn't see anything with the hood over his head, but he knew that Sister Raina was in the room, she of The Covenant, the elite soldiers of The Hand of the Seven Gods. Sister Raina had gone from captor to inquisitor, torturing him thrice daily for answers he didn't have, asking many variations of:

*Why were you outside The Kingdom of the Forgotten?*

*What are the Valkoer planning?*

*Do you have spies in The Hand?*

*What are the Valkoer planning with the portal?*

But Caleb couldn't confess to things he had no knowledge of.

So instead, he told her everything else. How he'd come from Earth. How until a few weeks ago, he didn't know even he was a vampire, Valkoer, whatever. How he'd been married to a wonderful woman whom he accidentally murdered after he reverted into a vampire in his sleep. How he had two brothers, one named John who tried to help him, and another, Jacob, who'd come from her world to do God only knew what. How he tried to kill Jacob and wound up following him through the portal to this world.

He told her these things daily, and was met with a world of pain nonetheless.

She'd punched him, sliced him, burned him, put clamps on his head and squeezed so tight he thought his brain would pop out, and had performed some medieval version of waterboarding. The only thing Sister Raina hadn't done, though she kept promising it was coming — severing his appendages.

*Is today the day?*

Her footsteps on the dirty stone floor came closer.

He flinched again, knowing she was near but not sure where.

Where would the first strike come from? His front? To his left or right? From behind?

Dread filled his broken body as Caleb turned his head, listening, attempting to determine which part of himself to brace for impact.

He felt a hand on the top of his head and shrieked.

But Sister wasn't hitting him.

She was removing his hood.

Raina gave no greeting. Just stood there, in her clean

white uniform, looking him up and down, mouth curled in contempt. He wondered how many uniforms she had — her last one was drenched in his blood.

She shook her head in disgust, looking down and seeing Caleb sitting in yesterday's filth. Nobody had come to rinse him with a bucket as they'd done on other days, so he was caked in piss, shit, and blood, drawing flies.

His chamber: a twelve-by-twelve cell in the bowls of some underground stone fortress, with barely enough light from torches along the walls to see the hate in his tormentor's eyes.

"So, are you going to tell me what I want to know today, *Valkoer?*"

"I've told you everything." Caleb's voice cracked.

"Not yet, but you will." Sister turned on her heel and left, without even bothering to close the cell door.

This was a first.

Caleb felt hope for the first time since being strapped to the chair. An open door equaled opportunity, if he could think beyond his constraints and find a way to get through it.

*Yeah, but if you do, you still have to get out of the dungeon and flee the fortress, past God knows how many guards.*

He cleared his head of negative thoughts, and forced himself to focus only on possibility.

It was peculiar how just moments ago he was ready to ask Sister Raina to end it all, but an open door had lifted his spirits.

*Got to think of a way out of these straps.*

He stared at the leather straps binding his wrists to the chair, searching for some frailties to exploit. The straps were thick leather with sturdy metal buckles, with no evident structural weaknesses.

*Come on, there* must *be something.*

Seeing nothing, Caleb began yet another attempt at wriggling free, looking around, eyes scanning the dimly lit room and flickering shadows, searching for something to use — some dropped tool or rock he could pick up with his feet. *Anything.*

But the area was clear.

The implements of torture were all on a table to his right, a good five feet away. May as well have been a mile if he couldn't break free from the straps.

He looked back down at his wrists, and a thought bubbled up from the depths of his subconscious.

*Focus on the straps and the buckles. Untie them with your mind.*

He wasn't sure where this thought was born — out of desperation or some forgotten past — but its origin didn't matter.

Caleb obeyed.

He focused on the strap holding down his right wrist — intently, as if doing so would compel it to unbuckle itself.

The strap slowly slid through the buckle, an inch or so before stopping.

Caleb stared, wide-eyed in disbelief.

*Oh my God. I did it.*

*I moved it!*

Part of him couldn't believe it, *refused* to believe it. Chalked it up to delusion. But he had to squelch that doubt. Had to focus again, try to push the strap's end through the buckle.

He stared at the buckle, willing it to move.

But whatever had budged it the first time wasn't cooperating now.

As if the taint of disbelief had stolen the magick.

"Come on. You can do this," he whispered to himself.

The strap's end began to slide again, pushing through the buckle.

*Yes, yes, yes!*

And then he heard footsteps — two pairs.

*No, no, no! Hurry, hurry!*

He stared at the leather strap, imagining it sliding through faster, but it was slowing down instead.

Footsteps were coming closer.

There was no way he could get the strap off before his tormentors returned.

He tried to shake the doubt from his mind, to tune the footsteps out and focus only on the strap.

Footsteps were closer still, now just inside his cell.

The strap began to move again, slightly faster.

*Maybe!*

Caleb was doused with a giant bucket of freezing water.

He gasped, spitting water as yet another bucket came.

And then another.

Ten men in white robes took turns dousing him with large buckets of freezing water. Caleb closed his eyes, unsure if this was further torment, or an attempt to clean him before Raina could continue her interrogation.

As bucket after bucket came crashing down, Caleb tried to focus on his right restraint, to unlock it while they were preoccupied.

He only wanted to unlock it, not escape with ten other people in his way. But if he could unlock it *just* enough, then maybe he could turn the tables on his inquisitor once he and Raina were alone.

Caleb had years of hand-to-hand training and could disarm nearly any assailant. He didn't know whether he could truly get the better of her — she was obviously a heavy hitter for this cult, and seemed, judging from his limited time with her, to thrive on violence alone. He had to assume Raina was an able fighter, though he'd seen no evidence of what she could do to someone not tied to a chair.

As the men with the buckets left, Caleb caught his breath and looked up at Raina.

"Well, you smell *a bit* less like an animal now," she said, then turned her back to him, walked over to the table, and slowly deliberated over which instrument to harm him with next.

"Hmm … should we use *this*?"

The cell door was still open.

She usually closed it during their sessions. Was this carelessness on her part or something intentional — a way of teasing freedom?

Nobody else was in the long, narrow, torch-lit hall outside his cell. It was graveyard-silent. Other than guards, Caleb hadn't heard anyone else in the dungeon since his arrival. He might have been The Hand's only "guest."

Raina's back was still to him, the doorway practically begging him to use it.

*Now's the time.*

As Caleb focused on the restraint, another thought came to him. His vampirism, and associated abilities, were latent, hidden by some spell put on him long ago. But now that he was able to remove his straps, perhaps his other abilities were now active as well.

Maybe he wouldn't need a weapon. He could simply lay his hands on Raina and drain her life. Same with any other bastard that got in his way.

But what then?

If he was a vampire again, wasn't he also subject to their weaknesses? If he escaped this place into daylight — impossible to know down in the windowless dungeon what time it was — would he burn to ash the instant he found an exit?

The right restraint fell aside.

Caleb's heart raced, watching Raina's shoulders move up and down as she fidgeted with something on the table he couldn't see.

With his right hand free, Caleb kept his eyes glued on Raina, and pulled the restraints from his left, praying she wouldn't hear him, or turn around before he was free.

His hands unencumbered, he bent down and slowly loosened his left leg's restraints. He didn't bother keeping an eye on her now — his neck hurt too much to look up while leaning down.

Right leg free.

Then the left.

Caleb started to sit up as he heard Raina gasp.

He looked up to see her hand on a dark blade similar to the one he'd thrust into Jacob on Earth — *the kind that kills vampires.*

Time froze.

Caleb felt like the proverbial wolf in the hen house as the farmer appears with a shotgun.

He launched himself from the chair, toward Raina with nothing but his bare hands and a prayer that his touch would kill her before she could stab him.

Caleb saw all his surroundings at once — the cell's four walls and open door; the empty hallway outside; the table with its many instruments, each one offering him a weapon to counter Raina's; and, of course, Raina, moving toward him, eyes going from wide-open surprise at seeing him free to a furrowed brow to match her gritted teeth, knuckles bone white on the blade she intended to plunge inside him.

Caleb also saw that they were on a collision course in which they'd both end one another, if he didn't change his trajectory.

Somehow, after seeing all these things in the splinter of

a second, he rolled to his right at the final moment, avoiding collision.

Raina went sailing overhead, and time seemed to catch up with itself. She slammed into the wall.

Caleb pounced like an animal atop her.

Her eyes snapped open.

*Too late, fucker!*

He grabbed her face with both hands, prepared to feed.

He closed his eyes, unable to truly enjoy what he was about to do. She was an enemy, but this was the theft of a soul, something he'd done only once in his life, while sleeping, to his poor, sweet wife.

He wasn't a monster like Jacob.

But survival left him no choice.

His fingers locked on Raina's face, an explosion of energy annihilating every one of his senses at once.

But this wasn't like before.

The energy wasn't feeding him so much as assaulting his every molecule.

He tried to break the connection to her but couldn't.

He was locked on.

Something was wrong.

He wasn't feeding from her.

He opened his eyes to see that she wasn't burning.

She was staring straight at him, shaking, eyes wide and afraid.

*What the hell is happening?*

"What are you doing?" she said, but her mouth didn't move.

She was inside his mind.

And then he realized why he couldn't kill her.

Raina was a vampire just like him.

NINE

Hope

THERE HAD BEEN no time to think.

No time to plan.

The giant wolves had come, and it was fight or flight.

Whatever fight might have been inside her vanished when Hope saw the wolves tear apart two Omega agents *and* their mounts.

She had to trust the horse's survival instincts to get her away.

It exploded into the woods in a thunderous gallop, and she did the only thing she could — hang on for dear life, hoping the horse wouldn't see her as an impediment to escape.

In Hope's youth — if it was, in fact, *her* memories and not the artificial ones created when John's people gave her a new name and false recollections — she'd ridden horses enough to know that once spooked, they stopped caring whether or not a human was around. The mount could decide to throw her off, maybe stomp all over her in an attempt to flee danger. She had to keep doing what she was doing: hanging on tight until the horse was calm enough for her to regain control.

Hope couldn't worry about John, Larry, or the others. Had to believe they could take care of themselves, or that their horses would take them to safety.

*What if all the horses are running in different directions?*

*What if we all get lost?*

It wasn't as if they had radios to communicate with one another on this planet. There were no cell towers, or even electricity as far as she knew.

Hope tried to shake the horrible *What-ifs* from her mind. There was no time for worries or self-pity. She had to focus on what was happening, what she could directly control — which wasn't much.

The horse was racing too fast and making too many quick turns for her to keep track of where she was, let alone how to get back. She was the passenger, forced to go wherever the horse wanted to take her.

She tried not to panic at the thought of getting separated from her group, or the possibility of her party being dead, but it was difficult, particularly with the thought of giant wolves owning the night.

Suddenly, her horse let out a high-pitched whine and pushed itself faster.

Hope turned around, wondering why the horse wasn't calming down as it put distance between itself and the wolves.

Then she saw:

A giant gray wolf was right on their heels, hot steam puffing from its nostrils, razor-sharp teeth glistening long in the moonlight, and glowing red eyes staring right at her.

*Oh God!*

Panic ripped at her insides. Hope felt like she and the horse were running in quicksand while the wolf was charging unfettered on smooth grass, quickly closing the distance between them.

She turned from the horror as the horse changed direction, heading into thicker woodlands.

Branches scraped her. She had a horrible image of a stray branch unseating her, the horse racing away, leaving her as a snack for the wolf.

Which, of course, was followed by a flash of Omega agents and their horses being torn in half by other wolves. She'd never seen anything like it — claws reducing life to meat in sickening seconds.

She stood no chance against something like that.

Few things did.

She dropped down, hugging the horse, clutching tightly and hoping her mount wouldn't be agitated enough to buck her off.

*Come on, come on!*

She dug her heels into the horse's side, as if it weren't already going as fast as possible.

She immediately regretted the decision.

There was an excellent chance that the horse, in its blind panic, had forgotten she was on its back. Now she'd reminded it.

Hope felt movement behind her and turned to see the wolf pouncing. Then everything went wrong.

The wolf landed on them in a heavy thud that knocked the wind from her body.

The horse, in a high-pitched scream, collapsed under the beast's weight.

They all rolled forward in one screaming, bumpy, knotted mess of flesh, fur, claws, and blood.

Somehow, Hope slipped out of the mess as the wolf and horse rolled into a line of trees.

The wolf shoved its muzzle into the horse's stomach

and tore, sucking down on intestines, guts, and flesh in a sickening slurp.

Hope lay on the ground, her Omega outfit covered in blood, working to catch her breath, unable to look away from the savagery as her mind raced to conjure some means of escape.

She considered playing dead but figured that probably wouldn't work with this monster. It seemed to be hyper-aware — it would smell her fear, or hear her beating heart. Maybe it wouldn't even care if she were dead — a fresh kill had warm blood, and its meat was not yet rotting.

As if sensing her parade of decaying thoughts, the wolf turned toward her, its crimson eyes sizing her up.

This was the first time she'd seen one of the wolves up close and still. Its details were even more unsettling when not cloaked in shadow or blurred by movement. It wasn't just that it was as big as her horse while also being more powerful. Nor was it the clawed feet, gaping maw packed with too many needle-like teeth, or glowing red eyes that looked like fire burned inside them.

Something else sent chills to Hope's core. Something she couldn't quite put a finger on, but if pressed she'd guess it as an intelligence greater than a mere animal's.

She wasn't sure why this terrified her so. Was it that this intellect made it a more capable killing machine, or that despite its acumen, the beast still chose such savagery?

The wolf stepped forward, its growl reaching into Hope's stomach, then her limbs, rendering her motionless.

The wolf's bloodied, razor-filled mouth broke into a sinister smile.

TEN

# John

JOHN'S BOOTS kicked up dirt and clay, every muscle in his legs firing like pistons, arms slicing the air like blades, propelled by a heart pumping so fast it would surely tear with exertion.

Or terror of what he might find once he caught up to Hope.

John's body raced faster than any human, his mind careening in a hundred directions, flooded with fear and regret.

*I shouldn't have brought them here.*

*I shouldn't have come here myself.*

*Fuck this war. Let The Guardians and Jacob sort it all out.*

*I'm tired of sacrificing the people I love, sacrificing* my life, *for The Guardians' and Harbingers' war.*

*I should've run away with Hope, Larry, and Abigail; built some fortress somewhere; and let the pieces fall where they may.*

As Hope's scent grew stronger, he inhaled traces of her fear blemishing the environment like psychic stains, which, of course, only heightened his fears of being too late. Of finding Hope's body ripped to pieces by the savage beast.

89

An ugly thought came to John, one he felt immediately ashamed of. Part of him preferred that Hope was killed by a person rather than some wild animal. At least he could find a home for his rage, avenge her death by destroying her killer.

But if a wolf killed her?

*That's nature, not man.*

How could you seek vengeance against the wild, of an animal doing what animals do?

John shook his head, trying to clear the terrible images of death and unfulfilled vengeance.

*She's not dead!*

*Stop assuming the worst!*

He kept running, chasing Hope.

## ELEVEN

## Larry

————

LARRY WOKE to the sounds of death all around him. A macabre song born in a nightmare — cries of the wounded and not-yet dead victims of the monstrous wolves, the tearing of flesh, the slurping of guts, and the spilling of blood serving as an gruesome melody to the carnage.

He vaguely remembered his horse rearing up and sending him flying off his mount to the ground where he hit his head on something hard.

He was about to get up, but felt woozy.

He fell back to the ground.

When he woke again, everything was silent.

Larry reached up, felt a wet spot and a giant lump on the back of his head, and turned, just enough to see that he'd hit a fallen tree.

He stayed down, scanning the battlefield for any sign of John or Hope, trying not to alert the wolves to his breathing.

So far as he could tell, he was the only survivor in the clearing littered with corpses of humans and horses ripped into barely recognizable shreds. The reek of blood and bile and shit was strong, practically choking him in its stench.

Larry fought the urge to vomit, gagging as quietly as he could.

He had to close his eyes to the grim environment. Focus on a way to escape, then find Hope and John.

A low growl demanded Larry's open eyes.

But what he saw made him wish he'd kept them closed.

There was a large gray wolf, only inches away. Glowing red eyes, bloody maw full of razor-sharp teeth, belly apparently not yet full.

It growled, the sides of its mouth curling up, revealing even more of its horrible teeth, black gums glistening with the slick remnants of Larry's comrades.

The wolf slowly padded forward.

Despite Larry's pounding heart and flooding adrenaline, his body was only prepared to stay frozen in place. His mind screamed at his limbs.

*Come on, move! Do something!*

He wasn't sure why the beast didn't rushed to capitalize on his paralysis, as if it were delighting in his torment.

Larry found the will to move — he'd make the wolf pay for not acting faster.

He reached down, grabbed the pistol tucked into the holster at his waist, raised it, and fired straight into the fucker's face.

Larry got off two shots before the beast yelped then spun around and ran.

Larry leaped to his feet, blood rushing to his head, making it hurt and turning him dizzy.

No time to find his balance.

While one wolf had fled, he could hear growling in the

woods ahead. Then they appeared, four of them, all staring at him, heads low, teeth bared, eyes burning bright.

Larry turned and ran deeper into the woods in the opposite direction.

The beasts followed.

Larry knew there was no way in hell he could outrun a normal Earth wolf, let alone these monstrosities. Nor could he shoot them all before one or two broke through and brought him down.

All he had was a pistol and a few shots left in that. His rifle was lost.

He had a few flash bombs in a pouch on his belt, but he wasn't sure how quickly he could get them loose while running for his life.

Four monster wolves against a fat dude wasn't a match he would likely survive.

Larry screamed as he ran, hoping that someone who could actually do something — assuming everyone else wasn't already dead — was within earshot.

But he had nowhere to run. No shack to hide in. No waterfall to jump off of.

*No escape.*

Only a swath of thinning trees in every direction.

He could feel the wolves closing in, could hear their thundering paws gaining on him.

He didn't dare turn; he'd surely lose all hope if he did. His legs would turn to jelly, and he'd collapse.

Then they'd be on him, tearing him apart, maybe fighting for scraps like some damned Otherworldly documentary.

He could hear the narrator's voice.

*Fortunately, the wolves had found the fattest of the species, so there'd be plenty to go around, perhaps there would even be leftovers.*

He screamed *John!* in his mind, hoping his friend was nearby.

Automatic gunfire erupted from Larry's immediate right just as he ran hard into something he couldn't see, knocking it, and himself, to the ground in a violent collision.

Deafening cries behind from the wolves.

Larry looked up to see the rippling air where the gunfire had erupted. Beyond the ripples, a dark shape taking form.

Not a shape, a person — Sanders, aiming an M16 at the wolves.

Then Larry saw something materialize in front of him — the thing, or person rather, that he'd run into: Emma Crowe.

She got up quickly, yelled, "Watch where you're going!" then ran toward him.

At first Larry thought she was going to hit him, but she grabbed his left hand instead.

Sanders cursed as the gun jammed.

The last wolf left had been starting to retreat, but must've sensed that the weapon no longer worked.

It turned, growling.

And moved, fast.

Emma tightened her grip on Larry's hand, pulling him as she launched herself toward Sanders.

*What the hell is she doing, trying to get us all killed?*

Emma's other hand seized Sanders by the shoulder.

Larry was confused as Sanders kept trying to unjam the gun.

But the wolf had stopped, head tilted, looking at them.

Realization dawned on Larry.

*It can't see us.*

He looked over at Emma, remembering that she and

her brother had shadow abilities. She was using hers to cloak them. *He* could see her and Sanders because they were touching and on the same frequency, or whatever the hell the Halfworlders called it. But the wolf could not.

Larry also knew that those powers rarely lasted long. The girl would soon lose her focus, and all three of them would become visible. Even then, the wolf could probably smell and hear them. Eventually, it would move toward the trio, or at least where its other senses told it they'd be.

Sanders got the gun unjammed, lifted her rifle, and fired straight into the monster's face.

The wolf howled and turned to run.

Sanders kept firing.

The wolf went down.

Emma released them, gasping for air.

"You have to hold your breath to do that?"

"Not all the time, but with three of us, yeah."

"Thank you," Larry said.

Sanders turned and nodded. "Yes, thank you."

Larry was about to ask if either of them had seen John or Hope, but then noticed that Emma was staring behind him.

*Oh God, not more.*

He turned, not sure his heart could take another attempt at escape. But this time he wouldn't need to run. Emma was staring at something already dead, and it wasn't a wolf.

The trail of blood the wolf had left behind in its escape now led to a naked man, lying facedown on the ground.

Sanders asked, "Is that a —"

Emma finished the question, "Werewolf?"

TWELVE

# Hope

HOPE SAT ON THE GROUND, frozen in the giant wolf's gaze, a jumble of life flashing before her eyes.

But unlike the movies where the heroine remembers sweet moments plucked from her life with soft, focused recollection — a few early memories with her parents, some struggles as a teen or young woman, or maybe a few romantic moments between herself and a lover or two — this was a torrent of recall, passing too fast for definition.

Even odder were those memories that didn't belong to her.

John's magick user had given her a new identity and created a fictional past. That had been confusing enough to sort which memories were hers and real versus the false and implanted.

But this was a deeper layer of confusion — memories of herself as a child, with people who weren't her parents. Places she'd never seen. And odd people and strange animals straight out of a fairy tale.

She tried to slow the memories, to excavate deeper and determine where they were coming from. If they weren't hers, whose were they? But they kept rushing by chaotically, so fast that it felt like she was in a projector room for a theater with a thousand screens.

The memories washed over Hope in a tsunami, drowning her senses — insights, sounds, and emotions, all at once and all too much.

She felt lost, adrift in nothingness, and lost sight of the danger literally breathing down her neck.

But then she was reminded by the wolf's low and ugly growl.

And in a moment that should have been filled with raw panic, desperation, and adrenaline, somehow peace bloomed.

She opened her eyes, and just as the torrent of alien memories and emotions had jarred her, so too had the serenity that spread over her in the face of certain death.

She tried willing her body to stand, fight, or run. To do *anything* that would prevent this beast from turning her into its meal.

But whatever panic she should have been feeling was gone.

There was only the comfort of death on its way.

It didn't make sense.

She met the wolf's eyes, and found herself doing the unthinkable, moving closer to better see the fire in its eyes.

The monster's gaze, which had been so terrifying just moments ago, now seemed majestic. Its eyes were tiny planets, living in fiery swirls of red, orange, and specks of black, all in constant, impossible motion.

Hope was awestruck by their beauty.

Without even meaning to she reached up to touch the wolf's thick, gray matted fur. She stroked it, smiling as she thought back to a dog she once had, unable to remember if it was truly her pet or another false memory.

Maybe it wasn't even a dog.

The only thing Hope knew, even though it didn't make sense, was that this wolf wasn't going to kill her.

As if the wolf had seen something in her, perhaps recognition of this awareness, it looked down, and softly whined.

Then it turned and ran, back into the darkness.

"What the hell?" she heard a man's voice from behind.

She turned to find John, staring at her.

# THIRTEEN

# John

"WHAT HAPPENED?" John asked, watching the wolf take off into the woods, leaving Hope unharmed.

"I don't know," she said in barely a whisper.

Hope stared at John, her body trembling.

He grabbed the gloves from his uniform pocket, slid them on, went to Hope, and hugged her tight, careful not to let the skin showing through his open helmet brush against her.

She said nothing as he held her. She barely recognized the embrace, as if he were hugging a stranger.

He pulled away and looked down at Hope who was staring past him and into the trees, probably in shock.

Perhaps she had snapped. It could happen in far less traumatic circumstances than staring down a giant wolf. Maybe this was the final straw. She'd been through a ton of shit in these last few weeks, least of all discovering that she wasn't Hannah, the false identity she was living as for a decade. Maybe her encounter with the wolf had shoved Hope over the edge.

If so, John wasn't sure how to bring her back.

He wasn't sure if he should try to comfort her or ask questions.

"Did you do something to scare it away?"

"No," she said, shaking her head, still staring past him.

"Did it hear me coming?"

"I don't know." Her voice was as lost as her gaze.

"You're okay now." He pulled her close, though she still wasn't receptive. As John hugged her, grateful that she was still alive, his mind kept circling the moment, trying to make sense of what happened.

Why would the wolf just leave? Surely, he hadn't scared it away.

He thought of Larry and the others, and felt guilty for not thinking of his friend sooner.

*Larry?*

"*I'm here, boss. Did you find Hope? Is she okay?*"

*Yes, she's good. What's the unit's status?*

"*Not good, John. We lost a lot of them.*"

*How many are left?*

"*I don't know. I'm with Emma. She managed to save me and Sanders, hid us from the wolves. But I think everyone else is either dead or took off.*"

*Shit. What about the horses?*

"*Also dead or gone.*"

*Fuck.*

This was a breath from a worst-case scenario — a few hours into their mission, and most of their unit was gone.

"*How far out are you? Can you find us, John?*"

*I dunno. Maybe a half hour walking. Just gather what you can in supplies, without getting killed, please.*

"*All right, John. See you soon.*"

Larry was shaken despite his bravado. Signing off without some smart ass comment clearly broadcast his terror.

"Larry's okay. So are Emma and Sanders."

"What about the others?" Hope's lost look was finally gone, and her voice was approaching something closer to normal.

"Dead or running. Too soon to tell how many others are left. But a lot of them are dead, and all the horses are gone."

Hope covered her mouth then from behind her hand said, "Oh my God. So what now?"

"We walk back, and regroup. After that, I don't know. Maybe we should head back home."

Hope met his eyes and shook her head. "No."

"No?"

"I want to stay."

John looked down at what was left of the horse, then back up at Hope. "After *that* you want to *stay?*"

"Something happened, John, and I'm not sure what."

"Scaring the wolf away?"

"No, before that."

"What do you mean?"

"You know how people say that their lives flash before their eyes when they're about to die? Well, I was seeing all these memories, but ... they weren't all mine."

"Well, of course they weren't. You were living another life for ten years."

"No, not that ... these were ... different. Not Hannah's life, but a childhood I don't remember having."

John didn't like where this was going. He wasn't ready to tell Hope that she was from this world. That she'd been used to smuggle one of the crystals to Earth. Not now. Not until things were closer to normal. They'd just reconciled after she learned that he'd had her mind wiped. He'd promised to never lie again, to include her in the decisions about her life.

He hadn't told her about her origin because he still didn't know much about it himself. It was one thing to learn that she'd lost a decade or so of her life to a lie, but to learn that her humanity was also false? That might be too much, especially given how shaken she appeared.

She locked onto his eyes. "Have you done this to me before? Was I someone else before Hope?"

"I met you as Hope," John said. Not a lie. "I don't know what you experienced, but I would guess that when Adam loaded you with memories, he might have given you some he decided not to use. Like extra programming? I'm not sure. I know some spells, but I'm no expert in memory wipes or re-creations."

She continued looking at John, then past him again. "No, I don't think it was him. I think it's something else."

"Do you think the wolf leaving had something to do with it?"

Again, she met his eyes. "I think so."

"How?"

"I don't know, but it was the weirdest thing. I was scared to death, and then, as all of these memories rushed through me, I felt so … *calm*. I was no longer afraid to die."

"Maybe it was your brain's way of finding peace in a horrible situation."

"Maybe, but it felt like something else."

"What?"

"Like I was just waking up for the first time ever."

She paused, then added, "I don't know what it was, but I need to stay here until I figure it out."

*Shit.*

# FOURTEEN

## Abigail



*THE VILLAGE* MUST *BE CLOSE.*

Abigail kept repeating the mantra as they traversed the narrow canyon pass, walls on either side vanishing into a thick, milky moonlit fog above. At least she *thought* it was fog. But they'd been following the land's incline through the night, so maybe they were high enough to actually be walking in the clouds.

They were following a river that was supposed to bring them to the village of Kovar and a witch who might be able to save her from the poisoning.

Abigail wasn't sure how much longer she could go on.

Her chest was tight; it was hard to breathe.

Her body was racked with pain, every stiff movement feeling as though something was breaking, as if her insides were turning into cement and motion was the only prevention, even if moving was the very thing that hurt most.

She thought of a story she'd read while in the monster's closet, about a boy lost in the Alaskan wilderness, exhausted and in search of shelter. He was desperate to sleep but knew that slumber would be final. That was how she felt now. Stopping for rest would be the last thing she ever did.

*I have to keep moving.*

*Just a little bit farther.*

Even though Talani had forced her to feed, the parasite inside Abigail didn't seem to be sharing the energy. It was fighting for its own life, damn its host. If they didn't get help from the witch soon, it would die and take Abigail with it.

The canyon walls started to widen ahead. Though the fog was growing thicker, making it impossible to see in the distance, Abigail took the widening as a promising sign that they were closing in on Kovar.

"This is where it's supposed to be, right?"

"Yes." Judith sighed, likely tired of answering the same question over and over since they entered the canyon what felt like ages ago.

Talani gave Abigail a smile that said, *Don't mind Judith.*

Judith always seemed cold and distant, but Abigail got the feeling that it was never personal. Yet now, since losing Solomon, she seemed even more remote. Talani had walked beside her a few times, attempting to raise her spirits, but Judith ignored every attempt, keeping her focus on finding Kovar. It seemed she was just hanging on long enough to get them to where they needed to go.

Abigail wondered if Judith would pull herself together before they left for Jonah. She wanted to do something, but if Talani — practically a daughter to Judith — couldn't get through, what hope did Abigail have?

In a way, Abigail was glad that she wasn't expected to help. It was all she could do to just walk. Abigail felt guilty for such a selfish feeling, particularly since she was the one slowing them down, knowing that if it weren't for her, they would've found the village, and its shelter from the sun, hours ago.

She felt like a third wheel, square and made of stone.

As the passage widened, Abigail felt hope — a sensation she thought she might never feel again.

*We're almost there!*

But as they stepped out of the canyon, the trio found themselves surrounded by trees in every direction, giant trees unlike any that Abigail had ever seen, all of them wider than mansions. Trees that would take fifteen minutes or more to circle around.

Even worse, they appeared to be at the base of a mountain, and their path continued its ascent with no sign of a village.

"What is this? Where's the village?" Abigail asked, her heart sinking.

"It's supposed to be right here. She didn't say anything about giant trees or a mountain," Judith said, her voice shaky.

Abigail wondered how much of an immediate threat the sun might be. They had cloaks and cowls, but how protective would they be in full daylight once the sun was high? She wanted to ask about the danger, but felt it might be a reminder that this was all her fault, and they might decide to leave her behind.

Abigail fought the urge to cry, but tears were welling in her eyes despite her best efforts. She looked at the ground, letting her cowl and long dark hair bury her face.

Talani said, "It has to be here. Right? We just keep walking."

Abigail didn't look up to see Judith's response, but hearing the others she followed, hoping they weren't slogging a path to their deaths.

THEY FOLLOWED the winding path through the woods up the mountainside as the plummeting temperature sent shivers through the group. Abigail thought she smelled the sweet scent of flowers, though she saw not a single bloom. The icy air didn't make it easy.

Their agonizing pace had slowed further, thanks to the mountain's steep incline and the path's twisted nature, navigating the massive trees, sometimes with several clustered together and occupying the width of an Earthly city block.

Abigail imagined a woodsman might be able to yield a town's worth of buildings with the wood from a single tree. Of course it would probably take him a month to chop said tree down!

She wondered how high the trees went — she could only see about ten feet up before the clouds obscured her view.

Given their width, the trees could be a thousand feet high, she figured.

Abigail wanted to ask the others what they thought, but the idea of talking, with her chest so tight already, felt like a punch.

Soon the rich brown-and-green ground gave way to white.

And in the snow, the path became even harder to follow, especially in the hazy blue of twin moons bleeding through the clouds.

Talani was the first to speak. "Is that the end of the trail?"

Judith scanned the ground, then shook her head.

"I can't tell."

Abigail felt her panic swelling again. "We've been

walking *forever* on this path! Are we going to have to turn around? I can't go back. I can't!"

Her chest tightened more.

Abigail gasped, certain she was about to suffocate, desperately trying to suck in air. But she couldn't draw enough to fill her lungs. Her heart was racing way too fast. Her skin felt like a million needles stabbing her at once. She cried out to Talani's mind.

*What's happening?*

Talani rushed to her, putting her hands on Abigail's back, rubbing up and down. "Calm down, Abigail. We'll find the path."

*No, no, we're going to die here. I can feel it!*

She continued to gasp for air, barely finding a breath.

*Oh God, I'm going to die right here!*

Judith walked over, though Abigail was only peripherally aware of her. Abigail's focus was narrowing, invisible walls collapsing around her. She pushed Talani and Judith away, desperate for space and still gasping for air.

"Calm down," Judith said, echoing Talani. "Close your eyes, and focus on my voice."

Abigail closed her eyes, but they involuntarily opened back up.

Her head spun around, eyes scanning the forest for enemies, certain that something was closing in. She screamed, dropping to the ground on her haunches, hands curled into claws.

*Something is coming!*

*Get ready to fight!*

She heard screams in her mind, not voices, not memories, perhaps not even human — animal-like shrieks, so loud she raised her clawed hands to her ears to drown the sound.

But she couldn't muffle the nightmares in her mind.

She kept gasping for air.

She felt lightheaded.

She *had* to run.

Had to kill.

Had to feed.

Noises of the women near her, whose names she suddenly couldn't remember, were inaudible blurs lost in her bellowing head.

The older one was approaching her, hands out.

"Get away," Abigail snarled, certain the old woman would harm her. She tried catching her breath as the younger girl approached from the other side.

Abigail swiped a clawed hand, yelling at her to go away, even though the words didn't come out as intended.

*Why won't they leave me alone?*

She turned to run, but Abigail's legs gave out beneath her.

She cried as she fell, face first into the freezing snow.

She heard movement behind her as she lay facedown.

She turned around.

The older woman was bending down, about to do something.

Abigail cried out, swiping at the woman with her hands.

"Away!" was all she could manage.

She gasped again, trying to suck in air.

The screams in her head grew louder.

The walls were closing in.

The woman reached down to touch Abigail's face.

Abigail tried to bite her, but then the woman's strong fingers found her mouth, and thrust inside.

*What are you doing?*

Abigail wanted to kick, but her legs refused to heed her brain's commands.

Abigail gasped, gagged, retched, vomit flooding her mouth, but the woman refused to move her fingers.

She looked up to see the woman's trembling body.

*What's happening?*

The walls closed in tighter.

Then darkness came.

FIFTEEN

## Caleb

*2011 ...*

At first, the interrogator, Raina, was in Caleb's head, digging through his memories.

He could feel her sifting through them like a catalog of his life's major events, with nothing he could do to keep her from peering in on his most intimate moments.

She stopped on a few from his childhood, including a time he'd stuck up for a smaller kid and knocked a bully on his ass. Then a time in his awkward teenage years when he'd cried because the girl he loved didn't feel the same. A sad time in his youth when Duncan Alderman had told him everything would be okay.

"Please," he said, standing beside her in his childhood bedroom, "stop."

"I just want to see the real you."

Raina did something to initiate another surge of memories then stopped on one that caught her interest.

He recognized it immediately.

"Please, stop. I don't want to be here."

She ignored him.

They were in the hotel room, *that night.*

Caleb was cradling his dead wife's burned body as he cried out.

He turned away from the scene, not wanting to relive the horror of having accidentally murdered his wife, having stolen her life in his sleep as the vampire inside him had been unleashed.

He closed his eyes, the sounds of his sobs cutting through the past into the present, causing him to cry again.

"So you *were* telling the truth?" Raina asked behind him.

He couldn't turn to meet her eyes.

"Yes. I told you that I'm not the monster you think I am. I haven't been on this world in a long time. I don't remember my life here, let alone my father or brothers. It was all taken from me, for my own good."

"Okay."

And then they were in darkness, still in some shared psychic space in their heads as if in a dream. The real world and the torture chamber was nowhere to be seen or felt.

Caleb looked at her. Her harshness was gone, replaced by a look of empathy.

"I'm sorry. It's not often I find a *good* Valkoer."

"So, you're a Valkoer too? How?"

"Well, since I saw your horror, let me show you mine."

The darkness shifted, and suddenly they were inside Raina's memories, standing in her childhood bedroom.

He wasn't sure how he knew where they were; he just did. It was as if some understanding of the memories was transferred along with Raina's shared vision.

The bedroom was small with one bed she shared with

her six-year-old sister, a dresser with a lantern and a toy boat atop it, and a closet with no door where meager clothes hung on a pole. The room was odd in that the only truly clear thing he could see was the bed, while everything else was slightly fuzzy, and in some cases shifting. One of the dresses in the closet changed from yellow to blue to red, as if Raina couldn't remember the exact color and was changing the memory as she recalled it.

The other thing that didn't change was the girl on the bed, lying there, covered up, asking, "Will you read to me, Raina?"

It was an alien bedroom on an alien world, but the scene was incredibly human — a younger kid sister wanting her slightly older sister to read a bedtime story.

The young Raina materialized in the room, standing in front of the window, staring out into the night. She looked maybe eighteen.

Younger Raina turned to her sister, whispered, "Hush," then ran to the dresser and extinguished the lantern, plunging the room into darkness before returning to her spot at the window.

Caleb walked over to her.

Suddenly, the older version of Raina was beside the younger, also looking outside.

"This is when they came," she said, looking at Caleb.

He looked outside the window to see a pair of figures getting out of a horse-drawn carriage.

The man, in a black coat and suit, was large and muscular, with an ugly monobrow and long dark hair. He looked like some of the swarthier European mobsters Caleb had run into while working at the Agency. His female companion was young, in her twenties, if that, with long blonde hair and a flowing black dress displaying ample cleavage. Something about her said prostitute, though Caleb wasn't sure if that was him inferring it or Raina's memories of the events flavoring the event.

"Who are they?" Caleb asked.

"His name was Hugo, the boss of the local criminal organization at the time. He was also Valkoer."

"And her?"

"Her name was Judith. One of his Valkoer women. He had several, and liked to bring them with him on jobs to help him."

"Help him *what?* Why are they here?"

Raina looked back at her sister, lying on the bed. Her eyes began to water.

"They're here to collect money my father owed them. But he couldn't pay, and so they're going to take something else."

Raina went to the bed and kneeled beside it, running a hand over her younger sister's head. But she couldn't touch in a memory, so her fingers went through the girl like a ghost.

Raina looked up at Caleb. "I wish I'd read to her that night. It wouldn't have changed anything, but our final exchange before this was me saying no."

Suddenly shouting downstairs.

Young Raina rushed to the bedroom door and locked it.

Her sister cried, "What's happening, Raina?"

"Shh," Younger Raina said, "let's hide under the bed."

More shouting downstairs, mostly words Caleb couldn't decipher, likely because he couldn't hear anything that Raina hadn't originally heard when this happened.

He watched as she hid her sister under the bed.

The younger girl called out, "You too."

"No, I won't fit," Younger Raina said. "No matter what

happens, keep your hands over your mouth and stay quiet, do you understand?"

The girl nodded, tears streaming down her face.

The doorknob rattled.

Young Raina looked up, startled, then back down at her sister. She put a finger over her lips, reminding her to keep quiet.

Caleb's heart raced, watching helplessly, wanting to yell at them to go out the window, that there was still time to escape.

But there wasn't.

He wasn't a time traveller, only a witness, unable to do anything to alter the past.

Older Raina's eyes were flooding with tears. But unlike Caleb having to relive his wife's death, she didn't turn away.

Raina watched as if it was her duty.

The door burst open. Hugo entered with the woman, followed by Raina's father, a skinny older man pleading, "Please, no. I swear, I'll pay you."

Hugo smiled, eying Raina up and down and licking his lips. "Oh, Reginald, why didn't you tell me you had such a lovely daughter?"

Caleb's stomach turned. He wanted to launch backward in time to knock the sick grin from the man's face.

The woman was wearing long black gloves. She put a hand through Young Raina's hair, "Oh yes, she *is* a lovely one, isn't she?"

*What kind of sick fucks* are *these people?*

Caleb looked under the bed to see Raina's little sister, but the girl was a blur. Perhaps because Raina hadn't been looking at her then.

She was too busy staring straight ahead so as not to

alert anyone to her sister's presence. The monsters didn't seem to know that there were *two girls* in the bedroom.

"Please, just give me one more week. I'll find the money."

Hugo spun around, his face twisted in an angry ball. "I gave you time! *Repeatedly.* But you keep lying. Keep stalling. How do you think that makes me look?"

"I'm sorry! It's been hard since my wife died. It's only me and —"

"Silence!" Hugo screamed, thrusting a finger at the man.

Reginald froze, staring down at the man's hand, obviously aware of the deadly touch poised to strike.

Hugo turned to Raina, eying her with his sick, lust-filled eyes. "Are you spoilt, girl?"

She was frozen, eyes filling with tears, her body shaking.

Judith, now behind the girl, holding a hand on her shoulder to keep her from fleeing, leaned forward, sniffing the girl's neck and hair.

"She's still a clean one," Judith said.

Hugo smiled, then turned back to Reginald. "Good news for you, Reginald. Your debt is now paid, in exchange for your daughter."

"No!" Reginald looked like he wanted to charge Hugo, but knew doing so would endanger both him and his family. Nothing worse than a brave man without a defense against evil.

Caleb wanted to ask what Hugo had planned to do with Raina, but as he thought it, the information entered his head. They would sell her into prostitution to the Valkoer Elite. They'd take turns raping her body *and* her mind. If she was *lucky*, they'd turn her first. If not, they'd leave her next to dead, a vegetable to be used over and again until there was nothing left to use. Actually, Caleb wasn't sure which outcome was lucky — to have your senses but be imprisoned, or to be slowly dying, oblivious to the hell?

"Please, just give me one more week. Please, you can't take my daughter!"

Hugo shook his head. "Too late. Your time is up, Reginald. Thank you for your business."

Hugo turned his back on Reginald, eager to eye his prize again, perhaps calculating the totals he'd get for her. Maybe he was even considering keeping this one for himself.

Then it happened.

Reginald ran at Hugo, a black blade in his hand, screaming as he charged.

Why he screamed, Caleb did not know, because it merely alerted Hugo to danger.

That would be Reginald's final mistake.

Hugo turned, quickly, his hand grabbing Reginald's knife hand.

And the feeding began.

Reginald screamed as Hugo's hand locked on, and the fire spread through his violently shaking limbs.

Raina screamed, tried to intervene.

Judith grabbed the girl violently by her hair, yanking her back and whispering into her ear, "Don't. He'll only kill you too."

The woman seemed to say this less as a threat and more of a warning.

Caleb looked at Older Raina, thinking she'd certainly be turned away as Hugo fed on her father's burning remains. But she stared on like a soldier, unable to flinch.

Caleb tried to look under the bed, but the little girl was

still a blur. He was afraid she'd scream; then Hugo and Judith would find her.

He didn't even want to wonder what would happen to a six-year-old, lest Raina fill him in on details he didn't want to know.

Hugo released Reginald, then opened his fingers, letting the man fall to the ground. Raina's father exploded into chunks of dust on impact.

Trying unsuccessfully to escape Judith's hold, Raina cried out, "Daddy!"

Hugo closed his eyes, basking in the glow of his feeding. Then they flicked open. He began to look around the room, then got up in Raina's face, so close Caleb was certain he was going to feed on *her* next.

But instead, he asked, "Where is your little sister?"

Caleb's heart sank as he looked under the bed, still a blur.

Young Raina lied, "She's at her friend's for the night."

Hugo looked Young Raina up and down as if trying to sniff out a lie. Caleb could see a thousand ways this could sour. He wanted to turn away, desperate to leave this memory. But if Raina was watching it play out, he had no choice but to join her.

Someone was suddenly yelling outside. The local authorities coming to save the day. Hugo turned to Judith. "I'll take care of them. You see if the sister is here."

Hugo marched out of the room, about to feed again. Caleb wondered if the local forces were prepared for what they were about to encounter, wondered how common it was to fight vampires.

Unlike last time, Raina offered no information, now staring at the past playing out, shaking and crying.

Raina's little sister had gone from a blur back into a

child. Staring up at her sister, hand covering her mouth, tears soaking her face.

*Oh God, she's looking at her.*

Judith noticed.

She stepped forward, bending over to look.

"Oh, you're just a wee one, aren't you?"

"Please," Young Raina cried out. "Please, take me. Just leave her alone."

Judith looked at Raina, weighing the request as Hugo, in the next room, murdered the men who came to rescue Raina's family.

Judith stared at Raina through an eternity of screams and gurgling as she slowly decided.

And in that moment, Caleb thought he saw something he'd seen many times in cases of domestic abuse. Judith wasn't just helping Hugo with his crimes; she was a victim herself, probably taken under similar circumstances.

Maybe that would be enough to give her pause, to disobey Hugo's instructions and spare at least one of the sisters.

But Caleb also knew something else from his time with the Agency — people under pressure rarely did the right thing.

"Sorry," Judith said, reaching under the bed to pull the girl out.

"Talani!" Raina screamed.

Then they were back in the present, in the interrogation room, staring at one another not as interrogator and hostage but fellow victims in an endless war of misery.

Caleb withdrew his hands and sat on the floor across from her.

"What happened next?"

"They sold me, turned me, and ... bad things happened. I don't know what came of Talani. We were separated immediately, and they said she was in a place where she was being cared for, not forced to do the things I was. But I don't know if that was the truth, or leverage to keep me in line. For all I know, they killed her. I've looked for a long time, but never found answers."

She wiped at her tears then continued. "After I don't know how many years, The Hand of the Seven Gods stormed into the place where I was being held and rescued a bunch of us. They killed our captors, but they never found Hugo, Judith, or Talani."

"I'm sorry."

"The Hand saved us. Saved me. I owe them everything, which is why I fight for them now. Why I …"

She looked at his wounds then down at the ground. "I'm sorry."

Caleb nodded. "I understand."

He thought about the things he had to do for his job on Earth, the times he may have gone too far. He hadn't tortured anyone, but he might have if given the chance.

"So, now what?"

"I'll talk to Prophet Malachi. Would you be interested in joining us in our fight against your brother and father? It wouldn't be too unlike the job you had on Earth."

Caleb wasn't sure he wanted to join anyone in anything, let alone some "prophet's" cult, but it seemed like the only option that might return his sense of freedom. Perhaps he could enlist The Hand's help in tracking down Jacob and killing him.

"Yes, I would."

# SIXTEEN

# Abigail

ABIGAIL WOKE IN DARKNESS, naked save for a sheet covering her body.

She was lying on a soft cloth-and-straw mat in a small room barely lit by a light floating in a glass jar on the floor beside her.

The wood had weird circular patterns. And, like the floor, the walls were wooden as well, with an odd texture she couldn't quite make out in the sparse light.

Her head foggy, she looked to her right and saw Judith sleeping on a mat beside hers. She also appeared to be naked except for a sheet covering her from the chest down.

*Or maybe she's dead?*

Abigail saw the same black veins she'd see on her own skin now creeping up Judith's arms, chest, and face.

*She's sick too?*

A voice in her head, familiar and comforting: *"Yes,"* Talani said. *"She took some of the poison from you, to save you."*

Abigail looked down to see that her own dark veins were almost gone. She could move her legs. She still felt like crap, but no longer on the verge of death.

*Did we find the witch?*

*Am I cured?*

*Is Judith going to be cured?*

A round wooden door opened. Talani entered then closed the door behind her.

"How are you?"

"Okay." Abigail sat up, raising the sheet to cover herself.

"Good," Talani said, walking over to a chair and grabbing Abigail's neatly folded clothes. "I washed them in the river."

Abigail noticed that Talani's clothes were also cleaned, patched, and sewn where they'd been torn during the fight.

"Where are we? How long have I been out? And why are we naked?"

"We're in Kovar. Turns out we were in the village, we just couldn't see it. They live in the trees. As for how long you've been out, I'm not even sure what day it is, but I'd guess maybe a few. As for your nakedness, the witches put a poultice on you both to extract the poison. They said not to bathe for a few more days. It's still working its magick."

Abigail had many thoughts and questions, bathing at the top of her list. How were they supposed to bathe here, or use the bathroom?

"The old-fashioned way," Talani said, reading Abigail's mind. "And no, it's not glamorous." She looked down. "Sorry, I didn't mean to still be inside your head. I was just waiting for you to wake up, and …"

"It's okay. I like having you in there. So, what did the witch say? Will I be okay? Will Judith?"

Talani went over and sat beside Judith as Abigail dressed. "The witch said you should both be okay, though Judith will take longer to heal."

"Why?"

"Because she's not young like us."

Abigail looked at the woman lying helpless with poison meant for Abigail coursing through her veins and marring her skin.

"I owe her," Abigail said.

Talani nodded. Then instead of speaking aloud, said into Abigail's head, "And she won't let you forget it."

"What do you mean?"

"Later," Talani said, still inside her mind. Then, out loud: "Before you get too comfortable, there's something you need to know."

"What's that?" Abigail asked, her stomach churning.

"The witch didn't do this for free. They want something in exchange for saving you both."

Abigail's stomach did another lurch. "What's that?"

"You're not gonna like this."

"What?" Abigail asked, annoyed at Talani for stringing it out.

The door opened, and someone, *some thing*, shambled into the room.

It was long, skinny, and covered in twisting gnarled roots and leaves. It looked like a human-sized tree. Its face was square and flat with hollowed-out pits for eyes. Except the pits weren't hollow so much as filled with a glowing green light that seemed to emanate from fissures along the creature's body.

Abigail couldn't help but be shocked by its appearance. She barely even realized that in her fear she'd fallen to a crouch, ready to run.

"It's okay," Talani said, easing her back to a sitting position. "They're safe."

Abigail stared at the thing, trying to figure out what it was, how it even worked. A chill ran through her. It was a walking tree, for lack of anything else to call it, but it had human-like appendages — arms, legs, and long, twisting fingers, all seemingly made up of dark reddish-brown bark, twisted limbs made of vines and foliage, and a gnarled mess that seemed to be dark mud or clay holding it all together. She wondered if the green light shining in its eyes and seemingly within its body were some sort of life force that propelled it, or something else she couldn't even guess at.

*"Hello, Abigail,"* the thing said as it stepped inside the doorway with a rustling sound. And yet the words weren't spoken, for it had no proper mouth. Instead, the creature projected the words into her head telepathically, same as Talani. And its voice sounded like her own.

Abigail wondered if it could read her thoughts and could see how creepy she found it.

"What *are* you?" Abigail asked.

*"We are the Druwan. We are pleased to meet you."*

Abigail didn't know what to do. Custom was to shake people's hand, but this wasn't a person, and she hadn't shaken a hand since long before she turned into a vampire that could kill with a touch.

"I'm Abigail. Do you have a name?"

*"No, we are all one. We've no use for names."*

"So, um, what are you? Are you like trees living inside of larger trees?"

Talani stifled a laugh.

Abigail realized that her question was too forward, and maybe offensive.

"I'm sorry."

*"We are Druwan, the oldest sentient life on this world. Despite appearances, we are not trees. We are custodians of the Sacred Woods."*

"Is that where we are now?"

*"Yes."*

"Are you the witch?"

*"No, she is one of the humans we allow to live here. She protects the Sacred Woods alongside us."*

"Thank you for saving us."

*"You are most welcome."*

"What was it you wanted in exchange?" Abigail asked, wondering what a tree-like thing could ask of them that would be as awful as Talani made it seem. Did it want them to stay there forever? Or to become whatever it was they were? Abigail might not mind staying with them if it was safe, but she had no interest in changing into yet something else.

*"We need you to find and kill a man in the Town of Jonah."*

"Who?"

*"His name is Baltazar, a crafter of tools and weapons."*

"What did he do?"

*"He is entering the Sacred Woods and using our trees, killing us for parts for his magick weapons. So far he has come alone, so I believe this is his secret. But it won't be long before others follow. And then they will destroy this place."*

"Why don't you just kill him when he's here?" Abigail asked.

*"We cannot kill. We value all life here."*

"But what about the witch, or some of the others? Couldn't you get some of them to do it?"

*"No killing in the Sacred Woods. Your friend said you were going to the Town of Jonah. There you shall end him."*

Abigail considered this, then asked, "Is he a bad guy?"

*"Bad?"*

"You know, *evil*. Is he evil? I can only kill evil people. I can't kill innocents."

*"We don't see things like you, in terms of good and evil. But to answer your question, this man has killed more than ten of our kind, and destroyed another twenty sacred trees in the past year. He's also a*

*werewolf who has been known to hunt humans. Would that count as evil to you?"*

Abigail looked up at the big tree's face. Though it was creepy, and though its face was missing expression without moving parts, and more or less a squarish block with glowing eyes, there was something she found cute about it now.

"A werewolf? Yeah, I'd say that counts as him being a bad guy."

*"Then you'll do it?"*

Talani answered, "Consider him dead."

*"The Druwan thank you."*

"You're welcome," Abigail said.

As the creature shuffled out of the room, Abigail couldn't help but think of Larry and her back home, searching through newspapers to find bad people that needed to die. Using her curse to help others felt good — except for the time Larry got it wrong and they killed that woman who hadn't really killed her kid.

Thinking about that only made her miss Larry, and John, all the more.

Talani nudged her, "Are you okay? You're thinking about your friends again, aren't you?"

There was no use lying since Talani could more or less come and go as she wanted in Abigail's head.

"Yeah. Don't you ever miss anyone from your life before this? Before becoming a vampire?"

Talani looked at the ground, as if thinking of someone specific.

"More than you know."

# SEVENTEEN

# Jacob

JACOB WAS STANDING ALONE in The Keep as the sun went down, looking out over the so-called Forgotten Kingdom. A warm breeze blew through The Keep, and with it came the stink of the city below.

It may have been The Forgotten City, a squalid town of crudely stacked buildings, bustling with too many people crammed together. It may have served as a surprisingly thriving commercial center, and several communities had made it a true home, but it was no Forgotten *Kingdom*, as Father called it.

Not like the majestic kingdom in the mountains that Jacob had known as a young child, before The Great Purge forced them, and most every other non-magick person, south as The North and their tech displaced hundreds of thousands of people and destroyed their homes. After four thousand years of fighting, the North had finally secured victory by secretly using The Hand of the Seven Gods to help them scourge the world of vampires and magick users, killing many while rounding up others to torture in the dungeons beneath the Stone Pillars in the capital city.

While Father had secured some form of victory by claiming this island as a "kingdom," it was a pathetic offering to pacify the only holdouts who could've prevented the peace treaty.

Jacob still hated his father for signing the Treaty, for not fighting harder. For betraying his own kind.

Calling this a kingdom was an affront to the Valkoer and those forced to live here.

It had been years since anyone in The Southern Realm had been to The North, save for The Hand of the Seven Gods, who kissed their rings and worshipped their tech and rules.

*As if any man could tell another how to live.*

Jacob looked past his shitty *kingdom* toward the northern horizon, but from this distance saw nothing beyond the tree-lined horizon and mountains to the north. Couldn't see skyscrapers, countless lights, zeppelins dotting the sky, or any of the other *wonders* of the modern age.

To be fair, he hadn't seen any of these so-called *wonders* himself. When he lived closer, in the northernmost part of The Southern Realm, Jacob kept mostly to his own land. While the lands were joined by a thin ten-mile natural bridge, his kind weren't welcome in The North, even before The Great Purge bled into The South, what with the constant warring.

Perhaps The North was more civilized, more homogenous, and more advanced, but what did it all mean in the end?

Jacob had seen plenty of amazing sights on Earth. While that planet was more advanced than The North of this world in some ways, it was less so in others. Still, the societies seemed similar enough to Jacob that he could lump them both with things he despised. Both civilizations laughed at the old ways and what they didn't understand, denying the existence of anything that didn't fit into their codified precepts of How the World Should Be.

Both worlds were blindly poking hibernating beasts whom they could never understand.

And they would pay.

*They'll all burn when I'm done.*

Jacob smiled at the thought of millions of people who thought they were so much better than him having to bow before he enslaved their so-called best and brightest, destroyed their armies, and made them regret ever making him feel like a monster.

*It will be wonderful indeed.*

Jacob's hand found his belt, and he withdrew the blade that his brother Caleb had stabbed him with. The blade that had nearly killed him. He looked at it, black onyx with tiny flecks of silver throughout. He liked holding onto something which had nearly ended him. It gave him a sense of mastery over his life, and fate.

A throat cleared behind him.

Jacob turned, startled, not used to anyone being able to sneak up on him.

Sir Tomas Barron stood in the chamber doorway. The young-looking knight wasn't wearing his usual black armor or weapons, but rather his formal clothing — a dark blue robe covering black pants and a shirt.

"Forgive me, my Prince, I wished to speak with you alone."

"Alone?"

It was highly unusual for Barron to speak with Jacob alone, let alone seek him out.

"Yes, my Prince. Could I have a moment of your time?"

Jacob sheathed the blade then considered Barron's request.

Jacob hated the man's overly polite mannerisms, which, along with his unnatural good looks, reminded Jacob of all the superficial humans he'd been around while stuck on Earth. .

"What is it, Sir Barron?"

The knight approached, hands folded before him.

"May I speak freely? Without fear of retribution?"

Jacob didn't know the man's game, but he'd better tread lightly.

"What is it?"

"I think your father is making a mistake."

Jacob's face flushed with a sudden anger. "You dare doubt your King's wisdom?"

"It's not King Zol's wisdom I question. Rather it is Viceroy Mason's, and his undue influence upon your father since you've been gone."

"What do you mean, *undue influence?*"

"For some time your father has been getting sicker. Not remembering things, prone to mood swings … more than usual, I mean. And he's been making decisions that seem less in line with the King Zol I've known most of my life and more in line with the political machinations of Mason."

"Examples?"

"The Hand of the Seven recently annexed Callen's Bay, a clear violation of the Treaty, and an incursion upon our brothers there, taking their homes, forcing them to come here."

"*Here?* They're craftsmen and fishermen, not monsters or magick users. Why banish them here?"

"Yes, but there was a family of lycanthropes living in the community. Or was, rather, until The Hand chased them away. They then seized the land under the premise that the people had violated the Treaty by harboring non-Humkoers."

"And what did Father do?"

"That's just it. Nothing. Normally he would've sent me or Mason to negotiate, to argue on behalf of Callen's Bay since they are our partners in trade. But he sent no one. Didn't even ask for a meeting with The Hand."

"And what of our *esteemed* Full Council? Did they not voice dissent?"

"You know that they're too scared to defy the King — or in this case, Mason, who argued to myself and the King that we ought to leave it alone. Argued that the citizens of Callen's Bay did, technically, break the terms."

"Since when are they enforcing *those rules?* Hell, they've got half a city of vampires, magick users, and other freaks living under the Town of Jonah. Are they going to pretend that nobody knows they're there?"

"I believe that exiles from here are given safe harbor."

"Of course. It's okay if they're a thorn in *our* eye, but nobody else is allowed to live in a normal home? They're going to close an entire town over one family of were-wolves? Had they been attacking anyone?"

"Not that I'm aware of, my Prince."

"So, why are you coming to me with this? What would you have me do?"

"It's not *this* I'm worried about. It's the future. If your father dies, I believe that Mason will make a play for the throne."

"But it is my birthright! How the hell does he plan to do that?"

"I believe he is telling your father not to use the crystals so that *he* may seize them. With control of the crystals, he can claim the throne."

"But why would he even do that? He is fat and happy in his empire of shit. He has no desire to fight our oppressors, or conquer Earth. Why seize the throne?"

"Because he is afraid of what you will do to this Kingdom once you take it."

"He told you this?"

"Not in so many words. But I read between the lines when he speaks to your father. Now that you're back, he's scared."

Jacob turned and looked out at the horizon, seeing the sun peeking over the trees in the distance, scorching the darkness with bright orange light. Soon it would bleach the remnants of night, and send his kind into hiding.

He really wished he'd brought Mr. Dark with him instead of telling him to wait on Earth to manage what was left of Harbinger. Jacob made a mental note to find another man, or woman, with his talents, so he could again enter the daylight fearless of death.

Jacob turned to Barron, eying the man so bold to approach him.

"How do you know I won't boil you under the sun for treason?"

"Because I believe *you* are our Kingdom's only hope of regaining our might. Because I have served your father forever, and it sickens me to see him wasting away, with someone exploiting his frailty. And because I believe you are the next King, and I will serve you faithfully, with my life if need be."

"Again, what do you propose I do? Kill Mason and take control?"

"No, Mason has made too many allies within the community, and, more importantly, outside our city."

"With The Hand, you mean?"

"Yes, my Prince."

"So, what would you suggest as a course of action, Sir Barron?"

"I say we wake your father up."

"Go on," Jacob said, a smile spreading across his face.

# EIGHTEEN

# John

THEY WERE DOWN TO SIX — John, Hope, Larry, Sanders, Emma, and one other, a forty-five-year-old Omega agent named Ralph Jenkins, a fireplug of a man they called Jenk. He was one of the toughest of the agents, as evidenced by his surviving the giant wolf attack. But he, like the rest of them, was shaken, bruised, and bloodied.

They stood in the cave's mouth, catching their collective breath after tracking down supplies lost in the chaos and reassessing the situation.

"Well, what the hell do we do now?" Jenk eyed their pitiful remainders with a disdain he couldn't disguise. "I vote we go back to Earth and regroup."

Sanders nodded. "I agree. This mission is a bust."

John watched Larry and Hope, trying to gauge where they were. While Larry definitely looked ready to go home, Hope did not. She was still taken by her visions with the creature, which now, in light of what Larry and Emma said, was likely a werewolf.

Emma was first to dissent. "We're not leaving here without Logan."

"We can't go in and save him," Sanders said. "We don't have the numbers."

"Fuck numbers. We *had* numbers, and now everyone else is dead or run off. You really think our odds will change if we come back with more troops?"

"Our primary mission has nothing to do with your brother," Sanders snapped back. "We need to secure the target and retrieve the crystals. We can't do that with just six of us."

"So, what, Logan means nothing to you? You're just gonna leave him here to die? I knew he shouldn't have ever agreed to work with you people. The Agency doesn't give a shit about anything but the almighty mission. Fuck the people who actually have to do the missions, right?"

Sanders, not used to such disrespect, let alone willing to take it from someone so young, got in Emma's face. "Don't you tell me what I give a shit about. We lost a lot of good people here today, and if you think that doesn't weigh on my conscience, then you don't know the first thing about me. Your brother knew the risks of working with us but believed in the mission enough to come anyway."

"No, you all coerced him into helping you. Same as always." Emma turned away, arms crossed over her chest. "You all can go back, but I'm not leaving Logan behind."

"I'm staying, too," Hope said.

John sighed. One of two things was apparently about to happen — they'd either split the team or all stay. Neither would work. Sanders was right: they didn't have the numbers, and no amount of earnest pep talks would change that.

He looked at Larry to gauge his friend's feelings, but Larry looked as defeated as John felt.

All eyes were on John, as if awaiting his vote.

"Well?" Sanders said, turning to him. "What do you think?"

"I think we're screwed no matter what we do here. Why don't you all return to Earth, and I'll stay behind and see if I can rescue Logan."

"If you go, I go," Emma said, hands on her hips.

"Me too," Hope added.

Sanders and Jenk both sighed.

Sanders said, "We're not going back to the portal alone. I *can't* leave you all over here."

"Then I guess it's settled," Emma said. "We're all staying."

But John had an idea. "How about this? We find Logan and the others, learn what we can about Jacob, then get back to Earth, regroup, and come at this fresh?"

Emma nodded. "My brother is the only reason I'm here, so that's fine with me."

Sanders and Jenk traded glances, then Sanders nodded. "Okay. Sounds good. Can you connect with your brother, or figure out where he is?"

Emma closed her eyes, focusing to find him.

John looked at Hope, found her gaze on the ground. He couldn't tell if she was avoiding eye contact because she disagreed with the plan and didn't want to go back without finding the key to whatever was locked away, or if she was simply lost in thought, and maybe remembering more. He'd have to tell her something about her past, and soon, before she remembered everything. He only hoped it wouldn't erode whatever trust in him she now had. She was the only woman he'd ever loved, but for her, he was a relationship she had a decade ago, in another life. He was surprised she was still with him, but he knew he couldn't push her too much without ruining everything.

"I can feel him," Emma said. "We're not far."

"Is he okay?" Larry asked. It seemed like a good way to let the girl know that they truly did care about her brother's welfare. John wasn't sure if he was being genuine or not. Larry had a lot more room in his heart than John did, if so. John had too many other priorities to care about Logan other than for whatever info he could provide to them. No, John was too concerned with finding Jacob and the crystals, finding Caleb, and finding Abigail to be overly sympathetic to Emma's sulking.

"Yeah, he seems okay for now," Emma said, "but we need to hurry."

Sanders looked at them all, likely with the same doubt John felt before the mission began, and nodded. "All right, let's go."

# NINETEEN

# Jacob

JACOB STOOD outside Father's chambers, lurking in the unlit hallway's gnarled shadows.

The living chambers occupied the castle's entire top floor and were limited to Zol's chamber, his servant's chamber, and Jacob's. The remaining rooms were unused, though Jacob was certain that Viceroy Mason would love nothing more than full-time access to the King.

Jacob rarely saw his father since coming home. At the end of the night, or often sooner, he'd retire to his chambers and do who knew what. Perhaps his illness begged for sleep.

*Or maybe he's avoiding spending time with me.*

*He won't evade me this time, though.*

Jacob figured he'd risk approaching Father one final time before trying the tactic he and Sir Barron had devised a couple of days ago. Jacob felt this was the right thing to do even if it might backfire and lay even more distance between them.

He heard Father's footsteps approaching from the other side of the door. The bedroom opened, and his father emerged in his robes, ready for his meeting with Barron and Mason.

"Father, may I have a word?"

Father's face twisted in annoyance. "This can't wait?"

"No, it can't," Jacob said, meeting Father's eyes.

"What is it?"

"I'd like you to reconsider my suggestion."

"Which one?"

"Using the crystals to reclaim our lands. Even if you don't want to invade Earth, I believe there are some here who would see this as a sign of weakness."

Accusing Father of frailty would anger him greatly. As expected, he snapped. "And how would anyone accuse me of weakness when they don't even know of the crystals' existence? Perhaps you should be more forthright in your accusations, Son. Admit that it is *you* who thinks I'm weak. The irony of *you*, who doesn't have the courage of his convictions to bluntly address me, accusing *me* of being feeble!"

"I'm making no such accusation. But I know how these things work. It's only a matter of time before people start talking. Some say they already are."

Father got in Jacob's face, eying him like a drunk in a bar searching for a fight. Despite the King's frail frame, Jacob couldn't help but see his father like he did as a child: bigger, stronger, crueler.

Jacob wanted to back down.

Wished he'd not started the conversation.

But now he was stuck, and didn't dare flinch.

"*They* already are, are they? And what are *they* saying, Son?"

It was now or never. This direct approach wasn't a part of his plan, and would likely make his plot with Barron even more difficult to execute, but Jacob couldn't help himself.

"They're saying that you're old, that you're dying, and making horrible choices. And that perhaps Viceroy Mason would make a better leader."

Jacob knew that attacking Mason's strength would only make his father stick by his right hand man all the more. But to paint Mason as a potential threat to the king, *that* could change the game considerably — if his father didn't see right through the ruse.

"Viceroy Mason and not *you?*" Zol chuckled. "I bet that's what has you so bothered, eh? That people know *you're* not leadership material?"

Jacob bit his tongue then drew a deep breath.

"I'm just reporting what I hear, Father."

"Yeah, and who's talking to *you?*"

Here, things could get tricky. If the old man's instincts were sharp, or his paranoia high enough, he might guess that Barron had been talking, and that could ruin their plans before they took flight.

"Nobody's talking to me. But I hear things while walking the city."

"You were never a good liar, Jacob. Let's just come out with it."

Jacob hoped he hadn't revealed any edges of truth. He hadn't felt the old man trying to pry inside his mind, and Jacob was far better than Father at telepathic warfare. No way the King could have sneaked in to find anything.

Jacob didn't respond.

"You didn't hear shite." Father laughed. "This is you taking a shot at the throne by hoping to remove your competition, turning me against Viceroy Mason."

*Shit.*

Jacob shook his head. "No. This is me worried about

you. Worried that you don't even see the snake slithering through your inner circle."

"You're talking about Mason?"

"Yes!"

"Envy doesn't suit you, Jacob."

"Envy?"

"Clearly, you're jealous of him. Let's not pretend otherwise. You've always been a petty child, feeling like everyone is always out to get you. And now you're extending that paranoia to me."

It was rich, Father calling *him* paranoid. This was a man who once executed his entire servant staff because someone had accidentally thrown out his kaikai berry shipment, claiming that the berries gave him vitality and that his staff clearly wanted him to fall ill.

"Just promise me that you won't let those crystals out of your sight. Do not let Mason give them to Elder Ponson, or whatever else *he* thinks you should do with them."

"I suppose I should just give them to *you*, right? You'll take *great care* of them, I'll bet. Only *Prince Jacob* could be the custodian of such power?"

*Yes. That's exactly right, you old fool.*

"No, *you* keep them. You are the King, not me. If I wanted the power, I wouldn't have returned home with the wizard's soul. I would have remained on Earth and raised an army of my own. No one could have stopped me. And *nobody* can stop you, Father. You just need to see the possibilities. Stop being blinded by whatever Mason is doing."

Jacob stopped short of giving the example of Mason not stepping up to save Callen's Bay. He wasn't sure how much was known beyond The Council, or even the King's two most trusted advisers. Saying too much could reveal Jacob's partner in what was to come next.

"Is that all?"

Jacob met the old man's eyes feeling two things at once — rage that Father never listened, and pity that the man was blind to what was coming.

*I tried to do the right thing.*

*I tried, but he refuses to let me.*

*So be it.*

"Yes, my King," Jacob said, looking down at the ground.

Father said nothing.

No *thank-you.*

No *I'll think about it.*

Nothing.

He simply left.

Jacob stood in the shadows seething.

*Oh well. I tried to do the right thing by my family. Now it's time to do right by me.*

# TWENTY

# King Zol

ZOL LEFT the hallway shaking his head, disgusted with his son yet again.

Something was wrong with the boy. Always had been. Even from early on, Zol knew it. He was soft, too needy of his mother's affection, too jealous of his brothers receiving attention, and too stupid to realize his weaknesses, always blaming others for his failings.

Jacob was too much like his mother, whose name Zol refused to ever remember again. Why had she not taken Jacob with the other two? Why leave behind such a failure of a child who would grow up to be a sorry excuse for the family name?

Perhaps it was one final *fuck-you* to him.

The woman had never appreciated anything that he had tried to do for her. Never appreciated how hard he worked to maintain a kingdom even as the world around them crumbled. Never appreciated him choosing her from among dozens of young women in the Calladian Mountains to make his wife, to give the gift of eternal life as a Valkoer.

She'd always seen herself as a victim, never recognizing opportunity for what it was.

And Jacob, as much as he hated his mother for abandoning him, was just like her: a victim, always looking to blame others for everything.

He was clearly jealous of Viceroy Mason, and likely the time they shared. But Zol refused to apologize. Calbot Mason was a longtime friend, one of maybe three men he trusted.

Zol would rather spend time with Mason, Barron, or even The Full Council than even an hour alone with his ungrateful, whiny son.

*Why* didn't *he stay on Earth?*

It wasn't as if Jacob was doing Zol any favors by bringing the wizard's crystals home. It was just one more problem to manage, a problem that Zol didn't fucking need right now.

Zol ran his hand over the pouch around his neck, concealed beneath his robes and shirt. They buzzed, warm to his touch, ready to be used however he wanted.

But he didn't need their power.

What use was great power when everyone was already leaving him alone?

He was right where he wanted to be, ruler of The Forgotten Kingdom, loved and feared by thousands. The Hand no longer bothered them. And war with The North, along with The Great Purge, was over.

Now was a time to rest.

A time to enjoy what he'd sacrificed so much for.

He had a place to live.

He had countless people to do his bidding.

He had power.

He could have any woman he craved, whenever he wanted.

His corner of the world might be smaller, limited to an island, but it was still his for the taking.

He no longer had to fight for it. While Jacob might have rose-colored memories of what their old kingdom was like, he never knew the battles waged to maintain that glory — against enemies within and outside the Kingdom.

He was too damn old for fighting. Let the others quarrel for scraps. He was content with his kingdom even if its appearance was less than majestic. There was an advantage to being king of a place that nobody wanted to rule. Nobody was aiming for his head. But if word got out about the crystals and their power, all of that could change in an instant.

And who would protect the crown?

Certainly not his whiny bitch of a son, Jacob.

He passed through one last corridor then came to his meeting chambers where Mason and Barron were standing at attention, eager to tell him something.

"What is it?"

"Someone came through the portal a few days ago," Mason said.

"Who?"

"Your son, John."

# TWENTY-ONE

# John

THEY'D BEEN WALKING along a wide dirt road for a few hours as the sun began to rise just above the horizon, painting the sky in violet and orange.

They could see hoof-prints and narrow wagon lines in the pre-dawn light, indicating they were on a popular, and hopefully safer, path than they'd started on.

Everyone was quiet for most of the trip. John imagined most of them were battling fear and processing grief over all they'd lost. John didn't know any of the Omega agents well but imagined that Sanders and Jenk had lost good friends to the werewolf attack.

Even Larry and Hope were quiet, trudging along with heavy uniforms and heavier packs.

John wasn't tired, yet, but he was getting hungry. If they didn't find enemies to feed on soon, there would be trouble. He'd planned well for the trip, feeding just a day prior to crossing through the portal. But after racing after Hope and the werewolf, he'd burned through his reserve.

And soon he'd pay.

He'd been walking point with Sanders but fell back in line with Larry and Hope, walking side by side.

"How are you two doing?" he asked, his voice low.

"They got a McDonald's around here? I sure could use a Big Mac, fries, and a Coke."

"Yeah, I'm not digging this leather, either," Hope said, taking a bite of jerky from their surviving supplies.

"Yeah, and nobody thought to pack any Mountain Dew? What is this shit?" Larry joked, holding up a bottle of water.

Hope laughed. "That would be water, Larry."

"What the hell is this *water* stuff? Is it like Mountain Dew without … you know, all the good shit?"

"I know this must come as shock to you, but water is a compound, which you'll find naturally occurring all over the planet. And, believe it or not, you rarely see it in fluorescent green. Mountain Dew is water with lots of caffeine and too many chemicals."

"What?" Larry joked. "You mean Mountain Dew doesn't rain from the sky, blessed by the kisses of angels on the way down?"

John smiled. "Great, now you ruined Mountain Dew for him."

"N0," Larry said, "you only made it sexier."

"Wait, I thought you packed a bottle or two," John said, clearly remembering giving Larry shit about it.

"I drank them right after we crossed over," Larry admitted.

Hope laughed. "You are so sad."

The three of them laughed, and Emma, who was behind them, started laughing too. It was the first time John had seen a smile on the glum teenager's face.

Laughter ceased when Sanders and Jenk shot back

stern looks at them: *How the hell can you all be laughing at a time like this?*

When Sanders turned her attention back to the road ahead, Hope covered her mouth, eyes watering. "Oh God, I can't hold it in," she whispered, which, of course, only made Larry's fit that much worse.

John fell back a bit to gauge Emma's temperament, and maybe dig into the source of the bad vibes he was getting from her. She'd been giving him the stink eye ever since they met. He had a decent idea why, but would have to broach the topic carefully to resolve it.

"How are you?"

"Okay," she said, no longer laughing, though the hint of a smile still played with her mouth.

"We're going to get your brother. I know Omega and The Guardians pissed you off, and treated you and Logan like shit, but they're not all bad. Sanders is one of the good guys, or gals, or … whatever; you know what I mean."

Emma looked up at John with a flash of accusation, "I'm supposed to take *your* word for it? John the Traitor?"

*And there it is.*

"We all had choices to make. They used you to get your brother working for them. They used Hope and someone else on me. But I was *trying* to do the right thing."

"By rounding up Otherworlders and Halfworlders and taking them to some black site to interrogate, or kill, them?"

"I didn't kill anyone who didn't deserve it."

"*Deserve* it?" Emma laughed.

"I only killed threats, people who were planning heinous shit or who had already done something unthinkable. People in league with Jacob, wanting to open portals and start a vampire farm on Earth."

"No, I saw plenty of good people taken, gone without

explanation other than the company line saying they were 'enemies of the state' or some other such shit."

"There were some bad apples in Omega, and now they're gone. But I promise: you, me, and Sanders, we're all on the same page. We all want the same thing."

"And what is that?"

"To stop a massacre of the human race."

Emma rolled her eyes.

"You don't believe me?"

"How can you know what this Jacob guy has planned? Did he tell you his plans to conquer the world whilst twirling his moustache like some movie villain?"

"You know how you and your brother share a telepathic bond? Same with us. I can see things he's thinking. I *know* what he wants. If you saw what I've seen, you'd be scared, too. Plus, he's more or less asked me to join him in taking over the world."

"If you have a bond, why not use it to *track him?* Why even involve my brother or me?"

"Because he can lock me out. I only get occasional glimpses, usually while sleeping."

"So, if you get glimpses of his thoughts, then it stands to reason that he gets glimpses of *yours*, too? Maybe he even knows we're here, that we're coming for him? Hell, maybe he sent the werewolves after us!"

For the first time, John saw fear in Emma's eyes.

"That's why I'm not sleeping until we find him. So I can be on guard, can sense any attempts at intrusion."

"But can't he sense that you're here? Is there any way for you to block that?"

"Yes, as long as I can maintain focus, I can keep him from sensing me. It's all in the spells."

"I hope so. For all of our sakes."

"We're gonna get through this, Emma. We'll find your

brother, and I'll make sure neither of you ever has to work for The Guardians again. Your obligation to them is over."

"Really?"

"I don't know what they used to pressure your compliance, but I don't believe coercion ever buys loyalty or the best results. If you work with Omega, it should be because you want to, not because they're holding something over your head."

Emma's eyes began to water. She turned away, not wanting John to see her wiping tears with the back of her hand.

"Thank you," she said, still turned away.

"You're welcome. I'm going to go check back in with my friends."

He caught back up to Larry and Hope, who were discussing the werewolf that had left Hope alone rather than killing her.

"What do you think it means?" Larry glanced at John with a knowing look that suggested he come clean.

Hope said, "I don't know. It's the strangest thing, but I feel like I've been here before."

Larry was looking straight at John, barely hiding it now. He may as well be holding a big fucking sign that said: *TELL HER THE BIG SECRET, JOHN!*

John would have to tell her, eventually, but this wasn't the time. It was one thing to reveal that she'd been mind wiped for nearly a decade to protect her, which in itself was a serious violation of trust. But to tell her that she wasn't even human? What would *that* shit to do to her? And would she believe that he didn't know until he found out she was a vessel made to hide one of the crystals?

He'd wanted to wait to tell her, until they were back home, in a safe and comfortable environment. A place where she had time to process the facts, at least the few he knew enough to tell her. And, if he was being honest, he wanted to wait until they'd spent a bit more time together. That their bond would be a bit stronger, not some tenuous thread it seemed to be.

Plus, it was quite possible that she could just snap.

John had seen these things go badly before — Otherworlders who'd had their Guardian-issued mind wipes not take. And when everything came back, it caused a mental collapse, psychic fissures. Otherworlder or human, the mind was fragile. To suddenly have something as fundamentally *you* as your past ripped out from under your feet, to be told that everything you believed was a lie, it was a core-shaking shock that could destroy even the strongest mind. And Hope had already been through so much.

Yet her memories seemed to be returning. If he waited any longer, there was no way he could help guide the process. She could have a total recall during the middle of a fight or flight for their lives.

And what then?

How would *that* be helping her?

John looked at Larry and nodded.

Larry returned the nod, then slowed his pace to give them space.

It was time to tell the truth.

# TWENTY-TWO

# Hope

"I'M *WHAT?*" Hope asked, certain she'd misheard him.

"You're not human," John said. "You're from this world."

"How ... how do you know this?"

"I found out when Jacob was looking for vessels holding the crystals. You were one of them. My father's wizard had used you, along with several other people, to hide the crystals, then sent you all to Earth."

"How long ago?"

"Probably when I came over with my mother and brother Caleb. Twentysomething years ago, I'm guessing."

"But — I have a family, friends, and ... No, it can't be true."

"Maybe he sent you over as a child. Maybe the people you grew up with were chosen to protect you; maybe they're from this world, too, I don't know. I don't know any more than what I'm telling you. But your *new* memories, they're from here."

None of this made sense, yet was it any more bizarre than any of the other insanity that had hurled Hope's life into chaos ever since John revealed himself as a vampire? No, and it certainly made sense of her strangest memories.

She tried to recall what had rushed through her mind during her encounter with the werewolf, but nothing would come. She saw flashes of animals that weren't from her planet. She remembered having a dog, though couldn't remember what it looked like. As for herself, she wasn't sure how old she was in her memories, other than very young. Perhaps five? Maybe younger? Hope couldn't see herself in the memories, only her hands holding stuff, and petting the blur of a dog.

"Why didn't you tell me sooner?"

"I just found out a week or so ago. And I didn't know when to bring it up. It didn't feel right to do so before we were back home and safe. I didn't want to do anything that might … I don't know, make things harder for you. I'm sorry."

A part of her was angry at John for keeping more secrets, but with everything that had been happening ever since he came back into her life, it wasn't as if they'd had any real time alone before being thrust back into action.

And he *was* telling her now.

"It's okay."

"Really?" he said, eyebrows arched under his helmet's open visor.

"Did you expect me to yell at you?"

"I don't know what I expected. It's been a long time since we lived together. Sometimes I feel like it was a different life, that maybe you went on without me."

"It's weird. It's like I've lived two lives. The last ten years as a florist, with a man I didn't really know, and then … when we were together in Saint Augustine. Even though it was like a decade ago, it doesn't feel like it. It's as if I woke up from a long sleep, and I want to pick up and carry on with my old life, but ..."

She tried to think of a way to say it without it sounding awful.

"But what?"

"There's a part of me that no longer feels like that person. I don't feel like Hannah the florist, or Hope the painter. I feel like someone entirely different."

She hoped that he wouldn't ask how she felt about him. She did love John, but there was a part of her that wasn't sure exactly how she felt about him now. A lot had happened.

He wasn't the John she'd known. The one she'd grown to love in that life before the long sleep. He was a vampire, someone she couldn't even touch without dying. A relationship with a man like that was impossible.

Thankfully, John didn't inquire. Instead he said, "What *do* you feel like? Do you think it's these new memories messing things up?"

"I don't know."

She said nothing more, and neither did John. Together they shared an uncomfortable silence.

She'd always loved his quiet demeanor. He wasn't like other men she'd been unfortunate enough to date — loud and obnoxious in their constant need for attention. John had always been confident, and didn't feel a need to fill silence with chatter. They'd spent many comfortable mornings lying in bed, neither of them needing to say anything — simply enjoying each other's company.

But *this* silence was the opposite. It was, in its own way, so loud that *she* felt a need to drown it with chatter.

She looked back to see where Larry was. He was always good for distracting conversation. But as she did,

Hope heard Emma say something that stopped everyone in their tracks.

# TWENTY-THREE

## Abigail

As JUDITH RECUPERATED, Abigail and Talani went to meet with the witch who had saved Abigail's life.

It felt good to be back in her clothes. Though the pants, shirt, and hood were provided by Judith and not the jeans and cozy shirts she wore at Larry's, there was comfort in knowing she could wrap herself in the cowl and hide her face if needed.

They were led through the tree's spacious inner hallways by one of the Druwan. It might have been the one she'd already met — it was hard to tell because they didn't wear clothes, all looked the same, and used Abigail's voice to telepathically speak to her.

Abigail marveled at both the intricately carved tree turned into what felt like a giant apartment building, and the tiny floating lights dispersed throughout the place. While small, about the size of a hummingbird, they emitted plenty of light. Surely she'd seen several thousands of them already. A single tree could probably host millions. There might even be *billions* spread throughout the other trees, if they, too, were occupied.

"What are those lights?" she asked their guide.

*"They're sheng-shee,"* the Druwan said inside her mind.

"What's sheng-shee?"

*"Tiny creatures made of light."*

"They're *alive?*"

*"Yes."*

"And you can tell them what to do?"

*"We don't tell them anything. They merely do."*

"Why?"

*"They feed on our air. The relationship is harmonious, as are all things in The Sacred Woods."*

"Cool!" Abigail said, her smile giant.

They continued along, passing many Druwan in the halls and open rooms along the way. Some seemed to be working together on projects unseen. Some were standing next to one another, gesticulating as if talking, though Abigail heard no voices, so she assumed they spoke tele-pathically to one another as well. Others were simply standing still and staring into space.

They also passed other people, those deemed special enough to share the Sacred Woods with the Druwan. Abigail wondered how many were like the sheng-shee, useful because of some cooperative relationship that bene-fited everybody.

Then there were the things that weren't people, or recognizable as even remotely familiar animals. Things she had no words for. Creatures that looked like crosses between all manner of species, a dog and a fish and a woman; a man and a bear; a spider and a cat. There were things her mind had no reference for, not even approxima-tions of what these things were — all going about their lives in this strange and wonderful home inside the giant trees that composed the Sacred Woods.

In addition to the sights, Abigail heard all sorts of

different sounds. Some seemed like languages; others were more primitive. And then there were the many smells. Sometimes good, occasionally putrid, and always offset by the sweet scent of the trees themselves, which was almost a blend of vanilla and cinnamon.

Talani was looking at Abigail with a weird smile.

"What?"

"Your face is all scrunched up funny. Is it the smells?"

"Yeah," Abigail said, hoping not to offend their walking tree companion.

If she had offended it, the Druwan didn't respond. Just kept leading them along the curving hallway.

Abigail looked down, embarrassed.

Talani teased, "It's okay. It's a cute scrunched-up face."

"Thanks."

"It's good to see you happy."

"It's good to feel happy, even if it isn't going to last."

"It doesn't have to be temporary. You can come back here. I've talked to the Druwan, and they said you could stay."

"Don't you mean *we* could come back?"

Talani frowned. "They won't let Judith stay."

"Because she's a vampire? We all are."

"But you're just a kid, Abigail. They'll let you stay."

"How do they know I'm not a thousand years old in a kid's body?"

"They can tell. And Judith has a reputation from when she was on this world before. She isn't welcome."

"Why not?"

Talani shook her head. "I don't want to get into it. Let's just say that *you* were the only reason we were even allowed here."

"Can *we* stay? While Judith goes to the Town of Jonah?"

"That's not how it works."

"What do you mean?"

Talani looked up at the Druwan, subtly requesting privacy, but the Druwan didn't take the hint. "Could we have a minute, please?"

The Druwan nodded then left them in a long curving hallway that seemed to be a transition point between two more populated areas.

"Not how *what* works?" Abigail asked.

"The bond between you and your Master, the person who turned you, is forever, until that person dies. It's like a parental thing, but with the parasites inside us."

"And?" Abigail asked, not yet putting two and two together.

"I'm tied to Judith because she turned me. I can never leave her."

"Why not? What will happen?"

"There's a psychic bond that must be maintained. It makes me weak if I go too far away from her for too long. I can get sick. I can die. But *you* can stay here. She'll let you. We can visit and make sure you're okay, that you don't get sick."

Something clicked in Abigail's head.

"Wait a second. You persuaded me to come here, and leave John on Earth. Does this mean that *I* will get weak, that *I* will die?"

"No, it doesn't have to be that way."

"What do you mean?"

"You can accept Judith as your Master."

"What?"

"There's a ceremony where you renounce your Master. Do that, and you can take Judith as your new Master. She will put her Darkness inside you. It will kill John's and break his connection. Then you'll be bonded with her, and me, forever."

Talani smiled as if to suggest this was something that Abigail should want.

Abigail backed away.

"What?"

"You tricked me!"

"No, I didn't. I swear."

"You didn't tell me that if I came with you I'd have to accept Judith as my *Master!*"

"You were miserable with John! He hadn't been around in ages. He was working with The Guardians, killing our kind! You were moments from ending your life. Do you remember, Abigail? Remember how sad you were?"

Abigail nodded but refused to meet Talani's eyes. She was angry, and clinging to her rage.

"You couldn't trust anyone!"

"I had Larry!"

"But he didn't understand you like I do. He isn't one of us. And he isn't a girl. We have a bond that you can never have with him, John, or anyone else. We're like sisters. You're the first person I've felt like that about since Raina."

"Who?" Abigail asked, looking up.

"Never mind."

"What happens if I don't accept Judith as my Master? Will I die?"

"I ... don't know. I've never seen someone go that long without eventually returning to their Master."

"How long does it take?"

"It's a while. Months, maybe a year, before things get too bad. It's different for everyone."

"What about John? Does *he* get sick when I'm not with him? Or if I were to let Judith become my Master?"

"It doesn't work that way. His is the dominant organism. It's not negatively affected by yours."

"So, I'm dead if I don't accept Judith? You basically tricked me, and now I'm going to die if I don't do what you want?" Abigail stared at Talani, wanting the girl to feel her anger, to know how deeply she was hurt by the betrayal.

"I didn't mean to trick you."

"But you didn't tell me."

"It felt like too much was happening at once. Telling you would've only given you reason to doubt what you needed to do — get away from John, and those other humans."

"It's not fair. You can't expect me to make a decision like this."

"You don't have decide now. We can wait until you show signs."

"Wait, you said that you couldn't stay here because Judith is your Master. So how could I stay?"

"I could have her come back from time to time to visit. That should be enough to renew the connection, so to speak."

"So why can't she do that for *both of us* then? You stay here with me?"

Talani shook her head. "She would be lonely without me."

Abigail wanted to say, *What about me? I'll be lonely without you.* But she didn't want to admit to it. Instead she asked, "What if I don't want Judith as my Master?"

Talani met Abigail's eyes. There was something in them that Abigail couldn't read. And she wasn't powerful enough to enter Talani's mind and read her thoughts without discovery.

"Will I die?"

"There are other options."

"Like what?"

"You can return to Earth, but I don't know what'll happen if we cross back through the portal after leaving all those soldiers dead. They might have something set up to capture us, or worse."

"What's the other option?"

"I can have Judith send a message home and ask them to … take care of John."

Abigail felt slapped in the face.

"*Take care of?* Do you mean *kill* him?"

Talani nodded. "If you kill the Master, then your bond is broken also. You won't get sick."

Abigail turned on her heel and walked away.

"Abigail!" Talani cried out.

Abigail kept walking, not knowing where to go but desperate to set distance between them.

*How can Talani suggest such a thing?*

Tears streamed down Abigail's cheeks. She picked up her pace, hating the thought of Talani seeing her crying.

She walked fast, not wanting to run and draw attention to herself. She passed two more tree people and an old man, ignoring them all, keeping her head down, hair covering her face as she went.

Talani ran after her, and because Abigail was still recovering and hesitant to run, she quickly caught up.

"Wait!" Talani grabbed Abigail's shoulder and spun her around.

Abigail's face was full of tears.

She hated people seeing her cry. Not just because it made her feel like a stupid little kid, though it did. She didn't want Talani to see the depth of her pain, or how much she cared for her.

"I'm sorry. I didn't mean to suggest we —"

"Why don't *you* kill Judith?"

Talani's hand wound back and slapped Abigail, hard.

Abigail stood, stunned.

Eyes unable to believe what they were seeing.

She ran.

Now uncaring of who might see.

As Abigail ran, tears continued to stream down her freshly smacked cheek, somehow making the pain that much worse.

Talani followed.

Abigail turned down a hall, making sure to keep her hands to herself as she ran past two animal-women things. They weren't human, but she wasn't sure what her touch might do, and didn't want any more innocent blood on her hands.

Her eyes seized on an open window at the far end of a long hall. Beyond it lay freedom, the Sacred Woods.

It was light out, but the woods were cloaked in clouds. She could probably avoid direct sunlight until nightfall.

Abigail wasn't sure how, but she'd find a way back the way they'd come. Find the portal and get back home.

If she ran into soldiers on Earth, she'd tell them who she was, and that she knew John who worked for them. She'd lie and say that Judith and Talani had kidnapped her.

Maybe they'd even believe her.

Then she could be reunited with John and Larry.

*Why did I ever leave?*

She reached the window and was about to leap out but got slammed by a blast of something before she could.

She hit the wall hard and fell to the floor.

She turned in time to see Talani approaching, fingers clenched, arcing with blue electricity. People, and other creatures, began to clear out, crying for help as they scattered.

Talani looked angry, coming closer to Abigail, like she might blast her again. Abigail was afraid, but not about to fight her friend, despite the betrayal.

Instead of hurting her, Talani dropped to the floor in front of Abigail and whispered, "Don't ever say that again."

"Say what?" Abigail asked, not remembering what caused Talani to smack her.

"Suggesting I kill Judith. If she hears you, she *will* end you."

Abigail had never seen such a serious look in Talani's eyes. Nor such fear. Her eyes were welling up. "I don't know what I'd do if I lost you."

Talani pulled Abigail into a hug.

Abigail was confused by so much, but Talani's hug felt true.

The girls cried, embracing for some time before two Druwan approached with a girl who looked no older than seven, and seemed to be human.

Her skin was paler than Abigail's, her hair long and white, her eyes big and violet. She wore a long green dress and a wooden necklace with an orange stone.

"Is something wrong?" the girl asked.

"Just a sisterly squabble," Talani said, standing up and helping Abigail to her feet.

The girl looked at Talani as if trying to determine the truth of her words. The child's expression was so serious, and the Druwan stood behind her as if *she* was in charge.

"Who are you?" Abigail asked.

"I am Mother. The one who saved you."

"You're the witch?" Abigail said, surprised.

"That's a Humkoer word, not mine."

"Then what are you?"

"Mother. Nothing more, nothing less."

The girl opened her arms, inviting Abigail to embrace her.

"I … um, I can't. I'm a Valkoer. I don't want to hurt you."

"You won't hurt me," the girl said, coming closer.

Abigail hugged the girl called Mother.

A warmth spread from the girl to her, to her skin, to her heart, to everywhere inside her mind.

Then, to Abigail's surprise, she realized it wasn't warmth but something else entirely: *love*.

# TWENTY-FOUR

# Abigail

ABIGAIL AND TALANI stood looking down at the clouds, above them the purple sky.

"This is beautiful," Talani said, except it came out more like *bee-yoo-ti-ful.*

They were standing with Mother atop a platform on one of the Sacred Woods' main trees. While Abigail had initially thought the trees were thousands of feet high, they weren't nearly as tall as their width suggested.

Despite the sun, neither she nor Talani were affected — thanks to some sort of protection within the Sacred Woods, the Druwan told Abigail before their ascent.

"So, are you as young as you look?" Abigail asked after Mother had told them a bit about the Sacred Woods and given them a tour of the Axis — the central tree where many of the people worked and lived.

"I'm four thousand cycles in age," Mother said.

"Are those like years?" Abigail asked. "Three hundred and sixty-five days?"

"Our cycles are different from year to year. It's essentially three seasons, which measure anywhere from one hundred to two hundred days.

"Still, you're way older than you look. Are you a Valkoer?"

"I don't know what I am. I was found as a baby by the Druwan in the First Tree, the tree that all others in these woods were born from. It was at a time when the Sacred Woods were dying. They took me in and cared for me, the first non-Druwan allowed to live among them. They planned to keep me alive until my mother returned, but she never came.

"Soon, the Woods flourished again. Legends say it's because of me, but I don't know if that's true."

"You healed me. And when I hugged you, I felt something I'd not felt in forever. I felt ... *love*. Is that why they call you Mother?"

"I think so. They all come to me for healing, to alleviate their pain. And I guess now I'm known as a witch out there. Which is fine if it scares people away."

She pointed out at the world beyond the woods, though Abigail couldn't see anything through the clouds.

"Do you have another name?" Abigail asked.

"The Druwan named me Mother. I don't know if it was an honor or if they were confusing daughter with mother. The common tongue isn't natural to them."

Mother moved her hands, and the wind picked up, dispersing the clouds around them.

As the clouds parted, Abigail got her first glimpse of the Sacred Woods from a bird's eye view.

Talani was right. It was *bee-yoo-ti-ful*.

Woodlands swallowed the entire mountainside in every direction, with one side mostly lush greens and the other white with snow.

She also saw the bright violet river they'd followed from

the valley. From this distance it sparkled like diamonds in sunlight.

"This is the only land untouched by The Great Purge," Mother said, then went on to explain how The Northern Realm had changed over the years, becoming a more advanced civilization while forcing out non-Humkoer, including the Valkoer, Were-Beasts, magick users, elves, and anyone else who didn't fit in with their new society.

There was a great war between The North and South with much blood spilled. Nobody thought it would ever end, until The Hand of the Seven Gods brokered a treaty between North and South.

"But I fear the peace will not last."

"Why is that?" Talani asked.

"Because of the portals."

"You *know* about the portals?" Abigail said, surprised. "How?"

"I've seen things since as long as I remember. The future, the present, and the past, it all arrives in my sleep. I spend most of my waking hours trying to decipher which is which on the grand time line. I saw you all coming through."

Abigail wondered if the bad guys could see them, too.

"I also saw King Zol's son, bringing with him a terrible threat."

"What sort of threat?" Talani asked.

"Something powerful. I'm not sure what it is, but it's something that could bring the war back. And this time, I fear it will consume our world *and* yours. If there is a war, the men will come here to destroy the Sacred Woods, and craft better weapons against The North's advanced mili-tary. The North, seeing this, will destroy everything and everyone here."

"Oh my God," Abigail said.

"How can you stop it?"

"That's why I asked you to kill the craftsman."

"That will stop your vision coming true?" Abigail asked.

"No, but it will put you in place for what's coming next."

"What's next?" Talani asked.

"I don't know yet. I only have the bits She shows me."

"She?" Abigail asked.

"The Goddess of Fate, one of The Seven Gods."

"As in The Hand of the Seven Gods?" Abigail asked.

"Yes, she is one of The Seven. But she doesn't speak to The Hand. They are a church of zealots who believe they're led by divinity, who use force to do their Gods' will. Of course that *just so happens* to coincide with their own."

Talani asked, "Why don't you tell this Hand of the Seven Gods to kill the craftsman?"

Mother looked up at Talani as if she hadn't been listening. "Because if they discover that this power is here, the war might come sooner."

"So, we're all screwed, either way," Talani said.

Mother's eyes closed and fluttered.

"Mother?" Abigail said. "Are you okay?"

"Another vision," she said after a moment. "There is a third option."

"What?" Talani asked.

"That you find the power. So neither the Valkoer or The Hand gets it."

"Us?" Talani asked.

Mother shook her head and pointed at Abigail. "No. Her."

"Me? What am *I* supposed to do?"

"You'll know when it's time."

"Why don't you just tell me now?"

"Because I have not seen it, and felt it only now. There is a reason you've been brought here. Both to this world, and to us."

"Why?" Abigail asked.

"To save us all."

"Me? I'm just a kid. What can I do?"

"More than you know. But first you must kill the craftsman. Can you do that?"

"How long will it take to reach Jonah?"

"A few days on foot. But I have a shortcut."

"A portal?" Talani asked.

"A portal between planes, yes, though not between worlds. Travel is faster, but I must warn you: There will be danger. You'll need to pass through the In-Between."

"What's that?" Abigail asked.

Mother met her eyes. "All of your fears and a lot of nothingness."

# TWENTY-FIVE

# Jacob

CROW'S NEST was one of several small agrarian communities living in the Freelands south of Golden Cove. It had been around for as long as anyone could remember, but had never blossomed beyond two hundred or so citizens.

Crow's Nest was the kind of place you came from, but not a place you stayed — unless you were stuck there. It had birthed a few reputable men who went on to better things — soldiers for The South in The Great Purge, a few scholars who went on to The Dark Islands, but most times, its sons went on to become servants of The Hand of the Seven Gods in The Citadel, and its women went on to marry The Citadel's wealthier residents who liked a less jaded, simpler woman. A stupid woman.

Jacob and his men stood on a knoll looking down at the dark village lit only by a few lanterns in windows, but most of its denizens were sleeping. Crow's Nest consisted of a few dozen small homes and farmlands circling a pathetic attempt at a town square.

This would be history's easiest conquest.

Jacob turned to Sir Tomas Barron, then to their company of six knights trusted to keep this mission secret. He looked the men up and down, all of them wearing their Forgotten Kingdom knight's black.

While Barron was a pretty boy who barely looked capable of fighting, let alone leading, his comrades were the ugliest, most violent-looking Valkoer Jacob had ever seen. The kind of monsters who wouldn't bat an eye at such a mission.

"Are you ready?" Jacob asked.

The six men were practically salivating at the chance to feast on innocents, and gave variations of nods, grunts, and yesses.

Ever since the Treaty, Valkoer were forbidden from leaving The Forgotten Kingdom to feed. Nowadays they could only feed on criminals, both local and those sent by The Hand of the Seven Gods for punishment.

While the criminals provided a fortifying nourishment, rarely did they supply the sort of memories one could enjoy. Most criminals lived painful lives full of memories that were best forgotten, not mainlined like a drug to the brain.

As his selected soldiers, with the exception of Barron, weren't royalty or the wealthier of the Valkoer who could partake in Esmerelda's secret stash beneath the castle, it had been a long time since Barron's knights had feasted on innocents.

This was like a holiday to these men, a holiday long in the waiting.

"Enjoy the feast, men," Barron said. "And remember, this is but a taste of what's to come in the next war."

The men charged into the night — fast, quiet, and deadly.

Jacob looked at Barron and smiled. "You, Sir Barron, have proved yourself worthy."

"It is my pleasure to serve you, *King* Jacob."

Jacob liked the sound of that. The man was surely working him, saying what he wanted to hear, appealing to Jacob's ego and desire to be recognized. But that didn't make the words any less pleasing.

"Let's feast," Jacob said, running into the night, hoping to trigger a war that would force Father's hand and expose his weakness.

# TWENTY-SIX

# John

"WE'RE CLOSE," Emma said, stopping and raising a hand. "I can feel my brother nearby."

They were at the bottom of a hill, the morning sun still an hour or so from making its appearance. At the top of the hill stood a walled city with a large dome and pillars at its center, flags flying on tall poles atop buildings screaming into the sky. Torches and moonlight from the two moons above lit enough of the city for John to observe.

From a distance it looked like an ancient Turkish capital, surrounded by a giant stone wall, lined with minarets and guard towers, fronted by an iron-looking gate. The Citadel Emma had mentioned?

"It's before the city," Emma said, pointing not to the city but toward a fork in the road. "There's a row of burned down houses. They're in there."

"Are they alone?" Sanders asked.

She closed her eyes, trying to focus.

"Yes. They're waiting for us."

Sanders and Jenk led the way with Emma right behind, and John, Hope, and Larry in the rear.

John kept looking at the city's tall spires, the giant dome high in its center. Something about it racked him with chills, though he couldn't explain what. He wondered if that was where Jacob and his father, the vampire king, were. If so, he was more determined than ever to return and regroup. Next time, they'd bring a real fucking army.

Larry looked at John and whispered, "So, what do we do if they tell us they've got a line on Jacob, and he's close? Are we really going to trudge all the way back to the portal?"

"Yes. We've got to get Emma and Logan to safety; these kids don't belong here. Then we get you two home."

"Nope." Hope shook her head. "I'm going where you go. You promised I could."

"That was before I saw how easily our troops were thinned by a pack of werewolves. Believe me, whomever they send with us next won't be any better. Hell, maybe worse."

"I made it through all right," Hope reminded him with a smile.

"Yeah, we don't know why that thing didn't slaughter you. Next time you might not be so lucky, or we'll run into something worse. But we are *not* taking a chance."

"But —"

John shook his head. "Can we *please* discuss this later?"

She started to say something, but John brushed her off, picking up his pace to catch up with Sanders, Emma, and Jenk as they turned right along the fork.

Trees grew thicker and narrowed the road. It was only a few hundred yards before it ended in a row of burned down buildings that look like they'd been singed to memory ages ago. Most were destroyed, but a few two-story stone structures were still standing, and mostly untouched by the fires.

Hope sounded annoyed as he walked away from her. Larry said something to lighten the mood, but John didn't hear what, too busy focusing on something else that was bothering him — Emma.

He walked a few feet behind her, watching. She wasn't walking fast like someone eager to see her brother. And her body language was all wrong. Shoulders slumped, fingers fidgeting, head down, but every now and again looking up nervously.

He caught up with her, closing in on her right. She was walking with her head down, hair falling over her face.

"You okay?"

She hesitated, only a second, but it was there all the same. She looked over at him, her eyes wet.

"What's wrong?"

Emma didn't answer, just looked back down.

John called out to Sanders and Jenk. "Wait!"

They turned.

Sanders said, "What is it?"

John looked down the road, at the buildings, then back at Emma.

"What's down there?"

"I'm sorry," she said. "They made me."

"Made you what? Who?" John asked, looking around.

He sensed movement to their right.

And to their left.

Emma said, "They said they'd kill him if I didn't bring you here."

"Who?" John repeated.

"I don't know, I —"

Jenk fell to the ground.

John spun around to see an arrow sticking out of his head.

More were coming, dark lines against the pale moon-light above.

"Ambush!" John screamed, raising his hand and sending a blast of energy into the air, knocking the closest arrows down.

He couldn't do that too many more times without being drained. They needed to escape.

They had no cover, so Sanders and Larry took off into the woods, firing as they went, Larry leading Hope.

John shouted at Emma, remembering her cloaking ability. "Hide yourself, and Larry and Hope!"

She looked at him, then vanished in a wisp of shadows.

John hoped that whatever was attacking them wouldn't sense her, or Hope and Larry once she cloaked them as well. Or that Emma wouldn't betray him, again, by delivering Hope to their attackers.

John cast a cloaking spell on himself, though his was nowhere nearly as powerful as the girl's, then darted into the woods after Larry and Hope, rifle raised, eyes scanning the thick woodlands.

He saw a rough-looking man wearing ratty-looking leathers, with unkempt long, matted dark hair, holding a sword and looking around with another two coarse-looking men behind him.

John raised his rifle and fired.

All three fell before they knew what was coming.

*That'll teach you to bring swords and arrows to a gunfight!*

John looked around for any sign of Emma, Larry, and Hope, but didn't see, or sense, anything.

Hopefully their attackers couldn't either.

John heard Sanders firing her rifle on the other side of the road, probably forty yards in the woods behind him.

Her gunfire stopped abruptly.

*Shit.*

Another three men appeared in the road, twenty yards away. One with a bow, eyes right on John in the woods, despite the shadow spell he'd cast.

The archer let loose.

John barely managed to drop to his stomach and evade the black arrow.

Another two whizzed overhead.

He looked up in time to see the archer notching another arrow.

He maneuvered his rifle out from under his body and took aim.

The gun jammed.

*Shit!*

The archer let loose.

The arrow hit John's shoulder but didn't pierce his uniform's thick leather.

His eyes met the frightened archer's.

John threw his stuck rifle to the ground, ripped off his gloves, and narrowed his eyes at the three men before him. He hopped to his knees, then surveyed the field.

*Let's go, fuckers.*

He raced toward them at top speed, hands pulsing with electricity in anticipation of the meal.

The three men's eyes all widened at the sight of John charging.

The archer dropped his bow and reached back to grab a blade from his belt.

*Too late.*

John leaped, hands finding the man's bare chest, locking on as he dragged him to the ground.

The other two men, to his right and left, had swords. They turned to John, who was now on top of their fallen comrade, sucking his life force.

One swung at John.

Though he wasn't even looking toward the man, John sensed him, and twisted his body to avoid the blow. He then raised a hand and shot a blast of energy into the swordsman.

The man went hurtling ten feet into the air with a scream as the ball of energy worked its way through his chest, and would soon burn through his internal organs.

The last swordsman thrust his blade at John. It wasn't a sword so much as a long and thin dagger that looked sharp enough to cut steel like paper.

John dodged, but not in time.

The blade pierced his uniform, straight into John's gut. But he was high on energy from the man's comrade.

He looked up as the man hurriedly tried to pull the dagger from John. The man's eyes were wide and white.

John bared his teeth in a growl, grabbed the man's arm before he could release the dagger, and began to feed off of him, too.

As he drained the man's life, and memories, he sought only one piece of information — *who planned this ambush?*

The man, like the one he took down, knew nothing other than the boss's orders: to capture the people that came through the portal, and keep John and Hope alive.

*You know our names?*

*It must be Jacob.*

John let the man's burned corpse fall to the ground, reached down and yanked the blade from his gut, then threw it to the ground.

He felt the man's energy coursing through him, already repairing the wound.

His eyes darted around in search of more enemies, and his friends.

As if in response, he heard a man shouting from the road.

"Come out and surrender, or I kill the boy."

John ran toward the voice. As the trees thinned he saw a hulk of a man standing beside two men with torches held up so John could see him. The man was eight feet tall at least, around five hundred pounds, and wore spiked armor over his blue skin. In his giant hand he held a crooked stone blade to the neck of a skinny young dark-haired boy in a torn-up Guardian uniform.

A boy who looked like a male version of Emma.

*Logan.*

"Surrender now, or Logan dies. You got until a count of five." The man's accent was thick and guttural, his words broken.

Standing beside the blue giant was a line of regular-looking men, most seeming like of the garden-variety mercs that John had already put down. Maybe twenty more, most on horseback, all armed.

There was also one more blue man, slightly smaller than the one holding a knife to Logan's neck, also wearing spiked armor, and carrying a giant spiked club.

John's eyes surveyed the situation.

It wasn't impossible, and if he could take down the leader, he'd scare at least a few away.

But he didn't know if he could do it without them harming Emma's brother.

"One," the countdown began.

John rushed out of the woods, hands raised.

"Okay, okay, I surrender."

The big blue man eyed him.

John's stolen memories from the soldiers already told him that Big Blue was Vashkar, the boss.

Though the men knew him as their boss, surely he

wasn't *the boss*. This had to be Jacob's handiwork. And if that were true, John figured he was safe to surrender. Jacob wasn't likely to kill him. Even if he did, John didn't care so long as he could keep Hope, Larry, and Emma alive.

"Where are the others?"

John wasn't sure if Vashkar was asking where *his men* were or where John's friends were. John hoped that Emma wasn't nearby hiding Hope and Larry. If so, how long could she be counted on to stay put? They had her brother at knifepoint. Anyone in her position would surrender.

John had to remove that option from the table.

John bluffed.

"Dead. Everyone's gone but me. You got me. Now let's go tell Jacob he won."

"Liar!" Vashkar pointed at John. "Two!"

"Don't do it!" Logan shouted.

John telepathically reached out to Larry.

*Don't let her surrender. Just stay hidden. I'll figure something out and save Logan. Tell her to trust me.*

"*Dude, she's not with me,*" Larry's said in his head.

*What?*

"Three!" Vashkar shouted.

"*She's with Hope.*"

"Four!"

*Where are they?*

"Stop!" Emma marched out of the woods, holding Hope's hand.

John held his breath as Emma and Hope approached the soldiers.

*Are you seeing this, Larry?*

"*You mean Papa Smurf on steroids?*"

*Can you line up a shot on that big blue fucker holding Logan?*

"*Already on it.*"

*On GO, you put him down, head shot if you can, along with any*

*of the other fuckers with bows or within swinging distance of Hope.
You got that?*

"*Ten-four, good buddy,*" Larry said.

John's eyes were glued to Emma and Hope as they walked forward.

John was at the edge of the woods, not within distance to get there in time to intercept anything aimed at Hope, especially if any of them were Valkoer or anything else that could match his speed.

He'd have to rely on Larry's shot.

Then he'd spring into action, try to get her out of there without touching Hope and accidentally killing her.

He wished he'd not thrown his gloves on the ground.

John started forward, slowly, since everyone was focused on Emma and Hope.

Vashkar took a step, smiling with a mouth full of sharp, ugly teeth. "Ah, you must be Emma?"

"Please let my brother go. I did as you asked. I led them here."

"Yes, you did. Thank you," Vashkar said, hand still on the blade at Logan's throat.

Vashkar turned to John.

John kept walking, slowly.

"Your brother Jacob is looking forward to seeing you, and this lovely woman, *Hope*, is it?" Vashkar laughed. "Funny that someone would name you the thing you're all out of."

John wanted to wipe the smug grin from his fat, ugly face. Make him choke on his fucked-up teeth.

Emma cried, "*Please*, let my brother go."

Vashkar looked at Emma, head tilted thoughtfully as if considering her request, then sliced Logan's neck.

Emma screamed, vanishing into dark wisps.

An arrow found her neck before she could completely disappear.

She fell forward, clutching the arrow, crying out, eyes wide on her brother as her body began to disintegrate.

*Now, Larry!*

A gunshot in the distance as Larry fired.

But Vashkar was gone.

There one second, then the next he was behind Hope, holding the blade to *her* throat.

All of his archers, at least eight of the soldiers, were aiming arrows at John.

Vashkar yelled, "Surrender, man with the gun, or she's next!"

*"What do I do, John? You didn't tell me this fucker was a teleporter!"*

John looked at Hope's terrified eyes and trembling lips, then up to the beast holding her against her will.

Their eyes met.

John vowed to take Vashkar's eyes out with his bare hands.

But that would have to wait. He had but one option.

*Surrender, Larry.*

Only after ordering Larry's surrender did John remember the soldiers' instructions — to kill everyone but John and Hope.

John hoped he wasn't sending Larry to his death.

Larry emerged from the woods, his hands raised, unarmed so far as John could see.

"Okay, I surrender."

As Larry marched toward one of Vashkar's men, John's heart pounded.

*Just be calm. They're not gonna kill you.*

*"That wishful thinking, or you got an inside track on my odds in Vegas, buddy?"*

*I know people like this.*

*"Yeah, but he just killed Emma and Logan. Clearly these fuckers like to kill more than your average army of lunatics led by a giant blue Smurf."*

John looked down at Emma's body and wished he could've done something to save her, anticipated what Vashkar might do. But at the moment he had two people closer to worry about — Hope and Larry.

John glared at the big blue man in charge still holding a blade to Hope's neck.

Her eyes locked onto John's, and he gave her a glance, hoping she understood that he had this under control.

"Don't kill him," John said.

Vashkar looked down at John with so much disdain, it seemed like he might do it simply because John asked him not to. Maybe cut Hope's neck for good measure, too, just to prove who was boss.

John continued his plea, "You're bringing us to Prince Jacob, aren't you?"

A glint of recognition in Vashkar's eyes.

"Jacob is my brother. That's why he told you not to kill me. Nor does he want to harm Hope. Fuck that up, and he'll have your head. So here's the deal: I'll play nice and go back with you. But if you hurt either of my friends, I'm not doing shit. I will *make* you kill me. And then you're fucked."

Vashkar laughed, but John could tell that he'd wormed into the monster's head, laying eggs of doubt. He was likely trying to find a scenario where he could kill Larry while still keeping John from fighting back. But short of incapacitating him, he had no options. And John was an unknown variable. These men didn't know how to bring him down without the encounter turning lethal. It would almost be easier to bring all three to Jacob. At least that's the conclusion John hoped everyone would come to.

Surrendering and going back to Jacob with these fuckers wasn't an ideal scenario, but definitely better than losing Larry. It would give John time to think of a way out.

Jacob hadn't killed John, despite having had a few opportunities. Surely that counted for something. Maybe Jacob could be reasoned with. Perhaps John could offer something to release Larry and Hope. Again, not ideal, but ideals were for people with options.

As Larry stood before Vashkar's men, one put a gun to his head and said something in a language John couldn't understand.

He seemed to be asking permission.

Vashkar looked at John, eying him a stone-cold glare.

John yelled, "Don't do it, or you're all dead. By me or by Jacob, either way, dead."

Vashkar grunted something.

The man grunted back, then used the gun's butt to hit Larry in the back of the head, sending him to his knees.

Vashkar looked down at John, still holding his blade to Hope's neck. "Fine. He lives ... for now."

Vashkar shouted something in another language as if commanding somebody John couldn't see.

Moments later, a horse and carriage arrived, driven by a surly looking man with a shock of red hair and a scar bisecting his face.

The carriage was a black metal box without windows — their prisoner transport.

"Walk," Vashkar commanded John, pointing at the carriage.

John hoped he wasn't making a mistake in not fighting, that he wasn't signing death sentences for two of three people he loved in the worlds.

# TWENTY-SEVEN

# Caleb

*2013 (Now)*

THE BIRDS GAVE IT AWAY.

Hundreds of scavengers circling the dark gray sky above the town of Crow's Nest, battling one another the ground, seeking to feast on scraps of flesh.

Earlier that morning, one of the couriers en route to The Citadel in Golden Cove had seen the birds and alerted The Hand, though the young man had been terrified to enter the town alone, sure the butchers might still be there.

Caleb and Raina led an expedition — twelve of The Covenant into Crow's Nest — as a nasty storm brewed above, bellowing thunder and crackling lightning at war in the swirling clouds. A cold breeze settled into Caleb's bones as he surveyed the corpse-strewn street.

In the two years Caleb had been working with The Covenant of the Hand of the Seven Gods, they'd dealt with rogue witches, the occasional werewolf, and a stray

Valkoer attack or two. But nothing had prepared them for this.

More than two hundred dead — men, women, children — killed in their beds, in the streets, or wherever they happened to be when the Valkoer came. So many dead that the vampires hadn't enough time to finish them all off. Some bodies were partially burned. Fortunate for the birds, who would otherwise have nothing but ashes to eat.

Caleb and Raina stood over a pair of ashen corpses huddled together — a woman with a child who was no more than three, frozen in time, their bodies scorched to husks.

"Have you ever seen anything like this?" Caleb asked.

"Nothing, not even during The Great Purge when the Valkoer were resisting capture, refusing exile to The Forgotten Kingdom."

"How many of them do you think attacked?"

"A dozen? More? This doesn't make sense."

"Maybe they're starving?" Caleb suggested.

To his left, a fat black bird was prodding its sharp beak inside a half-burned corpse until it found something and pulled, stretching tissue like a giant pink worm.

Caleb had to turn away. Something struck him.

Raina said, "They shouldn't be starving. Their numbers aren't that big and they have prisoners they feed on, not to mention whatever illegal arrangements they've got on the island or with others."

Caleb stared at the corpses feeling like he was missing something. Then it hit him. "They wanted these bodies found."

"What?"

"Why leave bodies *half*-burned? Why not finish the job?"

"Maybe someone came along and spooked them away?" Raina suggested.

"Who could've scared away a group that did *this?*"

"Perhaps the sun was rising?"

Caleb looked around. Despite his forensic experience, he couldn't guess time of death for bodies in this condition. Not without a lab or scientists to run tests.

One of The Hand, Brother Paul, came over as lightning ripped through the sky.

The first fat drops of rain began to fall.

"Brother, Sister, you must come."

"What is it?" Raina asked, following the man toward a barn whose doors had been ripped from their hinges, its livestock slaughtered with what appeared to be claws and blade markings.

"Drain the people *and* kill their livestock?" Caleb said. "It's like they were trying to send a message, but to whom? Do we know of any squabbles between these folks and the Valkoer?"

"None that I know of," Raina said.

"Do you think that there's a rouge group of Valkoer operating outside The Forgotten Kingdom?" Caleb asked.

"Anything is possible, but ..." Raina stopped when Brother Paul ushered them into the dark barn to show them what he'd brought them to see.

A boy, no more than eleven, still in his bedclothes, shaking, crying, sitting on the straw-covered ground, being comforted by Sister Celine.

Celine looked up. "We found him hiding behind bales of hay."

"What's your name, son?" Raina asked.

The boy looked up, his puffy eyes red as his nose. "Callum."

"Did you see what happened here?"

He nodded, swallowing a lump of grief. His mouth twisted to form words that he had to force past his lips.

"Th-they came after we w-went to bed. I heard my sister scream. Then my p-p-pa and ma. They were all in the same room. I was sleeping in the cellar because my uncle was staying in my room. I tried to go help, but my uncle *grabt* me, told me to hush, and hid me 'til it was over."

"Where's your uncle?" Caleb asked.

"They f-found him just as he was trying to secure the barn doors. Then they *kilt* him. I thought for sure they'd seen me, too, but they *din't*."

"Did you see them?" Raina leaned forward. "Did you see who did this?"

"'Twas the Knights that did this. The Black Valkoer Knights!"

Raina looked at Caleb and sighed. This wouldn't go down well with Prophet Malachi. This was a clear violation of the Treaty, and could give The Hand the excuse they needed to enter The Forgotten Kingdom and eradicate the Valkoer once and for all.

While they did want to take Jacob down, Raina didn't want a wholesale slaughter of everyone on the island.

But Caleb couldn't help think of the positives here. He'd been wanting to go into The Forgotten Kingdom to find Jacob ever since he arrived here two years ago. But the Treaty had prevented The Hand from just marching in and demanding to see the Prince. Additionally, the King and Council had all said the same thing, Jacob had gone back to Earth.

Caleb had wanted to follow him, but he was forbidden. Once you were a member of The Hand, you were a lifetime member.

You couldn't just leave when you felt like no longer doing your duty. Leaving could get you killed.

Caleb had no intentions of staying forever, but he couldn't leave until he was certain he'd found and killed Jacob.

While Caleb was originally biding his time until he could find Jacob, after which point he would find a way to escape, something had changed in the past two years.

He'd come to like this world.

Things were simpler.

People were *usually* kinder.

Caleb was making a difference, helping to protect towns from the monsters, wild things, and people roaming The Southern Realm.

*Was* making a difference, anyway.

This could change everything.

Again, the boy spoke. "What are you going to do about the others?"

"What others?" Raina asked.

The boy pointed toward a cellar door with a large piece of wood barring it shut.

"Who's in there?" Raina asked.

"The people they din't kill. They put them in there."

Raina's hand found her sword's hilt as she approached the cellar.

Caleb followed, drawing his silver and onyx blade. He'd grown proficient at wielding it, though he would've traded blade for gun in a breath.

But nobody in The South had guns, at least not the kind he was used to. They were forbidden in the Treaty, a way for The North to maintain power over The South, as The North had plenty of weapons, some rumored to have been brought over from Earth before the original portals were closed.

At the cellar doors, Raina motioned for Brother Lio to remove the bar. The big man hefted the bar aside and it dropped to the ground with a thud.

Brother Lio looked back at Raina and Caleb.

Raina nodded.

Lio leaned down and opened the door.

Something leaped out and on top of him — a Valkoer dressed in commoner's clothing.

Lio screamed as the thing feasted.

Another five Valkoer, all dressed like commoners, poured from the cellar, growling, heads darting back and forth as they surveyed the barn.

*Oh God, they turned the villagers. Turned them and left them as a trap.*

Movement to Caleb's right.

He turned to see the boy, Callum, calling out, "Dad?" arms wide as he ran toward one of the Valkoer.

"No!" Caleb rushed forth to throw himself between the boy and his father-turned-Valkoer.

*Too late.*

The boy ran right into his father's waiting arms.

And the father fed.

Caleb thrust his sword through the boy's back to end his suffering, then plowed it straight through the father's chest.

The swords were blessed silver with onyx designs forged into the blades, deadly to Valkoer and Were-Beasts.

Boy and father convulsed, burning alive at the end of Caleb's blade.

Movement to Caleb's left.

He couldn't pull the sword from the father and son, so he let go, drawing the dagger from his belt, turning to face a female Valkoer racing toward him.

She reached out, hands clawing at his face.

He ducked, not to avoid being burned since she couldn't harm him, but rather to avoid a telepathic assault, intentional or incidental, which might fatally distract him.

She went right over him.

He looked up as she sailed past, sticking the blade in her gut and slicing it open.

Hot blood painted him as he held the blade tight and her body crumpled to the ground just past him.

Raina screamed from somewhere behind him.

He turned to see her on the ground, struggling against a fat man choking her.

Caleb whipped the dagger across the barn, straight into the side of the fat bastard's head.

The fat man screamed, burning from the inside.

Raina shoved him off of her just in time to grab her blade and slice through another charging Valkoer.

Caleb spun around, scanning the barn for more danger, searching for his sword.

Then he realized he wouldn't need it.

Everyone was dead, except for him and Raina.

"Shit," he said, looking around.

Outside a woman's scream drew their attention.

He ran out into a torrential downpour to see four surviving members of his party, their hands full with a trio of Valkoer who had escaped the barn and backed them up against a wall.

Caleb was about to run into action, but he'd left both his sword and dagger inside the barn.

Moments after realizing he was screwed, Raina appeared from behind and tossed Caleb his sword.

They rushed into battle together, easily felling the final villagers-turned-Valkoer, then stood there drenched by the rain while recovering their breath in the ugly aftermath of two massacres. Caleb stared at the senseless slaughter, feeling sick, anger stirring in his gut.

"Do you think King Zol's men really did this?"

"It doesn't make sense," Raina said. "This would be an outright provocation of war. And he controls his people too tightly to allow for this."

Caleb spotted something among the dead, a body dressed differently, in dark black leathers with daggers strapped to a belt across his chest.

He walked over, Raina following, and looked down to see the man's dead gaze looking straight up, a black blade thrust in his skull. Black veins like spiderwebs beneath his skin as the blade's poison took root.

*Valkoer.*

On his left hand was a ring bearing the insignia of a lantern in a cave. He'd seen that ring enough times to know whom it belonged to.

Caleb pulled off the ring and showed Raina. "This is Under Harbor's Shadow Guild, isn't it?"

"Yes," she said. "Which means this *wasn't* King Zol's men. It was someone from the Town of Jonah."

## TWENTY-EIGHT

# John

THEY'D BEEN RIDING prisoner in the horse-drawn carriage for a few hours along bumpy roads to wherever Jacob was waiting. Rain pelted the metal walls and roof of the carriage.

John and Larry were on one side of the box, John's helmet confiscated before they shoved him inside, with Hope sitting across from them. They were bound together by chains and cuffs. John had tried to break free, but the metal was stronger than anything he'd broken on Earth. Magick didn't work to open the locks on the cuffs, either.

He shrugged to his companions, not wanting to alert the unseen man riding just above and in front of them.

Hope whispered, "Why does Jacob want us?"

"I don't know," John whispered back. "Maybe he's going to give me one last chance to join his *whatever the hell he's got going on.*"

"And if you don't?" Hope asked.

"I don't know."

Hope was quiet. Her eyebrows raised. "You wouldn't *actually* join him, would you?"

"I'd do almost anything to keep you two alive."

Hope shook her head. "You are *not* joining him. I still remember the way he looked at me, like he owned me or something. Need I remind you that he tried to kill us, John. I'd rather die than be anywhere near him."

"Nobody's dying," John said.

"So, you have an idea?"

John looked at Larry, who was uncharacteristically quiet, then turned back to Hope. "I always have ideas."

"Mind running a few by me?" Hope's voice was pitched higher than normal, the anxious tone she used for worrisome things — like whether they'd make rent, or when she was convinced that her paintings were terrible. It was hard enough to calm her when the stakes weren't life and death. Now, it might be impossible. But he had to say something to earn her trust, to make her believe that he'd find a means of escape.

"I'll figure a way out. I always do."

He gave her his most charismatic smile — the one that usually bested her defenses. The one that once ended with them kissing in bed after one of their very rare arguments.

But that was a long time ago, and the smile wasn't nearly as effective while being transported to your vampire brother intent on destroying the world.

She shook her head and sighed, looking down.

Larry finally spoke. "If John said he's working on something, you can trust that. I've seen this guy get out of way more fucked-up situations than this."

Hope looked at Larry and visibly relaxed. Perhaps he'd managed to do what John couldn't. Or maybe he looked so damn sad with the giant bump on the back of his head, she couldn't bring herself to argue.

Either way, mission accomplished — for now.

But as they neared their destination, John wondered if maybe this would be the one thing he couldn't think, or fight, his way out of.

# TWENTY-NINE

# Abigail

THEY STOOD in a large round chamber in the base of a tree with two of the Druwan and Mother kneeling on the ground before them, arranging small colored stones in a rectangle.

"What are those for?" Abigail asked.

"Materials for the portal spell."

"You need materials?" Abigail asked.

"Different spells cost different things, depending on the magick user. Some spells work with merely words. These are usually minor spells — telekinesis, minor confusion spells, and the like. Larger spells, such as this one, usually require a cost. A sacrifice of blood, or magickal items."

"So, those are magick rocks?"

"Not quite. They're soul rocks, containing the captured souls of our enemies."

Talani cut in, "I thought you didn't hurt people here."

"We don't. But we have friends who give them to us, helping to preserve the peace of our Sacred Woods."

"Ah," Talani said.

Abigail turned to Judith. "Can you cast a spell like this?"

Judith, who was looking much better than she had when Abigail first woke in the tree, with nary a black vein showing, shook her head. "No. I'm afraid my magick is minor in comparison."

Mother, not even looking up, said, "Don't be modest, Judith. You've performed powerful blood magick."

Judith's eyes narrowed on the child, but when she noticed Abigail looking, she shifted, and found an artificial smile.

"Nothing worth talking about," Judith said.

Abigail wondered how Mother knew what she'd done. Had she read Judith's mind while healing her? Or had she seen the future or past? If so, what had she seen?

Mother pushed one of the rocks into place then stood, stepped back, and turned to them. "Are you ready?"

Abigail nodded and looked at Judith and Talani. Both said, "Yes."

"Remember, the In-Between can be a very dangerous place. But only if you let it. Maintain your focus on the light, and keep walking … *no matter what you see.*"

"What might we see?" Abigail asked.

"There are wraiths in the In-Between. While they can't hurt you *physically* in the In-Between, but they *can* attack your mind, and use your fears against you. Remember that whatever things you see, they're not real. Whatever you do, do not stop. The longer you're in there, the morel likely you are to get lost."

"What happens if we get lost?" Abigail asked.

"Then you become one of them, the wraiths."

Abigail nodded. "Sounds simple enough."

Mother smiled. "I hope so. But just in case, please take this."

She reached into her dress pocket and pulled out a small black blade.

"What's this for? I thought you said the wraiths couldn't physically attack us?"

"It's not for the wraiths," she looked up at Judith and Talani, then back at Abigail.

Abigail frowned. "For them? They're my friends."

"The wraiths can use your friends against you. Just be careful."

Judith's lips pursed, but she held her tongue.

Talani looked uncomfortable.

Mother turned back to the stones on the floor and chanted in a language Abigail had never heard.

The air rippled as a crackling hum grew louder around them.

Abigail's ears popped. A black sliver in the world opened in front of Mother, glowing gold along the edges.

Mother turned to them. "It's ready."

"Thank you," Judith said, still showing some manners despite the tension between them.

Mother nodded, then walked away from the portal, glancing at Abigail one last time and mouthing the words, "Be careful."

Judith entered the portal first, vanishing into the sliver.

Talani looked back at Abigail, then held out her hand. "Together?"

"Together," Abigail said, grabbing her hand as she followed her new best friend into the In-Between.

THIRTY

# John

JOHN'S WHEELS KEPT SPINNING, stuck in the horse-drawn carriage on their way to Jacob.

He needed to find a way out of this. He could sense twelve other men escorting the carriage, most of them Humkoer, and two of the big blue men, whatever they were, including the leader, Vashkar.

John couldn't break the chains binding him to his friends, so escaping the carriage wasn't a possibility. The earliest he could act would be when they arrived wherever these men planned to bring them.

If it was a direct transfer to Jacob or his men, John would stand down. He wasn't sure why, but he felt there might be a way to reason with his brother, strike some sort of deal to keep Hope and Larry safe from harm.

But if the transfer *wasn't* to Jacob, and instead to someone else who would then bring them the rest of the way, escape might be possible.

It was agony to sit and wait while so much was out of his control. But better to lie low and not appear as a threat. Perhaps it would give their enemies a false sense of security, one that would open the door for a slip-up and offer John a weakness to exploit.

But John wasn't particularly good at waiting at times like this.

He looked at Hope and Larry, both their eyes bereft of any promise. He was desperate to lift their spirits. These might be his last moments with either of them if things went south.

"Larry, do you remember when you went to that dating service and got set up with that fitness instructor?"

Larry looked at John confused, likely wondering what the hell that story had to do with the end of their lives.

"You know, the Russian blonde? What was her name? Svetlana?"

"*Ukrainian*, not Russian," Larry said, starting to laugh.

"What happened?" Hope asked.

John said, "You want to tell it, or should I?"

"I'll tell it. You always fuck up the ending."

"If by fuck up, you mean tell it exactly as it really happened, then yeah, *guilty as charged*," John teased.

"Okay, as you may or may not know, back then I was a private investigator. Except I had more clients than Johnny Boy here. Suffice it to say, I was busy and didn't have time to meet women the *regular way*."

John interjected. "He means to say that he doesn't know how to meet women the *regular way*."

"Are you gonna keep interrupting, or can I go on?"

Hope grinned at John.

John waved a hand, "Please, continue, Casanova."

"So, *anyway*, this was when online dating was becoming a thing. I figured what the hell, right? So I answered a bunch of questions, built this profile so they could find the best match for me."

"Okay," Hope said, smiling in anticipation.

"And I got this hit from a hot Ukrainian in her early twenties. A fitness instructor who liked long walks on the beach, fine dining, and listening to classical music."

"None of which Larry's ever done by the way," John interrupted.

"Not true! I like all those things."

"Really? You've taken long walks on the beach?"

"Yeah, a few times I've had to follow people on foot to catch them in the act so I could bring photographic or video evidence to the client."

"What about fine dining? Your idea of fine dining is McDonald's."

"Hey, McDonald's *is* good food. And anyone who say's it's not is an elitist snob or lying to themselves. You don't sell eight zillion burgers if your shit sucks, am I right?"

Hope was laughing hard.

"So, anyway, we're gonna meet at this fancy restaurant called Walter's Bistro on the Beach."

Hope leaned forward, giggling.

"Now here's the part of the story where I should mention that I may have told a tiny lie while setting up my account."

John laughed. "*Tiny?*"

"Okay, maybe a *big* lie."

"Your application was a staggering work of fiction!"

"What did you lie about?" Hope asked.

"I *might have* said that I was really into working out."

Hope's eyes crunched together, throttling her laughter.

John laughed out loud. "Go on; tell her the rest."

"Okay, I *may* have *also* said I liked going on hikes and loved exploring the great outdoors."

John was about to piss himself. "He's not even telling you the biggest lie."

"What's that?"

"Okay, I *may* have used a picture from high school."

Hope lost it. "High school?"

"Hey, it's the last time I was skinny!"

"And she didn't notice that you were a teenager?"

"I was an early bloomer! I had a beard when I was fifteen."

"So, what happened?" Hope asked.

"Okay, so I go to this restaurant, and I'm sitting at a table waiting for her to show up. And I'm waiting. And waiting."

Hope pursed her lips to keep from laughing again.

"I see this woman walk by a couple of times eying my table like she's looking for someone. But she looked *nothing* like Svetlana. She was a brunette for one thing, not the chick with long blonde hair in her profile pic, but definitely fit, and was rocking this sexy little blue dress."

"And?" Hope said, waiting for the punch line.

"So after a few times she comes over and asks, 'Are you Larry?' And I said, 'Yeah, are you Svetlana?' She said, 'Yes' and extended her hand. Then there's this moment where I notice two things at once. First, the disappointment in her eyes. That she wasn't getting the strapping young go-getter from the photo. And then the second thing: her hands."

"What about her hands?" Hope asked.

"Man hands. And not just she was a girl that had manly hands like in that *Seinfeld* episode, but she had big, muscular man hands because … she was a dude!"

"No way!" Hope covered her mouth.

"Oh, yeah. Big man's hands, and a visible Adam's Apple. Of course then I realize her voice wasn't quite as feminine as I first thought."

"So, what happened?"

"We ate dinner," Larry said, his voice falling an octave.

"*And?* Did she know that you knew?"

"I wasn't sure. It was soooo damned awkward. On the one hand, no pun intended, here you have two people who obviously lied on their profiles, both too polite to call out the other's bullshit, going through with the date like it's just another ordinary Friday night."

"So, what happened next?"

"Okay, so here's where it gets a bit weird."

John was stifling laughter, not wanting to ruin the punch line.

"The date is going great. We wind up talking about a lot of cool shit: sports, movies, and she's telling me these crazy stories. She's fucking hilarious. But again, we're both avoiding the *elephants* in the room: that I'm a fat dude who looks nothing like his picture, and she's got a dick. So, we get to the end of the date, and I walk Svetlana to her car. And I should preface this by saying that I'm not gay. Nor do I have anything against gay people, trans, whatever. But it's not for me. I'm all about the ladies."

"Okay," Hope said, laughing.

"So, as I'm walking her to her car, there's this moment where I'm wondering how the hell I'm gonna get out of a kiss if she tries it."

"But you said she was pretty, right?" Hope said.

"Yeah, but I'm not into dudes. If I was gonna bang a pretty dude, I would've done John a long time ago."

John laughed. "Sorry, buddy, I've got standards."

"So I'm like freaking out inside with this whole inner dialogue — what do I do if she kisses me? What if she wants to see me again? I mean, we were getting along great, so it's not like I can say, 'Sorry, not interested. I'm into ladies, thank you.' Because there was this small part of me that was like, *What if she's not a dude?* What if she's just a very masculine lady? I mean, it's *possible*, right, and I don't want to offend her. And it's not like I can fucking ask, *Hey, are you a dude or a chick?"*

"*Probably* not a good idea," Hope said.

"So, anyway, end of date, we're at the car, and she comes in for a hug. And I'm like, uh-oh, the kiss is next, the kiss is next, what the fuck am I gonna do?" Larry paused, bit his lip to keep from laughing, and continued. "But then she just pulled away from the hug and said, 'Nice to meet you, Larry. I had fun.' Then she got into her car!"

"So, that's *good*, right?" Hope asked, "no awkwardness, no having to talk your way out of a kiss or a next date?"

"No, it *wasn't* good, because I was offended that she didn't try to kiss me, or ask for a second date!"

"*What?*"

"Yes, even though I didn't want the kiss, or the second date, I wanted *her* to want them."

"You're crazy," Hope said.

"That's not the end of the story. Svetlana was about to drive away when I knocked on her window and did that *rolling down* motion, then said, 'Did our date go well? I feel like we really hit it off, but you're all like, 'Later, dude,' and no exchanging numbers or anything?'"

Hope cringed. "Oh my God, how awkward."

"So, she looks up at me, and says, 'Sorry, Larry, you're a great guy and all, but I wished you hadn't lied in your picture.' And I was all, 'Me lie? Look at the pot calling the kettle black!"

"No you didn't!" Hope said.

"Oh yeah, I did. So then, she looks me dead in the eyes, and in a deep, manly voice says, 'Sorry, I'm just not into fatties.' Then she drove away and I was like, *What the fuck?*"

John and Hope burst out laughing.

Hope looked at Larry. "You are utterly ridiculous."

"Oh yeah," John agreed. "He's full of stories like that — surprising given how good he is at schmoozing. Then other times, he's like a man-child sent into the world without a clue."

"Oh, really? I'll have you know I —"

Suddenly, the carriage rocked to a stop, bouncing them violently against the walls.

Outside they heard the men yelling something in another tongue.

Then bloodcurdling screams.

Hope's eyes widened as she looked at John and Larry.

"What the hell?" Larry said.

More screams.

John sensed another presence. "The werewolves are back."

Larry looked at him, "The same ones or different?"

"I don't know. They're attacking the men."

"Why?"

"I don't know. Maybe they really like horses."

"What are we gonna do?" Larry asked. "We're stuck in here. If they open it, we're like a boxed snack for these fuckers."

Hope raised her hands, palms out in a calming motion. "No. I don't think they'll harm us."

"What?" Larry looked at Hope as if she were crazy.

John realized that they hadn't told him what happened earlier.

"I don't think they're bad. One of them cornered me, and, I dunno, I had this weird feeling from it, this sense of déjà vu or something, and it just let me be."

"You think you knew it from when you were a kid or something?" Larry asked.

"I don't know."

The screaming stopped.

Silence inside the box was deafening. John could hear their heartbeats racing.

Something clawed at the door.

John leaned forward, hands clenched, arcing with electricity, trying to put himself between the beasts and his friends.

The metal lock snapped.

John swallowed as the door creaked open.

An older muscular, heavyset man with messy hair and big gray mutton chops, maybe in his late fifties, stood in front of him, naked.

More men were behind him, some still in wolf form, others between changes.

"Esmee," the man said, looking at Hope. "It's true. You're back."

# THIRTY-ONE

# Hope

"Esmee?" she said, sitting confused in the carriage, chained to Larry and John.

The gray-haired man approached, shaking his head, tears in his eyes. It was hard to ignore his lack of clothing, having just shifted from a wolf to man, so she tried to maintain eye contact without being obvious. If the men had any shame in their nudity, they hid it well behind their casual manner while searching Vashkar's men for supplies.

"It's been so long. We thought you were dead."

"You know me?" she asked, feeling stupid.

"You don't remember?" the old man said. "I'm yer uncle, Gerald."

"Uncle?"

*Uncle?*

He reached down, shook the chains, then reached to the cuffs binding her hands together.

"You want that I should remove these?"

"Yes, please."

As his hands found her cuffs, she noticed the gray hair

running up and down his arms and wondered if he was the wolf who had cornered her.

"Are you the wolf that chased me down?"

He squeezed tight, and the cuffs snapped like brittle plastic.

"*Yer* friends?" he asked her instead of John and Larry, ignoring the question.

"Yes, please."

He set them free as the other men approached, standing behind Gerald.

"How'd you get into trouble with Vashkar?" Gerald asked.

"It's a long story," Hope said. "And I asked you a question. Were you the wolf that chased me? With the pack that killed our friends?"

Gerald looked down. "Yes. I'm sorry. We didn't know who you were at the time. We heard that someone came through the portal with weapons. We thought you to be with the prince's forces. Then I saw it was you, little Esmee, all grown up. Why did you come through the portal, and what does Vashkar want with you?"

John spoke. "What do you know about King Zol?"

Gerald spit on the ground. "Fuck him, his prince, and his *kingdom*."

John said, "Vashkar was going to turn us over to Zol."

"Why?" Gerald asked as the other werewolves dressed in the dead men's clothes and rifled through their saddlebags.

"Because I'm looking to kill his son, Jacob."

Gerald laughed. "*You?* Kill the prince? You hear that, men? This little man is gonna kill Prince Jacob. How you planning to do that? You couldn't even handle Vashkar and his men back there."

"They kind of had my hands tied, what with Vashkar holding a blade to your niece's neck."

"Pfftt," Gerald said with a wave as if *he* could've taken out all the men before the blade even had a chance to draw blood.

Hope didn't like the way her uncle was dismissing John. She was about to say something when John held her in check with a glance.

"Do you know where the prince is?" John asked.

"Sure," Gerald said, "in his castle in The Forgotten Kingdom."

"Can you show me the way?"

"That depends; are you taking my niece?"

"Yes. He's taking me."

"Then no, I can't show you."

Hope sighed. "Please."

Gerald raised both hands. "If I send you on your way, my sister will kill me."

"Your sister?" Hope asked.

"Yeah, yer mother, Abalena."

Hope's heart went still in her chest. "My … *mother?*"

"Yes. She's the one that sent us back out to find you. She's waiting for you back in the Town of Jonah. She thought you were dead. We *all* thought you were dead. You just up and vanished long ago. We always thought Zol had something to do with it, though we could never prove it."

One of the other men approached Gerald and whispered something in his ear. He looked to Hope, John, and Larry.

"Ride with us to Jonah, and tell us how you got here."

Hope looked at John and Larry.

John shrugged.

"Okay," Hope said as the men prepared their horses.

# Caleb

THEY REACHED The Citadel at noon and were immediately ushered toward The Council chamber, a large room where Prophet Malachi — founder and leader of The Hand of the Seven Gods — waited at the Round Table, with three Elders who served as the Inner Council. The Elders' names were a secret known only to Malachi — just one of many weird things Caleb didn't like about this cult.

Raina and Caleb took their seats at the table.

As Raina updated them on the situation at Crow's Nest, Caleb found himself staring at Malachi. The man was thousands of years old, but looked to be in his early forties. According to Raina, some Humkoer aged slowly, over thousands of years, while others matured at a more human-like rate. Nobody understood why, or even knew how long they'd live until around their twenties which way they would go. Those who aged slowly were considered blessed, and those who aged normally, cursed. More often than not, the cursed had lower stations — shopkeeper, farmer, soldier. The blessed were ushered into positions of importance — religious service, scholarly pursuits, knight-hood, or as stewards of the land.

Legends claimed that The Gods cursed people with short lives as punishment to those families involved in magick, which was seen as an affront to The Gods, men tinkering with divine powers. Of course, this seemed like more bullshit created by The Hand to control the people, to keep them from using magick and learning anything not approved by The Church.

Prophet Malachi was rail thin with a pointy jaw, a smug expression, and bleach-white hair. His eyebrows were so pale they were almost nonexistent. And his eyes so blue they looked almost fake.

On Earth, Caleb would've thought Malachi an eccen-tric, perhaps one of those pretentious fashion-obsessed androgynous artist types. But here, he was all business, and that business was his religion — The Hand of the Seven Gods, a cult that supposedly served as the figurative, and sometimes literal, hand of the *Seven Gods*, using its knights, The Covenant of the Hand of the Seven Gods, of which Caleb was now a part, to both enforce The Gods' rules and protect The Southern Realm.

The Citadel had seven worship chambers, one devoted to each God or Goddess, complete with a beautiful marble statue. A member of The Hand was also in each room to *guide* prayer and *make sure the proper Deity heard it*. A small donation was, of course, encouraged to ensure that the God or Goddess might be more inclined to act on the request. Some donations were money, and others favors.

Need luck? Pray before the idol for the Goddess of Fate.

Need better crops or a child? Pray to the Goddess of Fertility.

Need a bountiful fishing expedition? Pray to the God of the Seas.

Need someone dead? Pray to the God of the Night.

Of course, if the God or Goddess didn't act, it wasn't The Hand's fault. It was either the person asking or that particular God's wisdom, which could not be questioned.

It was masterful manipulation of the naive and frightened.

Back on Earth, Caleb had wondered how people could be so gullible. But here it sort of made sense. Many people were slaughtered during the four thousand year Great War. The North was invading The South, and many in The South were turning on one another, desperate for resources. Some smaller villages were rumored to have resorted to cannibalism. During those years most of the Valkoer and magick users, as well as any non-Humkoer, were either killed or escaped to The South.

It was a bloody war that could've been even worse had The Hand not stepped in and found a way to forge a treaty. The South conceded The Great War, agreeing to stay on their side of the ocean. The North would leave them to live their lives however they wanted so long as magick users and monsters were confined to The Forgotten Kingdom.

Being peacemakers had earned The Hand a tremendous amount of trust and devotion among the people of The South. The Hand had performed a miracle — reasoned with The North and forged peace among warring factions in The South.

It was hard to truly hate them. They *did* good things.

But they also did horrible things, such as using information learned during prayers to blackmail and manipulate others into doing their bidding. Like the mob, the KGB, and a cult coalesced into one.

Most days Caleb didn't mind being part of The Hand, as the good usually outweighed the bad. And, if Caleb had learned anything with his Agency job, sometimes good people needed to do bad shit to keep the *real bad guys* at bay.

It was a thin line — one Caleb felt he navigated well.

Sure, he had to pray to Gods he didn't believe in. Had to recite religious texts that seemed like silly fairy tales, and had to be around Malachi once a week during Inner Council meetings where he and Raina updated the Prophet and his Elders about secret missions that they would parse before presenting to the Citizens Council and the public who gathered in the chamber once a month. Other than that, it wasn't a horrible job.

And, if Caleb was being honest with himself, he rather enjoyed Raina's company — increasingly so as days went by.

It had been a long time since he'd been with a woman. He didn't even think he was capable of feeling anything for anyone after Julia died in his arms.

So he was surprised in recent months to find himself thinking about Raina when she wasn't around. Anticipating their missions, and feeling disappointed when she was tasked to do something else.

More than once he thought she might have caught him looking at her in that way friends shouldn't look at friends.

He wasn't sure if he was attracted to Raina because of their familiarity — she was the only woman he spent time with every day — or because they were both Valkoer living among Humkoer, a bond made all the stronger for the general distrust of their kind.

Regardless, Caleb refused to act on his feelings.

Aside from a few possible flirtations, she'd never given him an opening to take things further. And if he misread her signals, his job would go from mildly uncomfortable to thoroughly unbearable.

Plus, he didn't want to stop being around her.

So Caleb kept his feelings buried, just like his distaste for Malachi.

"What do you think?" Malachi asked in his nasally voice, breaking Caleb's thoughts of Raina.

"Think about what?" Caleb said, embarrassed as if the entire Council, and Raina, could see what, or rather *whom*, he was thinking about.

"Do you think this is a rogue group from the Freelands, or do you think they're from Under Harbor?"

Caleb nodded. "They *could be* from the Freelands, trying to incite war between us and Under Harbor. But I think it far more likely that this is the work of King Zol's men."

"King Zol?" said one of the Elders with an incredulous laugh. "Why would he incite a war he'd surely lose?"

"I don't know," Caleb said, though something about that notion *felt* right. "In either event, I'd post extra knights at each of the major cities."

Another laugh from the same skeptical Elder. "Post troops? I say we march into Under Harbor, round up the Valkoer, and end this problem before it truly begins."

"I think it's too early to react like that," Raina responded. "Especially if this is someone trying to get us to do exactly that."

One of the other Elders looked at Raina with a furrowed brow. "So, you're in agreement with Brother Caleb, that this isn't someone from Under Harbor? And what evidence do you have?"

"None," she said, though refusing to be meek in her response, "other than my gut saying that something isn't right."

"Something doesn't add up," Caleb agreed. "For one, why leave the bodies half-consumed? It doesn't take that long to finish feeding. And yet they left much of the town half-devoured, flesh still intact and drawing scavengers. It's almost as if they *wanted* the bodies to be found."

The Elder countered, "You said that they turned some people in a cellar, leaving them behind as a trap. Perhaps the goal was to use the half-burned bodies to lure us and hadn't counted on two of The Hand being Valkoer."

Caleb watched Raina look away, practically biting her tongue rather than blast back at the Elder's obvious disgust with their kind.

Back home, Caleb would've stepped in and defended them both against the man, but this wasn't his home, and Raina knew the games one had to play far better than he did. Besides, it wasn't as if she was normally shy in responding to criticism, particularly when other Covenant members gave her lip. But speaking to Elders and The Council required diplomacy, a skill that Caleb had never excelled at.

One of the Elders spoke, looking at Malachi rather than Raina or Caleb. "Might increased troops trigger undue alarm among the people? Perhaps cause them to question our efficacy in protecting them?"

"Good point," said one of the other Elders.

Raina looked right into Malachi's eyes. "There may already be some alarm once word travels about the massacre at Crow's Nest. If we don't increase troops and something *does* happen, then it'll look like we're not doing our jobs."

One of the Elders smacked his hand on the table with considerable force, his face turning red, "That is exactly why we should send The Covenant into Under Harbor now and respond! To prove we're not weak."

"We can't overreact, especially before we know all of the facts," Raina shot back.

The Elder dismissed her with a wave. "Fffftt! They're an illegal occupation flaunting their existence! They are only there because we allow it, with the provision that Jonah could keep the Valkoer and magick users under control. But clearly they are *not*. This is a provocation by an unruly child testing their limits. If we don't step in now, the problem will only get worse. We *will* lose the people's fear and respect."

"What say you?" one of the other Elders asked Malachi. "Should we station guards or respond as the Treaty mandates, by going into Under Harbor and demanding they turn over their Valkoer?"

Malachi sighed, stroking the white hair of his short beard.

"I'm inclined to a patient approach, see what we can learn before committing to a course of action that could negatively affect the Treaty. Let me consult with The Gods and see what They say. In the meantime, I suggest an allocation of troops to each of the cities under our protection."

"I agree," Caleb said. "And in the meantime, why don't you send Raina and me to Jonah, to find out what they know before we make any rash decisions?"

One of the Elders shook his head. "No, we don't let them know what we know. We must go in strong."

"Even if it's a mistake?"

The Elder glared at Caleb. "*Mistake?* We don't make mistakes. We are the divine Hand of the Seven Gods. We do as They instruct us. And *They* do not make mistakes, Brother Caleb."

One of the other Elders said, "I propose an allocation of ten troops posted per city."

"Ten?" Caleb repeated, unable to hide his disappointment. "You'll need way more than ten."

An Elder looked at Caleb with arched eyebrows. "And how many would *you* propose?"

His *you* implied that Caleb was an outsider whose opinion was not only unwelcome, but perhaps suspect given his biological similarity to the attackers.

"No less than thirty per city. Perhaps fifty at larger ones."

"*Fifty?*" the Elder chuckled with a phlegmy cough, as the other two men scolded Caleb with their eyes.

He was about to defend his suggestion when Raina cut in.

"We can certainly spare thirty men per city, can't we?"

One of the Elders looked at Caleb. "I'm reluctant to spread our resources thin at home, particularly when we don't yet know *all the details*. Who knows what we'd be leaving ourselves open to. Our first priority is to protect The Citadel."

The Elder turned and smiled with the slightest twinkle in his eye at Caleb when he said *all the details*.

Caleb wasn't sure if the Elder was cleverly using their rationale for not storming the gates of Jonah against them, or if he was implying something else — perhaps some sort of collusion between Caleb and Raina and the Valkoer enemies.

"If you want to accuse me of something, then say it direct."

The Elders all looked at Caleb as if he'd told them to fuck their Gods. No one spoke. Instead, Malachi glared at Caleb. "You will not address the Inner Council with a sharp tongue!"

In any other situation, Caleb would've told them all to fuck off. He didn't take shit from his superiors at the

Agency, and eating it from these self-important dicks was even less appealing.

But he also saw how quickly this could spin out of control without a bit of damage control.

"I apologize, Prophet Malachi, Elders."

He paused for dramatic effect, then met their judging gazes. "I'm sorry. I'm a bit emotional after this morning. Not only seeing all those dead men, women, and children, but losing several of our Brothers and Sisters has me feeling like I'm not doing enough. I just don't want to lose more good people to the insidious Valkoer. I'll gladly be stationed at any city you may find me useful."

He looked down at his folded hands, allowing his words of contrition to settle.

Malachi said, "You are forgiven, Brother Caleb. We are *all* on edge after the events of the past day. Please, excuse us while we weigh our options. Thank you, Brother Caleb, Sister Raina."

They stood, nodded, and left the Council chambers, Caleb feeling like a child reprimanded by the teacher.

"*Let's walk*," Raina said in his head.

Outside the Inner Council Hall, they continued past the worship centers, the pillars, the giant statues of The Seven Gods, and the marketplace until they were out of earshot of anyone in one of several manicured gardens.

They stopped in front of a pond, and Raina met his eyes.

"Well, what do you think they're going to do?"

"What do *you* think? You know them far better than me."

"They have to see the wisdom of increasing the guards at the major cities. Right?"

"I would hope so."

Caleb watched tiny white petals floating down from the

trees into the pond's bright blue water. Again he was reminded of how much he loved this place, though he hated the politics that ruled it. "Is there anyone we could talk to at Under Harbor, or in the Town of Jonah, who might be able to tell us if their Valkoer are responsible?"

"Yes, we could talk to Jonah."

"Do you think he would know? I mean, could his people sneak out and do something like this without his knowledge?"

"It's highly unlikely. Under Harbor exists because of him, because he took these people in when nobody else wanted them. He's earned too much loyalty for people to keep something like this a secret."

"I think we should talk to him. Before doing anything else."

"You heard what the Elders said. We can't just go talk to them."

Caleb shook his head. "I don't like this. I don't know if it's stubbornness, a misguided sense of infallibility, or worse. But to refuse a conversation before rolling in and rounding up Valkoer is *wrong*. You know that, don't you?"

Raina sighed. "It is not our place to question the wisdom of The Seven Gods."

Caleb looked at her, wondering how much was for show, in case someone was eavesdropping.

He moved the conversation into the privacy of their minds, something he'd rarely done, and always in the field when appropriate, unlike now, talking shit about The Hand.

*Come on, you don't really believe in all their superstitious nonsense, do you?*

Raina looked at Caleb as if surprised. *"Yes, yes I do."*

*Really? I thought you were smarter than that.*

*"What?"*

*I'm sorry. I didn't mean it like that. It's just … it's a racket, like any religion. A bunch of men getting together deciding how things should be, deciding what rules their supposed Gods have laid out, then using the naive followers to enforce those rules. It's been the same story forever, and I don't know, I guess thought we were on the same page.*

"The Hand saved me. I was in a dark place when they found me. I wanted to die. They gave me The Gods. A way to channel my fear, my self-loathing, my guilt for not saving my sister, to make something useful out of all these negative emotions. To help others."

*But you see the darker side of things, right? How they use information gleaned from confessions to blackmail and control people. How they interrogate and lock away supposed enemies of The Gods. Hell, you almost killed me because I was an enemy.*

"I'm sorry if you don't have the faith, and I will pray for you. But, I also understand. It took me a while to believe. And I'll admit that I don't always see the wisdom of their ways, but I trust in The Gods. I trust that we do more good than harm. And we are the only light in this world to battle the evils of people like your father and brother. The world needs us, and our Gods."

Caleb was surprised, and disappointed.

He also wondered how he could have developed feelings for someone who was so deeply engaged in this cult.

Caleb realized that Raina was seeing these thoughts, that he allowed them to flow into their shared conversational link.

*Shit!*

Her eyes narrowed on him, her lips pursed.

She swallowed.

"Whatever you think is happening between us, is not."

He looked down, feeling stupid and ashamed.

*I'm sorry.*

"And I'm not some stupid, naive simpleton being preyed upon by a cult. I don't expect you to believe what I believe to do your job. But I do expect you to respect me, and clearly you do not."

She sharply turned and began to walk away.

*Wait!*

She turned, eyes burning. "What?"

*I'm sorry. I don't think you're stupid. I respect you. I care for you a lot. I really do. And I hate to see people getting screwed over.*

*"I'm not being screwed over."*

*Okay, okay, let's just get past this, please. We need to focus on Under Harbor. Is there anyone you know there who could talk to us without it becoming a big thing?*

She looked down at the floating petals, and without meeting his eyes said, *"Yes, there is someone. A werewolf named Baltazar, who has always given me information. But if Prophet Malachi finds out …"*

*What if I do it?*

*"You?"*

*Yes. That way, if anyone gets in trouble, it'll be me, not you.*

*"It isn't just trouble you'd be getting into. You'd be seen as directly disobeying The Gods. You could be excommunicated, or, more likely, burned alive. I think we should wait and see what The Council decides."*

*Okay.* Caleb nodded.

Raina turned and left without a goodbye.

Caleb couldn't help but feel like he'd destroyed their friendship. Telepathy was a double-edged sword. While it had forged a bond between them that was stronger than most anything else he'd ever felt, it could be demolished with an errant slip of truth.

And Caleb was about to do something which might push her even further away: by going to the Town of Jonah himself.

# THIRTY-THREE

# Abigail

ABIGAIL DIDN'T KNOW what to expect as she entered the In-Between.

The trip through the portal from Earth to Otherworld was instantaneous, as if stepping through a doorway. This was more like stepping through a door into a hallway leading to another door.

Except there was no hallway.

Nor walls.

Nor a floor.

And if there was a doorway out, Abigail couldn't see it.

There was nothing but outer space all around them, brilliantly alive with yellows, reds, blues, greens, and a million colors in between, all set against a canvas of what seemed like the darkest blue. Galaxies, stars, planets, and colorful gasses that looked like watercolors spilled to the horizon in every direction.

And it was cold. *Ice cold.* Abigail's breath fogged the air in front of her.

For all the visual brilliance of light — and possibly life

— around them, the utter silence and absence of sound, including Abigail's breath, pressed on her head like a vice.

Abigail's stomach dropped, fear gripping her as she failed to find something solid to land on, stumbling forward, certain she'd fall and keep falling, spinning out of control into space, forever and ever until she was incinerated by a sun or swallowed by a black hole.

Abigail screamed without any sound.

*"I got you,"* Talani said in her head, reaching out to grab Abigail's arm, and helping her gain footing.

*"Just close your eyes, and hold my arm. I'll lead you,"* Talani said. *"We can't see the ground, but you have to believe it's there."*

*How do you know? Have you been here before?*

*"No, but Judith has, and she told me how to navigate."*

Judith appeared on her other side, putting a hand on Abigail's shoulder. *"We're not too far. Just keep steady."*

Abigail kept her eyes closed, walking shakily, taking small steps, knowing that a wrong one would send her stumbling again.

*Thank you, Talani.*

*Thank you, Judith.*

They continued walking as Abigail wondered how her friends were able to find and maintain *their* footing when she had so much trouble. Was it as easy as merely believing there was a floor there?

Suddenly, a shriek from somewhere.

At first Abigail thought she'd heard it outside of her head, but that was impossible since there was no sound. Instead, the noise had entered her head, unlike anything she'd ever heard — like a long, wheezing, high-pitched shriek.

Abigail opened her eyes and saw three large dark figures floating ahead. Like giant puffer fish crossed with octopi, black with purple lights inside their skin, long tentacles with more lavender lights on suckers.

Abigail stopped, not wanting to get any closer to the disgusting creatures.

From Judith: *"Ignore them. Keep moving."*

But Abigail was frozen. *I can't. They're scary.*

Talani: *"Remember what Mother said. They can't hurt us. Just keep walking. If it helps, keep your eyes closed. We'll guide you, Abigail."*

Abigail couldn't close her eyes, though. Couldn't stop staring. They were so disgusting with their slimy bodies and the way they floated, waiting, long tentacles undulating as if underwater and flowing with the ocean's current.

Talani: *"Close your eyes, Abigail. You can do this."*

Abigail finally squeezed her eyes closed and kept them shut, fingers tightening around Talani's hand.

Judith slipped her arm in the crook of Abigail's. *"That's okay, we're right here, honey."*

Judith's voice was calming, like Abigail's mother's had been — before she died. It felt warm and reassuring, and Abigail was glad she was there by her side.

As they walked, Abigail felt guilty for how she'd felt about Judith. She wasn't sure what it was about the woman — the occasional frost or the matter-of-fact manner in which she often spoke to Abigail — but there was something she couldn't quite place that kept her from bonding with Judith like she had with Talani.

Then again, sometimes Abigail sensed a distance between Talani and Judith, as though something wasn't quite right between them, either. Something that Talani was much too polite to discuss.

*Or too afraid.*

*"What?"* Talani replied in Abigail's head.

*Oh God, did you hear my thoughts?*

*"No, thought I heard you say something to me."*

*No, I was thinking about something. Can Judith hear my thoughts, too? Or only if I project them to her?*

*"Hear what?"* Judith asked. *"If you're asking if I can hear the horrible things you're thinking about me, then yes; yes I can."*

*Oh God, I'm so sorry,* Abigail cried out to them both. *I didn't mean anything by it. I'm just —*

*"You ungrateful little cunt!"* Judith snapped. *"What did you tell her, Talani?"*

Abigail felt awful, wondering how she could fix this before it got worse.

*"I didn't say anything. What the hell, Abigail? I thought you were my friend!"*

Abigail felt confused.

Judith and Talani were getting angry, and yet they were calmly guiding her. Talani hadn't changed pressure on her hand, nor had Judith pulled away. Actions weren't matching emotions.

Something was off.

Abigail opened her eyes.

And immediately wished she hadn't.

The floating octopus-fish were surrounding them, just inches away.

*Oh God!*

They were even more horrifying up close, and larger than they appeared, at least six feet tall and maybe eight feet wide, each of their tentacles at least another six feet or more.

And finally Abigail saw what appeared to be one giant purple eye near the bottom of each of their bodies, at the tentacles' origin. At least she thought it was purple, until realizing that was the eyelid covering the eye.

As they drew closer, all three shrieked louder at once.

*Oh God. Please, make it stop.*

They were closing in, and neither Judith nor Talani seemed aware, both still walking, holding Abigail's hands, eyes closed to the world around them.

*Look!* Abigail shouted over the shrieking in her head.

But they either couldn't hear or were ignoring her.

One of the tentacles bumped against her head.

It didn't hurt Abigail so much as surprise her.

She yelped. Though she didn't make a sound, all at once the three creatures opened their eyes to reveal giant, bright white lights, beaming right at her.

Tentacles whipped back and forth in a frenzy.

Abigail screamed.

She broke free from Judith and Talani, then ran.

Shrieking grew louder behind her.

Somewhere beneath it all, Abigail thought she heard her friends call for her. She wanted to turn but couldn't.

If she stopped or slowed or turned around, she'd see one of those creatures coming at her with its big horrible bright light for an eye.

Mother had been wrong.

If these things could bump into her, they could physically hurt — or kill — her.

Ahead she saw a black slit floating, a portal, either the one she'd entered or the one they'd been seeking. Either way, she didn't care.

She raced toward it and dived in.

She fell on her stomach, hitting the nonexistent ground hard enough to knock the wind from her body.

She was in a bedroom, small and sparsely decorated with a bed, a dresser with a lamp and a toy boat, and a few items of clothes hanging in a closet.

There were two light-skinned black girls: one, who looked to be about five, was in her bed.

An older one, maybe sixteen or seventeen, stood at the window, staring out.

Something bad was about to happen.

"What's wrong?" Abigail asked.

Neither girl responded.

Abigail went to the window and saw a carriage with a big, scary-looking man standing outside of it. Beside him, a woman.

A chill ran through Abigail as she realized it wasn't just a woman, but a younger-looking version of Judith.

"Judith!" she yelled out the window.

Neither man nor woman heard her.

Same for the girls in the bedroom.

"Hey," Abigail said, reaching out to grab the older one's arm, "can't you hear me?"

Abigail's hand went right through her.

The little girl in the bed cried out, "What's happening?"

Abigail heard her voice and knew in an instant that this wasn't just some little girl. It was Talani as a child.

Abigail had somehow gone back in time. Or was seeing something that happened.

"What's happening, Raina?" Little Talani asked.

The girl, obviously her sister, told her to hide under the bed.

Abigail watched in horror as the scary man came in and killed Talani's father. As Judith put a blade to Raina's neck.

Then the big man left, leaving Judith and Raina alone, with Talani safe under the bed.

Judith saw the hiding girl.

Raina begged her to leave Talani alone.

"Sorry," Judith said, reaching under the bad and pulling Talani out.

Raina screamed. "Talani!"

SUDDENLY, they were no longer in the bedroom.

Abigail was in another large room, dark red, with many chairs and couches. A long bar occupied the far wall. Men in suits stood in front of a stage where girls were lined in a row, dressed all in white, like simple wedding dresses. They all looked like teenagers, a few maybe in their early twenties. Each girl held a numbered card. It didn't look like any numeral Abigail had ever seen, yet she somehow recognized it as a number, despite not knowing its value.

Men were eying the girls, some licking their lips as if ordering steaks. Abigail had, of course, seen that sort of sick desire before. In Randy Webster's cold, dark eyes.

In the back of the room, two doors opened, drawing all eyes.

"Wait, we've got two more," Judith said, entering the room with that frightening man. He held two leashes, and as he walked, Abigail saw Raina and Talani on their ends, also dressed in white. The man smiled as if showing prized dogs.

*Oh God.*

Abigail's heart was breaking as they led the girls onstage. A fat tattooed woman sitting to the left of the line wrote more numbers on cards then handed them to the girls as if conducting a simple business transaction.

Abigail glared at Judith. "How could you?" she said, even though the past couldn't hear her.

She wished she could kill Judith right there. Grab a bottle of wine from one of the tables, bash it into her face.

Abigail watched in horror as Raina and Talani stood on the stage.

Talani was shaking, crying.

Raina held her hand tight. "It'll be okay," she said, making a promise she couldn't possibly keep. "We'll get through this."

Though Abigail was too far from the stage to hear Raina, she could hear the words as if they were being whispered in her ear.

*We'll get through this.*

The fat woman stood and paced in front of the girls.

"Welcome to tonight's auction, distinguished gentlemen. You'll see that we have quite the beauties tonight. All are guaranteed clean. Even the little one." She laughed, putting a hand over Talani's head.

Abigail wanted to kill the pig bitch, even more than Judith.

"So," the woman continued. "Let's start the bidding with this beauty from the small village of Crow's Nest. This farm girl can tend your crops in the day, and your cock at night. We'll start the bidding at one hundred."

Abigail was sickened as the men's hands shot into the air, waving wildly like kids waiting to be chosen by the teacher.

*We'll get through this.*

One by one, men claimed their prizes then went to a stairway beyond the bar to *truly* claim them.

All the girls had been sold — or perhaps rented; Abigail wasn't sure — except Raina and Talani.

Talani was crying, shaking as Raina clutched her hand.

*We'll get through this.*

Abigail wondered if the young girl knew what was about to happen, or only that men were going to buy her.

Abigail had once been naive enough to not know what sick men wanted. She missed that innocence, but was glad that she'd never be tricked again by a smiling man's lies.

The fat woman said, "And, gentlemen, we've saved the

best for last. Two pristine beauties. Sisters, no less. One so young she's not so much as a single hair down below."

She lifted Talani's dress to show the men.

Talani cried out, trying to push her dress back down.

Abigail turned away.

*We'll get through this.*

The men laughed.

Abigail wanted to kill them, too.

End everyone in the godforsaken place, except Talani and her sister.

"And because the wee one is a bit young, we're selling them together."

A few groans in the audience, while some of the men seemed thrilled at the prospect of buying both girls.

"We'll start the bid at one thousand."

Nearly every hand was raised.

"Do I hear one thousand one hundred?"

And so it went until the price reached two thousand, with one hand remaining.

A beautiful dark-haired woman in a long black robe and long black gloves was holding her right hand high. Abigail noticed a rose tattoo on her cheek.

"Two thousand," she said, looking around.

The men seemed scared to counter her offer.

The fat woman on stage asked, "Two thousand? Do I have any more bids?"

The dark-haired woman stared the men down.

Not a single man raised his hand.

"Sold to Esmerelda," said the fat woman.

As Esmerelda approached the stage, Talani cried. Once there she looked down at the girls, and said, "Think happy thoughts, girls."

Then the women and girls, as well as the room they were in, were gone.

. . .

AND BACK IN the sprawling nothingness of the In-Between.

Instead of being surrounded by stars, the sky was dark save for a large glowing white ball of energy that seemed like some kind of moon-sun swallowing much of the sky and casting a milky white luminescence on rolling desert sands as far as she could see in every direction.

*"Abigail!"* she heard Judith and Talani screaming in her head.

She opened her eyes and saw them running toward her, bathed in beams of light coming from the giant eyes of the big black floating things chasing them.

Talani pointed urgently behind Abigail.

*"Turn around. The door is behind you!"*

Abigail spun around and saw the portal, a thin black gash surrounded by gold light.

*"Go, go, go!"* Talani yelled in her head, though Abigail could barely hear her over the shrieking octopi.

Abigail went to the portal, was about to cross through, but looked back to wait for her friends.

*"Go!"* Talani yelled.

The things shrieked louder, and as they did Abigail thought back on what she'd seen — how Judith had destroyed Talani's and her sister's lives. How she sold them to some woman who did God only knew what.

How could Talani stay with her, let alone think of her as a *mother?*

Abigail again wished she could've gone back in time to be there, instead of being a mute witness. She would've killed Judith, and all the other horrible people in that room, right then and there. Finish the whole lot of them, and save the innocent girls.

Abigail reached into her pants pocket and palmed

Mother's blade, its blackness buzzing warm in her hand, full of deadly promise.

*"What are you waiting for?"* Talani yelled as she and Judith drew closer, about fifty yards away, with the floating terrors right behind them, their tentacles wildly shaking in the bright light.

*She can't come,* Abigail projected to Talani. *It's time for her to pay.*

*"What are you talking about?"*

*I saw what she did to you and your sister. How she sold you.*

*"Abigail, it's not as simple as that. Please, don't do anything."*

They were thirty yards away.

The shrieking in Abigail's head grew louder.

*She's not coming with us. She is staying here!*

*"No!"* Talani yelled. *"We will talk about it. But please, trust me. Do NOT do this."*

*She hurt you. And your sister. She has to pay.*

*"If you do this, Abigail, you aren't just hurting her. You're hurting me. Is that what you want?"*

Ten yards away, the shrieking now louder than anything else — raking her ears and agitating her entire body, like a violent itch that could only be scratched with cruelty.

Kill Judith to avenge the girls, and sate the screaming in her brain.

*We'll get through this.*

The noise demanded action.

The past demanded blood.

Talani and Judith were only a few feet away.

Abigail gripped the blade, eying Judith to time her strike.

Judith had no idea what was coming, staring toward the portal, running straight to it, trying to escape the octopi-things.

*We'll get through this.*
*Three.*
*Two.*
*0 —*

Talani suddenly changed everything by dodging in front of Judith, slamming into Abigail hard, forcing her backward through the portal, and landing on top of her.

ALL AT ONCE THE shrieking died.

They were in what looked like an underground tunnel, light flickering from lanterns fixed to the wall.

Abigail tried to look around, but Talani was atop her, reaching up and grabbing Abigail's chin, turning it as if to kiss her.

And in that moment so close, Abigail, oddly, almost *wanted* her to. Their eyes locked. Talani's eyes were wide, scared.

Talani cried, *"Please, don't."*

Abigail was confused.

*Don't what?*

Something shifted in Talani's eyes, and Abigail's terror grew as she feared that Talani saw her thoughts ... and the kiss she wanted.

*"Please, don't kill Judith."*

*Why?*

*"I'll explain later. But please, if you love me, just trust me."*

And there it was — the word *love.*

Abigail hadn't thought of how she felt about Talani as love. At least not at first. She only just met her, and Abigail didn't like girls that way, certainly not enough to kiss them.

But then again, the world of people she'd known until now was so limited — her parents, both dead; her uncle, who sold her to the pedophile, Randy Webster; John, whom she loved like a father, but who left her alone with Larry; Larry, whom she loved like a brother, but whom she betrayed. And then there was Katya — her first real friend — killed by Abigail's own hand.

Her every form of love had either died or been corrupted or betrayed.

But here was yet another chance.

Maybe not romantic love, but a sisterly love. Something she could call her own, and maybe fill the void in her heart.

And she didn't want to screw that up.

Their eyes still locked, it felt as if everything hinged on this moment.

Talani repeated, *"Please, Abigail. Don't hurt her."*

Abigail swallowed.

*Okay.*

Talani sighed, then leaned in and kissed Abigail softly on the cheek.

She then climbed off Abigail.

Abigail looked up at Judith, who was distracted by someone else in the hallway — a man with a sword drawn on them.

# Interlude - Jacob Aage 13

Jacob was sitting in the garden, throwing rocks into the pond after finally giving up on levitating them as VVessolff had been trying to teach him, when he saw the brown men carrying the large box through the castle's iron gates.

The men were dressed from head to toe in golden silks, indicative of the Jska tribe from No Man's Land.

Jacob hopped up and raced toward the castle entrance, eager to get a closer look at the men, and maybe see what they were bringing his father.

The Forgotten Kingdom was a twelve-day walk from No Man's Land, or three days by horse, unless they'd used a magickal portal. In any event, they'd never been to The Forgotten Kingdom, so Jacob wasn't the only person with eyes on the men. Everyone watched their approach, met by the King's Guard at The Citadel gate.

They were ushered through, accompanied by two guardsmen.

Jacob followed closely, wondering why they were here and what they had brought. The Jska tribe was known as having the finest craftsmen of The Southern Realm, often working with gold and other rare metals. Father had many of their decorations already in the castle, but nothing custom made. This must be special. And his little brothers were off with Mother visiting the market, so Jacob would be first to see the treasure.

He could hardly contain his excitement as the men were led to Father's visiting chamber. Jacob sneaked in behind them, then ducked behind the red velvet curtains lining the walls to avoid being seen by Father or the guards.

He listened as the men spoke, but it wasn't the common language, or any of the others that Jacob had learned.

King Zol greeted them in their tongue. Jacob couldn't tell what he was saying, but judging from his big, booming voice, which he only used for important people, Father was happy to host them.

Jacob peered through the curtains as the men pulled back the wooden planks and then the linens that covered their gift.

Jacob leaned forward, hoping for a better look, when he slipped, taking the curtain down with him.

The guards approached, yelling.

Jacob's heart raced as he tried to pull the curtain off of him to prove he wasn't an enemy, but he was too tangled in the fabric.

*They're going to kill me!*

"It's me, it's me, Prince Jacob! Don't kill me!"

One of the guards yanked the curtain off of Jacob. The other stood with his sword drawn, face twisted into an angry red.

Jacob looked up past the guards to see Father glaring.

"What are you doing?" he screamed, standing from his throne.

"Sorry, sorry, I just wanted to see what they were bringing."

"Get out!" Father scolded, pointing toward the exit.

Jacob slunk out of the room, red-faced and feeling stupid.

~

Two weeks later, Jacob woke early and sneaked into his parents' sleeping chamber to see the Jska's gift.

It was a mirror, and quite beautiful, or so he'd heard — from his brothers no less. Jacob had begged his parents to see it, but they refused, saying he had to wait. Their way of teaching him patience, and not to sneak around where he wasn't allowed, or at least that's what Mother said. Jacob thought it was just Father's cruelty, denying his son something simply because he could.

Jacob had tried to play it off to his little brothers, saying that he didn't care about the "stupid mirror," but the reality was that he'd become obsessed.

He started planning, first to try and gain entry while Father was elsewhere in the Kingdom, but the King often locked his chambers during the day. Jacob decided that he'd sneak inside while they were sleeping.

He crept into the dark bedroom, carefully making his way past their bed to the mirror standing beside the open window, reflecting the full moons outside.

The room was dark, bathed in a blue, milky light that illuminated enough of the golden frame for Jacob to be impressed. The Jska had carved mountains and flowers along the frame, a design that wrapped around the rear. Jacob walked around the back of the mirror to see a giant raven, his house sigil carved to sit atop their old Kingdom in the Calladian Mountains.

Jacob reached out to touch the design, marveling at the softness on his fingertips.

It was just as beautiful as his brothers had promised.

Jacob walked back to look at the mirror's front, and caught his reflection. He was thirteen and still horribly awkward, his dark hair already receding. His eyes were sunken caverns in his moon-like face. He turned to make his way back out of the bedroom.

Suddenly, movement to his right.

Father, getting out of bed.

*No!*

"What are you doing in here?" he bellowed.

"I'm sorry, Father! I just wanted to see the mirror."

His mother woke. Sleepy, she said, "What are you doing in here, Jacob?"

"He is looking at that fucking mirror," Father snapped, grabbing Jacob by the back of his shirt, shoving him toward the bedroom door.

"Sorry, I just wanted to see if it was as beautiful as —"

"*Yes*, it is beautiful. You want a closer look? *Here!*"

His father shoved Jacob against the glass, almost hard enough to break it.

Jacob whined.

Father grabbed the back of his head and shoved his face harder against the cold surface. "You like that? You like that fucking mirror? Here, maybe you can't see."

He pressed harder.

Jacob cried out. "Sorry!"

"Stop!" Jacob's mother cried out, trying to insert herself between them.

"Stay out of this!" He slapped her with his free hand.

She slunk away, lest she face more of his wrath.

Father put both hands on the back of Jacob's head,

then pulled him back so they were cheek to cheek staring into the mirror together.

Father's eyes were dark and full of hate — more hate than a father should ever feel for his son. A hate that Father seemed to reserve mostly for his firstborn.

"You getting a good look?"

"Yes!" Jacob cried.

"Good because this will be your last look. If I ever see you using my beautiful mirror to reflect your donkey face again, I'll break the mirror and use it to gouge your eyes out, do you understand me?"

"Yes!" Jacob cried.

"Yes, what?"

"Yes, my King."

Father shoved him to the ground, then kicked him hard in the ass. "Now get out of my sight, you fucking mule."

# THIRTY-FOUR

# Jacob

JACOB WAS RESTING IN BED, after barely being back at the castle for two hours, when he heard a loud crash.

He woke, startled, then realized it was only thunder outside.

He lied back down, eager to catch some shut-eye. But his search for sleep was interrupted by another noise — three sharp raps on his chamber door.

Still tired from the assault on Crow's Nest, despite having fed well on the wretched souls, he opened the door to a pair of knights, dressed in their armor and looking stern.

"The King would like to see you."

"I'll be there after I sleep." Jacob started to close the door.

A hand intercepted the door before it could close. "Now."

Jacob tensed. Had Zol found out already? Did he know Jacob and Barron had been behind the attack? That might explain why Barron wasn't the one at his door.

"Okay. May I at least get dressed, or shall I stroll in there nude, maybe give you all a show?"

Jacob made a point of smiling as he waved his hand over his cock.

The men looked away. One of them murmured, "Go ahead, but be quick about it."

Jacob closed the door, and dressed in his most comfortable, flowing black garb, trying to keep calm as he prepared for what was to come. He had to assume that Viceroy Calbot Mason got in Father's ear, but had no proof. The men they took to Crow's Nest were Barron's best, hand selected, loyal to the New Order that would rise after the coming war — whether Zol was willing to lead it, or if Jacob claimed the throne.

JACOB FELT the knights at his back as they marched him down the long hall to the King's Royal Chambers.

Footsteps echoed off the long and narrow walls. The entire floor felt ominously empty, particularly for such an early hour. This floor was usually filled with various workers, people waiting to appear before the King with requests, proposals, or offerings.

But the entire floor was empty save for Jacob and his escorts.

*Where is everyone?*

They arrived at the double doors.

Mason stood outside the doorway, arms folded, glaring at Jacob. Jacob ignored the man's stare and waited for him to open the doors.

He did, and Jacob entered, stopping when he saw Sir Barron's decapitated head, its eyes staring up at Jacob, on the red carpet leading to his father's throne.

He started to turn, but Father's knights blocked him, swords drawn.

Mason, standing between the guards, smiled.

*Shit!*

Jacob turned to face Father sitting on his throne and glaring at his son.

Mason closed the doors behind Jacob.

Jacob walked slowly forward, his eyes on the ground as he tried to figure out who ratted him out. He raised his eyes, covertly seeking any means of escape.

Jacob could already imagine Mason calling for his head, could see it added to the pikes placed in the center of town an example of what happened when you betrayed the King.

*If the King would kill his own son, what might he do to us? We'd better not fuck with the King!*

The only blessing, if there were any to be counted, was that Barron's head was the only one staining the carpet, meaning that maybe they had yet to discover who else was involved. Perhaps Jacob was being called forth to supply answers.

But their eyes were suspicious. Perhaps Barron *had* given him up. Whatever the case, Jacob's plan to cause a war had clearly hit a major snag. Maybe they wouldn't behead him. Maybe they'd turn him over to The Hand of the Seven Gods for judgment.

Jacob approached the throne, stopping ten feet from Father's glaring countenance. He was dressed in his black robe, and wearing his crown — this was official business.

Father stared down at Jacob for what felt like an eternity. Jacob hated the disappointment in his eyes. The look had been there ever since childhood but seemed to have festered in severity. Now, Father was looking at him with pure disgust, practically sneering.

Jacob looked down.

"You have one chance to tell the truth, Jacob. Do you understand me?"

"Yes, my King," Jacob said, still unable to look up.

He could feel the two guards and Mason behind him, reveling in the moment. Mason was probably aroused.

Father cleared his throat. "Did you participate in the attack on Crow's Nest?"

Jacob's fate in a question. Should he offer the truth that, yes, he was not only a part of the attack but orchestrated it from the start? Or should he lie — say that he had nothing to do with it? Or perhaps a variation on the truth, saying that Barron had talked him into it?

*What do they already know?*

Despite the single head on the floor, he had to assume they knew everything. Father had likely plucked the memories from Barron's mind, and this trial was a formality before delivering punishment to Jacob.

Still unable to meet Father's eyes, Jacob spoke softly. "Yes, it was my idea, my King."

"I knew it!" Mason shouted from behind.

Jacob didn't give the fucker the satisfaction of turning around.

He stared at the floor, waiting to hear what Father would say next.

"Why would you do that?"

"Because Barron and I saw an opportunity to seize power, to make our Kingdom strong again, to reclaim our homeland."

"By starting a war?" Father's voice cracked in disbelief.

"Sometimes you must do something bad to achieve something good."

"Under whose authority?" Father bellowed.

Jacob still couldn't meet his eyes, nor answer the question.

This was crumbling fast. He could sense his father's wheels turning in search of a punishment. Jacob had to play humble if he expected to avoid the worst of this, or even survive.

"I asked, *under whose authority?*"

"We were trying to save the Kingdom."

Mason shouted from behind: "The Kingdom doesn't *need* saving!"

Jacob responded, though not turning to fully dignify his outburst. "The Kingdom *does* need saving, from you, Viceroy Mason! He has been making you weak, my King. You don't hear it, *but I do*. The people are whispering behind your back, wondering if you're still the same King they know. Wondering why you've bent to The North, bent to The Hand of the Seven Gods, bent to anyone who poses any threat?"

"I bend to no one!" Father shouted.

Jacob laughed without looking up. He could tell by Father's huffing breath, the old man was getting angry, his face turning red.

Mason shouted, "You dare to mock the throne?"

Jacob finally looked up at him, meeting the man's red eyes.

Jacob smiled and said, "Fuck the throne."

Father's eyes widened.

Father rose, stepping towards him.

"How dare you? I ought to have your head!" Father yelled.

Jacob fell to his knees, crossing his hands over his chest, bowing his head down, begging forgiveness.

"I'm sorry, my King. I'm sorry ... *Father.*"

Jacob kept his head down, sobbing, pleading, "Please, I

was trying to do the right thing, trying to make you proud of me."

He kept his head down, still pleading for his life. He could hear Father above him, his voice starting to calm.

"Please, Father. I will accept whatever punishment you deem fit, but please, don't kill me. I am your last son, and live only to serve you."

The silence stretched. Jacob didn't dare look up or back, but he imagined Father conferring with Mason in nods and gestures.

"Please, Father," Jacob repeated, his voice cracking.

It was custom when one begged at the King's feet to keep one's head down and wait for him to turn away or offer his hand. And if you were fortunate enough for the King to offer his hand, you took it, kissed it, and thanked him for his generous mercy.

Jacob waited, head down, for what felt like forever, hoping that Father would not turn away.

He felt Father's hand on his shoulder.

Jacob kept his head down, and reached up blindly, feeling for his hand. He took it.

"Thank you, Father," he said, starting to rise.

He finally managed to turn his face to Father. He met his eyes ... and slid the blade into his father's gut.

Father's eyes widened as he gasped.

Jacob pulled his father to him in what appeared to those watching from behind nothing more than a father-son hug, driving the blade deeper as he embraced him.

Jacob reached under Father's shirt, found the crystals in the pouch hanging around his neck, ripped the cord, and seized the power.

Father gasped, trying to say something but stammering on his words. Jacob whispered in his ear, "Mother was right to leave you. You are nothing. And now you will die."

Jacob pulled the blade from Father's gut, and watched the man collapse to the floor, clutching his wound.

He spun around, grinning as he greeted the two knights and a horrified Mason.

Mason pointed at Jacob and shouted, "Kill him!"

The men started toward him, swords drawn.

Jacob raised the pouch, feeling the crystals' warmth spreading into his body.

"Stop!" he commanded.

They stopped.

He could see confusion in their eyes as they wondered why they'd followed such a ridiculous order, and why their bodies were obeying his, instead of Mason's, instructions.

"Kill him!" Mason shouted even louder.

"No." Jacob smiled at Mason. "Kill the Viceroy."

The guards turned on Mason, swords now drawn on him.

His face was an incredulous delight, eyes bulging as he screamed at the men. But no amount of tortured bellows would stop the knights from obeying their Master.

"Make him suffer, *please*," Jacob hissed.

Mason screamed as one of the men slid a blade across his gut.

Earth had a saying about laughter being the best medicine. But clearly, whoever made it up had never heard the music of their enemies being disemboweled.

# THIRTY-FIVE

## Caleb

THE TOWN of Jonah was a half-night's horse ride east of Golden Cove, nestled in The Southern Realm's uppermost northeastern peninsula.

The small town was well secured on its south and west sides by a giant stone wall, on its north and east by sailors and guards stationed along the fishing and shipping docks.

If Golden Cove was known for its sprawling views of the nearby mountains and seas, dazzling architecture — golden towers, elegant spires, and voluptuous domes — and its buzzing sea of bourgeois citizens, then the Town of Jonah was its opposite in nearly every way.

The town, once called Fisher's Bay, was a low-lying, cobbled-together village that seemed to exist under perpetual fog and rain. Instead of dazzling architecture, the hamlet was dappled with common homes, mostly a dingy gray or stygian blue with weather-beaten and aging facades.

Unlike Golden Cove, where people seemed to present some idealized — or holier — version of themselves, what you saw was what you got in Jonah: no-nonsense, hardscrabble men and women who had no time for the nonsense of Golden Cove's citizens.

The Town of Jonah had been renamed for Jonah Montaine — a pirate who'd nearly lost his life during The Great War defending the hamlet against The North. It was one of only two towns, along with Golden Cove, to avoid surrender when The North invaded.

If not for Jonah's support of Golden Cove's navy, the entire South may have collapsed before The Hand of the Seven Gods managed to carve out a treaty. Their steadfast defense of The South had earned them undying respect not just from The Hand of the Seven Gods but also from King Zol. It also earned them respect from rulers in The North, which eventually led to the Town of Jonah having a lucrative shipping and fishing deal with The North, making it the second most powerful city in The South, after Golden Cove.

Because of this power and respect, both The North and The Hand overlooked the Town of Jonah's criminal underbelly.

Beneath the city lay an entire town called Under Harbor, a network of tunnels, homes, bars, and black market shops that served as home and catered to criminals on the run, banished Valkoer, other freaks from The Forgotten Kingdom, and exiled members of The Hand of the Seven Gods.

The town's existence was technically in violation of the Treaty, but because of Jonah's storied history, and its legendary patriarch, everyone looked the other way. But there were also pragmatic reasons for allowing the town to exist, serving as a pressure valve for the other cities. Without it, tensions surely would have risen to more infighting and perhaps had a destabilizing effect on the current power structures. Additionally, it kept many of the undesirables occupied with the black market's various underground activities — sex, drugs, and magick you couldn't get anywhere else outside of The Forgotten Kingdom.

Caleb arrived at the gates, claiming to be a craftsman from the Freelands seeking a good time. While he'd been to the Town of Jonah several times to meet with people on behalf of The Hand, he'd never come alone, or visited Under Harbor.

He tried not to be nervous at the thought of being underground, though it would be difficult given his claustrophobia.

Within minutes he was ushered toward a bar that served as one of several secret entrances to the underground city.

Like all visitors, he had to check his weapons at the door, but that was fine — he wasn't planning to fight. Besides, Caleb could always buy weapons in one of the many underground markets, and use the power of his touch if needed.

While Caleb had accessed his powers during Raina's capture, he hadn't yet fed. And thus he'd never completely reverted to his vampire side. He still had some of his abilities, such as telepathy and minor telekinesis, but not the deadly touch. Nor did he have Raina's weaknesses, such as aversion to sunlight or needing to feed. Raina wasn't sure how some of his powers could surface without all of them. Then again there were no examples in this world of cured vampires, even temporarily reverted ones such as Caleb. For most Valkoer, you turned when you were a teenager then were cursed forever.

But Caleb had turned once, when he accidentally killed his wife, and *had* been reverted.

Ever since he laid his hands on Raina, he felt the power

calling. He felt a desire to feed, but he'd not yet given into it.

He felt that if he did he would become full Valkoer again. And without his brother, John around to help him, it would likely be his last day as a human.

But he was pretty sure that the power was there if he needed it.

Caleb spent the first part of the evening in a bar drinking and schmoozing, attempting to subtly find information on the werewolf Baltazar. But mining details from secretive criminal types was always a gamble — the more questions you asked, the more people suspected your intentions. And as much as criminal types might fight with one another, there was a loyalty against the powers-that-be.

A few people had told him that his best bet was in talking to Oomar, a gambler who spent most nights in the back room playing cards and getting drunk. Oomar knew everything about everyone in Under Harbor, and if you got him in a good enough mood, he might reveal what you wanted to know.

Caleb found his way into the game, figuring if he put up a few good hands then lost, Oomar night take a shine to him.

Oomar was a short dark-skinned man with wild, long brown curly hair and an eye patch over his right eye. He was playing with two other men, all of them piss drunk but in good spirits, laughing and joking whether winning or losing hands.

Caleb had tried to bring up Baltazar a few times, but had to tread carefully, as these men could spot a fishing expedition, and Caleb didn't want to wind up shanked in an underground bar. None of his attempts to steer the conversation seemed to be working, as Oomar and his men would either ignore the comments, change the subject, or sometimes start laughing as one of them laid down a hand strong enough to gather the others' money.

About a half hour in, and having had a few too many drinks, Caleb was ready to give up his search, maybe look for someone else who could steer him toward Baltazar.

"Well, thank you, gentlemen, for taking most of my money, but I need to get going," he said, starting to stand.

"Leaving already?" Oomar asked. "Me and the lads was going to hit Desire's Soma Den. Why don't you join us?"

"I should probably save some money for supplies, or else my old lady will kill me when I get home. I came here to *win* money tonight, not lose my ass!"

"Where'd you say you was from?" Oomar asked, looking over a bottle of green alcohol as he swished its contents then finished it off.

"Kindwood." Caleb named one of the Freelands' few villages, small enough not to be commonly known, but large enough that you could conceivably be from there without belonging to a specific family — something that could screw you if you ran into someone from a smaller town, where everyone truly did know everyone else.

"Never been. Bet you all don't have soma dens like this, though. You've really gotta experience it, my friend. You'll forget all about your old lady, right, fellas?"

The men laughed. A guy named Will agreed. "Ain't no woman as sweet as the girls working here. And the soma ain't bad, either."

Soma was a sweet-smelling tobacco and opium-like drug that was big underground. Caleb had never smoked it — the drug was frowned upon as one of many "scourges of the heathens," but he knew from others that it was good shit, put you in an especially friendly mood, and might just loosen Oomar's lips.

Plus, it had been forever since Caleb had taken his pills, and though he'd kicked his addiction, he never truly stopped craving that opiate bliss, or felt an escape from the pain.

Pretending to be a bit drunker than he was, Caleb said, "How sweet are these girls?"

Hank raised his almost-empty glass, said, "The sweetest! Cleanest in all The Realms!" then polished it off.

Caleb pretended to think it over, then finally said, "All right, you twisted my arm."

Hank slapped Caleb on the back. "I knew he couldn't say no!"

Oomar laughed. "No real man can say no to Desire's!"

The other man, a red-headed bear whose name Caleb still didn't know, laughed and raised his drink, "To Desire's!"

The men stood, each leaving cash on the table to cover their tab, and Caleb followed them out of the bar.

Underground tunnels varied in width and height ranging from road wide where several people and even small horses could navigate to narrow and short enough to permit only a few people through at a time. No matter how big or wide the tunnel, or how well lit with torches or lanterns, they all felt claustrophobic to Caleb.

And the longer he was down here, the more anxious he became.

He wanted to ask the men how they could live underground, but thought it might come off as rude, particularly since most of the people in Under Harbor were there because they had nowhere else to go. And, a few times during the night, he'd sensed disdain for outsiders. This was a place for the marginalized and they didn't take kindly to their oppressors coming round acting like they owned *this* place, too. On the flip side, places that catered to tourists often had to hide their resentment, choosing commerce over spite.

Oomar and his men had been cordial enough, though. Caleb reminded himself to soothe his anxiety as he followed them through ever-narrowing tunnels. But it was difficult when fear began to whisper into his ear.

*They're probably on to me and bringing me somewhere to rob and kill me.*

The walls soon felt even closer, the air even harder to breathe.

Caleb paused to catch his breath.

Oomar stopped, turned and said, "You all right, mate?"

The other two men also stopped and turned, all now eying Caleb suspiciously.

His heart was racing. Breath shallow.

He tried to slow his breathing, closed his eyes to focus.

He put his hand to his head to exaggerate inebriation rather than reveal his swelling anxiety.

"Just think I drank a bit too much."

Oomar slapped his back, "A bit of soma will cure what ails ya, come on."

Oomar lightly pushed Caleb onward, staying by his side as they continued through the tunnel, followed by Oomar's friends.

Caleb could practically feel their eyes, their hands on the blades at their belts.

*This is a trap!*

*Run!*

He ignored his growing panic.

He tried to focus on the moment — no matter what, these were men, and he was something more. He could kill them in an instant, if need be.

*Yeah, unless they've got those onyx blades.*

*Then we're fucked.*

There was no way to tell what kind of daggers waited in their sheaths. Suddenly he wished he'd not checked his weapons above.

The tunnel turned, and they reached a passage so narrow that the only way through was one at a time.

Caleb stopped, his heart about to burst out of his chest.

The passage, a sliver of a space, was barely wide enough to squeeze through. Barely tall enough to walk down without ducking.

Oomar saw him eying it and patted him on the back. "If Kruk can fit through here, you can, now git!"

Kruk must've been the big redhead.

Caleb looked into the passage, definitely dark enough to kill someone, with a scant blur of light at the other end.

"Guests first," Oomar said, ushering him forward.

*Yeah, of course you want me up front. Better to stab me.*

Caleb met the man's eyes, and wasn't sure if it was his anxiety or not, but Oomar seemed to be at the edge of his patience.

Caleb looked again at the passage — more like a crevice — and turned to Oomar.

"Okay," Caleb said, squeezing sideways inside.

As he pressed himself through, the cold rock walls on either side seemed to be closing in on him. The slightest tremor and surely the walls would collapse.

*Does this place have earthquakes? Well, obviously they wouldn't be called earthquakes here.*

He looked back, certain that the other men were still on the other side, that they'd tricked him into entering a death trap.

But Oomar was right behind him.

*Move, fast, or he's going to stab you and leave your body to rot.*

Caleb quickly shimmied his way through the passage,

then sucked in a deep breath as he arrived safe on the other side — a wide chamber with many glowing blue lanterns.

At the other end of the chamber he saw a violet doorway in the rock. Beside the door, a black wooden sign with a drawing of a moon with sensual red lips, and, in English, the words *Desire's Soma Den*.

Caleb sighed with relief, then noticed two halls to the right and left where people were streaming into the den, which meant that the narrow passageway wasn't the *only* way to reach the place, just the most fucking difficult.

He wanted to turn and yell at the men, asking why the hell they made him take that route but figured it was either a shortcut from where they were coming, or they were fucking with him. Either way, yelling wouldn't get him any closer to what he needed.

Oomar smacked Caleb's back again. "Get ready, Kindwood, you're about to have the time of your life!"

Caleb smiled uneasily as they led him through the door.

The first room inside the den was a piece of surrealistic painting.

Caleb had expected another small room carved into the subterranean rock, the roof almost pressing down on them.

Instead, the room was sprawling, scattered with tables seating a myriad of odd-looking people and creatures sitting, smoking, and drinking.

But it wasn't the room, nor its Otherworldly inhabitants, that nabbed Caleb's attention.

It was the ceiling, which was at least a hundred feet above, with roiling misty clouds atop it. And hanging from the ceiling, poking through the gray clouds, were trees, growing upside down.

Swirling golden lights floated around the trees, like strands of Christmas lights without strings, painting the mist and lighting the room with a warm glow. Caleb didn't know if this was magick or some natural phenomena, and was lost trying to make sense of what he saw.

Oomar noticed Caleb's awestruck expression. "Hey, Kindwood, you wanna look at the trees, or find yourself a woman?"

Caleb laughed. "It's just … so beautiful."

To his left, Hank said, "You haven't seen nothin' yet, friend."

"Come." Oomar led them past several tables. A few people looked up and nodded or greeted Oomar as they passed, with the large man returning quick, cordial greetings but wasting no time getting to where he needed to be.

The room's rear had a large winding black iron staircase. Oomar led them up, through the trees and fog, until they reached a landing leading to another chamber.

This room looked like a hotel lobby, with a woman greeting them from behind an oblong desk. She had long golden hair, looked no more than nineteen, and wore a blue silk robe revealing ample cleavage.

"Welcome, gentlemen," she smiled. "How many rooms?"

"One suite," Oomar said.

She told him it would be two hundred bits — quite a sum.

Caleb reached into his pants to pull out his coin pouch.

"Put your money away, Kindwood, I've got ya."

"You sure?" Caleb asked, surprised by Oomar's generosity. He was about to spend half of what he'd won from Caleb.

Oomar smiled, but there was only darkness in his eyes. "It's not every day we get royalty in here, Prince."

Caleb was about to turn and run.

But Hank stepped behind him, stone-faced, hand gripping a black blade.

Oomar looked at Caleb. "Now, now, let's not turn a lovely reunion into an ugly event."

"*Reunion?*" Caleb repeated, confused.

Oomar was no longer looking at him, his eyes fixed behind Caleb.

Caleb turned to see Jacob standing there, dressed in all black, smiling.

"Well, hello, Brother."

# THIRTY-SIX

# Abigail

THE MAN with the sword was large and old, with a big, bushy gray beard. He was wearing drab gray clothing with thick padding, and a wide belt with a sheath dangling from it.

"Who are *yu*?" He stared at them cautiously, looking as if he were on his way somewhere when the portal opened and the three girls suddenly appeared.

Judith stepped in front of Abigail and Talani.

"My name is Judith. We have come at the request of Cassandra Rollusulo. We came with her brother, Solomon. She is expecting us."

The man looked at them for a moment, and in a thick accent asked, "Where's 'er brothu?"

"He died trying to get us here. Attacked by bandits."

"Hand over *yur* weapons," the man said, "drop 'em on the floor. Then I shall take *yu* to Cassandra."

Abigail and Talani looked at Judith for guidance. She nodded, removing the sword from her sheath.

They laid down their weapons, though Abigail slid the blade Mother had given her deeper into her sleeve. She wasn't about to surrender her only protection against Judith.

"Come along, then." The man sighed then led them down the hall, leaving their weapons on the floor.

They walked in silence for about ten minutes, navigating underground tunnels, wide-open chambers with makeshift shops, and passersby — some human-looking like them, and many others looking very different, though not nearly as different as the things in the Sacred Woods.

Abigail wanted to ask questions, but the old man didn't seem all that talkative. So she kept her mouth shut, thinking instead about what she saw in the In-Between — how Judith had been a wicked person, capturing Talani and her sister only to sell them. She was a monster, just like Abigail's uncle, and she wanted to deliver the same justice she'd dealt to him.

Why had Talani begged her not to kill Judith? How could she protect the woman who destroyed Talani and her sister's, lives?

It didn't make any sense.

Abigail had once read about something called Stockholm Syndrome, where kidnapping victims fell under the spell of their captors. Sometimes the people were broken down over time; other times it was an odd natural reaction. But Abigail couldn't imagine ever feeling that way about the man who had kept her in his closet and raped her repeatedly. There was never a day she didn't want Randy Webster dead. Nor a day she didn't pray for him to die. There might have been days where she changed the prayer, asking for her own death instead, thinking that might be easier on God. But never did she fall under the demon's spell.

She looked at the back of Talani's head, and the side of her face, as she walked beside Judith.

*Why isn't she walking with me?*

*Is she mad at me?*

Abigail wondered if Talani was somehow bewitched by Judith. Or was there some other reason to defend the woman? She considered sending a message but was afraid to do so right next to Judith.

Talani had said Judith couldn't hear them so long as they blocked her out, as Talani had taught her. But what if she'd been lying? What if it was something that Judith had told Talani to tell Abigail?

Abigail also couldn't stop thinking about the offer — to accept Judith as her Master. Not only would she be saved from whatever might happen to her being far away from John for so long, but Judith could make Abigail appear older.

As much as Abigail wanted to be older — perhaps in her early twenties — she wouldn't let Judith be her *Master.*

No way, no how.

Of course that led Abigail to her conversation with Talani, about how a vampire separated from its Master would eventually get sick and start to die.

Abigail felt fine now, but what would happen once she fell ill? If they couldn't return to Earth, then she'd never see John again. Even if she managed to get home, what if she couldn't find him? He hadn't heard her calls before, and that's when he knew she was living with Larry. If they'd moved on from that house, she might not even be able to find John. Then she'd have to make a choice: die or allow Judith to be her Master.

Then Abigail thought of a reason that might make sense. Maybe Talani was defending Judith because she was the only person Talani knew who could become Abigail's Master. Maybe Talani didn't know how to do it, or couldn't. Maybe she was only keeping Judith alive to protect Abigail.

Abigail felt a crushing sorrow at the thought.

She also felt even more lost from John and Larry than ever before.

As they followed the old man through the subterranean labyrinth, Abigail felt a sudden horrible certainty that she was going to die in this place.

She looked at Talani, walking to Judith's right, and felt awful for whatever was happening between them.

She wanted to apologize, though she wasn't sorry for wanting to stick up for Talani. But she wanted to say sorry all the same.

*Maybe she's not mad. Maybe she's weirded out because she saw that I wanted her to kiss me.*

*Oh God, I hope she doesn't hate me.*

Abigail already felt alone. If she upset Talani, too, she couldn't see a reason to keep living.

She'd be alone, in a strange world, a monster that could never grow up, never have friends, and never know real love.

If Talani told her they couldn't be friends, Abigail might just step out into the sun and end it all.

She hastened her pace and fell in step to Talani's right.

Talani looked down at Abigail, eyes red as if she'd been crying.

Abigail reached out for Talani's hand.

Talani smiled; their fingers braided.

Abigail felt a smile spread across her lips.

Everything felt right again, if only for the moment.

Then they came to a blue door in a wall. It read *Madame Cassandra, Seer of All.*

The old man knocked. "Cassandra, I've got someone that says yu was waitin' for 'em."

The door opened almost at once.

In the doorway stood a woman who looked to be in her early forties, with long jet-black hair, in an all-black dress. Her eyes were red and puffy.

Judith spoke: "Hello, Cassandra. I'm afraid I've got bad news."

"I already know," Cassandra said, wiping a cloth against her nose and blowing. "Please, come in."

# THIRTY-SEVEN

# Hope

THEY ARRIVED at the Town of Jonah just before noon. The prisoner carriage pulled into a stable, the doors opened, then Hope, John, and Larry disembarked.

Her uncle, Gerald, thankfully now dressed, said, "Welcome to the Town of Jonah, second-best city in The Realms."

"Second?" asked Hope. "What's the first?"

"Under Harbor, of course. The town beneath the town. *That's* where all the interesting people reside."

He walked them through a secret doorway in the back of the stable, then down a rock stairway into the underground city, explaining the town's origins and how it was home to exiles from both the religious Golden Cove and The Forgotten Kingdom — King Zol's city of criminals and monsters.

"But this is a peaceful place," he said as they passed a tavern where six people were fighting, breaking glasses and cursing. "Well," Gerald said with a grin, "more peaceful than Zol's city, anyway."

Hope stared at the man, still unable to reconcile that

he had been the giant wolf who attacked them. "Uncle Gerald, can I ask you something?"

"Anything you want, sweetie."

"How did you become a werewolf?"

He laughed. Then, with obvious pride he said, "The right way — was born into it."

Hope suddenly had an awful thought. "My mother … Was she a werewolf?"

"Gods no. The curse didn't touch her."

"And me? I'm not a werewolf, am I?"

Gerald laughed so hard he fell into a fit of coughing. "Don't ya think you'd know if you was a werewolf?"

"I don't remember anything before going to Earth. And even then, I'm not exactly sure what's what."

Gerald turned and shot John and Larry both dirty looks. "These two men have anything to do with that?"

"No," Hope said, both annoyed at the man's persistent need to attack John, and also somewhat touched that she had family here so willing to stick up for her. "I lost my memories before I went over. How old was I the last time you saw me?"

"I dunno. Still quite young, not yet a woman."

"How did you recognize me?"

"We always recognize our kin. Plus, you look just like yer mum."

They continued walking for some time, Hope marveling at the underground city's interesting architecture — halls and rooms carved into the ground, without looking like subterranean hovels. Instead, many of the places they passed had wood flooring, running water, and even gardens somehow growing underground without daylight. Perhaps the most surprising part of all was how bright the place was. Lanterns were everywhere, but most were lit by something that didn't look like lamp oil, but rather glowing rocks and, in some cases, tiny floating glowing things that might have been Otherworldly fireflies giving off far more illumination than their Earthly counterparts.

Along the way to her mother's, they passed all sorts of odd-looking people with every manner of clothing. She saw blue people like that man who had captured them, she saw a pink woman who was walking around naked with no obvious genitalia, and she saw all sorts of people who resembled humans, many looking savage, as though they'd cut you to get whatever scraps you might have on you.

They finally came to a hallway with three doors on either side, each painted a different color, stopping in front of a blue one. Gerald knocked.

"Who is it?" said a woman's voice.

"It's me, Abalena. I've got her. I've got Esmee."

The door opened, and the woman appeared.

Just as Gerald had said, Abalena *did* look like Hope, just slightly taller and older.

She was wearing a long blue dress with an intricately woven flower design, azure threads woven through her hair, and a cornflower pinned where the threads began.

Her eyes were green, the whites of them tinged with red, as if she'd been crying.

Hope absorbed all of this in the split second before the woman threw her arms open and sobbed, pulling Hope into a hug.

Hope collapsed into her embrace, though missing memories prevented her own flood of emotions. Hope's mom, the one she remembered from her childhood, was a fifty-six-year-old woman named Mary, living in Palm Beach, Florida.

"Thank The Seven Gods. You're home!"

Her hug was strong. Her scent, sweet like flowers and something else, maybe perfume.

Abalena pulled away, holding Hope's face in her hands, staring deeply into her eyes. "I can't believe it. Oh, how you've grown into such a beautiful young lady!"

She kissed her on both cheeks, then hugged her again.

They stood that way until the moment yawned into something awkward. Finally, Gerald broke it up.

"Ya gonna let us in, or we just gonna stand here in the doorway all bleeding day?"

Hope laughed, small and honest.

Abalena ushered them into her home, a small, cozy place with wood-carved knickknacks on every shelf, and paintings on every wall.

She led them to chairs and a large leather couch in the living room, then asked if anyone wanted drinks.

They all said yes.

As her mother entered an adjoining kitchen, Hope kept staring at the paintings, all of them brushed in a similar style, and seemingly by the same person.

*She paints. Just like me!*

Hope followed the paintings along the home's far wall leading into a hallway and two other rooms. The paintings in the hall were all of a little girl — one on horseback, one in a field of flowers, and another floating in water.

The one with water had the word *Esmee* painted into the ripples, and beneath it the shape of a heart.

Hope felt something break inside her, thinking of the agony her mother must have gone through after she vanished so long ago. Though Hope had no memory of the woman, or their relationship, and had never had a child of her own, she could still imagine the pain of losing a daughter, of not knowing all these years whether she was dead or just stolen.

Tears welled in her eyes as she continued down the hall.

Then she saw a painting that nearly stopped her heart.

A painting she knew all too well because *she* had painted it, or one just like it, more than a decade ago in Saint Augustine.

A painting of John, nude, hovering against a dark violet background of churning storm clouds, hands outstretched with red rings of light swirling around them, suspended by two large white angel's wings.

She reached out to touch the painting, to dispel the sudden feeling that this was only her imagination.

It wasn't. The painting was as real as the wall that held it.

"Mother," she called out, the word feeling foreign on her tongue.

"Yes?" Abalena said, stepping into the hall.

"Did you paint this?"

"Yes. I painted them all. Why?"

Hope grabbed her mother's hand, led her back into the living room, and pointed to John.

"You painted him."

Abalena stared, then nodded. "You're right."

She smiled as if this was something that happened all the time. That it wasn't weird to paint a man she'd never met, a man from another world that her daughter had fallen in love with.

Hope said, "I painted him too. Painted the exact same painting more than ten years ago."

Abalena smiled. "You're a painter?"

"Don't you find it the least bit odd that we painted the same exact thing even though we hadn't seen each other in forever, and you'd never met him before?"

"We have the gift," Abalena said, as if Hope should understand what that meant.

"What gift?"

"We can see things that others can't. It's why that wizard took a shining to you, hoping to develop your skills."

"Wizard? What wizard?"

"VVessolff. Back when we lived under King Zol's rule. He had taken you as an apprentice of sorts, even though you were only a stable girl."

John stood and approached them. "She was an apprentice to The Last Great Wizard?"

"Yes, though I wish I'd never agreed to let her train. Had I know he'd vanish, and take you with him, I never would've let him near you. What happened, Esmee? Did *he* take you to Earth? Or was it that vulgar Prince Jacob?"

"It's a long story," Hope said. "I think I'll need that drink."

Hope sat between Larry and John on one couch while Gerald and Abalena sat in chairs opposite them, everyone sipping a warm beverage with heavy, aromatic spices, but not unpleasant, as she told her story — how she'd been a vessel for the wizard who had helped King Zol's two other sons escape, then hiding his soul inside six crystals buried in people he trusted whom he sent to Earth where the King could never reach them.

She then told them everything else, ending with why they were here — to retrieve the crystals.

Abalena shook her head. "No, it's too dangerous. If they have all the crystals, as you say, then they're unstoppable. There are no magick users left with a tenth of VVessolff's power. The Hand either killed or imprisoned them all."

John interrupted, "Imprisoned? Who?"

"There was a man here until late last year named Morloth. He lived in Under Harbor for some time after The Great War was over, Jonah hiding him from both The

North and The Hand when they were cracking down on magick. They purged anyone with true powers. But Morloth managed to hide among us for a while. Until one day The Hand sent its Covenant here to capture him. I don't know if Jonah had betrayed him or if someone else sold him out to collect a bounty, but either way, he's gone."

"How powerful was he?" John asked. "Could he fight the Valkoer?"

"If anyone could, I suppose it would be him, but I don't know how he could be found."

"We'll figure that part out," John said, his wheels obviously turning.

"Please, Esmee, stay here," Abalena said. "We have so much to catch up on, so many years stolen. Everyone thought you were dead, but I never gave up believing."

John asked, "Can you get me a meeting with Jonah?"

Gerald nodded. "I was gonna ask you to come meet him, anyway. You need to tell him what you told us about the prince and the crystals. If it's true, this might be the first place King Zol strikes seeing how Jonah is housing exiled enemies of the King."

John looked at Hope and Larry. "Can you two wait here?"

Larry looked momentarily disappointed not to be going along. But then he nodded. Hope figured that John must've sent him some telepathic message to stay behind and look after her.

John gave Hope a weak smile and said, "I love you," before following Gerald out of Abalena's home.

Hope returned to getting to know the mom she never knew she had.

# THIRTY-EIGHT

# Abigail

CASSANDRA HAD TURNED out to be quite nice. She worked as a seer, which Abigail guessed was like a psychic, though she had never believed in clairvoyants before, at least the kind she saw on TV that could tell the future. Cassandra had, however, claimed to have seen her brother die in a vision.

Cassandra said that she could set them up with a shop and a place to stay — if they didn't mind working on an underground farm.

Abigail was surprised that you could grow anything underground, but apparently some fruits and vegetables could grow pretty much anywhere on this world. Talani and Abigail's job would be to pick the fruit, wash it, and place it in boxes to go topside for sale at the market, with some of the rarer fruits shipped to The North. Judith's job was a bit different, and Cassandra asked to be alone with her to discuss it — which, to Abigail, meant it probably involved some sort of criminal element.

As Judith and Cassandra talked in the shop, Talani and Abigail were given permission to explore the general market level — the one they were already in — so long as they didn't take stairs to any other level.

Cassandra had said "any other level" as if all sorts of untold horrors awaited on every floor but this one.

Which, of course, made Abigail curious. But not enough to go exploring — at least not right now.

She and Talani were walking through a large open marketplace filled with stalls and tons of people buying and selling. Abigail was surprised by how many citizens lived underground. The girls talked about Under Harbor, Abigail wondering if they could actually kill the man they were supposed to take care of, Baltazar, and Talani saying that they had to because they "made a promise." Abigail kept hoping that Talani would lose interest, but it seemed like finding and killing the man was something she actually wanted to do.

"So," Talani asked, holding up the two coins that Cassandra had given them both, "how much do you think this'll get us?"

"I dunno," Abigail said, still holding hers in her pocket. "I am thirsty, though."

"Me, too," Talani said, looking around for a place that sold drinks. "I guess we're not going to find any soda fountains."

Abigail giggled. "Larry would *hate* it here."

Talani didn't respond, instead pointing to a stall where some people were standing around talking and laughing. They were holding large glasses of pink liquid. "Think it's lemonade?" Talani asked, already heading toward the stall to find out.

Abigail followed.

The stall was manned by a short blue man with bushy black eyebrows and big tufts of hair.

He reminded Abigail of a Smurf, so she had to choke back her laughter.

"What can I get for ya, ladies?" the man asked in what sounded a lot like an Irish accent, not that she'd ever heard one in real life.

"What are those pink drinks?" Talani pointed to a couple of women standing nearby sipping from them.

"Those are Miquari fruit drinks, guaranteed to cure whatever ails ya!"

Talani winked at Abigail, "Oh really? *Anything?*"

"Headache, body aches, nerves, coming down with a foul temper, or a bit of the runny tummy, Miquari fruit drinks will cure ya quick!"

"Wow, sounds like snake oil," Talani said.

The blue man didn't get the reference, or that Talani was being sarcastic. He kept on smiling. "*Snake oil?* I didn't know snakes produced oil, and if they do, who would *drink* such a thing?" He made a face like he might vomit. "No, these are Miquari fruit drinks, straight from the Calladian Mountain region. Practically dripping with magick."

"Magick?" Abigail asked, "what kind of magick?"

Talani spoke inside Abigail's mind. *Come on, this guy is a snake oil salesman; don't buy the hype.*

"Oh, all kinds of magick, me lady. As I said, it cures everything, but" — the blue man leaned closer in a conspiratorial whisper — "*it also delivers whatever your heart desires.*"

Talani grabbed Abigail by the arm. "No thank you, sir."

"Wait," Abigail said, resisting her friend. "How much is it?"

"One piece if you drink it here, four if you take the glass."

Abigail fished into her pocket, pulling out both silver coins. She looked at Talani, "Want one?"

"No," Talani said, giving the blue man a dirty look.

"Just one, please, and I'll drink it here," Abigail said handing the blue man his piece.

He put the money in his pocket then turned around, grabbed a glass, brought it to a big wooden barrel atop the table behind him, turned a spigot, and smiled as it filled with the pink, frothy juice.

"Here you go, me lady," he said, handing it to Abigail with flourish.

She liked him. Sure, his juice might not be a cure-all or magickal, but he had a nice smile, and was friendly.

She walked toward where the other people were standing, off to the side of the man's stall, lifted the drink to her nose, and deeply inhaled.

"Weird," she said, thrusting the glass toward Talani to smell.

Talani waved it off. "I don't want to smell that."

"You have to," Abigail said, "it smells like oranges and vanilla!"

Talani looked at her suspiciously, then took the glass to her nose.

Her nose wrinkled before a reluctant smile spread across her face.

"You're right, it does!"

"Wanna taste it? You can have some."

"Nah, you drink the *magick juice*," she said, rolling her eyes.

"Fine." Abigail grabbed the glass and turned her nose up at Talani. "I'll drink the whole thing."

She lifted the glass again, stopping just short of drinking it, and looking closely at the thick glass. She could see tiny seeds — purple, orange, red, and yellow —

floating in the frothy white bubbles, and the glass wasn't particularly cold.

She hesitated.

"Gross, eh?" Talani asked, smiling.

Abigail couldn't let her friend be right. She shook her head, "Nope, just admiring before I drink it."

"Uh-huh," Talani said. "You keep telling yourself that."

Abigail lifted the glass to her mouth and took a deep gulp.

At first, she gagged, but then, as its flavor flooded her senses, the drink tasted even better than it smelled. She couldn't quite place the flavor. It didn't taste like orange *or* vanilla, but it was sweet and creamy, even if not very cold.

"Well, how is it?"

"Good!" Abigail said with a huge smile. "*Very* good!"

She took another swig.

"Yeah, is it magickal?" Talani asked, with a grin.

"Ha ha," Abigail said, finishing the drink in two more huge gulps.

She surprised herself with a loud burp.

"Eww," Talani said. "Soooo gross."

Abigail laughed, then so did Talani.

People were starting to stare, but Abigail didn't care.

"You sure you don't want one?"

"Fine," Talani said, her body language and face both begrudging.

Abigail laughed. "I knew you would."

After Talani finished her drink, and Abigail had another one, they decided to walk the huge courtyard surrounded by shops.

It was filled with gardens, a small babbling brook, and a few trees that stretched to the rock ceiling, and seemingly through it.

She was considering ways to bring up the whole Judith thing when something small and black ran past them, ducking into a nearby thicket.

"Was that a kitty?" Abigail asked excitedly.

Talani looked at her, "A kitty?"

"Yeah, a cat. I think I saw a cat run past us."

"You act like you've never seen one before."

"Not up close, I haven't."

"What? Are you for real?"

"Yeah. My mother was allergic to cats, and Randy wasn't exactly a be-kind-to-animals sort."

Talani smiled. "Wow. I can't believe you never saw a cat. Come on, let's see if it'll let you pet it."

Abigail followed Talani toward the bushes, and squeed with delight when she saw the tiny thing with big blue eyes looking up at them, mewling.

Talani bent down to pick it up carefully.

For a moment Abigail was scared that Talani's touch might kill the cat. But nothing happened.

The cat didn't hiss or bite, and let her pick it right up.

She handed the ball of fur to Abigail. "Here, you hold it."

Abigail opened her hands and brought it up to her chest.

The cat let out a tiny cry, its blue eyes looking up at Abigail.

"Oh my God, it's soooooo cute."

Talani smiled as Abigail gingerly stroked its head.

The cat started to vibrate, purring so loud that it made Abigail laugh.

"I think it likes you."

"You think?" Abigail asked, looking down. It was so light and tiny in her hands. "You think he, or she, is a newborn? Where's your mommy, little guy?"

The cat mewled again.

"Think he's hungry?"

Talani shrugged, looking around. "Maybe Mr. Magick Fruit Drink Guy has some milk he can give us."

"Good idea," Abigail said as she headed back to his stand.

The man was dealing with another customer, so Abigail waited, petting the cat, an overwhelming feeling of joy swelling inside her.

When it was her turn in line, she asked, "Excuse me, do you have some milk to give this kitten? He looks hungry."

The man looked at Abigail oddly. "You want to *feed* the cat?"

"Yeah, why not?" Abigail asked.

"It's a cat," he said as if the answer was self-evident.

"I know it's a cat, mister. Do you have any milk?"

The man shook his head. "No, you'll be hard pressed to find *milk* in these parts."

Abigail sighed. "Well, what else do kittens eat?"

He looked at Abigail as if she were crazy.

Talani came up behind them, smiling like she was as happy as Abigail to have found the cat.

"What's wrong?" Talani asked, sensing something between the blue man and Abigail.

Abigail turned to her. "He doesn't have any milk. And when I asked what else cats eat, he just sorta looked at me," she turned to see the man still looking at her, and she pointed, "like that!"

Talani burst out laughing.

Abigail laughed too, though she wasn't sure why. Suddenly, everything felt hilarious.

Talani repeated Abigail's question, asking what else cats eat.

"I dunno, find a mouse," the man said, dropping his kind demeanor then turning his attention, and phony smile, to another customer in line.

"What did *I* do?" Abigail said, surprised by his reaction.

He walked over to her and whispered, "Maybe you all had a bit too much of the juice if you think it's funny to harass me with games, asking if I have milk for a damned cat."

He abruptly turned. Abigail thought he looked like a Smurf again, and started laughing hysterically. *Angry Smurf!*

People began to give her and Talani dirty looks.

Which, for some reason, made everything so much funnier.

Abigail couldn't stop laughing.

Nor could Talani.

"Go on," someone nearby said, "take your cat somewhere else."

Talani looked at Abigail, her eyebrows narrowing. "Man, people *really* don't like cats here, do they?"

"Come on, kitty, let's take you somewhere else, where people can appreciate you!" Abigail said, turning with a huff.

They began walking back the way they'd come.

"You think we can keep him?" Abigail asked.

Talani's eyes widened, and she started laughing louder and harder.

"Oh my God!" she said.

"What?"

"I just realized why everyone is looking at us funny."

"Why?" Abigail asked.

"People don't keep cats as pets here."

"They don't?"

"No. I mean, some farmers keep them to chase vermin away, but they're not really pets like we think of them back on Earth."

"Oh," Abigail said with a frown. "That kinda sucks."

Talani burst out laughing again.

Abigail, not sure what was so funny, joined in, unable to help herself. She laughed so hard she began to cough.

Suddenly, likely in response to Abigail's cough, the cat leaped away and ran down the hall away from them.

"No, kitty!" Abigail said, chasing after it. "I'm sorry."

Abigail ran, trying to keep up, but the cat was too fast, disappearing around a bend before Abigail reached it. She turned the corner and found three forks in the path, tunnels leading straight, left, and right. But Abigail couldn't tell which one the cat had gone down.

"Crap!" she said as Talani caught up. "I lost the kitty."

Talani pointed to her nose. "I can smell her. This way," she said, pointing straight.

They ran as fast as they dared in the narrow dark hallway, past several closed doors that seemed like they might lead into homes, until the hallway ended at a stairwell.

Abigail looked at Talani. "Can you tell which way she went?"

"Down, I think."

Abigail started down the stairs.

"Wait!" Talani said, "Remember? We're supposed to stay on this level."

Abigail sighed. "Oh, yeah."

She looked down the dark stairwell, suddenly sad that the cat was gone.

"I scared it away," Abigail said, her lip trembling as her eyes welled up with tears.

Talani began to cry too.

"The kitty's gone!" Abigail cried louder.

"I'm sorry," Talani said, coming over and hugging Abigail.

They stood there, pathetic and crying, until suddenly Talani started to laugh.

"What?" Abigail asked, pulling away with a hopeful smile, thinking maybe the cat had come back.

"Oh my God, that drink isn't magick; it makes us an emotional mess! I never cry. Especially over a cat!"

"He's a cute cat," Abigail argued, her feelings hurt, though she didn't know why.

Then she started laughing, too.

"Never drinking that stuff again," Talani said, still laughing.

Abigail looked back down the stairs, feeling horrible that she scared the cat off of his level.

"What if he gets lost? What if his mommy can't find him down here? He might starve."

"Please," Talani said. "Stop. Don't make me cry again!"

"I don't want the cat to die," Abigail said, still crying. "We need to go find it."

"But Cassandra told us not to go upstairs *or* downstairs."

The way she emphasized "or" made Abigail laugh — which sent Talani into hysterics, too.

Abigail clenched her jaw. "I don't care what she said. She's not the boss of us."

Talani really started laughing at that, which made Abigail giggle like crazy.

"Fine," Talani said, "but if we die, I'm gonna kill you."

Abigail laughed as they descended the stairs in search of the kitten.

# THIRTY-NINE

## Caleb

CALEB OPENED his eyes to a blurry world.

He was in a bed, in a dark room, but couldn't remember how he got there or where he was.

A woman's hand stroked his chest.

Slowly, she came into focus, the blur receding.

A fireplace's warm glow lit enough of the room for him to see her — a redhead with bright green eyes, long hair, and freckled cheeks.

"Hello," she said in his tongue, with a thick accent suggesting it wasn't her language.

"Where am I?" he asked, confused but feeling a deeper bliss than any he'd ever felt.

The thing about pills, or any opiate, was there was never a time like your first. After that, you were caught in a hopeless loop of chasing the next high, needing more drugs to inch closer to that first time. But over time, your senses dulled and the drug could only help you feel normal.

But this, whatever he'd been given, erased all that.

This was like tapping into some cosmic bliss that

spread warmth and a deep feeling of love through his entire being.

Though some part of Caleb knew he should've been concerned that he didn't know where he was, or whom he was with, most of him didn't care.

He only wanted to feel more of the bliss.

He reached over, cupping the girl's left breast, then running his hand down her stomach.

She sighed as he slid his fingers along her lips.

He was instantly hard.

He wanted to be inside her more than he wanted to know where he was, whom he was with, or how he got here.

He climbed on top of her, looked into her beautiful eyes, captivated by her slightly crooked smile.

He leaned down, kissed her, gently at first, then devouring her mouth as every fiber of him exploded with joy.

He thrust himself inside, watched her eyes roll back in her head.

He leaned down to kiss her again, practically growling.

Her fingers clawed into his back, and the pain was euphoric.

He wouldn't have cared if she cut him. Hell, he almost wanted it.

Wanted to be part of her, one with her, to ravish her, to … consume her.

Her eyes locked onto his.

"Hurt me," she said in broken English.

Something animal snapped inside him.

His eyes locked onto hers, too.

He smacked her face.

She smiled, biting her lip.

"Again," she said.

He thrust deeper, harder, suddenly wanting to both fuck *and* hurt her.

His hands found her throat, and he choked her.

And as he did, he grew harder still.

A part of him tried to make sense of this. He'd never had violent fantasies, but as Caleb hurt this woman, something inside him was responding — exploding, a flood of endorphins, and what felt like a hundred other chemicals in his brain, suddenly energized in a way he'd never felt.

He felt *alive* like never before.

He looked down at the woman, and squeezed tighter.

Her eyes were glassy, like she was wasted, too.

"Harder."

He obliged, both in fucking, and choking.

Her eyes suddenly bulged, panicked, as if just waking up to what was happening.

She made a noise, began to squirm out from beneath him.

A part of him knew he should let go, but that part had lost control.

Something else was guiding him.

Something that didn't know mercy or empathy.

He kept thrusting, harder, faster.

She reached up, trying to pull his fingers away from her throat. Clawing at his hands and arms, trying to scrape at his face.

He growled, ignoring the pain, feeding from it, fueling it to fuck her harder.

As her face turned red, then purple, he found himself unable to stop, thrusting faster, until he was about to release.

But then something happened.

His hands locked on the girl's throat, and he sucked the energy from her.

He could see her memories rushing by, feel her energy coursing through him.

And as he came in a shattering orgasm, her body burned with him still inside her.

Then whatever was controlling him let go.

And Caleb was alone with what he'd done.

He screamed, pulling himself off of the girl as her body turned to ashes in the bed.

He looked down at his hands, and had a sickening flashback.

*Julia.*

He'd taken his wife's life in his sleep, while dreaming. An accident he had no control over.

But this … This was different.

It was as if he did have control, as if he *wanted* to do this.

He shook his head.

*No, no, no.*

He heard a clapping, and realized he wasn't alone.

He spun around to face the shadows.

Jacob sat in a corner, his eyes practically glowing in the darkness.

Caleb remembered where he was, though still not how he arrived. The last thing he remembered was turning around to see his brother.

How did he get into bed with the woman? What had Jacob done to him?

"Doesn't it feel good to finally embrace what you are?"

Caleb's fists balled at his sides, and he rushed toward his brother, eager to kill him.

But then he froze, unable to move.

Caleb couldn't see for certain, but felt Jacob smiling.

"Now, now, is that any way to treat your long-lost brother?"

"What did you do to me?"

"I'm helping you become what you were meant to be. To find your true nature. And might I say, you … *performed* quite well."

"I didn't do that," Caleb said, shaking his head. "You … you somehow got in my head and controlled me."

Jacob laughed, raising his hands. "Okay, okay, you got me. But didn't it feel so good? I know you were there, experiencing it, just like me. And it was pretty fucking awesome, am I right? I forgot just how good sex can feel."

"That wasn't sex. That was …"

"Please, enough with the hysterics, Brother. You enjoyed it as much as I did. Or," he said, looking up and down Caleb's naked body, the stickiness all over his cock, "maybe more?"

Caleb wanted to cover up, but his body refused to obey his mind.

"Sit," Jacob said.

Caleb fell backward on the bed, forced to comply.

"You and I are going to talk. And you're going to tell me what I want to know. Do you understand me?"

"Fuck you."

Suddenly, Caleb's body was standing again, marching toward Jacob, against his will.

As he got closer, he wanted to reach out, strangle the fucker.

But Caleb was merely a marionette under his brother's telepathic instructions.

Jacob reached into his jacket, pulled out a blade — silver and sharp rather than black.

He handed the blade to Caleb.

Caleb's fingers closed around the hilt.

He wanted to drive it through Jacob's eye socket, straight into his brain.

Jacob laughed as Caleb struggled to break free. "You so desperately wish to kill me. What did I ever do to you? I spared you, brother. I liberated you from that cunt of a mother and this is how you repay me?"

Caleb grunted.

"Sit back on the bed."

Caleb's body turned.

*No, no, stay. Kill the fucker!*

His body continued to disobey.

He sat back on the bed.

"Stab yourself in the gut, Brother."

Caleb laughed.

*Yeah, right.*

But then his hand turned the blade around.

*No, no, no!*

His fingers tightened around the grip.

He then thrust the blade into his own stomach.

Caleb screamed.

*You fuck!*

"Silence!" Jacob commanded.

Caleb shut up, whimpering as his warm, sticky blood drizzled over his fingers and the hilt of the blade.

"Now, as I said, you will tell me everything, Brother. Beginning with how the hell you came to be part of The Hand of the Seven Gods."

FORTY

## Raina

RAINA HAD TRIED to take care of things on her own when she noticed that Caleb had left Golden Cove.

She tried to contact him telepathically, but he was either ignoring her attempts to connect or something had happened to him.

She only knew that he was in Under Harbor, not responding.

She would go on her own, but a horrible feeling lodged in her gut finally got the better of her. She'd gone to Prophet Malachi and told him what she thought Caleb was trying to do. He immediately assembled a team, riding to Under Harbor with twenty of their best soldiers on horseback led by himself and Raina.

She was wrapped head to toe, hood covering her face in shadow, masking what little sun bled through the cloudy late afternoon sky.

The ride had been mostly silent, but she could tell that Malachi was pissed. At Caleb for undermining his authority, and at her for not coming to him immediately after

Caleb mentioned going to Jonah to investigate the Valkoer attack on Crow's Nest.

As they approached the Town of Jonah, Malachi finally said, "Do you trust him?"

"Caleb?" she asked, looking back to make sure the others were out of earshot. Caleb had already suffered difficulties with the more strident members of The Covenant who took issue with his role — the last thing she wanted was to offer ammunition to their dear leader, who apparently also doubted his loyalty. It was one thing to have one Valkoer in The Covenant, two was a bit much for many, and some of their hate was seeping through in their interactions with her. Fortunately, Raina was The Covenant General, and her title still held enough power to prevent abuse. But she had no doubt that people were always angling to take her position away by other means.

"Yes, Caleb. Do you think he went behind our backs, conspiring with the Valkoer in Under Harbor?"

"To what end?"

"He knows some of our weaknesses, those of cities in The Southern Realm. He could deliver information to plan more attacks, and destabilize our leadership. If The Hand of the Seven Gods can't keep the people safe, then perhaps the rabble will begin to reconsider their allegiance to The Seven Gods. There are other groups out there that would love to take our supporters — The True Believers, The Freemen's Association, The Faith Alliance, and The Doctrine Promise — not to mention King Zol's own rotten kingdom."

"I can't see Caleb doing that. He has helped us secure many towns against evil threats. And saved many lives. It's what he did on Earth. It's who he is. He has lost a lot, and that pain drives him."

"Like you?" Malachi said, with an arched eyebrow.

"What are you implying?"

"Nothing," he said, a smile belying his thoughts. "But does he have the faith?"

"Yes, I think so," she lied.

"Really?" Malachi asked, eyebrow arched yet again. "Then I must doubt your ability to honestly assess him. Which means that either you've lost your ability to read people, or just Caleb specifically. And if it's him specifically, then we must ask, why? Do you love him?"

"No," Raina scoffed, glaring at Malachi. "I serve The Seven Gods."

"Good. Because I was starting to wonder if you'd forgotten your vows to The Seven Gods."

She didn't like the smug way Prophet Malachi was eying her, as though he knew some truth that she refused to admit. Like he knew her better than she knew herself. She wanted to wipe that smug grin from his face.

Something changed in his expression. The smile faded, replaced by something cautious, and Raina was afraid that maybe she'd revealed too much. That he saw her true feelings.

She'd done so well over the years hiding her growing distaste for the man and his ways. She did believe in The Seven Gods, and in their mission. Her faith in the religion was never in question. But her faith in its leader was, which presented a dissonance she couldn't quite reconcile. How can you have faith in a religion but not the man who birthed it? If one was corrupt, how could the other be innocent? Was he a fraud, as the heathens accused, making a religion just to control others?

Or could he have started off with the best intentions, truly inspired by his encounter with The Gods so long ago, then fallen off track, warped by the day-to-day shite that wore away at everyone's souls like rain against a mountain?

They came to the gates of Jonah as the sun set behind them and dismounted their steeds.

The gates were open but guarded by six men on the ground who checked anyone attempting entrance. Several additional guards were lined along two towers on either side of the gates, arrows ready to fell anyone attempting to force their way in.

The lead guard, an old heavyset man with a thick beard, instantly recognized Malachi. He approached and said, "Hello, Prophet Malachi. How may I help you this evening?"

"I'm here to see Jonah about an urgent manner."

"Of course," the man said, waving Malachi and Raina through, taking their weapons as was procedure.

The guard tried to stop the rest of the men from following, but they ignored his attempts to get in the way.

"Prophet Malachi, we must ask that your men stay behind, as we have no proper escorts for so many people."

Malachi turned, slowly approaching the man, measuring him.

"We are The Covenant of the Seven Gods. Surely, *we* don't need escorts. Right?" He said this with a smile and threatening eyes.

The guard looked down. "No, sir."

"Very well, then," Malachi said, leading the way into Jonah.

~

THE GUARDS, all of them with their weapons, waited just inside the city gates while Raina and Malachi went to meet Jonah.

They arrived at a dark tavern by the sea called The Lonely Fisherman, where Jonah could be found most hours, drinking or sometimes tending bar. He was the town's leader, but very much a man of the people. *Perhaps too much*, thought Raina. Being that accessible, especially when you spent much of your time drinking or smoking soma, seemed like it would eventually erode the people's respect.

But the folks in the fishing town were a different breed than most in The Southern Realm, and Raina was reasonably certain that there was nothing Jonah could do to lose his people's respect. His legend was too great, and lesser men had ruled with weaker lore to their name.

They found Jonah in the back of the bar sitting alone at a table with several empty glasses of lager before him, and another two full ones ready to go. A soma pipe sat to his left, and in front of him, a leather-bound book he was writing in.

He looked up and quickly closed the book as they approached, adopting a smile that said he was happy to see them. But, like Malachi earlier, the smile didn't match his eyes.

He stood and offered his hand. "Welcome to Jonah, Prophet Malachi and Sister Raina. What brings you to our town?"

Raina could tell by his body language that something was happening.

Malachi said, "I wish we were here under better circumstances. Could we have a word with you, alone?"

Jonah looked around as if he'd lost something, then turned to Malachi. "Yes. Come to my office."

Jonah grabbed the soma pipe, his book, and one of the two full steins, then led them through a door in the rear of the tavern to his private office.

The back of the tavern was as grimy and dark as the rest of the place, but Raina had seen worse.

They took seats around a small, wobbly circular table. Jonah wiped two decks of cards aside and onto the floor, then set his drink and pipe on the surface.

"I'd offer you a drink, but I know better. Would you like some water?"

"No, thank you," Raina said.

Malachi didn't answer, getting right to business. "We're looking for one of our Brothers. Caleb. Have you seen him?"

Raina watched the man's face for any sign of deception.

"No, can't say that I have. What makes you think he came here?"

He didn't seem to be lying about Caleb, but the man was definitely hiding something. She could feel it like a horse hidden under a sheet.

Malachi said, "Caleb was on his way to Under Harbor, hoping to speak to an informant and find out about a Valkoer attack on Crow's Nest."

"Ah yes, I heard about the attack. A true shame. A pleasant town that never did anything to anyone."

"Yes," Malachi said, "and we have reason to believe that the Valkoer responsible are from Under Harbor."

"*Here?*" Jonah laughed, then took a swig of his drink. "Impossible."

Malachi turned his head slightly to the side. "*Impossible? Why do you say that?*"

"Because nobody here would ever do such a thing." Jonah set his mug on the table with a thud. Lager splashed, but no one looked at the mess. The men's eyes were locked, broaching a messy conversation.

Malachi folded his hands on his lap. "You're a good man, Jonah, and you see the best in your people. It's an admirable trait. One I aspire to myself. But I can't help seeing the unrepentant people for what they are: *wicked*."

Jonah crossed his arms over his barrel of a chest. "I'm not repentant, nor do I bow to The Seven. Am *I* wicked?"

Raina considered intervention before this turned into a battle of egos, but anything she said now would be dismissed by Malachi, especially considering her ice was already thin.

Malachi took a moment before responding, then, "*All men* are wicked who do not come before The Seven. That's not a slight on you, Jonah. You are an admirable man, and a great leader of your people. I respect that. But you, like anyone, are prone to men's frailties until you allow the light of The Seven into your soul. This is a fact, not a judgment."

Jonah's smile disappeared. He stared silently at Malachi, eyes red and glassy, arms still folded over his chest.

Malachi didn't take the bait. He simply returned the man's stare, hands folded on the wobbly table, fake smile on his face, looking as calm as one used to calling the shots.

Jonah finally broke. "What is it you want?"

"I want to talk to Baltazar. Caleb was meeting with him."

Jonah nodded. "I spoke with him an hour ago. He said nothing of your Brother's visit."

"Just the same, I'd like to talk to him."

"And if you don't like his answers, what then? I'm not turning over any of my people, not until I can conduct an investigation. I hope you will recognize our sovereignty."

Raina wondered if Malachi would get into an argument over the town's independence. While the Town of Jonah was recognized as a free town under its own jurisdiction, it also operated under a treaty that forbade the existence of Under Harbor. Both towns existed because everyone looked the other way. But the Kingdoms *could* take issue with the secret city and revoke the Town of Jonah's inclusion as a recognized city or invoke sanctions that would instantly cripple the town's trading and economy.

Malachi didn't argue the matter. He simply nodded and said, "I'm not here as an enemy, Jonah. I'm here in the spirit of cooperation, hoping to prevent more massacres in The Southern Realm, and rule out anyone in Under Harbor. Because if it's not your people, then it's King Zol's, and I'm sure you can see how *that* can be a problem for all of us."

Jonah uncrossed his arms and nodded.

"May I speak to Baltazar?"

Jonah finished his drink, stood, then stuffed the pipe into his pocket and pointed toward the door. "Let us talk to him now."

~

THEY DESCENDED into Under Harbor and followed a series of tunnels toward the shopping district, finding Baltazar at his smithing shop hunched over a grinding wheel, sharpening a long silver sword. Behind him, leaning against the wall, were another two dozen swords waiting to be sharpened.

She wondered if this was normal business or if he was preparing his people for war.

Baltazar was a bear of a man. Nearly seven feet tall, broad-shouldered, and with long dark brown hair and a long scruffy beard. Despite his terrifying appearance, he was soft-spoken and clearly intelligent. In Raina's past conversations with him, he was as likely to talk about history and philosophy as about weapons or war.

He looked up from the grinding wheel and sighed, almost as if he were expecting Malachi and Raina, then stopped his work.

He walked over and shook Malachi's hand, then Raina's. She couldn't help but focus on the Shadow Guild ring on his finger — the lantern in a cave, signifying the group as the only light in an otherwise dark world. She supposed that even thieves and assassins had to feel like they were part of something noble, though she couldn't quite nail the moral acrobatics required to think stealing and murder were actions of light and not the essence of darkness they claimed to illuminate.

"Good evening, Brother and Sister."

Jonah said, "Prophet Malachi and Sister Raina would like to talk to you about what happened at Crow's Nest."

"I figured you would come round sooner or later. Hold on a moment."

He went to the shop's door and locked it, then led them to the back, into a dark storage room packed to the ceiling with shelves stocked with weapons, metals, stones, leather, and everything else he needed to run his shop. It was a rat's nest — Raina wondered how the man ever found anything.

Baltazar invited them to sit at a small wooden table with four chairs around it.

Raina sat last, putting her chair in position to see the door behind Malachi, in case this was some sort of trap.

It wasn't that she didn't trust Baltazar, but one never knew what sort of people were running the show in Under Harbor, or what leverage they might have to turn Baltazar against former allies. Jonah was the ostensible leader, but there were several organizations and factions at play — the merchants, the Magick Guild, the Shadow Guild, the Arcane Philosophers, and a half-dozen more.

The Shadow Guild ran the black market, was composed mostly of thieves with connections to crooks and swindlers in The Southern Realm's many other kingdoms, but the guild's true real power was the assassins operating within. And Baltazar was their unofficial leader.

Malachi asked, "So, what do you know about Crow's Nest?"

"I heard it was Valkoer that did it. There was allegedly someone from the Shadow Guild, or at least a Valkoer with a Shadow Guild ring on his finger, aye?"

"Yes," Malachi said.

"Who was it?"

"We didn't recognize him. Are any of your men missing?"

"Not a one. First thing I did was ask around, check in with the Valkoer living here. Nobody is unaccounted for, nor does anyone know anything."

Malachi shifted in his seat, crossed one leg over another. "So this *wasn't* a sanctioned Shadow Guild mission?"

"Gods no. Why would we ever attack Crow's Nest? It's a tiny farming community, one that supplies food to our towns here."

"I don't know, maybe one of your associates wanted to take over the farms, control supply *and* demand?"

Baltazar's brow furrowed. "If you think I'd allow that, then you don't know me well, Prophet Malachi. There is a code, even among assassins. At least *here* there is."

"Of course," Malachi said, "no offense intended. But you can see why I must ask."

"Of course."

"So, does anyone know anything? I mean, surely

*someone* has to be talking? You don't have a massacre like this without *any* rumors!"

"There are always rumors," Baltazar said, "but if you want *facts*, I'd suggest looking south."

"South? Do you mean the Forgotten Kingdom?"

"I do."

"What makes you say that?"

"Who would stand most to eliminate Under Harbor?"

"The King?" Malachi asked.

"He's been looking for ways to shut us down for years. The more people he loses to us, the more knowledge we have of his inner workings. He fears the inevitable."

"What's that?"

"An uprising within his city."

"And what would you know about any such uprisings?" Malachi asked with a mischievous grin.

"You can talk to the Arcane Philosophers. I refuse to get involved in *that* mess."

Baltazar went on to tell them a bit about how exiles from The Forgotten Kingdom were actively trying to make the King look bad, but it seemed like mostly minor things to Raina. They'd never kill an entire town of people to destabilize Zol's kingdom. It wasn't even a matter of ethics, Baltazar explained, but merely logic. The ends didn't justify the means in this particular case. This wasn't the way they wanted Zol to go down.

"It's got to be someone else," Baltazar said.

Raina asked, "So you think *King Zol* would sanction an attack on Crow's Nest just to have us, or The North, step in and retaliate against Under Harbor?"

Baltazar looked at Raina as if she were daft. "Does it seem that far-fetched? This is a man who, before the Treaty, routinely hung enemies of the Kingdom in the town center. Destroying a tiny hamlet would cause no lost sleep."

Raina saw the logic, though she didn't acknowledge it. Nobody beneath the Prophet could ever undermine his position, especially in front of others outside The Church. She looked at him, waiting for a response.

"That makes sense, Brother Baltazar. Thank you for your wisdom."

Raina noticed that Jonah, who had been tense and on the edge of his seat the entire time, finally seemed to relax. This led her to wonder how much control Baltazar, as soft-spoken as he was in person, exerted over Jonah. Was Jonah afraid of the man, or of the Shadow Guild? Or was he just relieved that the likelihood of a political shitstorm in Under Harbor and the Town of Jonah seemed to signifi-cantly recede now that Baltazar had turned their focus on King Zol?

"There is one other matter I wish to discuss," Malachi said.

Jonah's tension returned. Baltazar stayed calm.

Malachi continued, "Have you seen Brother Caleb?"

"I have."

Malachi uncrossed his legs. "You have?"

"Yes, he was seen entering a soma den in the dark district earlier, as reported by one of my spies. I know nothing beyond that, save for the fact that he has yet to leave."

"Can you take us there?"

Baltazar looked at Jonah for a moment, as if seeking permission.

If Jonah nodded or gave any affirmation, Raina missed it.

Baltazar then said, "I think it's best for our relationship that we not be seen together in public, at least not in the dark district, lest people figure out that I'm giving you information."

"Fair point." Malachi nodded then looked at Jonah. "Will you take us?"

Jonah nodded. "Sure."

As they were about to leave Baltazar's storage room, he said, "Hold on a moment. You shouldn't go unarmed."

He went to a bench where several blades were laid in a row, then brought them two, silver and onyx. "This'll take care of Valkoer and werewolves. Just try not to kill any of my clan."

"Thank you," Raina said, wondering what they were walking into.

# FORTY-ONE

# Abigail

THEY'D BEEN FOLLOWING the cat's scent for nearly thirty minutes, down several levels and hallways, when Abigail finally found the courage to ask what had been on her mind since the In-Between.

"Why are you still with Judith?"

Talani didn't look at her, just kept walking ahead of Abigail.

For a moment Abigail wasn't sure if she'd heard, but then she wondered if Talani was ignoring, or mad at, her.

Abigail kept following her for another minute, working the courage to ask again, or maybe reframe her question into something less direct.

But she didn't need to.

"I don't know how much you saw, but she's not the monster she used to be."

"I saw her with some bad man. They came and took you and your sister away. Then they sold you to some terrible people. That *is* what happened, right? Because if it is, I'm not sure how anyone could ever make up for that."

"She was under Hugo's control. He was an evil man who had been her mother's pimp, for lack of a better word. She grew up in a brothel in Skelltown, a place long since burned to the ground by The Hand. Judith's mother died when she was twelve, and left her with nowhere to go."

"Why didn't she just leave?"

"You don't leave a man like Hugo. He had minions everywhere. She had no resources and would've spent a lifetime looking over her shoulder. She took the only option she saw. Agreed to be with him. He turned Judith, made her a Valkoer, used her to find other young, vulnerable girls."

"She didn't have to do that. We all have choices."

Talani kept looking straight ahead. "That's easy to say when it isn't you. Anyway, Judith did this for several years, and felt a little more dead inside with every girl turned. Then she found my sister and me."

Talani grew quiet as they entered a more populated hallway, waiting until they were alone again before continuing.

"She found us, sold us to this woman named Esmerelda, who works for King Zol, providing slaves of all types to his kingdom's Elite. I don't know what happened to Raina. I was only allowed to leave my room to eat and bathe, always in small groups and under constant guard."

"Were you ... sex slaves?"

"Yes, but sometimes worse."

"Worse?"

"Some of the men had very particular tastes, seeking ever younger, even more innocent children. Not for sex but rather the theft of their memories. Sometimes they'd do it in the way you know, and leave the child more or less dead.

But there was also another way — turning a child into a Valkoer to keep them alive, in perpetual bondage, there for the plucking of memories. And then, of course, there were the ones who double dipped, stealing both our bodies *and* minds."

Abigail's stomach churned at the thought. As awful as Randy had been, he could never truly get inside her mind. Abigail's thoughts were *hers*. She had a place to hide during the worst of it — reliving good times with her family, thinking of the books that Stacy had sneaked into the closet for her, and even the odd friendship they'd developed over time.

Thinking of Stacy, Abigail realized that Randy's girlfriend was probably a lot like Judith — a prisoner of a monster she couldn't escape, an accomplice in his evil, but a victim just the same.

As they turned down another empty passage, Abigail asked, "Is that what happened to you?"

Talani stopped and turned to Abigail, tears in her eyes. "For five long years I was locked in a room, serving men, sometimes women, several per day, giving a bit of myself each and every time until there was almost nothing left. I felt desperate to die."

"I'm sorry," Abigail said.

"Then one day all the kids were brought out for a 'special' client. It was the first time they'd ever done anything like that. And I was reminded of the time we were all put on the auction block, and for a moment I was excited, thinking I'd see Raina, even if only for a few minutes while they paraded us before this important client. But she wasn't in the group. And I sat there looking at all these other kids, some of them my sister's age, others even younger than me, all of us ghosts.

"There were about twenty of us, waiting, most of us

probably scared. Special clients were allowed to get away with even more than the usual ones. Then he arrived, and I felt like someone stabbed me in the gut. It was Hugo, and Judith.

"I felt this panic as he looked us over, praying he wouldn't recognize me, wouldn't pick me. I don't know why, because, as I said, at this point I was already being abused several times a day, so it was really just another drop in an endless bucket of misery. But, for some reason, I was terrified that I would be chosen.

Talani paused, wiping tears from her eyes.

"You don't have to finish," Abigail said, even though she wanted to know more, and how this tied into her falling in with Judith.

Talani continued, staring at the floor. "He brought me back to my room, and the whole time I kept hoping he wouldn't recognize me, that *he* had sold me to Esmerelda. It wasn't about me, but I didn't want him to remember who I was, that he had murdered my father. I didn't want to give him those memories of me seeing my father die, of the horrible hate I felt for him, how I had wished him dead every day for five long years. Nor did I want him taking my memories of my father, of my mother, of my sister. They were *mine*, and enough horrible people had already taken them, lived them vicariously. I couldn't stand the thought of him having them.

"So we went back to my room, the three of us, and the whole time I'm plotting my way out. And here's the part where I should mention the poison."

"Poison?" Abigail asked.

"Sometimes the people who came in to see me didn't want my memories or my flesh. Sometimes they just wanted to talk. They were usually sad people who hated what they'd become. Some were turned into Valkoer against their will. Others were born into it, but saw it as a curse. At any rate, about four months prior, a sad young man came to me. At first I didn't remember him — all the faces, except the very worst, sorta blend into one over time — but then he reminded me that he'd seen me three months earlier. His father had paid for him to use Esmerelda's service to get laid, but when he saw me, saw how young I was, he couldn't go through with it. Nor did he want to take my memories. Instead, we talked. I don't remember about what, but apparently I made some sort of impression on him. He said he couldn't get me out of his mind, and how wrong it was for me to be there.

"He handed me a small bottle and said it was 'a way out.' A poison that would instantly kill me, and end my nightmare.

"At the time, I thanked him politely, but wasn't sure if I was really ready to die. A part of me was still holding out hope of seeing Raina again. I didn't want to leave her in this world, or in this terrible place, all alone.

"So, as Hugo and Judith came into my room, Hugo went into the adjoining bathroom to get himself ready. Judith stayed with me, sitting in a chair. I guess she was going to watch whatever Hugo planned to do. She was looking at me weird, and I wasn't sure if she recognized me or not. Meanwhile, I was inching my way toward the pillow where I'd hid the vial of poison. Hugo came out, naked, and eyed me with a twisted smile.

"Hugo went over to Judith and kissed her, maybe getting himself worked up, or maybe getting *her* worked up, I don't know. I took the opportunity to grab the poison. My hands were shaking. I didn't want to die. I didn't want to leave Raina behind, but at the same time, I couldn't take another day — I couldn't take what Hugo was surely going to do to me. I unscrewed the cap and was about to down the bottle when Judith screamed, 'She's drinking something!'

"Hugo turned, saw the vial, and smacked it out of my hand. It flew into the wall and shattered, its dark liquid splashing the wall and my bed. Then he turned and asked me what it was.

"I told him. He smacked me, harder than any of the others had ever hit me. He said, 'Oh, you're gonna die today, all right, but not before I'm done with ya.'

"He began tearing at my dress, ripping it off. Then he threw me on the bed and began to choke me.

"He was probing my mind, trying to find my most secret memories.

"I could feel him inside my head, like fire spreading through my brain. I knew it would consume me. And after it had, he'd take my body. But then she stood up."

"Judith?"

"Yes, I saw her from the corner of my eye, and then the black blade as she buried it in his head.

"For a moment I didn't think it did anything. His eyes went wide, but he wasn't dead. He stood, turned around, and looked like he was going to kill her.

"But then he dropped to the ground, black lines running through his skin, his body convulsing.

"Judith looked at me, told me to take her hand, that we were getting out of there."

Abigail stared at Talani, unable to find a single word to express the heartbreak, or the understanding now dawning on her.

"She saved you."

"Yes. And after that, we fled to Earth. This was before the portals had all been closed by The North. Judith promised to make it all up to me. To make things right. She replaced Esmerelda's parasite with her own, becoming my Master. It was a long time before I finally trusted her. I tried to escape, but she always found me. In time, I understood that Judith wasn't all that different from me. She was weak, being controlled by a monster. Later she told me that when she saw me at Esmerelda's, in that room with all the other girls, she recognized me in an instant. She'd regretted recruiting every girl she had, but for some reason, I stuck out more than any other. And when she saw me again, she knew it was her chance for redemption."

"But you never found your sister?"

"No. The portals had closed, and we couldn't return, until now."

"Do you think your sister is still alive?"

"I don't know. It was so long ago. If they didn't turn her, she'd probably be dead of old age by now. Unless she was among the blessed who could live for ages, but I doubt it. And if they *did* turn her, I'm afraid what she'd be like after all this time. Perhaps it's better to think she died long ago."

Abigail reached out and hugged Talani. "I'm sorry."

After an awkward moment where Abigail wasn't sure if she should break the hug or not, Talani blurted, "There it is!"

Abigail pulled away just in time to see the kitten turning a corner at the end of the hall.

"Come on!" Talani said, running after the cat.

Abigail followed right on her heels.

They chased the cat through several more halls then up a few flights of stairs before watching it slip through a narrow passageway.

Talani slipped and fell on her butt as Abigail continued forward through the narrow hall.

Halfway through, she heard a voice that stopped her.

Abigail stopped, paralyzed in the narrow crevice,

staring straight ahead at the last person in the world she expected to see — a naked, bloody man. But he didn't capture Abigail's attention so much as the man behind him.

*Jacob!*

# FORTY-TWO

# John

GERALD LED John to the city above Under Harbor, to the tavern where Jonah could most often be found.

They were met inside by an short old woman who looked worried. "Gerald!"

"What is it?"

She eyeballed John suspiciously.

"It's okay," Gerald said. "He's with me. What is it?"

"Jonah went into Under Harbor with Prophet Malachi and Sister Raina. Jonah looked nervous."

"How long ago did they leave?"

"Just a few minutes."

"And do you know where they went?"

"I overheard them say something about the soma den, and about what happened at Crow's Nest."

"Well, that can't be good."

John cut in. "What's wrong?"

"Everything," Gerald said, turning on his heel and heading toward the stairway back underground.

John followed.

FORTY-THREE

# Caleb

*"WALK,"* Jacob commanded in Caleb's head.

Caleb could only obey, stumbling naked and bloody through the soma den lobby, with Jacob right behind. He wasn't sure which scared people away more, the sight of a naked man stabbed in the gut, or the knife he was still holding with a white-knuckle grip ready to strike again. As people took notice, whatever high or sexual bliss they were enjoying vanished, and sent them screaming in flight from the lobby.

He could feel Jacob's perverse satisfaction, an opposite reaction to Caleb's horror.

Caleb was usually the one to calm the frightened, to chase away whatever boogeyman might be threatening someone. Now *he* was their boogeyman. They were afraid of *him*. It was as if Jacob had reached deep inside his psyche and found one of few things that would hit him where it hurt most.

Caleb tried to resist Jacob's instructions, but could no better oppose him now than earlier when his brother

309

extracted everything Caleb knew about The Hand of the Seven Gods from his brain.

Jacob was rooted deep into his mind. Death was the only escape.

If Caleb could kill himself, he would have.

But he was stuck, being a sick marionette for the twisted fuck that shared his biology, and nothing more.

He prayed that he would bleed out and drop dead before Jacob could hurt anyone else.

But Caleb needed to stay alive, needed to find a way to warn Raina that he'd been compromised. But Jacob didn't dare try to connect telepathically with Raina while Jacob was in his head. Jacob might use the connection to lay a trap for her.

He hoped just thinking about it didn't raise the idea in Jacob's mind.

They approached the exit, and Caleb wondered what they would do next. Continue this macabre parade through Under Harbor, scaring people, maybe until someone killed him?

Jacob, reading Caleb's thoughts, responded.

*"Don't worry, Brother. I won't let anyone kill you. We're going to pay a visit to Jonah. I need to find a few people here, people that fucker's been hiding from me. You have time, right? No pressing appointments? No? Good."*

*Fuck you.*

Jacob laughed out loud. *"Someday you and I will look back on this moment with fond memories, as the beginning of the end. And you can say you were here when it all came down. And, yes, I did overhear that whole thing about Raina. That's a pretty good idea, calling her. Maybe after we're done with Jonah."*

*No, please don't!*

Jacob didn't respond.

They stepped through the doorway and into the

hallway outside the soma den. Caleb looked around help-lessly for something, anything, he could use to fight back against the puppeteer behind him.

*There must be something.*

And then he saw something in the narrow passageway whence he came. A girl. And not just any girl.

The little girl that John had been on the run with ages ago.

*Abigail!*

*What are you doing here?*

And as soon as he saw her, he felt Jacob's excitement.

*Shit. I tipped him off.*

Caleb wanted to shout, *Run! Run away!*

But his mouth belonged to Jacob.

Jacob dropped Caleb to the ground like a sack of meat. Then he went after Abigail.

# FORTY-FOUR

# Abigail

ABIGAIL SCREAMED as the bloody naked man fell to the ground and Jacob locked eyes with her.

He was just as she remembered when he took her captive two years ago — tall, pale, bald, with dark evil eyes, and dressed in all black.

He was also smiling. Again.

*Oh God, that smile.*

She remembered how helpless he'd made her feel. How he probed inside her mind, and how she'd been unable to stop him.

How cold and sick she felt with him in there, sifting through her memories as if they were belongings and he an intruder. How scared she'd been that he would stay in her head forever, taking it over, taking *her* over and turning her into something else.

Every instinct screamed for her to run. Fast and far. *Do NOT let him catch up.*

She turned in the tight crevice to flee.

But Talani was blocking her way.

"Move!" Abigail shrieked, batting and shoving Talani with her hands. "He's coming!"

"*Who's* coming?" Talani said, looking up and over her. *Why won't you move?*

Abigail kept shoving her. "Go! Go! Go! Go!"

Talani turned, but Abigail could already hear the man in black's footfalls drawing closer.

Her flight through the passageway, which might have been a hundred feet, suddenly stretched into a thousand, slogging to a crawl.

But Jacob's time didn't slow like Abigail's.

The man seemed to move even faster.

*Come on. GO!*

She pushed herself, shoved at Talani's back, urging her forward.

Despite the muscles in her scrawny legs feeling pushed to their limit, the world was a drip.

She kept her eyes on the other end of the passageway, the exit, not knowing what she'd do once she and Talani reached the other side. Jacob wasn't fat enough to get stuck — she'd have to figure out a solution once there.

For now, she just had to focus on getting out.

Getting her and Talani to safety.

They were almost out of the passageway.

It was maybe twenty feet away.

*Yes!*

*Yes!*

*Ye —*

She fell.

*No!*

Jacob landed atop her.

# FORTY-FIVE

# John

GERALD PICKED up his pace as they navigated the dimly lit cloistered warrens composing Under Harbor on the way to the soma den.

"What's going on?" John asked. "What's this Crow's Nest thing?"

"A group of Valkoer attacked a small farming village called Crow's Nest, left most of 'em dead. Rumor says it was someone from here, but I'm not buying it."

"And who are Prophet Malachi and Sister Raina?"

"They're from Golden Cove, capital of The Southern Realm. Prophet Malachi is the head and founder of The Hand of the Seven Gods, the big church here who all the other towns and kingdoms more or less pay off to protect them from, well, people like us."

Gerald winked at John. "And they've got the biggest army in The South. So probably not people you'd want to be making enemies of."

"You think they're here to start something?"

"Or finish, as they likely see it. Only a matter of time

before this was bound to happen, but hopefully it won't come to that."

"Through here," he said, pointing at a passageway.

They stopped at the sight of a young black girl running out of the passageway screaming.

The girl turned, looked back, and saw that whatever she expected to see wasn't behind her. She ran back into the passage, still screaming.

John raced forward to help.

# FORTY-SIX

# Judith

JUDITH SAT across from Cassandra at her kitchen table, drinking a juice that was giving her a pleasant buzz while Cassandra filled her in on life in Under Harbor.

Though the city was underground, it actually held more citizens than the aboveground Town of Jonah. Under Harbor was like the proverbial small town where everybody knew everyone's business, except here a lot of people's business was criminal. Still, it wasn't as bad as all that. Like any small town, you had a wide variety of people and political groups to navigate to avoid getting on the wrong people's bad side. Screwing up here wasn't like messing up in other places. Exiled from Under Harbor left most people with nowhere else to go. Other kingdoms didn't allow magick users, witches, monsters, or the other deviants that called Under Harbor home, so the exiled were forced to become vagabonds, or settle in the Outlands — a place that wasn't particularly hospitable to lone wolves, or small families, unless one was adept at fighting bandits.

"I think we'll do fine here," Judith said. "Thank you again for taking us in. You didn't have to do this."

"Of course I did. You made my brother happy, not an easy task. He loved you, and wanted the best for you. You must be something special."

Judith took another drink, allowing her buzz to ease the pain of losing Solomon. "Nothing special, believe me. If you knew me before I met Talani, and before your brother found me, you'd have wanted me dead. I was a horrible person."

"I know. He told me all about your past. About how Hugo controlled you."

"I can't blame other people for my choices. I just have to try and make enough right ones to correct the wrong. To try and make enough of a difference to enough people's lives that it outweighs my many sins."

"See," Cassandra said, smiling, "a good person. Most people would allow their pasts to break them. But you refused to give up. You fought back. You saved that child. And it looks like you've found another."

Judith smiled. "Abigail? She reminds me a lot of myself when I was her age. And she gives Talani a sister …"

"What is it?" Cassandra asked after Judith had stopped.

"It's my fault that Talani and her sister were sold to Esmerelda. And she split the girls up. I'm guessing her sister is long past dead, but I suppose I owe it to Talani to try and find her. Do you know anyone who can help me? I'd like to do it before telling her — in case I'm unearthing a tragedy. I don't want Talani to dig up old ghosts if they're only going to hurt her."

"I might be able to see. Would you give me your hand?"

"So you really *are* a seer?"

Cassandra arched her eyebrows. "Why would I claim so if not?"

"On Earth we had these so-called psychics who claimed to see things, but they were all frauds looking to take people's money and exploit their hopes and fears."

"*All* of them?" Cassandra said with a smile. "Surely *some* of them must've been real."

"Perhaps. But none that *I* ever met."

Judith was about to offer her hand then jerked it away. It had been so long since she'd been around anyone who wasn't Valkoer that she'd nearly forgotten what her touch would do to anyone else.

"It's okay," Cassandra said. "I'm protected."

"How's that? Spell?"

"No," she said, reaching into a box on the table and pulling out a black glove.

"So you don't actually need to make contact with my skin to see things?"

"No," Cassandra said, slipping on the glove. "Now, place your palm on the table."

Judith did so cautiously.

It had been a long time since she'd let anyone into her head that wasn't Talani or Solomon, and granting entrance to another made her anxious, even if it was Solomon's sister.

Cassandra placed her gloved hand on top of Judith's open palm, then closed her eyes.

"I want you to remember the moment when you took Talani and her sister. Can you remember?"

"Can I *forget* is the better question."

Judith thought back to the night, as she'd done too many times to count, usually under the influences of guilt and alcohol.

She remembered Hugo instructing her to find the

hiding sister. Remembered seeing Talani, so young, so scared, trembling under the bed. Remembered her sister, Raina, pleading not to take her.

A part of Judith had wanted to leave the girl undiscovered. But she wouldn't have gotten away with it. Hugo had told her to find the girl, and wouldn't let it go. If she hid the girl, and he discovered her disobedience, he would have probably killed her. When Judith was lying to herself, she liked to think she was protecting the girls. Her way of thinking was that Hugo would've found them anyway. And if Judith had betrayed him, he would've been so mad he would've killed both girls in front of her, just to teach her a lesson.

And that might have even been true.

But there was also a part of Judith — and this was always the hardest part to face — that had *wanted to* find the girl, had *wanted to* give the girl to Hugo, had *wanted to* please him. Because then, maybe he'd love her a little bit more. Maybe he'd stop treating her like property. There had been times when he'd been tender. Times he seemed to actually care for her. She had wanted more of those times, even if it meant doing horrible things like stealing children from others.

She hated that sad stupid part of herself with a bitterness that even the sweetest of tastes could never fully blot out. So many times Judith wished she could go back and change what she did.

The world was full of magick, but there was no way to change the past.

"The older sister's name is Raina?"

"Yes."

"Can you focus more on her face in your memories? I want you to really see her as she was that night."

"Do I have to?" Judith sighed, already feeling her eyes well up with tears, her throat constricting.

"Please, just once more. Focus."

Judith did.

"It's her."

"Huh?"

"It's Sister Raina of The Covenant of the Hand of the Seven Gods."

"She's alive?"

"Oh yes."

A scream ripped through Judith's mind.

She yanked her hand back from Cassandra's and sat up straight, her senses suddenly hyper-aware.

"What's wrong?" Cassandra asked.

"Talani's in trouble!"

Judith leaped from her chair and ran out the door.

# FORTY-SEVEN

# Abigail

ABIGAIL CRIED out as Jacob pounced on her. He was on top of her, hands on her shoulders and pinning her down.

She flashed back to the last man to hold her down like that, and panic spread through her like fire, through every muscle, washing over her mind and rendering every thought but one to ashes.

*Fight!*

She kicked, flailed, clawed, and twisted, trying to bite the man's arms.

"Get off of me!" she growled.

She must have hurt him: his eyes bulged, and his mouth twisted into a grimace of rage.

"Stop it!" He pulled her up by the shoulders, then slammed her back repeatedly, sending Abigail's head into the ground, over and over.

Fear turned to pain, clouding the edges of her vision as her body went limp, limbs refusing to heed her commands.

In her peripheral vision, she saw Talani running toward Jacob, screaming.

She tried to warn her away — Jacob was too powerful. She needed to get help.

But Abigail couldn't warn her, couldn't even focus to string together a coherent telepathic message.

She was already slipping into the darkness.

*No, I have to hang on. Got to get up. Help her.*

Jacob saw Talani coming at him, and stood up to intercept her attack.

He would kill Talani. Abigail had to stop him.

Abigail struggled to move her arms, to push herself up from the ground, to find a way to get between he and Talani.

Every attempt was slow, and shaky. It hurt just to lift her head.

Then she saw something else, behind Talani.

Not something, *someone.*

Not just someone …

*John!*

Then she fell back.

# FORTY-EIGHT

# Talani

TALANI SCREAMED, racing toward the man hurting her Abigail.

He looked up, and instead of running away, barreled straight for her.

Talani had meant to leap on the man, grab his head, then suck his life out before he could defend himself.

But she missed as he sidestepped her at the perfect moment.

As Talani started to sail past him, her momentum halted as he grabbed her by her hair and yanked her to the ground.

She fell hard on her back, gasping for air.

Then he was on top of her.

His evil dark eyes met hers. His hands throttled her throat.

*Why isn't he dying?*

Then she realized. He was Valkoer, too.

He smiled. "And who might *you* be?"

"Fuck you," she growled.

He squeezed tighter. "Wrong answer."

He let go with one hand, reached down to his belt, drew a black blade, and waved it in front of her, delighting in Talani's terrified eyes.

"Ah, so you do know what this does," he said, smiling. "Good. I wanted to see the fear in your —"

Suddenly he went flying off of her as a blast of hot, bright white light erupted above, temporarily blinding her.

Running footsteps behind her.

She clenched her fists, and focused on the sound, bracing for attack.

She leaped to her feet and, as her eyes adjusted to the blast's blinding effect, turned to see another man in all black, with long dark hair, run past her, then drop down beside Abigail.

Talani remembered the man from Abigail's memories. The "angel" who saved Abigail from Randy Webster, then had saved her again by turning her into a vampire.

*John!*

"What happened?" he asked, cradling Abigail's motionless body, blood pooling around her skull.

FORTY-NINE

# John

---

"HE WAS SHAKING HER, slamming her against the ground!" the young teen said, eyes wide, helplessly staring at Abigail.

So much blood seeping from her head.

John looked up to see Jacob standing, shaking off the energy blast.

Their eyes met.

Jacob gave him a sinister smile then nodded.

What that meant, John didn't know.

He looked down at Abigail, limp in his hands, barely clinging to life, then up at Jacob who stood there as if saying, *Your choice, Brother. Save the girl, or come get me.*

Did he save Abigail or chase the monster who held the fate of worlds in the crystals?

Gerald stood next to John, growling, "Want me to get 'em for ya?"

"No," John said, not wanting to send another person to their death for a battle that belonged to him.

Jacob turned, walking back from where he'd come. He bent over, then picked up someone John couldn't quite see. It was a man, naked and bloody, on the verge of death.

John focused harder, and the shadows started to pull away from the figure's face.

*Caleb!*

"What are you doing with him?" John yelled.

Jacob slung Caleb over his shoulder. "He's my brother. I'm taking him home."

The air in front of Jacob began to hiss and crackle, black and purple lights blinking as a portal opened before him.

A tiny sliver, taking up the width of the passageway. In it, John saw nothing but blackness and swirling lights.

Jacob started to enter. "Care to join us, Brother? Make it a family reunion? I'll see if we can scrounge up some barbecued something or other."

John looked down at Abigail's tiny body.

He needed to cast a healing spell if he wanted to save her. *If* he could save her.

But Jacob was right in his sights. As was Caleb. He could chase Jacob now, and end it. Get Caleb back, recover the crystals, and kill Jacob once and for all.

Suddenly a woman's voice behind him. "What happened?"

He turned to see a pale woman with long white hair and red glasses — one of the vampires who had crossed through the portal with Abigail, the ones who had taken her to this godforsaken world.

"Judith!" the teenager said. "Abigail is hurt, bad. We need to do something!"

Judith came toward John, looking down. "Who are you?"

John didn't answer.

He turned back to see Jacob stepping into the portal and the darkness beyond.

The portal began to close.

"I can go after him," Gerald repeated his offer.

"Are you immune to Valkoer touch?" John asked.

"*Resistant*, not immune."

"Then stay here."

John's heart was racing as he looked back down at Abigail then again at the portal.

The blonde was obviously Valkoer, and could maybe heal her. But she stole Abigail, persuaded her to cross over to this world, and was responsible for her now lying unconscious, on the brink of death.

He couldn't leave Abigail with her, even with Gerald as a bodyguard. He watched the portal closing.

He closed his eyes, and instead of focusing on the missed opportunity, he began to recite his most powerful healing spell out loud.

"What are you doing?" the teenager asked.

Judith hushed her, indicating that she knew exactly what John was doing: saving Abigail's life.

# FIFTY

## Raina

BALTAZAR LED them to the soma den. But as they were about to enter the seedy locale, a commotion behind them drew Raina's attention.

She turned toward the noise coming from a narrow passageway opposite the den entrance.

And in the passageway was an oval patch of black sky with stars, floating as if someone had plucked a piece of the sky and hung it in the corridor.

*A portal!*

Jacob was stepping into the portal — a man she recognized from Caleb's memories, with a naked man slung over his shoulder. Even without seeing his face, she knew it was Caleb.

"There!" She pointed to the portal.

Malachi drew his blade and raced forth.

Raina was right beside him, her dagger ready. Then she took the lead, closing in on the enemy.

Jacob stepped into the portal. It rippled and faded, starting to vanish from sight.

She picked up her pace, desperate to get there before it vanished.

"Wait!" Malachi said, failing to keep pace beside her. "It's unstable."

"I'm not going to let him take Caleb!"

She was ten yards away, close enough to hear the portal's crackle and hum.

She pushed herself to run faster, propelled by a cocktail of adrenaline and fear.

"Caleb!" she called out, drawing nearer.

But the portal was almost gone.

She pushed harder.

*Almost …*

*There.*

Ten feet away, blackness and stars were barely visible. She could see *something*.

Seven feet away.

It was almost completely gone.

*Must*

*Reach*

*It*

Raina made one last push, and leaped into the portal.

Time seemed to slow around her, and in that elasticized moment, she could feel the portal's vibration on her skin, in her hair, like ice all over her, as if she'd left the warmth of Golden Cove for the frozen mountains of Calladia.

Then the sensation was gone, as she slid face-first onto the passageway ground.

The portal was gone.

She'd failed.

But then she looked up and saw the last person in the world she thought she'd ever see — the woman who had stolen her and Talani.

Judith stood with three others — a teenage girl, and a man holding a small girl on the ground, blood pooling around her.

Raina felt like she'd arrived after a battle, obviously one with Jacob that these people lost, and a girl's life was on the cusp.

But none of that mattered.

She could focus only on Judith, the woman who'd stolen her life, the woman responsible for every horrible thing that had ever happened since. The monster who stole Talani.

Raina screamed and raced forward with her blade.

Malachi screamed something from behind her, but the world outside Judith was only a blur.

There was just Raina, Judith, and a millennium of pain.

Judith stared, like a helpless animal with nowhere to run and no defense to mount, as Raina ran right at her, blade tight in her grip.

Raina closed the distance in seconds.

More yelling, this time from the teenage girl.

But none of them would save Judith from vengeance.

Raina struck, plunging the blade into Judith's heart.

Raina fell on top of Judith, whose eyes were wide and surprised.

She started to say something, but Raina grabbed the blade, pulled it out, and stabbed her again — in the gut, the chest, and finally her face.

"Die! Die! Die! Die!" she screamed, still stabbing.

"Stop!" the teenager cried out, pulling Raina from Judith.

Raina spun around, launching herself at the girl, blade thrusting forward.

And then time slowed again.

As the blade arced toward the girl's stomach, just inches away from ending her life as well, their eyes met.

And Raina felt as if she'd been hit in the chest by a battering ram.

*No.*

*Impossible.*

*But ...*

"Talani?"

The blade was centimeters from gutting her sister, and momentum made stopping impossible.

Raina couldn't stop, but she did manage to drop the blade before her fist slammed into Talani's stomach, sending her sister sprawling backward to the ground.

As she fell backward, Malachi grabbed Talani in a choke hold. Seconds later, he brought his own knife to her side.

"No!" Raina screamed.

Malachi stared at her. "What?"

"She's my sister!" Raina sobbed as she fell to the ground.

Talani looked at her, eyes wide. "Raina?"

Raina burst into tears as she hugged her.

After a moment, Talani pushed Raina away, and made her way to Judith.

# FIFTY-ONE

# Judith

JUDITH FELT her life slipping away as she brushed her fingers over the knife wounds, assessing the damage.

There were too many, all too deep. Blood ran over her fingers, sticky hot.

She was losing blood fast, and because Raina had used one of the cursed black blades, the poison was destroying her ability to heal herself.

She was going to die, and knew it the moment she saw Raina.

She watched the sisters hug, and felt tears stinging her eyes.

Talani and Raina were finally together again.

Maybe they could find a way to make up for lost time. They had an eternity, assuming they could avoid getting stabbed with onyx.

As she watched their embrace, darkness clouded her vision.

And in that darkness she saw something moving toward her.

A new panic rose, though she couldn't explain it. She was already dying; what other danger could there be?

She wondered if the stories of an afterlife were true. She'd heard many through her scattered years, on this planet and on Earth.

She believed a great many things, had seen so much, but when it came to a God, she had no belief.

No Heaven, no Hell, just nothingness.

But a new thought terrified her.

*What if I'm awake for the nothingness? Not alive but aware of the nothingness forever?*

And would it be like the In-Between? Icy, endless, and full of nightmares?

Before now she thought she'd be okay with dying. She'd lived a long life, longer than most had any right to. And she was okay with it ending.

But she wasn't okay with an eternity in Hell, Limbo, the In-Between, or whatever else might be waiting.

And the panic of that possibility now swelled inside her.

More movement in the shadows, coming closer.

*What if its the souls of all the girls I destroyed with Hugo? Not just their souls, but their families' souls as well? Waiting to greet me as I go from this world to an endless hell.*

*No, no.*

Another shape approaching.

Judith flinched, then relaxed when she saw it was Talani.

Talani looked at the wounds, as if seeing their severity for the first time. Her eyes widened.

"Oh no. No, no."

She held her hands over Judith's wounds, urgently whispering a healing spell.

"It won't work," Judith said.

"Then we'll get you to the Druwan. They healed Abigail. They can heal you. Come on."

Talani began to lift Judith.

Judith cried out in pain. "No, don't."

Talani gently set her down, then turned and called out to the big man who had come with John. "Can we get a horse and carriage?"

Raina intervened. "What are you doing?"

"Saving her," Talani said.

"What?"

"She's not the person you think she is."

Talani started to explain why Judith didn't deserve this death, and while the words were touching, they were muddled as darkness clouded her hearing and even more of her vision.

The thing creeping in the darkness moved close enough to feel it. A chill spread through her body, her limbs becoming numb and unresponsive.

She flashed back on her life, all the horrible things she'd endured as a child at the hands of monstrous men. Horrors she herself had inflicted on countless men, women, and children while helping Hugo to capture them.

She saw Talani arguing with Raina, trying to save Judith's life.

Talani was the start of the only life she wished to remember. The life where she met Solomon, and discovered what love truly was. The family she had crafted from tragedy — she, Solomon, and Talani. A family that helped others like them. A family that was the antithesis of the horrors that had once tried to shape her.

*This is who I am.*

*This is how I want to be judged — if there is such a thing as judgment.*

But could such sins ever be erased no matter the number of a person's good deeds?

She thought of the horrible In-Between, and the floating psychic monsters that tried to break her. She could feel something moving closer.

*Go away. Just go away!*

She closed her eyes, tears streaming down her face.

"Judith?" Talani said through the muddled ocean in her ears.

Judith tried to open her eyes and see the girl, but found only darkness.

She tried to open her mouth, but couldn't.

*No!*

"Judith?" Talani repeated, now sobbing. "Judith!"

*I'm here!* Judith screamed telepathically.

But she could only hear the crying.

She could no longer feel the link with Talani. Her comfort was severed, and she was helpless, listening as Talani mourned her in some faraway world she'd never be part of again.

Judith was no longer in her body.

Was in a pure darkness, floating, free of constraints.

Talani's cries were already dimmer.

Judith struggled to stay close, but they hurt too much to hear. She didn't want Talani to feel such pain in losing her.

Judith cried, though she had no eyes.

She still felt an aching loss, though she had no brain to recall what was missing.

*How can I be and yet not be?*

She looked around the darkness, searching for something, anything.

But she saw only nothing in every direction. Despite the vast emptiness, she felt it closing in, almost crushing her shapeless form. She needed to get away, but where, and from what?

She willed herself into motion, flying through the void, though without a body, or visual cues to signify movement, Judith couldn't be certain she was moving at all.

She wasn't sure if she was in the In-Between or somewhere else. Judith was only certain that she wasn't alone.

And that something was watching.

# FIFTY-TWO

# Jacob

JACOB LAY in the darkness of his father's massive bed, now his, holding the amulet over his head, staring in awe at the glowing red crystals that had come together into a single shape, looking almost like a heart. Not the romantic hearts gracing greeting cards on Earth but an actual human heart.

"So, Wizard, now that our common enemy is dead, what should I do with you?"

"*Set me free,*" said a man's voice, surprising Jacob.

He dropped the crystal and jumped out of the bed, looking around, fists ready to tear someone apart.

But Jacob was alone in the giant garish chamber.

He looked down at the amulet and smiled. "Was that *you* talking to me, Wizard?"

"*Surprised, Prince Jacob?*"

"I suppose I shouldn't be. I knew you were in there. I know that you gave me power. Why haven't you spoken to me before?"

"*Because you didn't speak to me.*"

"But you were there? Aware of what was happening?"

"If you're asking if I'm aware of the horrible things you've done, then yes."

Jacob was nervous to sit, not knowing what the amulet might do, and so stood a respectful distance from the bed. "I take it you don't approve of what I've done?"

"It's not for me to judge."

"Surely you have opinions?"

"They don't matter."

"You're right, Wizard. They don't. So what are you asking? To be set free?"

"Yes."

"And how would I do that?"

"Simply command me to leave my vessel."

"And what will happen to you then?"

"My soul will go to the In-Between, like all passing souls."

"Why would anyone want that punishment when you can be here, or Earth, among the living?"

"It's hard to enjoy the freedoms of the living without a body, wouldn't you say?"

"Fair point. So here's a better question, why don't you just leave the vessel now? Why have you allowed me to use you as I wish?"

The wizard said nothing.

"You can't disobey me, can you?"

"No."

Jacob sat on the bed, picked up the amulet — glowing from red to orange in his hand — and held it up to his eye for closer inspection.

Light swirled within the crystal. He wondered if this was what a soul looked like out of its body.

"Why can't you disobey me? Why can't you merely do as you wish?"

Again, the wizard was silent.

"It's the spell, isn't it? It was made to protect the vessels. And in this case, I am your vessel, even though you're not inside my body. Am I right?"

The wizard said nothing.

"So why would I set you free when you are of so much more use here, serving me?"

"Because you know it is wrong."

"Wrong?" Jacob laughed. "You know who you're talking to, right? You used to scold me when I would use the magick *you* taught me to hurt vermin. You said it yourself, I'm a wretched, wretched person."

"You offered your father a chance to live, to join you. You did the same with your brothers. That doesn't seem like a *thoroughly* wretched person to me. I think there's a part of you that knows the right thing to do, and that part of you is what's hesitating now."

"Hesitating with what?"

"Your plans."

Jacob harrumphed. "What do *you* know of my plans?"

"I can see inside your mind, Jacob. You can't hide your thoughts from me. You couldn't as a child, but it's even harder as a man. You want revenge for everything The North did to you and your people. You want to destroy The Hand of the Seven Gods for their betrayal of the Valkoer and The South, not to mention a host of other sins before The Great Purge. And you think you wish a return to Earth so you can enslave the human race. But we both know different, don't we? A part of you wants the violence to end. A part of you sympathizes with the innocents — the same part of you who murdered that poor girl in Esmerelda's den rather than leave her to suffer. The same part of you that doesn't want to become a monster like your father."

Jacob hurled the amulet across the room.

It hit Father's precious gold-framed Jska mirror, sending a spiderweb of cracks across the surface.

Jacob flinched, bracing for punishment before his mind reminded his body that he no longer had to fear Father's wrath.

"You don't know me!" he yelled at the wizard.

"Why are you upset? I'm complimenting you for your mercy. A mercy your father never had. You got what you want. Your father is dead. The Kingdom is yours. *You* have the people's respect. *You* have the entire kingdom and all that your position affords. *This* is what you dreamed of as a child, is it not? Taking over the throne?"

"I'm no longer that child, and the throne is not enough. I'm tired of being subjected to other people's rules. *You can't do this. You can't go here. You must stay on this tiny shithole of an island. You must sit and watch your brothers and sisters die out as a species. Must, must, must, must!* Fuck your musts! I refuse to obey anyone ever again. They will all bow to me, bow and serve … or die."

"This isn't you, Jacob. This is your grief. This is your pain talking. But *you* are better than this."

"Fuck you," Jacob said, "you don't know me. But you will soon enough. And you're going to help me realize my plans."

Jacob walked to the mirror, caught his reflection in the fractured glass. His eyes were wild, full of fire, and a confidence he'd not felt in years.

He smiled at his reflection, bent to retrieve the amulet, slipped it around his neck, then tucked it under his shirt.

"It's time you see just how little you know the real me."

Jacob spit on the mirror, then turned on his heel and headed downstairs. Time to visit his little brother.

# FIFTY-THREE

# Abigail

ABIGAIL WOKE in an unfamiliar bed to the muffled sounds of people talking.

A lantern's dim light revealed a small bedroom, a woman's judging from the decorations on the dresser and hangings on the wall.

Her memory was foggy as she tried to figure out where she was, *and* how she got there. She sat up, slowly, so as not to make a sound and alert whoever might be nearby.

Abigail noticed that she wasn't wearing the same clothes. She was in a white cotton dress, probably some kind of sleepwear, with no socks or underwear.

She stepped onto the cold stone floor, and focused on the voices outside her door, trying to recognize them.

Men and women talking, cordially. A good sign.

She cupped her hand against the door, listening more intently. There were at least seven or eight voices. She could sense even more people behind the doorway.

Then she heard a laugh she'd never forget.

She opened the door and ran out, yelling, "Larry!"

She ignored everyone else in the large room — there

were plenty — and ran right toward Larry, stopping short before hugging him, since her arms and legs were fully exposed.

She couldn't hug him, but bounced like a giddy little girl.

"Abigail!" he shouted, smiling. "Oh my God, I thought we'd never see you again."

*We'd?*

Abigail felt him before she saw him.

Her angel.

John.

He was standing next to a woman with long dark auburn hair, and a large older man who reminded her of a bear.

She ran to John.

He opened his arms, picked her up, and pulled her into a big, deep hug.

"John," she cried into his shoulder, "I'm so sorry I left."

"It's okay," he said, rubbing his hand along her back. "Everything is okay."

She kept crying into his shoulder, the weight of the past two weeks unspooling in his embrace. From accidentally killing that family and burning their house down to Katya's unintended murder to nearly dying on this world, it all washed away in a torrent of tears now that John was with her again.

"It's okay. I'm here now, Abigail. We're all here, and everything will be fine. But first, there's someone I want you to meet."

He set her down, then put a gloved hand on the woman's shoulder. "Abigail, this is Hope."

Abigail's only recollection of Hope was in her first vision when she and John first met and were hiding in that motel, back when he still had amnesia. But Abigail hadn't forgotten what she looked like, and she was even more beautiful in person.

"Hi," Abigail said, awkwardly waving, knowing she couldn't hug the woman without turning her to ash.

"I've heard so much about you," Hope said, smiling, tears in her eyes. "I'm so glad to finally meet you."

"Me too. I mean glad to meet you, not for you to meet me. Um, you know what I mean," Abigail said, laughing.

She wasn't sure what to say next. Did Hope know that John was a vampire? That *Abigail* was a vampire? She probably knew everything, considering she followed John to this other world.

Abigail looked up at John. "Did you come here to find me?"

"That, and something else."

"What?"

John explained how Jacob had crystals that held a powerful wizard's soul. With them he could do pretty much whatever he wanted. John had come to Otherworld with a group of people to stop Jacob, but most had been killed along the way. He also told her that his good brother, Caleb, was here and had been working with The Hand of the Seven Gods, but he'd been taken by Jacob, and now they were going to go rescue him.

Then, Abigail remembered.

"Jacob! He ... he had me again!"

Talani had been with her. Abigail looked around the room, but didn't see her. "Where's my friend? The girl I was with when Jacob came after me?"

"Talani?" John said, "She's in one of the bedrooms, resting."

"Is she okay?"

"Yes, she had a long day, and lost someone."

"Who?"

"Judith."

"Judith died?" Abigail felt a tightness in her chest. As much as she'd wanted to kill Judith not too long ago, that changed the moment she learned what the woman had done for Talani. Now Abigail only felt loss, and pain for Talani.

"How did she die?"

"Talani's sister killed her."

"Her *sister?* Talani's sister is *alive?*" She spun around the room, heart racing, excited, wanting to meet her. Wanting to see the two of them finally reunited.

"Yes, she's in one of the bedrooms resting with her."

Abigail looked around the room they were in — large with no windows, and several doors presumably each leading to bedrooms like the one where she'd woken. A bulk of the main room had tables, chairs, and a small kitchen area, though it had no refrigerator or other appliances. There was probably no such thing as electricity, though the world did have proper toilets and running water, of sorts.

At the far end of the room was a large double door made of metal.

"Where *are* we?" she asked. It didn't feel like Under Harbor.

"We're in Golden Cove, in one of the barracks of The Covenant of the Hand of the Seven Gods."

"Why are we here?"

"Because it's safer, and they're going to help us kill Jacob, then get Caleb back."

# FIFTY-FOUR

# Talani

TALANI HAD WANTED to sleep alone, needing time to digest everything that had happened. But when she admitted to her fatigue, Raina had insisted on resting in the same room, reluctant to leave her side.

They'd barely spoken since Raina showed up and killed Judith, with Raina telling her to wait until they were alone. She wasn't sure if her sister distrusted John and his group, or her own Prophet and the others in Golden Cove.

At any rate, Talani's stomach was in full churn as they were led to a room in The Citadel's underground barracks.

The moment the door closed, she let loose.

"How could you do that?"

"What?" Raina asked, as if she didn't know.

"You killed Judith without hesitation, without questioning, without any —"

"She deserved it."

"No, she *didn't*. She isn't the same person who took us."

"Looks the same to me! Hell, she hasn't aged a day. Nor have you. Well, too much. So I'm guessing she turned you?"

"She saved me. From a horrible situation."

"Yeah, well, that must've been nice."

Raina turned away, maybe to hide her tears.

Talani could only imagine the hell her sister had been through, how long she'd been a slave serving the sick desires of terrible monsters. Talani knew she *should* show sympathy, but something inside her refused to offer the thing her sister might need most.

Instead, Talani said, "It's not *my* fault she didn't save you. She tried, but we couldn't find you. And too many people were coming after us. So we went to Earth, where we've been ever since. She risked everything to save me."

Raina didn't say anything. Didn't look at her. Perhaps she was thinking about it, maybe even feeling regret.

Finally, Raina looked up at her. Eyes wet but not crying. "So, what? You want me to *apologize* for killing her? I can't. Nor can I forgive her for what she did to us. To you."

"I'm fine! She didn't do anything to me. She was like a mother. She —"

Raina slapped Talani across the face, eyes glaring at her.

"She is *not* our mother!"

Talani rubbed her hand where Raina had hit her. It stung, even more because her sister had done it.

Now it was Talani trying not to cry.

"I didn't say she was. But I don't even remember our mother! I was too young when she died, and it's been forever. Judith was the closest thing I had to family for a long time."

"*I* am your family, not *her*."

"I didn't say you weren't."

Before she could continue, Raina said, "I'm tired."

She lay on the bed's right side, fully dressed, not even covering herself with the sheets.

Talani was left standing there, wanting to finish the argument, but unable.

She seethed, and was tempted to push back, force her sister to finish the conversation, but then, staring at the back of her sister's head, Talani thought back to the night Judith had come with Hugo. The night Hugo killed their father. And the look in Raina's eyes when Judith dragged Talani out from under the bed. The pain in her voice as she begged for her sister's life, offered her own in place of it.

Yes, she killed Judith, but hate didn't drive her so much as love.

And while it hurt, Talani could understand.

Talani lay down on the bed to Raina's left, also leaving her clothes on, cold and covering herself with a sheet, her mind swirling around the pain of Judith's passing.

She was finally reunited with her sister — something she'd only imagined in her wildest dreams — and yet Talani had never felt more alone.

She still had Abigail, assuming she'd be okay, and it seemed like she would be. But Talani was still surprised by the emptiness she felt in the aftermath of Judith's death.

She wondered if this was a normal reaction of loss, or if it was because her Master's connection was severed. The parasite in her no longer had a bond — maybe she was feeling *its* loneliness.

She'd never thought of the disgusting creature inside her as having feelings or emotions. It had always seemed to push her primal thoughts — to feed, to fear, to fight — never something so complex as *loss*.

As Talani's eyes grew heavy, she wondered if Raina was asleep.

She imagined her sister saying, "I'm sorry" just as she was about to drift off.

But the apology never came.

After a while she heard Raina get up. She thought to follow her out to the main room, maybe make amends.

But sleep's hold was too strong.

# FIFTY-FIVE

# John

Sitting at a table, watching Abigail and Talani smiling and joking while Larry and Hope were doing the same with Abalena, John wished like hell they weren't on the brink of war.

But that's exactly what he was planning while sitting at a round table with Prophet Malachi, Raina, Gerald, and Jonah.

Malachi had a map of The Southern Realm spread atop the table, with red Xs on the land just west of The Forgotten Kingdom's island. "These are the tunnels they've been using to smuggle stuff in and out of the city. They'll be guarded, but I doubt they'll be ready for The Covenant's full force."

"Can we get any other cities to join?" Jonah asked Malachi.

"We need to keep this as insulated as possible. We don't know if they have spies in the other camps or not. We keep it simple. The Covenant and your best men," Malachi said to Jonah.

Jonah nodded. "I've already sent word to Baltazar to assemble some men."

"Just the wolves, right?" Gerald asked.

"We can trust his Valkoer," Jonah snapped.

Gerald didn't press, but John could tell that the matter wasn't settled, and he'd likely discuss it further with Malachi and Raina out of earshot.

Malachi looked at John. "We *will* recover your brother. But I need to know something."

"What's that?"

"When were you going to tell me about the crystals?"

John looked up at Gerald, who shook his head and said, "*I* didn't say anything."

John looked at a smiling Malachi. "So you *do* know about the crystals?"

John nodded. "And how do *you* know of them?"

"I have spies everywhere, John. Not much happens in The Realm without my knowledge. So, when were you planning to tell us that Prince, or I suppose I should say King Jacob, now that he has killed his father, has a powerful weapon that could destroy us all?"

John wasn't sure what he hated more, Malachi's smug expression, his stupid white eyebrows, or his arrogance disguised as piety. But he kept his emotions in check, not giving his host, or his army of fanatics, a reason to turn on him and his comrades.

"He won't get a chance to use it. I'll see to that."

Malachi smiled. "You're a confident man, not unlike your brothers. But what do you have beyond confidence? Surely not a magick crystal?"

"No," he said, pointing to his head. "I've got this."

Malachi smiled and folded his hands on the table. "So, you're planning to outsmart him?"

"What do you want me to say? That I'm going in with

nothing, that we may as well give up? If that's what you're looking for, you've come to the wrong place. I've lost — *we've* lost — a lot fighting this man over the years, and I'm not going to lose anymore. He will die, and I'll see to it."

John met Malachi's eyes, refusing to flinch until the other man looked nervously down.

"Okay," Malachi said, "let's say you do kill him. What do you plan to do with the crystals?"

John caught a glance from Raina that made him approach this question cautiously, with a lie.

"I'll destroy them."

"You can do that?" Malachi said, eyebrows raised.

"Yes."

"And you're just going to give up all that power. Some would say the power of a *God?*"

John had been briefed in whispers by Gerald on their way to Golden Cove that The Hand of the Seven Gods was a lot like The Guardians on Earth, highly opposed to magick and responsible for destroying what they found, often along with the magick users themselves.

John said, "Not the power of a *God*, the power of a wizard, a man. A man whose power does not belong in this world, or on Earth."

"On that we do agree," Malachi said. "Except one small thing: I want the crystals, to make sure that they are *properly* destroyed."

*I'll bet you do, nut job.*

John had no doubt that Malachi craved the power for himself. No man in charge of an entire religion, or who claimed to speak for The Gods, could be trusted with so much power. In that way he was even more like the Guardians than John initially thought. They too liked to keep a lot of the artifacts that they deemed too "dangerous" for mere mortals.

*Hypocrites, all of them.*

From what Gerald told him, Malachi had already been a part of The Great Purge, using his *Gods'* will to pursue people like John and Gerald. Their truce was only in force because of The North's power, and the Town of Jonah's stalwarts. But if that much power shifted to Malachi, everything in The Southern Realm could come tumbling down.

But John couldn't refuse Malachi. He had to lie through his teeth.

John leaned forward. "You were surprised a moment ago when I said the crystals could be destroyed, so how is that *you* plan to destroy them?" It wasn't confrontational so much as an attempt to mine a seemingly honest inquiry about the crystals' destruction.

"I'll speak with the Elders, and possibly come to you for assistance, if you would?"

"Yes, I'll help however I can. The sooner they are destroyed, the sooner our worlds will be safe, and we can go home."

Malachi nodded, then continued to go over their plan.

As Malachi planned and Gerald and Jonah argued about a few points of contention strategy wise, John met Raina's eyes. She looked desperate to tell him something, but fuck if he knew when they might get a moment alone.

Then John realized that he had other options.

He reached out to Abigail.

*Abigail, don't say anything out loud. Just tell me telepathically if you can still hear me.*

"*Hi, John. I can hear you. What's up?*"

*I think Raina wants to tell me something, but can't around Prophet Malachi. I need you to let Talani know, and the next time they're together, have her find out what it is, okay?*

"*Ten-four, good buddy,*" she said with a giggle.

It felt good to hear the girl's raspy, happy laugh. For a while he was afraid he might not ever hear it again.

*Larry teach you that?*

"*Yeah. Did I say it right?*"

*Yeah, you did. Ten-four.*

John continued listening as Malachi planned their assault on King Jacob's castle for the next morning at dawn, but he was mostly listening to figure out his own best time to break free from the group. He wasn't about to let Malachi's men get the crystals, or allow anyone else to kill the King.

# FIFTY-SIX

# Caleb

CALEB WOKE in a dungeon that made the one in The Citadel seem like a resort.

It was dark, the walls and floor were stone and cold, with black iron bars so close together, you could barely slip a hand through much less attempt an escape. If he walked to the cell door, Caleb could see a long hall with many cells on either side. But he felt alone, and hadn't heard a single sound. Caleb was curious, but he wasn't about to call out and inquire. He might not like the response.

At least he wasn't confined to a chair, or chained up. A small thing to be thankful for, sure, but in times like these you took your blessings where they came. Another blessing was that he wasn't forced to sit in the cell naked. When he woke he was dressed in clean gray pants and a matching shirt.

He hadn't seen anyone since waking, about six hours ago he figured, and was getting hungrier by the minute.

There was no food in his cell. Just two metal buckets. One with water, and another that was probably his toilet.

He had thus far resisted the urge to use either.

Instead, he spent his time trying to think of a way out of the dungeon, and fruitlessly trying to reach Raina telepathically.

Caleb assumed he was in Jacob's castle in The Forgotten City, though he couldn't remember anything after his brother conquered his mind in the soma den.

He looked down at the bandages covering his wounds. Someone had cleaned him up and dressed his wounds — clearly Jacob didn't intend to let him die in the cell.

*So what* does *he want from me?*

Caleb remembered Jacob forcing him to confess all he knew about Golden Cove, The Citadel, and The Hand of the Seven Gods. But Caleb didn't think he knew much that Jacob could exploit. You couldn't exactly sneak into the city with a secret password, and Golden Cove's guards were everywhere. Jacob and his men would be swiftly defeated if they attempted invasion. Caleb figured they must have known that, or they would have tried to attack before now.

*Maybe they want The Hand to come to them. That's why they have me.*

That made sense.

A part of Caleb smiled at the thought of killing himself to rob their leverage, making it hard, if not impossible, to lure The Hand into a trap.

But fuck that. Caleb wasn't ready to die.

Not before he saw to Jacob's final breath.

Caleb smiled at the thought of killing his brother. Then he thought of his other brother, and wondered if John was here, too.

Caleb remembered seeing the girl, Abigail, just before he passed out. If she was here, then had John come, too? And if so, why? Had they come to save him? And if so, did they just arrive, or had they come two years ago when he crossed over?

Suddenly, Caleb heard a voice in the cell beside his.

"It's funny, when I used to watch movies on Earth, I always thought it was stupid when the bad guy would confront the good guy and tell him his diabolical plans. I'd think, *Just kill him and get it over with already. Don't give him time to attempt rescue.* Didn't you think that was stupid, Brother?"

Footsteps, then Jacob was standing in front of his cell. "Well, didn't you think it was stupid?"

"Yeah," Caleb said, standing up and approaching the cell door. "Yet here you are, about to do the same thing?"

Jacob laughed, his dark eyes twinkling. "That's what made me think of it. But then I thought, no, this is different. Because I'm not the bad guy. I mean, sure, I am *to you.* But that's a temporary thing, a paradigm shift waiting to happen. In time you'll come around to my way of thinking."

"And what way is that?"

"That the time for false gods has ended."

"You know what, I *do* agree with you. Fuck those false gods! Why don't you let me out so we can discuss it?"

Jacob laughed again. "I like you. You've got one hell of a sense of humor, unlike the boring prick *other brother* of ours."

Jacob made an exaggerated sad face, then smiled again.

The man was truly insane.

"So, you're not going to let me out to talk so we can discuss this?"

"No, sorry, Brother. Perhaps after I'm done."

Caleb knew that Jacob only said this in hopes that Caleb would ask when *what* was done. He hated giving him the satisfaction, but damn it, how could he not.

"When *what's* done?"

Jacob smiled, reached down the front of his black shirt, and pulled out a glowing red heart-shaped amulet dangling from a gold chain.

"You see, this right here is the collected crystals of the wizard who helped you and your brother and your mommy all escape to Earth. He hid his soul to avoid my father's wrath. And who could blame him, really? Dad *was* a bit of a cunt. Anyway, he hid these magickal crystals in people, which I'll say is pretty damned clever, then shipped them off to Earth so Daddy wouldn't find them. But I'm not Daddy. And, as you can see, I *did* find them, and ripped them right out of the fuckers. Now I've got them all in this pretty little necklace."

"Good for you."

"Oh, you got that right! You just don't know *how good* yet. You see, these crystals give me all kinds of power. This wasn't just any wizard, but The Last Great Wizard, and now all of his power is mine!"

"And what are you going to do with all that power? Something positive, I bet? Maybe feed the homeless, help some unwanted children find good homes?"

Jacob let the amulet fall back into his shirt as he laughed. "You and I are going to get along well, Brother. I truly believe that. And that's why I'm here telling you of my *evil diabolical plans*." He held up his fingers doing air quotes for that last bit. "That's a bit redundant, isn't it, evil *and* diabolical? I mean, really, I could've just said diabolical and that would've pretty much covered things, right?"

"I know you must have a point — these walls aren't gonna stare at themselves."

"Yes, the point is that I'm going to go destroy The Citadel. Then I'm going to destroy The North. And then, I'm going back to Earth to give it a much-needed enema."

Caleb nodded. "Sounds like a plan to me. Why don't you let me out? I'll help you get into The Citadel. You can't just stroll right in there, ya know."

Shadows fell over Jacob's face as he worked some dark magick.

Caleb wanted to take a step back, but didn't want to show fear.

"Oh, I know *I* can't just walk into The Citadel." The shadows fell from Jacob's face, and Caleb gasped. It was like staring into a mirror. Jacob had shifted his appearance, and now looked exactly like him.

In Caleb's own voice Jacob said, "*I* can't. But *you* can."

# FIFTY-SEVEN

# Hope

As JOHN and the others plotted and planned on one side of the room, Hope, Abigail, and Larry sat at a small circular table near the rear, talking with Hope's mother.

Though she kept calling her Esmee, Hope couldn't yet think of herself as anyone other than Hope. Hell, sometimes she still thought of herself as Hannah Quinn, the life she'd lived for the past decade after John's friend had wiped her mind.

*I'll be Hannah. I'll be Hope. But I'm not Esmee.*

Most of the conversation had been Abalena telling them about her world, how bad it had been before Under Harbor offered sanctuary for magick users, thieves, freaks, and seers such as herself.

Abigail, wearing the white garb that Raina left for her, sat in a chair with her knees tucked under her chin, listening intently.

Abigail suddenly lit up, "Ooh, we met a seer named Cassandra. Do you know her?"

"Yes," Abalena said. "We're good friends."

"Cool," Abigail said, then looked around awkwardly

like she was expected to carry the conversation but didn't know what else to say.

Larry, being Larry, broke the ice by asking a question that Hope couldn't bring herself to ask.

"So, Abalena, you're a seer? Why didn't you see what was going to happen to Hope, er, Esmee? That the wizard was going to take her away, hide a crystal inside her, then ship your daughter to Earth?"

"I can't see everything, nor do I pretend to understand the will of The Gods who gift it to me."

"But you can see the future for people you read for, right? So you do have some control over it? If I come to you for a reading, can't you touch my hand or do whatever it is you do and see something?"

"Yes, usually," Abalena said, showing a surprising amount of restraint given Larry's questions, which another person might interpret as accusatory. But she smiled through it all, her voice melodious and warm.

"So, why didn't you look into your own daughter's future?"

"Because I don't read people close to me. There's nothing worse than seeing a fate you can't change. I'd rather not know."

"I call bullshit."

Hope nearly gasped, but Abalena took it in stride.

"To which part?"

"That you can't change fate. If you knew the wizard was going to take Esmee, you could've kept her home that day, or maybe never let her be a stable girl for the King, let alone the wizard's apprentice."

"Even if I had known, there's nothing I could've done."

"Because of fate?" Larry asked sarcastically.

"No." Abalena's voice became stern. "Because VVessolff hand selected Esmee to be his apprentice. He knew of my abilities and knew early on of Esmee's natural talents. Selection was an honor. And even if it weren't, you don't refuse the King or his wizard."

"My talents?" Hope said. "I'm a seer, too?"

"I don't think so. But you had other abilities early on: moving objects with your thoughts, reading people's minds, even charming them."

Larry looked at Hope, suddenly happy like a big shaggy dog. "Okay, girl, you need to teach me that shit yesterday."

Hope laughed. "As soon as *I* remember it, I'll teach you."

"I can unblock your mind," Abalena said.

"What?" Hope said, caught by surprise. "You can?"

Larry leaned forward, hands folded over one another.

"It's one of my services, though more people need me to help them forget."

"Can I forget Justin Bieber?" Larry joked.

Abigail giggle-snorted, and Larry gave her a wink.

Missing the joke, Abalena looked at Larry oddly, then continued talking to Hope. "Would you *like* to remember?"

"More than you know. How do we do it? How long does it take?"

"Tonight, as you sleep, I will slumber beside you and go inside your mind. I'll remove the blocks, assuming they're not too difficult. And if all goes well, you should wake up in the morning remembering everything, though sometimes it takes a few days or more."

"Some blocks are too difficult?"

"Some are locked, where only the person who created the block can unlock it."

"Don't you think VVessolff would've done that, made

it impossible for me to remember? He was this 'great wizard,' after all."

"Perhaps, but sometimes I can still get through if I'm able to forge a strong enough connection with your dream self. And given that we're blood, I think I'll have an advantage over the *Last Great Wizard's* locks."

Hope began to feel anxious. She *wanted* to remember. It was the very reason she urged John to stay rather than retreating to Earth after the werewolves decimated their team. On the other hand, she didn't know *what* she might be remembering. Or the effect it might have on her psyche. She was already having difficulty remembering which memories were hers and which belonged to the fabricated Hannah. What if remembering more was too much?

"Is it dangerous?"

"Not at all. Well, not *usually*."

Larry cut in, "*Usually?*"

"There's always a chance someone will go mad when you enter their thoughts. Sometimes the mind can't handle the breach, and a person snaps."

Hope's stomach began to feel wobbly. "What kind of chance?"

"Very small, or I wouldn't be suggesting it."

Hope looked at Larry, "What do you think?"

"I dunno. Maybe ask John?"

She looked over at him, leaning forward, eyes intensely focused on the plan of attack against King Jacob. She hated to burden him with her decision. He was about to go after a man with the power to destroy two worlds, and needed to focus.

"No need to bother him. I'll do it. Tonight."

Hope prayed she wasn't making a mistake.

# FIFTY-EIGHT

# Abigail

AFTER A WHILE, John left Prophet Malachi, Raina, Jonah, and Gerald's table, then came back to sit with Hope, Larry, and Abalena. It wasn't long before Abigail began to feel like a fifth wheel as the adults talked. She hadn't felt that way before, but now that John was speaking, and specifically to Hope, Abigail began to feel ignored.

She was thrilled when Talani emerged from the bedroom, finished with her nap.

She leaped up from her chair and ran to greet Talani with a hug.

Talani, smiling a huge grin, hugged her back. "You're okay!"

"Yep! All better!" Abigail said, leading her to a chair in the corner, where they could talk in private.

"So, that's your sister, huh?" Abigail pointed to her, sitting with the Prophet and Gerald. "She's so pretty. I like the cool blue symbols on her face. Is that paint or tattoos?"

"Paint, I think. Didn't you see a few of the others with other colors on their faces?"

"Yeah," Abigail said.

Abigail then noticed that Talani wasn't smiling as much as someone who just reunited with their long-thought-dead sister should be.

Abigail was about to ask if something was wrong, then thought of what it might be, and felt stupid for being all smiley with Talani still in mourning.

"I'm sorry about Judith."

"You don't have to pretend," Talani said, kinda pouting. "I know you didn't like her."

"I didn't like what she did to *you*. But you loved her like a mother, so my feelings don't matter. If you say she was a good person, I believe you. And she had been nice to me. Heck, she saved my life. So no, I'm not glad she's gone. I feel awful."

Neither of them spoke until Abigail finally found the courage to say, "So, are you mad at Raina?"

Talani met her eyes, then wiped away a tear. "Yes. She didn't even apologize for killing her."

"I'm sorry." Abigail frowned. "Not that it helps."

After another silence, Talani asked what had happened during her nap. Abigail filled her in, telling Talani that they were going to attack King Jacob before dawn, meaning they'd have to get some rest soon.

"Great, I'm not even tired."

"That's okay, we're not going."

"What?" Talani said, brow furrowed. "What do you mean *we're* not going?"

She stood and marched over to John and the others. Abigail tried to stop her, but was too late.

Talani pointed at John. "What do you mean we're not going tomorrow?"

John's eyes widened in surprise. Larry, Hope, and Abalena all looked uncomfortable.

"It's not my decision. It's the Prophet's. Children are staying here, where it's safe."

"*Children?* I'm older than you by a thousand years or more! I'm going. And so is Abigail."

Abigail, standing behind Talani, cleared her throat, "I don't wanna go."

Talani spun around. "What?"

"I don't want to go. I want to stay here with you."

"What are you talking about? King Jacob tried to take you from me. Gods only know what he would've done to you! He needs to die, and this sorry lot needs all the help they can get."

Raina stood and approached. "John is right. It will be hectic enough without you and Abigail there. You must stay."

Larry, Abigail's chubby bearded man-child friend butt in, "If it makes you feel any better, I'll be here too."

Talani ignored Larry with a vicious eye roll.

Abigail cringed.

Talani, hand still on her hip: "This is bullshit! I am *not* staying here like some baby in need of protection."

Prophet Malachi's chair flew backward with a squeak as he stood. "Silence!"

While his normal voice wasn't all that commanding, this booming thunder demanded attention, and made Abigail nervous.

"This isn't up for discussion. This is a matter of The Covenant of the Hand of the Seven Gods, and I refuse to listen to petulant whining."

Talani looked at Raina. "You're going to let him talk to me like that?"

Malachi snapped again. "What part of silence do you not understand, *girl?*"

Abigail gently took Talani's shoulder, but she shrugged

Abigail off, glaring at her sister, then Malachi. "I can fight just as well as any of your soldiers, if not better."

Malachi gave her a cocky smile. "I'm sure you can, young lady. But you have not trained with my soldiers, nor do you know our methods."

"And *he* has?" Talani pointed to John.

"He has trained on Earth with The Guardians, a group much like our own."

"I'll bet," Talani snorted.

"Come on," Raina said, getting in Talani's face, pulling her aside and trying to calm her.

Prophet Malachi's judging gaze burrowed into Abigail's skin. He could barely hide his contempt, though she wasn't sure if it was because Abigail was a kid, a vampire, or maybe because she was friends with Talani the trouble-maker. In any event, she wanted to shrink from his glare.

"Come," Malachi said to Raina. "We've more planning to do."

Raina turned to him and nodded.

Suddenly Abigail remembered the favor that John had asked of her — to see if she could get Talani to ask Raina what she wanted to tell him.

Abigail relayed the message to Talani, but didn't get a response, nor did she accept Abigail's attempt at connection.

Talani was too angry at her sister, and still glaring at Malachi.

*Come on, Talani. John needs to know.*

But Talani was either ignoring her, or didn't hear. Perhaps she was distracted by Raina insisting that every-thing would be fine, and that she had to trust her.

*Come on, answer me!*

And then it was too late.

Raina went to Malachi, and followed him out the door.

# FIFTY-NINE

# John

JOHN WATCHED as Abigail tried to calm Talani. He needed to ask if Abigail had been able to get anything from Raina before she left with the Prophet.

He approached, cautiously, Talani glaring at him like he was the enemy.

"I'm sorry," he said. "You're right. You should be able to fight. But, at the same time, I'm glad you'll be here. Someone needs to protect Abigail."

With a clenched jaw Talani said, "Then why don't *you*, if she's so important?"

"Because Jacob is my brother. My problem, and nobody else needs to die to solve it. I wouldn't be able to forgive myself if you or Abigail got hurt."

"This isn't about your feelings," Talani said.

"It's not about yours, either. And I'm not about to argue with the Prophet. He is giving us an army to fight with. We *need* it. And he was gracious enough to let us stay here, where it's safe."

"It was safe in Under Harbor, too."

"Actually," Gerald said from across the room, where he

was talking with Jonah, "it's safer here. At least we know who our enemies are."

*Sheesh, these werewolves have good hearing!*

Talani sighed and rolled her eyes.

John struggled not to smile at her pouting. She didn't want to be seen as a teenager, but certainly acted the part. Abigail, who was now forever eleven, seemed infinitely more mature.

He met Talani's eyes with his sincerest expression. "I want to thank you for being there for Abigail when I wasn't."

"You mean when you left her all alone."

John tried to hide his annoyance. "The Guardians forced me to help them. If I didn't, they would've turned Abigail into a killer slave, doing their bidding. I left to spare her."

Talani blinked, shedding some of her anger.

"So, again, thank you for being there for her. For being a friend. I can tell she likes you a lot."

Talani looked down at Abigail whose eyes were tearing up.

Abigail nodded.

"I need to ask you two things," John continued.

Talani nodded.

"First, did your sister give you any messages for me?"

Talani shook her head. "No. Why would she do that?"

"I get the feeling she was trying to tell me something. Can you reach her now?"

Talani closed her eyes, trying to reach out. "No, I can't get a connection with her. I don't know if it's because we have different Masters, though that shouldn't be a reason. I found Abigail, after all. But I can't find my sister."

"Okay," John said. "I tried and couldn't reach her,

either. Let me know if you are able. Now, here's the more important thing."

"What?"

"If anything happens to me, I want you to do your best to get Abigail, Hope, and Larry back to Earth — or at least to safety."

"What do you mean, if *anything happens* to you?" Abigail asked.

"I don't know what will happen tomorrow, but I need to make sure you're all safe. Can you promise me that?"

Talani nodded. "Of course."

"Forget that bullshit about the Prophet. *This* is the main reason I want you to stay behind. You're strong. A fighter. I saw in the surveillance video of you cutting through those soldiers guarding the portal."

Talani looked down, maybe ashamed of those innocent deaths.

Abigail started crying. "I don't want anything to happen to you."

He knelt and hugged her, hearing her sobs in his ear. He patted the back of her head. "Me either, Abigail. Me either. I'll do everything in my power to get back."

He caught Hope watching their embrace, and knew saying goodbye to her would be equally hard.

As everyone got settled for bed, John told Hope he'd be right back, then caught up with Larry, ducking into his room.

"Yo, don't even think of bunking with me, Bro."

"You wish."

"Well, you do have *purty* hair."

"Fuck you, Larry," John said with a laugh.

John closed the door for privacy.

The grin fled Larry's face. "What's wrong?"

"After we leave in the morning, I need you to get with the girls and let them know I might not make it back."

"What do you mean?"

"Malachi wants the crystals, and I can't let him have them. If I can't convince him to part with them peacefully, I'll have to make a run for it."

"I don't know, man, maybe you should wait until you all get back here, then try and get them."

"No. I don't want you all caught in the crossfire if shit goes south. I'll send you a message if that happens, and you can get your asses out of here, head for the portal."

"I don't wanna leave without you, man. Please, let me go with you tomorrow."

"No. I want you here to make sure nothing happens to them. Don't worry, I'll do everything possible to meet up with you all once I ditch the cult."

"How will we find the portal?"

"Here," John said, reaching into his pocket and pulling out a map. He handed it to Larry. "Gerald drew this."

"You told Gerald about your plan?"

"I had to trust someone else."

"You sure you can trust him?"

John telepathically said, *Shh, the dude has wolf hearing!*

Larry laughed, then winked. "Okay, then I *definitely* trust him."

"Thank you, Brother," John said, hugging Larry.

"Don't you fucking die on me tomorrow. I'm really not cut out for this single parent shit, especially if we're gonna have *two* moody teenagers around."

John laughed.

~

JOHN WENT to the room he shared with Hope and was surprised to find Abalena in a third bed pulled up beside Hope's.

Even though he couldn't sleep with Hope because the barracks had no Queen- or King-sized beds, nor could he touch her, John was still looking forward to being alone with her on what might be his last night alive. There was still so much he wanted to say before marching to war. But her mother was a wet blanket on it all.

"Um, what's going on?" he whispered.

Hope reminded him that her mother needed to sleep beside her to clear the barriers to her memory.

She looked at John, smiling, eyes optimistic. "Isn't that great?"

"Yes," he lied, "great."

Truth was, John wished she could wait until this whole thing with Jacob was done. He needed to focus on finding his brothers. But now he'd be worrying about Hope's psyche after her memory returned. He needed to be there to help her if things soured. But he couldn't stay.

Yet one more thing to advise Larry on in the morning.

He thought of telling her no, asking her to wait, but the look in her eyes, the smile on her face — it was the happiest, most hopeful he'd seen her since Saint Augustine. And he couldn't bear to destroy it.

He forced himself to smile. "Goodnight, Hope. I love you."

"I love you, too."

For the first time since their reunion, John felt the weight of those words, her truth behind them, and the terror that he wouldn't survive to see Hope again.

SIXTY

## Hope

Hope dreamed of a vast black sky filled with stars.

She was walking, on a cold ground made of black sand as far as she could see in every direction. A leash bit into her neck and throttled her pace.

She looked back to see that the leash fixed her to Abigail.

Hope slowed to let the girl catch up. Abigail drew closer, and Hope noticed her closed eyes.

"Abigail?"

The girl said nothing.

Kept walking in silence.

Hope remembered that she was supposed to be here with someone else. She looked around for any sign of her mother.

"Mom? Abalena?"

Nothing.

Not even an echo of her own voice.

As Hope looked down at the sand, a shadow passed overhead.

Startled, she looked up to see a large object floating

maybe fifty feet above them. She thought of a giant whale floating through the sky.

Her heart raced, and a chill ripped through her.

*What the hell is that?*

More of its shape took form against the stars — Hope realized it was less a whale than something resembling a giant octopus with trailing tentacles.

She needed to run.

"Come on." She yanked on Abigail's leash. "We need to get out of here!"

Abigail stopped dead in her tracks.

"Come on!"

Abigail stood there, eyes closed, not moving or saying a word. Only then did Hope notice that the girl's lips were sewn shut.

Startled, Hope went for a closer look.

But then a shadow forced her to look up.

The creature was descending.

"Oh God, Abi, we've gotta go!"

As the thing drew nearer, every pore in her body sizzled with fear.

Abigail finally spoke, though not with her mouth. "There's nowhere to hide. He's coming."

"Who's coming?"

Abigail's eyes flicked open, black as the sky above and ground below.

Jolted, Hope stumbled back and lost her footing, falling backward to the ground, and then through it.

She screamed as she continued to fall through the sand, then plummeting through the void, bracing for a fall with a ground she could not see.

Then she woke in a gasp, back in the real world.

John was sliding on his boots across from her.

"You okay?"

She looked around, shook off the nightmare. "Yeah."

"Well? Do you remember anything?"

Only the endless black desert and the horrible octopus thing. Abigail with black eyes and a cryptic warning.

"No."

Abalena sat up. "I tried, but I don't know if I got through."

"What did you see?" Hope asked.

"Nothing. Absolutely nothing."

Grinding metal gears screeched from the main room.

# SIXTY-ONE

# John

John ran into the main room to find the others, some dressed and ready to go, others still in their sleeping clothes, staring at the still-closed front doors.

"What's going on?" John asked as Gerald approached the door.

"Fuck if I know." Gerald grabbed both knobs and threw the doors open to a wall of metal bars.

Raina and Prophet Malachi were on the other side, standing in front of men with hands on the hilts of their swords.

"What's the meaning of this?" Gerald snapped.

"We're going without you."

"What?" Jonah stumbled past John, looking hung over.

Malachi stood there with his smug grin. "I thank you all for your help in planning the raid, but I think it best if we go without you."

John joined Gerald and Jonah at the door. "What the hell is going on?"

Malachi met his eyes. "Quite simply, I cannot trust that you won't take the crystals."

"Are you kidding me? I said I would give them to you."

"Yes, but your lips and eyes do not agree."

Suddenly Talani was right next to John, yelling at her sister, "What the hell, Raina?"

"I'm sorry, but we must take precautions. The crystals can't be trusted to anyone but The Hand."

John said, "If you go alone, Jacob will kill you all."

Malachi smiled. "We are The Hand of the Seven Gods, and nothing will stop us from delivering our Gods' judgment."

Talani pleaded, "Raina, don't let him do this."

"I'm sorry." Raina stared past Talani, trying to hide her emotions.

"John is right," Talani yelled. "You'll die if you do this without him."

"And without me." Gerald pounded a fist against his chest. "My brothers won't help you fight if they don't see me there."

"Yes, they will," Malachi said. "They'll have no choice."

John grabbed the bars, trying to bend them, but having no luck. "You're making a mistake, Malachi. You don't know my brother, or what he's capable of."

Malachi met John's eyes. "And you don't know our Gods or what *they* are capable of."

Turning to leave, Malachi said, "Raina and Kero will keep you company until we return."

~

JOHN SPENT twenty minutes begging and pleading with Raina, and even the other guard, a young man who couldn't be more than sixteen, to let them go.

Raina stood stone-faced and frozen, having given up

on arguing about ten minutes in, at first repeating, "I have nothing more to say," and then saying nothing at all.

John and Gerald both tried to bend the bars and break the wall, but nothing gave. The barracks seemed to double as a dungeon.

John pulled everyone aside, to the room's rear, and said, "Does anyone know of another way out?"

None of them did.

Talani said, "Maybe I can reason with her."

"It hasn't worked yet." John shook his head. "And she probably thinks she's protecting you. Hell, maybe she is protecting you. A man like Malachi doesn't leave someone in charge whom he doesn't have leverage over."

"Fuck his leverage," Talani said, storming past John toward the large barred door.

John looked at the others, shrugged, then followed.

But upon arrival, a third guard approached Raina and Kero, out of breath.

"Sister Raina, you must come to the gate."

"What is it?" she asked.

"You must see for yourself."

Raina left Kero in charge.

John looked at Talani, then back at the gate.

Talani approached him, looking to charm the young man. "Hey, Kero. How would you like to do the right thing?"

But the guard refused to meet his eyes, likely instructed to avoid a Valkoer's charms.

# SIXTY-TWO

# Raina

RAINA MARCHED to The Citadel gates and froze in her tracks when she saw the man conversing with the guards — battered, clothes wet and bloodied, but alive.

*Caleb!*

She ran up to him, arms wide, pulling him into a huge hug.

"You're alive!" she cried, not caring that the others could see her emotions. If any of them had shit to say tomorrow, she'd kick their asses then.

"How?" she asked.

"I escaped," he said, rubbing his head.

His cheeks were bruised, and a long cut ran the length of his forehead, blood crusted around it. His eyes looked hollow, like he'd not only seen a ghost but had battled it back into Hell.

"How did you escape?"

"One of the guards dropped his caution, and I made him pay. Then I found an old drainage tunnel and took it to the island's edge before swimming to shore."

She hugged him again.

He was cold, shaking, and not exactly returning the hug. Raina imagined the torture he must have endured while held by the King.

"Did they hurt you?"

He nodded.

"Did you give up any information?"

He shook his head. "Nothing."

"Good. Let's get you cleaned up, and you can tell me everything."

She tried to send him a message telepathically, but could only connect to static. It was like he wasn't even there, despite standing before her.

She wondered how badly they hurt him. Extreme psychological duress could definitely impair a Valkoer's ability to communicate telepathically.

She escorted Caleb into The Citadel. But before taking him to his room she said, "I have a surprise for you."

"What is it?"

"Your brother is here."

"*Brother?*"

"John."

Caleb smiled. "*Really?*"

"Yes, do you want to see him?"

"Gods, yes."

# SIXTY-THREE

# John

---

JOHN HAD GIVEN up on also trying to charm Kero, and was back in the rear talking to Larry, Gerald, and Jonah while Hope and Abalena occupied the girls and tried to calm Talani.

John asked Jonah, "Do you trust Malachi with the crystals?"

"Gods, no."

Gerald said, "A bastard like *him* getting ahold of that kind of power … It could be worse than King Cunt Jacob getting it."

"Shit." John shook his head. "We've got to find a way out of here."

"You prepared to fight your way through the entire Hand, or whatever's left behind?" Gerald asked.

"How many men are we talking?"

"Maybe two hundred, I'd guess."

Jonah laughed. "I could kill two hundred of these pussies with one hand tied behind my back."

John smiled. He liked the old man's attitude, both old

men's attitudes, actually, but thought he might be overestimating his skills.

John said, "I don't want to get anyone else killed. Maybe we wait until —"

A familiar voice beckoned: "John?"

John turned to the barred doorway and saw Caleb, battered and torn, but alive.

"Caleb!" John ran to the door.

His brother smiled, reaching through the bars, stroking John's face. "It feels so good to see you again, Brother."

John looked at Raina. "Can you open the door, please?"

Raina shook her head. "I'm sorry."

"Just let me in," Caleb said, turning to Raina.

"I can't open the door until Prophet Malachi returns."

Caleb turned to Raina, his brow furrowed. "Just open the door, bitch."

Her eyes went wide. "*What?*"

Then John saw Caleb's blade, moving swiftly, piercing Raina's neck.

John screamed.

Talani's scream was a whimpering echo.

Raina dropped to the ground, then Caleb turned his attention on the young guard, fumbling with his sword.

Kero was too late.

Caleb grabbed him by the neck and began to suck his life away.

*Oh God, Jacob turned him!*

Caleb dropped the spasming, burning boy to the ground, then turned back to the door.

"You fucker!" Talani screamed, reaching through the bars, trying to claw at him.

Caleb stepped back, laughing. "Oh boy, Brother, you've got a live one there, eh? Better in the sack than Hope?"

Something was wrong.

The man in front of him looked and sounded like Caleb, but it wasn't his way of speaking.

"*Jacob?*"

Caleb's smile faltered. He pouted, then sarcastically said, "Never could pull one over on you, Johnny Boy. But you've gotta love this amulet's little tricks."

Caleb tugged at a necklace, pulling it out of his shirt to reveal a glowing red amulet — the crystals formed into the shape of a heart.

Wisps of darkness moved over Caleb's face, then parted. Jacob smiled. "Hello, Brother."

John gritted his teeth. "*You.*"

Suddenly, screams behind John.

He turned to see two portals opening, with Valkoer and other monstrosities pouring forth.

John couldn't go to war, so Jacob had brought it to him.

# SIXTY-FOUR

# Hope

At least a dozen men dressed in black armor spilled through the portals, black swords drawn. Behind them, three tall, spindly creatures — inky black, with long limbs, claws for hands, and hollowed-out eye sockets — twitched into the room. Their mouths were open maws of blackened razor-sharp teeth as they shrieked, heads bobbing, as if using sound to search for prey.

No one moved as the men, whom she assumed to be Valkoer, surrounded Hope and her friends. Neither the Valkoer nor the monstrosities were striking, obviously waiting for Jacob's order.

"Do I have your attention, ladies and gentlemen?" Jacob asked them.

"What do you want?" John shouted.

Hope exchanged glances with Talani, who was standing in front of Abigail protectively. She looked at her mother, frozen behind Gerald.

John and Jonah were at the gate, waiting to hear Jacob's answer.

He finally spoke: "I want you to come home. There's a

place in my kingdom for you and your friends. Simply accept me as your Master."

"Never!" Abalena screamed.

Hope turned to beg her mother's silence before something silenced her.

*Too late.*

One of the black creatures charged, thrusting a clawed arm through her chest.

Hope screamed and raced toward her mother, without even knowing how she could help.

The creature turned its empty eyes to Hope as she neared it, opened its maw and hissed. It swiftly withdrew its claws from Abalena, leaving her guts splashing out of her body and onto the floor.

Hope froze again, meeting her mother's wide eyes. Time turned to ice as her mom mouthed something incomprehensible, then collapsed to the ground.

Hope couldn't move.

Movement to her side told Hope what her mother was trying to say:

*Look out!*

She turned to see the other monster barreling toward her.

Hope braced for impact, but none came.

Instead, Gerald thrust himself between her and the creature. But his blade was no match for the monster's hook.

A claw ripped through his stomach and drilled out through Gerald's back.

Then all hell broke loose.

# SIXTY-FIVE

# John

JOHN SPUN around when he saw the wraith chasing Hope, and threw himself toward her.

Gerald got there first, and lost his life because of it.

Hope was frozen, shrieking as she stared at Gerald and her mother's bodies.

Larry grabbed Hope and pulled her back toward the front door with Jonah, who had somehow managed to kill two knights already. Larry and Hope picked up the fallen soldiers' swords as more knights surrounded them.

Talani launched herself at the Valkoer Knights, with Abigail right behind her. Talani had no weapon that John could see, but Abigail did — a black Valkoer-killing blade.

Talani managed to turn one of the men's swords against his companion, then wrested it out of his hands and turned it on its owner.

*She's right — she can fight.*

The murdering wraith turned its attention to John, sockets staring hard as it opened its mouth wide, shrieking blades into his ears.

John wasn't sure where the other two wraiths were but

hoped that Larry was protecting Hope — if he *could* protect her from the monsters.

John clenched his fist until he felt a ball of energy filling it. He swung, unclenching as it neared the monster's face. The blast of energy ripped a chunk from the wraith's gnashing maw and sent it hurtling to the ground.

But the wraith wasn't dead and scrambled to stand.

About to counter, John spotted a sword slicing the air, coming straight at his face. He fell back, swept with his feet on the way down, and managed to topple the attacking Valkoer Knight.

As the knight tumbled, John reached for his fallen sword.

The wraith met him instead, slamming into John and sending him flying backward.

The wraith fell to all fours and charged like a giant monstrous bull.

# SIXTY-SIX

# Abigail

JACOB'S MEN were wearing black armor to protect their bodies, but they weren't wearing helmets. Abigail stabbed the first knight through his eye, driving the blade into the back of his skull as Talani took on two knights herself.

Blade still lodged in him, the dying knight took Abigail down with him as he fell backward.

As Abigail struggled to remove the knife stuck in his skull, she looked up to see John fighting a wraith. Behind him, Larry and Hope backed up against the door, Jacob smiling, watching the horror unfold from the rear. Raina lay dead like a broken toy on the ground outside.

Abigail wanted to kill him. For all he'd done to her and John, and Talani's sister. She was glaring at Jacob, and he was glowering back. A cold wave rolled through her, and for a moment she was frozen.

The blade finally came free with a sickening plop.

Then a shriek behind her.

Abigail turned to see one of the monsters coming right at her, mouth wide open and screaming, claw swinging.

She had no time to move.

It was inches away, and she was still frozen.

Abigail closed her eyes.

She heard an unholy scream, followed by a thump, then looked up to see Talani standing over the creature, sword driven into its back, body twitching.

"Thank —" Abigail started.

But then one of the monsters grabbed Talani around the throat, pulling her back.

Abigail screamed, finally finding the will to move, and leaped to her feet, blade ready to murder anything that stood in her way.

## SIXTY-SEVEN

# Hope

HOPE AND LARRY stood back to back, swords drawn, fending off two knights on either side of them.

She wasn't sure where Jonah had gone, and didn't dare move her eyes from the man in front of her, a giant bushy-bearded beast who looked like he wanted to slice her from gut to neck with his blade.

"Don't let them touch you," Larry heaved over the clanging swords. "They're all vampires."

She could feel his back against hers. It was a comfort to have an ally *literally* at her back, and worrisome that if one of them was pushed too hard into the other, or if their feet got tangled, both would fall.

Hope had never fought with a sword, but was somehow managing to parry away the knight's strikes, even if she'd yet to deliver a blow.

It felt fluid as she swung, her instincts like razors, and the blade's hilt like a gift in her hands.

More memories poured forth: her as a child fencing with the wizard. And for the first time, she could *see* him: old and short but with surprisingly dark shaggy hair and piercing gray eyes. She could almost hear his voice telling her to concentrate.

And then, lost in the flashback, her real world was gone.

Her sword fell to the ground.

The knight's eyes lit with opportunity.

He thrust his blade forward.

Hope dodged, and the sword missed her.

Only to find Larry's back.

# SIXTY-EIGHT

# Larry

LARRY FELT Hope fall away behind him.

*Shit!*

He thought she was hit, and was trying to think of a way to dodge the pecker in front of him while also turning to help her.

An explosion of pain pierced his back.

He screamed. Agony came in a flood.

His hand seized up, and he dropped his sword.

The knight in front of Larry thrust a blade through his gut.

Stabbed, front and back.

The men pulled their blades out at the same time. Larry fell to the ground, choking on blood and his final few breaths.

# Hope

HOPE GRABBED her blade and went after the knight who had stabbed Larry in the back, horrified to see a second knight pierce him from the front.

She screamed as something else took over her actions. Suddenly, her body just knew what to do. She swung the sword hard, lopping the closest knight's head clean off.

She stared at the body as it staggered headless, blood spurting from its neck like some ghastly joke.

She looked away, only to see her mother's corpse.

*No, can't think about that now. I can only avenge her.*

She saw Larry crumpled, facedown on the floor, blood pooling beneath him.

She couldn't tell if he was moving, or take the time to check as the other knight was coming straight at her.

Gripping her sword with both hands, she swung and met his blade. Their eyes clashed as a thunderous clang screamed through her hand and up her arms like lightning. But she wouldn't drop her sword again.

They pulled away at the same time, eyes locked,

engaged in a deadly pirouette of thrusts, countermoves, and feints.

Movement swirled around her, pained screams, clashing blades, and the shrieking of monsters, all threatening to dizzy her mind, as did the horrible truth that her friend was dying on the ground.

But she couldn't lose focus. Not again.

The first time had nearly cost Hope her life.

It might be costing Larry his.

## SEVENTY

## John

_______

JOHN ROLLED out of the way as the wraith came at him, but not before it reached out and sliced at his left thigh.

"Fuck!" John screamed through gritted teeth.

He couldn't be certain of the wound's depth, but his pants were ripped and blood was spilling.

The monster quickly turned back on him as John clambered back to standing, shrieking as it charged again.

John threw up his hand and shot a blast of energy, this time hitting the wraith in its gut.

It fell back howling, a hole blown through its insides.

The wraith was down.

John looked around, surveying the chaos, heart sinking at the sight of Larry lying facedown in a pool of blood.

And Hope fending off a Valkoer Knight, wielding a blade like a seasoned swordsman.

He was about to help her when Abigail cried out behind him.

John turned to see a wraith dragging Talani into the portal.

Abigail screamed, "No!" then ran in after her.

*Fuck!*

John took another quick glance to find Jonah fending off two remaining Valkoer, and a wraith. He could probably use help, but given that all the rest of the Valkoer were dead or dying, perhaps the old man could finish them off.

Something was missing from the scene.

Then John saw the empty hall outside the barred doorway. Jacob wasn't there.

*Where the hell is —*

He felt the blade at his neck, and Jacob's voice in his ear.

"Hello, Brother."

# SEVENTY-ONE

# Hope

HOPE WAS BLOCKING the knight's every strike, but he was pushing her back against the wall with every attack.

She tried to push *him* back, but couldn't manage.

The wall was closing in behind her, but she didn't dare look.

*What will I do when he gets my back to the wall? How can I counter or dodge him then? I'll have nowhere to go.*

Her heart was a bomb, seconds from detonation. Every sense was focused on the beast of a man before her. His rusty eyes, scarred face, and yellow teeth practically champing to end her. She imagined him licking his lips, eager to feast on her flesh.

She could feel more memories stirring, bubbling to the surface. Visions commanding her sight, voices demanding her ears.

*No. I must focus.*

Jonah fell to the ground, then two Valkoer pounced and fed.

Her stomach was an elevator in free fall.

*Focus on your enemy!*

The knight swung again. Hope parried, and again stepped back.

She slipped on blood.

Her foot gave way.

She fell on her back.

The knight charged in with his sword.

"Stop!" a man bellowed.

The knight froze above her, as if a force compelled him against his will. Hope stared at the man, his eyes wide in their sockets, seeming confused.

He looked behind Hope, toward the command, eyes darting back and forth as if desperate to resume what he was doing.

But his sword was frozen overhead, his body still.

Jacob was standing behind John, a blade to his neck.

Her stomach finally found the floor.

She wanted to vomit.

Jacob grinned. "So, now that we got all *that* out of the way ..."

# SEVENTY-TWO

# Abigail

ABIGAIL CHASED Talani into the portal, and found herself back in the In-Between.

It was slightly different this time — even colder, with black sand on the ground in every direction. The sky was ink and stars, some blotted out by the horrible floating things.

In the distance she saw one of the monsters who had taken Talani, now carrying the girl over its shoulder instead of holding her by the throat.

Abigail wanted to scream for her return, but didn't want to alert the monster. So she ran, cursing the sand for slowing her, and pushing herself to run harder.

But the monster was faster.

Abigail didn't know where it was taking Talani, but she could feel that wherever it was, she could never catch up.

"Hey!"

The monster stopped.

Abigail kept running.

It was nearly fifty feet away, and as she drew closer,

Abigail remembered what Judith had said: The monsters can't hurt you in the In-Between. At least not physically.

If that were true, could *she* hurt *it?*

Abigail was about to find out.

Ten feet away, the monster dropped Talani to the sand.

Talani's eyes were closed.

Abigail hoped she was passed out rather than dead.

"Get away from her!" Abigail yelled, waving her knife at the monster, trying to scare it away.

The monster stood seven feet away, looking down at her with its wide empty sockets.

*Can it see me without eyes?*

She held her breath, and stopped waving the knife to see its response — maybe it *saw* movement or sound. Maybe staying still would make her invisible.

It was even more hideous up close. Its black skin was wet and slimy. Its clawed hand looked like some sort of sharp black bone jutting out from its flesh.

The monster continued to stand there, staring down at Abigail.

She looked down at Talani at its feet. Abigail could see her chest and stomach rising and falling, still breathing.

She had to reach Talani and get her away from the monster.

Abigail inched closer.

The monster stayed frozen, staring ahead.

She moved a bit to her left, slowly to avoid all sound, and waited to see if its head followed.

Still, nothing.

*It can't sense me.*

*I can do this.*

Abigail inched closer.

Three feet away.

She'd bend down, slowly gather Talani in relative

silence, then tiptoe away, assuming she could carry her friend who was bigger and weighed more than Abigail.

*I can do this. I've got vampire strength!*

Inches to go.

Not having a sheath, she bit down on the hilt of the blade as she squatted, sliding her hands under Talani, keeping her eyes on the monster.

If the creature breathed, she couldn't hear it.

She couldn't hear *anything* save her own breath, which she was trying to stifle, wishing for a wind or anything that might mask her movement.

But the In-Between was as silent as it was cold.

As she slid her hands fully under Talani, sand fell away with a whisper.

The monster's head turned quickly toward her, mouth open wide as if it was hearing with that instead of eyes.

*No, no, no, no!*

She paused, praying that it wouldn't jump on her.

Again it was still.

She kept her eyes fixed on the monster, and lifted Talani.

Her knees cracked.

The monster's head turned slightly downward, but still its body didn't move.

*Good, good, just gotta move quietly.*

Talani wasn't too heavy, but quietly moving away would take a lot longer than Abigail wanted.

She slowly turned from the monster.

She then began to walk, slowly as humanly possible.

*That's it.*

*Nice and easy …*

*and quiet.*

*One foot in front of the other.*

*Just keep —*

Talani suddenly screamed, thrusting her arms out, elbowing Abigail hard in the face. She fell with Talani atop her.

The monster's mouth opened wide again, as if its jaw were unhinged.

Then it screamed — a high-pitched shriek like knives in Abigail's head. She covered her ears to muffle the sound.

The monster moved closer.

Shadows descended.

Abigail looked up to see the floating nightmares sinking toward them.

# SEVENTY-THREE

# John

JOHN FELT the blade at his neck, and flashed back on Vashkar slicing Logan's throat, and how helpless he'd been to stop it.

Again he felt helpless. Not to save his own life. He didn't think Jacob would kill him if he didn't have to. But he might kill Hope, and make John watch.

And that would be worse than death.

"What do you want from me?"

"As I said before, dear brother, I want you to come home. Caleb is waiting for us."

"Fine. I'll come with you. But let her go."

Jacob was quiet, perhaps considering the request.

Hope's eyes were wide, terrified, as she stood helplessly in front of John. A Valkoer Knight stood frozen behind her. Another knight and wraith headed back into the portal.

John hoped they didn't catch up to Abigail and her friend.

Jacob finally responded. "Maybe, if we were back on Earth, I might let her go. But we're not, and without you, she won't get back on her own. It isn't safe out there for a woman. How about she comes with us? We can be one big happy family, with me as your Master."

John swallowed his disgust.

He'd say anything now to buy time.

"Okay."

Hope's eyes were wide in terror.

John hoped she trusted him to find a way out. If not, he'd have to kill his true love before Jacob could turn her.

Then he'd kill himself.

# SEVENTY-FOUR

# Abigail

ABIGAIL AND TALANI WERE TRAPPED, a screaming monster in front of them, and floating nightmares descending.

"Run!" she yelled at Talani.

Abigail turned to run, but a second monster was behind her, its mouth open and shrieking.

She fell to the ground, hands tight against her ears, barely able to muffle the sound or drown the pain.

Not knowing what else to do, she let out her own unearthly scream, "Stoooooop!"

The monster stopped screaming.

And for a moment, Abigail felt hopeful. Then she felt its claws closing around her, picking her up. She tried to fight back, but her body went limp.

*No, no, no, no.*

*I can't move.*

*It's controlling me!*

The other monster was gathering Talani. She yelled, "Put me down!" but made no moves to stop it either. They were both helpless.

Abigail screamed again, but the monsters didn't care.

They began walking, to where God only knew.

Abigail continued to scream the entire time. She caught Talani looked back at her, eyes crying.

*"Sorry, Abigail,"* Talani said in her mind.

Suddenly, a woman's voice in Abigail's head: *"You can fight them."*

Abigail thought it was Talani, but when she spoke again saying that Abigail could fight them, she realized that it wasn't.

*"Judith?"*

*"Yes."*

*Aren't you dead?*

*"I'm here, Abigail. Stuck in the In-Between."*

*How can I fight them?*

*"Attack their minds."*

*I don't know how.*

*"Yes, you do. Just focus on their thoughts."*

Abigail closed her eyes, felt for a connection, and was surprised to immediately find it. Most people felt like whispers, whose thoughts she could sometimes overhear. These things sounded like static, a frayed signal on an endless loop. *Maybe* it was their language.

Abigail could feel the door opening into their minds.

She forced her way in.

And found herself standing in a void, utter darkness all around her. She couldn't see anything, but felt the walls around her as if in a labyrinth as big as the world. But the walls weren't made of wood, concrete, or steel. They felt wet and alive, like tissue. Brain.

She pressed on one of the nearest walls — squishy to the touch.

She drove her hand through it.

The static grew loud.

Whatever she did hurt the thing.

"Put me down," she commanded.

The static continued, a buzzing beneath it.

She punched another wall.

*Shriek.*

She punched again and again and again.

The shrieking and static grew in concert, a cacophony, like nails pounded through her ears. But she didn't care.

Abigail kept punching, then she grabbed ahold of the fleshy walls and turned her focus from punching to absorbing.

To feeding.

The thing screamed.

Abigail laughed.

She felt her body drop, both in the psychic space and the In-Between.

She opened her eyes, disconnected from the monster whose body was burning from the inside.

Abigail launched another mental attack on Talani's monster, and doubled her victory.

As the monsters burned, Abigail and Talani shook off the numbness and regained control of their bodies.

"You did it," Judith's voice spoke as if beside them.

"Judith? Is it really you?"

"Yes, Talani."

"Why can't I see you?"

"I'm afraid my body is gone. But I'm here with you nonetheless."

"Thank you," Abigail said. "But we need to get back to John. Can you help us find our way?"

As they searched for the portal, Abigail told Judith about the amulet, and how they had to stop Jacob.

Talani had questions, like why Judith was here, and if there were other dead people around, like maybe her sister or father.

"I don't know why I'm here, nor do I know if there is anyone else. You're the first people I've seen — everything else has been wraiths or psychopis."

"Psychopis?" Abigail asked.

"The floating things. I remembered their name. They're like the wraiths, but can't breach the portal into our worlds. Here, they rule. Ignore their attempts to trick you, and you'll be fine."

"Can we fight them telepathically?" Abigail asked.

"I wouldn't try. They're much smarter than the wraiths."

They continued walking until they saw the portal they'd come through.

Just on the other side of the portal, Jacob was holding a dagger to John's throat, leading him toward the other portal.

Abigail grabbed her blade, about to leap through.

"Wait," Judith said. "Not yet. If he sees you, he might kill your friends. Run behind the portal and wait until they come through. I'll shroud us in shadow."

They waited, crouched behind the portal, shrouded by Judith's magick even though she wasn't physically with them.

They watched as Jacob marched John and Hope into the In-Between.

Abigail tensed, craving attack but not sure what to do. Jacob was so much more powerful than she or Talani were.

She gripped the knife tight in her hand hoping it would be enough.

But first she'd have to sneak up on them.

They waited, watching as Jacob cruelly joked with them about the fun they'd have as a family together.

After they put some distance between them, Abigail and Talani stood up.

As they approached the portal to pass it, Abigail looked through and immediately felt as if someone punched her in the heart.

"No," she whispered, pointing.

"Oh my God," Talani gasped at all the bodies.

Abigail's eyes welled up, but she stifled her tears. She had to stay strong so they could surprise Jacob.

But then she saw a body that broke her: *Larry.*

"No!" she cried out, jumping through the portal, into the remains of the massacre, scrambling over corpses.

Talani followed, "We're gonna lose them!"

But Abigail couldn't focus on anything other than the sight of one of her best friends, dying or dead.

She dropped to the ground beside Larry and turned him over, careful not to touch his skin.

His eyes were closed.

Blood spilled from his closed mouth.

"Larry?" she asked, her voice cracking.

He didn't respond.

Abigail stared at him, listening for a pulse, or a breath, or anything.

*Nothing.*

"No, no, no!" she cried, leaning over, resting her head on his chest as if he might hear her and wake from the dead.

She looked up at Talani, also crying.

Talani cried, "I'm so sorry."

Abigail shook her head. "No."

"What do you mean, no?"

"We can't let him die."

"We're too late."

"Are we?"

Talani looked confused. "What do you mean?"

"They brought me back from the dead. Turned me. Can we do it to him?"

"I don't know." Talani swallowed. "I've never turned anyone."

"But Judith has."

"Yes."

Abigail stood and walked to the portal.

She stepped halfway in, and made sure she couldn't see Jacob, John, or Hope. "Judith. We need your help."

# SEVENTY-FIVE

# Abigail

ABIGAIL KNEELED DOWN BESIDE LARRY, his blood staining her pants, as she stared at him, hoping that this would work.

His eyes were closed.

He had no pulse.

He was dead.

How long had he been dead?

How long did she have?

She didn't know anything other than she had to try.

Talani stood half-in and half-out of the portal as Judith instructed her on the means to turn a person.

Abigail recited the spell.

Then she leaned forward, parted his lips, and kissed him as her parasite split, then crawled into Larry's dead mouth.

Abigail closed her eyes as the creature slipped from her mouth and into his. She would vomit if she saw it. Abigail was still disgusted by the thing living inside her, even though it was the only thing that kept her alive.

"It's in," Talani said.

Abigail opened her eyes, watching Larry's face, waiting, hoping, and … *praying*.

She felt like a fraud coming to God for help, especially after the deaths on her hands. She'd once been an innocent little girl, victim of a horrible uncle, victim of a fate that stole her family, and victim of the rapist Randy Webster.

But Abigail was no longer a victim.

She was a perpetrator, killing to survive.

And while she had only intended to kill bad people that God Himself would probably agree deserved to die, the blood of innocents also stained her soul.

And what God would listen to a monster's prayers? Especially when her request was to help her create another just like her?

Minutes stretched, and faith turned to tears.

She looked back at Talani. "Ask her if he should be awake by now."

Talani slipped out of sight then returned, looking gravely at the ground.

"I'm sorry. She said it's too late."

Abigail's lip trembled as tears began anew.

"I'm so sorry," Abigail cried, bending to kiss Larry on his forehead.

She swallowed her knot and stood.

She looked down at Larry one last time, remembering the good times, the many nights they sat in his van talking about stupid things and things not so stupid. How he'd never really treated her as a kid but more like a slightly younger sister.

In many ways, she was closer to him than John, and she couldn't imagine living without his laugh or his stupid jokes. Living without *him*.

"Goodbye, friend." she said.

She turned and met Talani at the portal.

Talani hugged her. "I'm sorry."

"We both lost people today. Let's go make that fucker pay."

Talani pulled away from the hug and nodded. "Yes, let's."

They were about to step through the portal when they heard a gasping behind them.

# SEVENTY-SIX

# John

"IGNORE THE THINGS ABOVE," Jacob instructed as they stepped into the In-Between, a vast and endless black desert beneath a starry sky that looked like no sky he'd ever seen.

"What is this place?" Hope asked, walking a few paces ahead of John, who still had Jacob guiding him forward with a knife at his throat.

John had been looking for a moment to escape but had yet to find one that wouldn't end with his throat slit.

And if he was dead, Hope would be lost to Jacob for eternity.

Jacob responded. "It has many names: the In-Between, the Void, the Null, Purgatory, Limbo, and, I suppose some humans might call it Hell."

Hope was shivering, her breath like smoke as she spoke. "Where are we going?"

"This is a shortcut to your new home, The Forgotten Kingdom. But don't worry, it's only temporary. Once I am your Master and I know you won't leave my side, you'll be able to find your own Kingdoms. If you want to make one on Earth, we can arrange that. Or perhaps you'd like to go to The North on this world. I hear its tech makes Earth's look like the Dark Ages."

John risked talking. "Why is it so important for you to be our Master? Why not just let us go?"

"Because, John, we're family. I know you probably don't remember much of your life before Mother stole you away, but we were all once a happy family."

"Really? Is that why Mother left the King? Because she was *happy?*"

"The wizard clouded her mind. Made her think Father was bad. Sure, he had his issues; who doesn't? But he treated her okay ... well, much better than he treated me, anyway."

John sensed a thread to pull at. He wasn't sure what it would get him, but he had to try something before they reached the Kingdom.

"How *did* he treat you?"

"It doesn't matter. He's dead now, and the past is behind us. What we do with the future is all that matters. I'm going to liberate our people, John. No longer will we live in the shadows, slaves to those who fear us."

John wanted to get back to discussing the King, knowing there was something there to use against Jacob. He was getting flashes of memory, too, from Jacob — of exactly how terrible he'd been treated by their father. He didn't think Jacob was sending him the memories so much as they were seeping out of him, perhaps because of this place.

"You know my adopted father treated Caleb and me like hell, too?"

"I know all too well. I answered your brother's prayer and killed him for you. A gift. You're welcome."

"Thank you," John said, then let the silence stretch.

"I'm sorry we were taken. That the King took it all out on you. That wasn't right. If I could go back in time, I'd change it."

"Well, you can't. And damn it, stop pretending to give a fuck about me. I know what you're doing."

"What?" John asked coyly.

"You're pretending to know what it felt like, feigning concern. I know you don't care about me, and I get it, what with me being a 'psychopath' and all. But I hope that you'll see that I'm not the monster you think I am. *I spared you.* And Hope. I spared Caleb, too! Would a monster do all that sparing?"

"No," John said.

"That almost seemed genuine."

John didn't respond. He was losing whatever foothold he thought he might be gaining in Jacob's mind.

"It's okay. You don't have to like me now. But you will once I am your Master. You'll both come to love me."

Hope asked, "What kind of love is one not given freely?"

"What?" Jacob said, turning to Hope.

"How can it be love if you *force us* to love you? That's not *love.* That's pathetic."

"Shut up," Jacob growled.

Hope stopped. "No. I won't."

*What are you doing? Stop it!*

"Excuse me?" Jacob said.

"You're nothing but a bully!" Hope said, hands on her hips.

She was reminding John of Talani. *Too much* of Talani.

"Stop it," John said.

She stared past him, straight at Jacob. "Tell me, does it feel good to be a bully? Does it feel good to be no different than your daddy?"

Jacob pressed the knife to John's throat, harder, piercing the flesh. The blade stung, and he winced, feeling its poison seeping into his bloodstream.

"Shut up and walk, or I'll kill you both right here."

"No, I don't think you will," Hope said. "I don't think you *can*."

Jacob laughed, his voice shaky, "I don't think this bitch likes you too much, Brother. Or likes living, for that matter. You want to tell her to shut her mouth or should I shut it for her, permanently?"

Did Hope have a plan? Or had she decided that it was better to die than let Jacob win? If Hope thought she could agitate him enough to toss John aside and pursue her and that John could grab him from behind and save the day, she was misreading Jacob's volatility, and how close he was to losing his shit and killing them both.

"Please, Hope," John said, "just stop."

Suddenly, a voice spoke in John's head — Abigail's.

*"John, let her keep going. Judith is guiding her."*

*Judith? What?*

*"Trust us,"* Abigail said.

Hope stood her ground. "No, I refuse to be quiet! What kind of man needs to force people into loving him? What kind of *pathetic* excuse for a man? Boo-hoo, Daddy didn't love me. I'm gonna take it out on the world. *You. Are. Pathetic!*"

Hope spit toward them.

Jacob pressed the knife harder against John's neck.

"Another word, and he dies."

Hope's eyes locked onto Jacob's.

"Go ahead. You're gonna do it anyway."

Jacob stuck the blade into John's throat.

# SEVENTY-SEVEN

# Hope

HOPE WATCHED JACOB SNAP, thrust the blade into John's neck, and toss him to the black sands.

John fell, clutching at the blade, unable to pull it out, twitching wildly as poison spread through his body. Judith had said they could save him but only after retrieving the amulet.

Jacob's eyes, dark and full of rage, narrowed on her.

"Look what you made me do!"

All humor was gone from his voice, replaced by an ugly mottled rage. He seemed to believe that *she* had made him stab John.

And now she would pay.

He rushed forward, hands reaching out to end her life.

Behind him, he never saw the blurs approaching.

Abigail and Talani pounced on Jacob from behind.

He gasped in shock on his way to the ground.

Abigail slid her blade toward his neck.

But instead of cutting him, she sliced the necklace, and the amulet, free.

It fell into the black sands, instantly buried by all the dirt kicked up in their quarrel.

Jacob growled, likely realizing what they were trying to do. He swung his arm, knocking Abigail twenty feet back.

Talani plunged her blade into Jacob's chest, but it made a terrible scraping against the light armor under his shirt.

He grabbed Talani by the throat and started to choke her.

Hope used the distraction to drop to the ground, and scrambled on hands and knees, hands digging, searching for the necklace.

Jacob tossed Talani into the air like a doll.

Hope didn't have time to see if Talani landed safely, or where Abigail was. She was fishing through the sands, trying to locate the amulet.

Jacob turned on her, opened his palm, and sent a wave of energy that sent Hope hurtling backward.

She fell hard on her back then scrambled to her feet.

Abigail was up beside her, eying Hope for guidance.

But Judith gave it instead.

"Attack!"

Abigail and Talani rushed him again, though both were unarmed.

Jacob became a blur, grabbing Talani, swinging her by the arm with a sickening crunch of something breaking, before sending her straight into Abigail, causing them both to collide in a painful heap.

Hope saw a glimmer of gold, about five feet in front of Jacob.

She was only three feet away, scrambling forward, diving, hands outstretched.

Jacob thrust his hand upward, and the necklace vaulted into the air before Hope's fingers could close around it.

She gasped and hit the ground hard, black sand kicking up into her mouth.

Jacob looked down at her, smiling as she spit the sand out.

The necklace floated before him as if he were taunting her, keeping it just out of reach.

Hope felt something tighten around her neck.

Jacob wasn't touching Hope, but was somehow choking her anyway, lifting her into the air with his mind. She kicked and tried to grab at invisible hands, but couldn't feel anything to pry away.

Jacob's smile widened, growing darker as he levitated her.

She tried to claw at him, but the monster was just out of reach.

The grip on her neck tightened.

Behind her, she heard one of the girls running to launch another attack.

Jacob raised another hand, and the movement stopped.

Hope turned to see that Jacob had Abigail in a floating choke hold as well.

He brought the girls together then looked at them both, shaking his head. "Never have I met two bigger pains in the ass. I don't know if I should kill you or make you my thralls."

"Fuck you," Hope gasped, the grip around her neck still getting tighter.

He stepped closer, necklace floating beside him, mocking her and Abigail both.

He looked at Abigail and smiled. "I think I'll keep you." Then he turned to Hope. "But you, my dear, must go."

He reached out to choke her himself, and drain her life.

Hope looked down at John, still idle on the ground.

*I'm sorry I failed.*

Someone shouted, "Hey, Captain Fuckface, make that *three* pains in the ass!"

Jacob turned to see Larry standing about ten feet behind him, trying to draw his attention. "Oh, you want to play, too, fat boy? Hold on, just after I kill this bitch." He reached out and grabbed Hope's throat, his skin touching hers.

She flinched, preparing to burn alive.

A flood of childhood memories surged through her mind. Among them was VVessolff casting a spell that made her invulnerable to the Valkoer who had often threatened her as a stable girl.

Jacob's eyes widened as if to ask why she wasn't dying.

She smiled.

He never saw the flash behind him — Larry racing faster than he had any right to be running.

Larry stabbed Jacob in the back.

Jacob screamed, managing to send an energy blast into the ground that knocked them all about ten feet away from the impact site.

Abigail and Hope landed next to one another.

Jacob was still standing, reaching back and pulling the blade from his back. "You're all going to die," he said, walking toward the still-floating necklace.

Hope remembered one other thing. She reached out and compelled the necklace toward her.

Jacob's eyes widened as the amulet landed in her hand.

"Give me that!"

Warmth spread through Hope's hand as the amulet glowed bright blue. With the warmth came more memories, too many to corral, most of them pleasant.

She felt as if she were reunited with an old friend.

*"Esmee?"* she heard VVessolff's voice in her head.

"My name is Hope now."

*"Welcome home."*

"Thank you. Can you please take care of this pathetic King?"

*"Gladly."*

She felt the amulet's warmth spread through her entire being.

She'd never felt more alive, more powerful.

Jacob stood shaking.

"No. What are you doing?"

"What your mother should've done before she left," Hope said, approaching Jacob.

He tried to move but was met by Larry, Abigail, and Talani behind him, blades in their hands.

Hope used her newfound powers to raise him up in the air in a choke hold.

He turned back to Hope, gasping. "Please," he begged, eyes crying, "all I wanted was to be with my family again."

"Hold tight. You'll be with family again real soon … *your parents.*"

Her right hand glowed orange, bright as the sun, if not as hot, though Hope felt no pain.

Jacob flinched when he saw it, tried to break free.

He was as helpless as she was.

Hope raised her glowing hand. "This is what you get for fucking with *my family.*"

She placed her radiating palm on his face.

Jacob screamed as his flesh melted, then turned to ashes.

As his body fell to the ground in clumps of ash, Hope ran over to John.

He was still shaking, black webs like corrupted veins spreading under his skin.

Her hand no longer glowing, she reached down and

pulled the blade from his throat, then rested her hand on his neck to heal him.

# SEVENTY-EIGHT

# John

JOHN WOKE to a warm sensation spreading throughout his upper body.

His eyes opened, and he saw a figure standing above him, basked in light coming from the flying monstrosities above, hair flowing out. And, with his blurred eyes, he would've sworn he saw angel wings.

He remembered the painting that Hope had made of him as some sort of gothic angel or something more than a decade ago.

Except he wasn't the angel, now.

She was.

Hope kneeled down beside him, reaching for the blade on his throat, then removed it.

Then she put a warm hand on his neck.

He jerked away, trying to protect her. "What are you doing? You can't t-touch me."

"Yes, I can," she said, smiling.

"What?"

Behind her stood Larry, Abigail, and Talani.

"Where's Jacob?"

"Dead," Hope said.

"What? Who killed him?"

Larry smiled. "You've got yourself one badass chick here, dude."

John looked at Hope confused. "You killed Jacob?"

Then he saw the amulet around her neck and put two and two together. That still didn't explain how she could touch him.

*Unless …*

"You're not a vampire, are you?"

"No," she laughed. "Turns out that I've always been invulnerable to Valkoer touch."

"No shit? Really?"

"Really," she said, leaning down to kiss him.

It had been more than ten years since he'd kissed, let alone touched, her, but it was as sweet and perfect as he remembered. The sort of kiss that can only come from your soul mate.

He pulled her into the sand, never wanting it to end.

Larry cleared his throat, trying to get their attention.

John broke away from the kiss. "What?"

"If you think that's something, wait until you hear what happened to me!"

~

# EPILOGUES

## JUDITH

AGAIN, Judith found herself alone in the void.

But she no longer felt like her long life had been a total waste. Yes, she had done many terrible things, but in death she had a chance to atone and right some of her wrongs.

She had managed to save Talani, Abigail, John, Hope, and Larry. Perhaps she had helped to save two worlds.

Not that she expected The Gods to reward her. She was stuck here, forever it seemed, to live with the consequences of her sins.

Part of her wished that Talani and Abigail could stay in the In-Between with her, or that she could return to her world, if only to see how their lives fared from here.

They were with good people now — John, Hope, and Larry — people with good souls, who risked their lives to save those that they loved.

But for Judith there was no going back.

No way through the portal, no body to return to even if she could. And asking the girls to give up their lives to keep her company in eternity was selfish.

She gave a reluctant farewell, wished them well, and told them both that she loved them.

Back to an eternity of loneliness.

She thought of Talani's question, asking if Judith had run into any other souls in this Limbo.

She hadn't.

But she couldn't be the only one here. It didn't seem right that it would *only* be her and a bevy of monsters.

She remembered though that the monsters were once souls like her. She wondered how long it would take her to become another of their number.

*Please don't let me become one of them.*

Judith continued to wander the void without a body, or souls to keep her company, for what felt like forever.

After a while, she forgot what Talani and Abigail looked like.

A while after that, who knew how long with time so different, Judith forgot their names.

One day, as if such a thing existed in Purgatory, she heard a voice.

"Judith?" a man said behind her, somehow familiar.

It took a moment, but the name found her like a lost song lyric.

"Solomon?"

"You're almost here."

"Where?"

"Just follow my voice, and you'll find me."

Judith followed his voice until she saw a dim white light ahead.

"What is it?"

"Just follow."

She gathered speed until the light took form.

"Is that —" she asked, unable to finish, too much in awe of the giant glowing white tree, floating in the middle of the nothingness like a planet. Surrounding the tree were millions, if not billions of tiny lights, gold and white, floating like petals in the wind.

"What is it?"

"The After," Solomon said.

As Judith moved closer, the tree grew even larger, its branches twisted and full of leaves and flowers, glowing in countless hues.

Closer, she saw they weren't flowers but miniature worlds, hanging by branches.

*Impossible.*

"Here," Solomon said, directing her toward a planet flower with a purple hue. "I'm here."

"What do I do?" Judith floated in front of an apple-sized world.

Then again, it was hard to tell size with no form of her own. Perhaps in her current incarnation of nothingness, she was giant.

"Touch the world," Solomon said.

"I don't have hands."

"Don't let that stop you," he said with a friendly laugh.

Judith floated closer to the world, could see clouds on the surface, green fields and streams below. Like an ornament on the world's largest Christmas tree, with a world inside it.

*Impossible.*

She floated closer, then imagined herself reaching out.

As she did, the floating light petals formed an arm for her.

She looked down, feeling tears of joy, if not actually crying them.

She moved her fingers made of tiny light petals, and laughed. "All I do is touch the world?"

"It's all you do. Then we'll be together again."

"What is this? Where are we?"

"That's for you to find out."

She reached out and touched the world, and as she did an explosion of light rushed her from every direction.

Judith screamed, certain that the light was consuming her, that this was some sort of cruel trick.


THEN DARKNESS.


NOT JUST DARKNESS, but cold water.

*I can feel. I have a body!*

And the sound of sloshing waves.

And then she heard Solomon. "Judith."

She opened her eyes.

Solomon stood there. He was in a different body, as was she, but it was him all the same.

And though this wasn't her home, she was home none-theless.

~

## CALEB

"YOU REALLY WANT TO DO THIS?" John asked Caleb as they, along with Hope, Larry, Abigail, and Talani stood at the top of The Citadel tower under the waning moons, watching the burning pyre of the mass funeral in the center of Golden Cove.

"Yes," Caleb said. "These people need a new leader. Someone without the dogma of their Gods."

It had been a week since John saved him from the dungeon. A week since they'd tried to revive Raina, and the others, but even Hope's miracle amulet couldn't raise someone who had been dead for as long as Raina had been lying there on the ground.

"Are you sure you trust me with this?" Caleb patted the amulet now beneath his shirt.

Hope said, "The wizard chose you. Said he saw into your soul, and that you can do the most good with it."

Caleb hated having the responsibility. "What if I fuck up? What if it corrupts me?"

John joked, "Then we'll come back and kick your ass."

Larry hit John's shoulder, "I think you mean *Hope* will come back and kick his ass."

Hope laughed, flexing her muscles.

Caleb laughed, then asked John. "Are you sure you all don't want to stay and help me? I could grant you seats on the New Council."

Larry said, "Hmmm, I've always wanted to be a politician."

"Oh God," Hope said, laughing.

"Hey, I'd be a good politician. At least you'd know I'm gonna tell it like it is!"

Abigail raised her hand, "I'd vote for you!"

"See, Abigail's got my back!"

John said, "She's not old enough."

She threw her arms across her chest pretending to sulk.

Caleb laughed, but found it hard to enjoy their victory

with so much work to do. With alliances to make and mend. With an entire North he knew nothing about to deal with. Then he had to figure out what to do with Jacob's Forgotten Kingdom or Under Harbor for that matter. He wouldn't make the same mistakes that The Guardians made on Earth, hunting down and criminalizing people for simply existing. He'd need to find a way to integrate them back into society, then deal with the blowback.

The more Caleb considered it, the less he thought himself up to the task. But the people of Golden Cove begged him to lead, especially when they learned that he'd killed King Jacob — a small lie perpetuated by John, but needed to forge a new history.

~

## JOHN

THE FIVE OF THEM — John, Hope, Larry, Abigail, and Talani — returned to Earth through the portal. Then it, and all other portals, were closed by Caleb on Otherworld.

John's mandatory meetings with The Guardians, now led by a man named Arthur Parish, apparently one of the old guard, a Pioneer from centuries ago, were thorough debriefings of everything that had happened on Otherworld. Art, and several others, questioned John and his companions for days.

John said enough to keep them satisfied — Jacob was dead, and Caleb had everything under control. But the crystals were destroyed. *Whoops.*

Art didn't seem to believe him, but what could he do?

On the fourth day, John was finally allowed to have his friends in the meeting for a final debriefing.

They were sitting in an underground war room in Washington State, bright white and filled with monitors, a large table, many officials and agents from agencies John had heard of, and several he hadn't, sitting around it. It was, for lack of a better word, the new cabal that called itself the Guardians.

Art started the meeting by thanking the group for their service and having an assistant hand them each fresh credentials with new identities so they could start their lives over, and a check from the government for "services rendered."

Judging from the raised eyebrows, the checks were all as generous as John's.

"Thank you," John said.

The assistant then handed them folders marked *CONFIDENTIAL: TOP SECRET*.

Before anyone could open their folder, John raised a hand and told his friends to keep them closed.

"What's this?" he asked Art.

"Your new assignments."

John felt punched in the gut.

"What?"

"The Guardians, and Omega, have suffered serious losses. You are the only proven fighters we have left. You did what nobody else could do: stopped Jacob and closed the portals. We need you. Your country needs you."

John held up his hands. "I'm done. I told you all this was my last job."

"You can't be *done*," Art said, his voice too stern for John's liking — as if the man was talking to property not a person. "You are a Guardian for life, son."

John shook his head. "No. That was my old life. Now I'm choosing a new one. And if you, or anyone else from the government, tries to stop me or my friends, you'll wish we never came home."

John stood, grabbed his new identity, and his check, and started toward the exit.

"You can't just leave here."

John turned on his heel and rushed toward Art, forcing the frightened man to stumble backward into the table. John raised his hand, threatening to take his life.

The room filled with gasps.

John half expected someone to pull a gun, but he glared at them all, his eyes a dare.

"Do we understand each other?" John growled.

Art nodded.

He looked at the others, waiting for their nervous nods as well.

"Good," John said. "Thank you for your generosity."

Then he left the room with his friends.

~

*SIX MONTHS LATER ...*
*Saint Augustine, Florida*

JOHN WOKE up early to make breakfast for the others as the sun was setting.

He liked making breakfast, and sitting around the table for meals with his new family.

They were living in a beautiful restored house in the historic district, not too far from his first place with Hope. A five-bedroom house shared with Larry, Abigail, and Talani — one big weird family.

Hope was painting again. He loved seeing her passion breathing.

John and Hope managed to meet up with old friends, including Sergei and his boyfriend, Stephan, who still ran the art gallery, and *still* had one of Hope's paintings on display. Hope had tried to find her adopted mother, but she'd died of cancer three years prior.

Larry spent most of his nights on Xbox playing Call of Duty and yelling at foul-mouthed teenagers. Seemed that being forced to sleep during the day and be up all night didn't really change Larry's lifestyle all that much. If anybody was suited for life as a vampire, it was Larry.

On the nights he wasn't playing video games, he was sitting in front of his new computer set-up, going through a national database he'd created of people who needed to die.

Nothing he loved more than traveling the country cleaning up the streets. Sometimes he even got Abigail and Talani to join him, but only when he was one hundred percent certain that the person was really guilty. Certainty was rare, but when it happened he ran through the house like a kid on Christmas morning, shouting, "We've got one!"

The smell of sausage, eggs, bacon, and pancakes filled the kitchen. As John plated breakfast and his *family* gathered around the table, he looked at them with an overwhelming feeling of joy.

It had been a long road to get here, and no, things weren't always perfect, especially having two *teenagey* girls living under the same roof, but it was a hell of a lot better than he had any right to expect.

Usually they broke bread discussing the night ahead, and what they had planned. But tonight Hope began breakfast by looking around the table. "Um, do we have any more chairs?"

John looked at their circular table. There was enough room for five chairs, exactly. "Um, no, why?"

"I think we're going to need a new chair, or maybe a new table."

"Why?" John asked, confused.

Hope reached into her shirt pocket, retrieved a plastic white stick, and handed it to John.

At first he didn't know what it was, then when he saw the two pink lines and realized. "You're …!"

Hope's eyes welled with tears of joy.

John's eyes were watering, too, as he hugged and kissed her, saying, "Oh my God, I can't believe it."

"What?" Abigail asked, always eager to know what was happening.

"I'm pregnant," Hope said.

"What?" she shrieked, smiling. "I'm gonna be a sister?"

Talani said, "Hey, you're already my sister."

"I mean to a baby," Abigail said, running over to Hope and trying to feel her belly.

"There's nothing to feel yet, I don't think," Hope said.

Talani and Larry both came over and hugged her, too.

As they sat to eat, conversation turned to names, with Abigail wanting to name the baby Angel.

Hope, being polite, but obviously not liking that name, said, "Maybe."

Talani offered, "Jessica" and "Raina."

"How do we know it's gonna be a girl?" Larry said. "I say we name him something manly, something that says 'WINNER.' Like Larry!"

Everyone laughed.

And as they did, John felt like the world's most fortunate man, surrounded by these people whom fate invited into his life.

One didn't choose the family they were born into any

more than one chose their fate. But sometimes, if you persevered, survived the hell you were born into, and didn't become too scarred by life, you'd live long enough to create your own version of a family, one bound not by circumstance or fate, but by love.

## THE END

If you loved reading *Available Darkness* then you'll definitely want to check out the Platt & Wright lush dark fantasy tale *Fornevermore*.

Get Fornevermore: Season One

# About the Authors

**Sean Platt** is an entrepreneur and founder of Sterling & Stone, where he makes stories with his partners, Johnny B. Truant, and David W. Wright, and a family of storytellers.

Sean is the bestselling author of over 10 million words' worth of books, including the Yesterday's Gone and Invasion series. Sean is also co-author of the indie publishing cornerstone, Write. Publish. Repeat. and co-host of the Story Studio Podcast.

Originally from Long Beach, California, Sean now lives in Austin, Texas with his wife and two children. He has more than his share of nose.

**David W. Wright** is the co-author of edge-of-your-seat thrillers including the best-selling post-apocalyptic series *Yesterday's Gone*, the paranoid sci-fi *WhiteSpace* series, and the vigilante series, *No Justice*, as well as standalone thrillers *12*, and *Crash* which was recently optioned for a movie.

David is an accomplished, though intermittent, cartoonist who lives in [LOCATION REDACTED] with his wife and son [NAMES REDACTED.]

He is not at all paranoid.

He is "the grumpy one" on *The Story Studio Podcast* with fellow Sterling and Stone founders, Sean Platt and Johnny B. Truant.

You can email him at <u>david@sterlingandstone.net</u>
We swear, he almost never bites. Unless you feed him after midnight.

# Also By Sean Platt

**The Dead World Series**

Dead Zero

Dead City

Dead Nation

Dead Planet

Empty Nest

**The Beam Series**

The Beam Season One

The Beam Season Two

The Beam Season Three

**Robot Proletariat Series**

En3my

Robot Proletariat

The Infinite Loop

The Hard Reset

Cascade Failure

Reboot

**The Tomorrow Gene Series**

Null Identity

The Tomorrow Gene

The Tomorrow Clone

The Eden Experiment

**Karma Police Series**

Jumper

Karma Police

The Collectors

Deviant

The Fall

Homecoming

**Yesterday's Gone**

October's Gone

Yesterday's Gone Season One

Yesterday's Gone Season Two

Yesterday's Gone Season Three

Yesterday's Gone Season Four

Yesterday's Gone Season Five

Yesterday's Gone Season Six

**Tomorrow's Gone**

Tomorrow's Gone Season One

Tomorrow's Gone Season Two

Tomorrow's Gone Season Three

**Available Darkness**

Darkness Itself

Available Darkness Book One

Available Darkness Book Two

Available Darkness Book Three

**WhiteSpace**

WhiteSpace Season One

WhiteSpace Season Two

WhiteSpace Season Three

**Stand Alone Novels**

Burnout

The Island

Crash

Emily's List

Pattern Black

Devil May Care

The Secret Within

The Sleeper

Last Night Never Happened

I Am John Tidor

# Also By David W. Wright

**Cold Vengeance**

Cold Vengeance

Cold Reckoning

Cold Retribution

**Hidden Justice**

Hidden Justice

Hidden Honor

Hidden Shame

Hidden Virtue

**No Justice**

No Justice

No Escape

No Hope

No Return

No Stopping

No Fear

**Karma Police**

Jumper

Karma Police

The Collectors

Deviant

The Fall

Homecoming

**Yesterday's Gone**

October's Gone

Yesterday's Gone Season One

Yesterday's Gone Season Two

Yesterday's Gone Season Three

Yesterday's Gone Season Four

Yesterday's Gone Season Five

Yesterday's Gone Season Six

**Tomorrow's Gone**

Tomorrow's Gone Season One

Tomorrow's Gone Season Two

Tomorrow's Gone Season Three

**Available Darkness**

Darkness Itself

Available Darkness Book One

Available Darkness Book Two

Available Darkness Book Three

**WhiteSpace**

WhiteSpace Season One

WhiteSpace Season Two

WhiteSpace Season Three

**Stand Alone Novels**

12

Crash

Emily's List

Threshold

The Secret Within